Praise for
SUSAN MALLERY,
whose "prose is luscious and provocative" (*Publishers Weekly*),
and her acclaimed novels

"Susan Mallery's gift for writing humor and tenderness make all her books true gems."

—*Romantic Times*

"Susan Mallery writes an unforgettable combination of humor and sizzle."

—Christina Dodd, *New York Times* bestselling author

"Witty dialogue, plenty of romantic tension, and delicious characters."

—*Publishers Weekly*

"Mallery skillfully conducts an intense emotional journey . . . in this richly textured, poignant tale."

—*Booklist*

"You can never go wrong with Ms. Mallery's fascinating storytelling."

—*Romance Reviews Today*

"A book that simply refused to let me set it aside."

—*Fresh Fiction*

"Wonderful and engaging, a love story meant to be read over and over."

—*Reader to Reader*

ALSO BY SUSAN MALLERY

The Best of Friends

Sunset Bay

The Marcelli Princess

The Marcelli Bride

The Seductive One

The Sassy One

The Sparkling One

Married for a Month

SUSAN MALLERY

Sweet Success

POCKET BOOKS
New York London Toronto Sydney New Delhi

Pocket Books
An Imprint of Simon & Schuster, Inc.
1230 Avenue of the Americas
New York, NY 10020

This Pocket Books paperback edition November 2023

POCKET and colophon are registered trademarks of Simon & Schuster, Inc.

For information about special discounts for bulk purchases, please contact Simon & Schuster Special Sales at 1-866-506-1949 or business@simonandschuster.com.

The Simon & Schuster Speakers Bureau can bring authors to your live event. For more information or to book an event, contact the Simon & Schuster Speakers Bureau at 1-866-248-3049 or visit our website at www.simonspeakers.com.

Interior design by Erika R. Genova

Manufactured in the United States of America

10 9 8 7 6 5 4 3 2 1

ISBN 978-1-6680-1745-6
ISBN 978-1-6680-1746-3 (ebook)

To those wonderful people who make
Godiva chocolates, my favorite of which is
their incredible champagne truffles.
You were an endless source of inspiration.

Dear Reader,

I can't tell you how much it means to me that so many readers have asked for *Sweet Success* to be reissued in print. This one is for you!

Sweet Success was originally published in 2001, and I left this book pretty much as it was back then. I hope you'll savor the side dish of nostalgia that comes with the delicious main course—a heartwarming romance between Ali, a small-town chocolatier with a habit of rescuing strays, and Matt, a business tycoon hiding from his painful past by posing as an itinerant handyman.

Ali and Matt exist in a world where cell phones aren't ubiquitous, people can't rely on GPS, and getting a website is a cutting-edge idea. But one thing will never change—the always fascinating and often infuriating push-pull of a man and woman falling in love.

Enjoy!

Susan Mallery

chapter one

"Hey, Ali. I found you a man."

Allison Thomas blinked sleepily and thought about hiding her head under the pillow. However, the phone pressed against her ear might get in the way.

"Was I looking for one?" she asked.

"Sure. You've been bugging me for weeks." There was a pause, followed by an impatient sigh. "Ali, it's me, Harry."

Ali pushed the pillow away and sat up. "Harry?"

Her sluggish brain pulled together random bits of information. Harry, the local handyman. Her business downstairs. How Harry had been teasing her with the promise of doing actual work for weeks on her business downstairs. "Are you finally going to build my shelves?"

"Nope. I've hired me a new guy. If this one works out, I think he'll stay around and buy me out."

Ali resisted the urge to roll her eyes. Harry was always hiring some new guy, and anytime an employee stayed longer than a week, Harry became convinced he'd finally found someone interested in buying his small handyman business.

"I hope that happens," she said sincerely. "In the meantime, is he going to do some work for me?"

"Sure thing. I've already sent him over to start your shelves. I'll be by this afternoon to check on his progress."

"Okay. Great." She was drowning in office supplies, cooking supplies, and mailing containers. She needed more stock space in her storage room. While Harry wasn't known for hiring the brightest bulbs in the chandelier, how hard could it be to make a few shelves and paint some walls? She could probably do it herself if she had the time, which she didn't. "When can I expect him?"

"He should be there any minute."

"Okay." Ali blinked, then sat up straighter in bed. "What? Like now?"

"Yeah. He left about fifteen minutes ago, but he's walking."

Ali glanced down at the soft cotton T-shirt that barely came to midthigh. Underneath she wore exactly nothing. Her hair was a mess. *She* was a mess, and not the least prepared for Harry's helper. She swore under her breath.

"Next time give me a little more warning, Harry," she said.

"You're welcome."

His cheerful reply set her teeth on edge. She hung up the phone, then scrambled out of bed.

It was nearly eight, and on a normal morning she would have been awake for hours. Or at least since seven. But work had kept her up well past midnight. Again.

Ali pulled off her sleep shirt and tossed it onto the four-poster, brass bed. She grabbed underwear, a bra, jeans, and a T-shirt that proclaimed her "Queen of Everything" and dressed. When she dug in her closet for sneakers, she found one and had to waste precious minutes searching for the mate. Damn. One of these days she was going to clean up the floor in here and get a shoe organizer, the kind with the clear front so she could see where everything was. Or, if she really went wild, she could hire one of those anal-retentive people who made their living organizing other people's lives. That was what she *really* needed. A reorganized life. In the meantime she would settle for a pair of matching shoes.

"Gotcha," she murmured, spotting a familiar green shoelace sticking out from under the bed.

She skipped socks and shoved her feet into the shoes, sidestepping the circling of her black-and-white cat, Domino. Ali then turned around to stare into the mirror. As usual, her long dark hair was a tangled riot of curls. On models in magazines the disarray looked artful. On her it looked like a scary "before" shot in a makeover. No time, she thought and rooted through the piles of clips, makeup, and jewelry on the top of her dresser until she found a scrunchy and fashioned a quick ponytail. She could imagine how awful she looked—no makeup and a thick bushy cat's tail of hair. Not to mention the T-shirt and jeans faded from too many washings. Ali shrugged. She was busy, which meant she didn't always have time to make a fashion statement. Okay, she never had time, and any statement she made shouldn't be repeated.

Less than two minutes later she dashed out of the bathroom and headed downstairs, just in time to hear someone impatiently pounding on the back door.

"I'm coming," she yelled, jogging through the stockroom.

But the person on her back porch wasn't Harry's

mystery helper. Instead, her mother—tall, slender, and perfectly groomed—stood there, with a pale, leashed pig at her side.

Ali sighed. Most people were allowed to start their day with a cup of coffee and a few minutes to peruse the local paper. She had to face her mother.

"Took you long enough," Charlotte Elizabeth Thomas said as she pushed past her daughter and into the rear room of the shop. "Miss Sylvie and I thought we'd stop by and have coffee after our walk." Her mother's gaze narrowed. "You didn't even brush your hair this morning. And what is that you're wearing?"

"Jeans, Mother. A denim fabric made into slacks for both women and men."

"Sarcasm does not make you more attractive, Allison."

Charlotte Elizabeth bent down and unfastened the leash from Miss Sylvie's collar. The nearly albino pig trotted over to Ali and snuffled at her scuffed sneakers. Ali wasn't sure if it was a greeting or a criticism, nor did she want to know. Charlotte Elizabeth turned and headed for the kitchen.

"We did an hour around the pond. The doctor said that with proper exercise, the heart condition won't be a problem," Charlotte Elizabeth called over her shoulder. "I prefer walking here, rather than in Los Angeles. The sea air is very refreshing, and there isn't any smog."

Ali trailed after her mother, following her into the kitchen, then watching as Charlotte Elizabeth worked, filling the coffeepot with water and pouring it into the machine. After she added six scoops of flavored coffee, she shut the front flap and hit the start button.

"I'm relieved to hear the positive medical news," Ali

said, trying to muster some enthusiasm and sincerity. They were, after all, talking about the pig's heart, not her mother's. But while Ali didn't understand her mother's devotion to the large, ungainly animal, Charlotte Elizabeth and Miss Sylvie were inseparable.

How did an otherwise intelligent, articulate person make such a poor pet choice? Why couldn't her mother be like other people's eccentric relatives and just collect dozens of cats or small dogs? Ali could understand the appeal of a stray. She'd had several herself over the years. But a pig? And not one of those cute miniature ones. Miss Sylvie was several hundred pounds of pale, sunburn-prone pork on the hoof, or whatever it was that pigs had.

Charlotte Elizabeth patted her pig's large back. "I think this new sunscreen is going to work. Did I tell you about it? I found it in a catalog. I do so love mail order. The sunscreen is organic and practically guaranteed not to produce an allergic reaction. Something I worry about, don't I, sweetheart?"

Miss Sylvie grunted in response.

"You could carry it here in the store."

Ali looked at her mother. "The sunscreen?"

"You like natural products."

"This is a sweet shop, Mother. Chocolates, cookies, scones, and muffins. Not a sunscreen kind of place."

"I suppose not. Although it wouldn't hurt you to expand. Speaking of which—muffins, I mean, not expanding—do you still have those low-fat ones in your freezer?"

"Yes." Ali pointed to the freezer at the far end of the huge kitchen. "I baked about four dozen and sold maybe three in two days."

Her mother opened the door and gazed at the labeled

packages inside. "Three dozen is excellent. That's seventy-five percent of what you baked. Not bad for a new product."

If only, Ali thought. "No, Mom. I sold *three muffins.* I had to freeze the other forty-five."

She'd learned her lesson. Low-fat anything did not sell well at Decadent Delight. People traveled great distances for her gourmet chocolate and when they got here, they didn't want to think about healthy foods or saving calories.

"At least they won't go to waste. I thought instead of a scone, I could start giving Miss Sylvie a low-fat muffin." Her mother glanced up and smiled. "She does so like a treat with her coffee in the morning."

Ali stared at her mother's beautiful face. Charlotte Elizabeth had wide hazel eyes, a small nose, and a perfect mouth. There was a symmetry to her features that left lesser mortals feeling deformed in comparison. Despite being nearly sixty-five, her mother had smooth and practically wrinkle-free skin. Some of that was the result of carefully planned surgery, but most of it was just great genetics.

Ali, of course, took after her father.

Charlotte Elizabeth found the large container of muffins and took one out. She set it on a plate, then put it in the microwave tucked in the corner of the counter near the double metal sink. While she waited, she glanced through the open doorway leading to Ali's storeroom and frowned. Her sharp gaze took in the stacks of supplies for the store, the office, and the kitchen. Unopened bags of sugar nestled up against boxes of mailing envelopes.

"That place is a disaster. You should get some shelves in there."

"Funny you mention that," Ali said, but figured there

was no point in explaining the renovation was already planned. In fact, Harry's helper should be arriving any minute. *Please God,* she thought sincerely, *let him get here and rescue me from the force of nature that is my mother.*

The microwave beeped at the same time the coffeemaker gave a discreet chime indicating it had taken grounds and water to produce warm, liquid magic. Miss Sylvie came trotting in from wherever she'd been and grunted with pleasure.

"Just a moment, darling," Charlotte Elizabeth said. She cut up the muffin and blew on it to cool it down. Then she poured coffee into a saucer and blew on that as well.

"Did you ever treat me this nicely when I was a child?" Ali asked as she watched the ritual.

"Of course. Don't you remember?"

"Not really. I think Rick and I got shortchanged. Miss Sylvie gets a lot more attention." Ali was only half kidding. Did her mother's behavior still fall in the "normal" range, or did it slip over into a more scary category? And was any of it due to old age? "Mom, have you been getting forgetful lately? Are you taking your hormones?"

Charlotte Elizabeth set the saucer and the plate on the floor and stroked her pet. "If you're trying to imply there's something wrong with me, I won't listen. I lavish love on Miss Sylvie because I don't have grandchildren to spoil. I'm nearly sixty. I deserve grandchildren."

"Sixty-five," Ali said patiently, knowing she only had herself to blame for the tirade about to rain down on her like a winter storm. There would be flashes of both lightning and thunder, not to mention dark clouds and chilling temperatures. They'd been over this material countless times before. Why hadn't she let well enough alone? So her mother had a strange relationship with a pig. Was that so unhealthy?

"Don't try to distract me with the truth," her mother said as she poured herself a cup of coffee. "As I was saying, if you had bothered to get married and have babies of your own like other people's children do, I wouldn't be alone. But no. You wanted a career and a business. I had to get a pig so I would have something to spoil and cuddle in my old age."

Ali glanced at Miss Sylvie's considerable bulk. The pig was cute, especially when her mother dressed her up in seasonal jackets and rakish hats, but she was far from a lap pet. "How exactly do you cuddle her?"

"You know what I mean."

Actually Ali didn't, but she figured it wasn't a good time to ask. Nor did she really want to know.

"Do you want coffee?" her mother asked.

Ali nodded. She needed the jolt of caffeine to keep her wits about her. Charlotte Elizabeth was many things, but she wasn't stupid. And she could be stubborn when she didn't get her way. If Ali didn't distract her soon, she was going to be hearing about the woes of being grandchildless for the rest of the morning. To make matters worse, Ali was less than a week away from turning thirty. Fortunately, Charlotte Elizabeth wasn't one for keeping track of birthdays, and this year she would be in Los Angeles on Ali's birthday weekend. With a little luck, her big "three-zero" would pass in unrecognized silence. Of course if Charlotte Elizabeth *did* manage to remember, Ali would never hear the end of it.

In Charlotte Elizabeth's mind, turning thirty without

a husband or even the hint of a man in her life was a fate worse than death. It was worse than a new wrinkle.

Ali's private guilt on the subject of grandchildren didn't help. In the recesses of her mind, she knew she owed her mother grandchildren and much more.

"You look very nice," Ali said abruptly.

It was a feeble first attempt to change the subject, but the best she could come up with under pressure. Fortunately, it was also true. Her mother wore a pink jogging suit that should have looked frumpy and added the appearance of an additional ten or fifteen pounds to her slight frame, but this was her mother she was talking about. Of course Charlotte Elizabeth managed to look both stylish and reed slim. Maybe it had something to do with her having been an actress for many years. Charlotte Elizabeth always had the correct outfit for every occasion and the psychic knowledge to know exactly when to wear it.

"Don't for a moment think that I've gone so senile that you can distract me with a silly compliment," her mother said, glaring at her. "What about my grandchildren?"

Ali groaned. It wasn't that she didn't want a child. She did—desperately. But on *her* terms and schedule. Not her mother's.

Taking a breath, she threw out another subject to distract her mother. "I really wish I looked as great as you."

"You could with a little effort."

"Time is the one thing I don't have a lot of."

"Time and effort aren't always the same thing. You could get your hair cut or change how you dress. Take a lesson from Clair, who always looks elegant. *She's* not too busy to make herself attractive."

Ali winced. Done in by her best friend. Damn. To make matters worse, Ali couldn't even claim her life was too complicated by comparison, either. Clair managed to be nearly as put-together as Charlotte Elizabeth while raising two kids, being married, chairing a major charity in Los Angeles, and occasionally assisting her husband in his winery. Oh, and she was pregnant. All Ali could claim was a candy store and a cat.

Charlotte Elizabeth studied her daughter critically. "You're 5'6", which isn't model tall, but it's not so short you have to worry about styles not looking right on you."

Ali closed her eyes and sighed. Her mother was on a roll, and she had no one to blame but herself.

"You have my breasts and my legs," Charlotte Elizabeth continued. "Both of which are spectacular. I can't tell you how many times I was asked to pose topless. I refused, of course. It would have been tacky. But it wouldn't kill *you* to show a little cleavage sometimes, or a bit of thigh. And you have lovely large eyes, dear. Take advantage of that. Get a makeover. Or I would be happy to—"

Miss Sylvie finished her morning coffee and muffin and came snuffling for more. The pig managed to do what Ali hadn't been able to and distracted her mother. "No, darling. That's all you get. You need to watch what you eat. Your heart, dear. Remember?"

Miss Sylvie's little pig eyes seemed to dampen with disappointment. She went back to snuffle at the now empty plate.

"What about my grandchildren?" Charlotte Elizabeth demanded again.

Ali didn't know which was worse. The "I want grand-children" speech or the makeover speech. "Leave me alone. If you want pretty, find a model. If you want grandchildren, go talk to Rick."

Her mother made a moue of disapproval. "First, it's not nice of you to say that. Rick is a lovely young man, but he's my stepson, not my child by blood. It wouldn't be the same."

"So telling you to go rent a grandchild wouldn't work either? I bet Clair would loan you one of hers."

Charlotte Elizabeth sighed. "You know, I always tried to be a good mother. Wasn't I there for you? Didn't I bake cookies for you and always ask about your day?"

"You did ask me about school, but I don't remember you baking."

Charlotte Elizabeth considered. "All right, but I *paid* someone to bake, so there were always cookies at home. That counts."

Actually, in Ali's mind it did count, but she wouldn't dare give that point away to her mother. "Find me a husband, and we'll talk grandchildren. Until then, leave me alone."

As soon as the words were out of her mouth, she wanted to call them back. She knew better than to issue a challenge to anyone in her family, especially her mother.

Perfectly shaped eyebrows arched toward perfectly trimmed bangs. "Really?" Her mother drew out the word for nearly four seconds.

Ali scrambled to regain lost ground. "No. I was kidding. Ha ha. Pretty funny, huh? Had you going, didn't I?"

Charlotte Elizabeth was not moved.

Fortunately at that moment, someone knocked on the back door.

"That would be Harry's helper," Ali said. "Harry sent him over to build me some shelves."

"Allow me," Charlotte Elizabeth said and headed toward the rear of the building.

Ali stared after her and tried to figure out why her mother would care about the handyman. Charlotte Elizabeth preferred her world to move in an effortless manner. She didn't want to be bothered with the details of repairs or construction. She just wanted—

Ali swore out loud and raced after her mother. Harry's helper—did the poor man have a name?—was a new guy in town. Ali had just issued a challenge. If the man had most of his own teeth and no really large hump on his back or his nose, Charlotte Elizabeth might just try to—

Ali came to a stop. Too late. Conversation drifted in through the half-open storeroom door, and she could only stand there, frozen, humiliated, and eavesdropping.

"Tell me, Mr. . . . Baker was it?"

"Yes, ma'am. But you can call me Matt."

"All right. Tell me, Matt, are you married?"

Ali closed her eyes and leaned against the doorframe of her storage room. This wasn't happening. Really. If she just visualized another scene, another place, or perhaps even another time, she would find herself magically transported there. She would not be in her own place of business being humiliated by her mother.

Something breathed against her foot. She glanced down and saw Miss Sylvie checking out her shoe again. Apparently the muffin hadn't been satisfying.

"I'm only asking because my daughter, Allison, is very lovely. She's also single. Not because there's anything wrong with her. She's been busy."

Strangled laughter forced its way up Ali's tight throat. Busy? Was that the best her mother could come up with to explain her lack of male companionship? Busy? As in "If only she could get that last sock drawer organized, she could see to her personal life?"

Ali heard someone clearing his throat, and she guessed it wasn't her mother. The masculine voice that followed confirmed her guess. "Ma'am, I'm just here about the shelves."

"Oh." Pounds of disappointment thickened Charlotte Elizabeth's voice. "You don't like women. I understand. Well, my son Rick is gay, although I think he's in a committed relationship right now. My daughter is the stubbornly single one in the family." She paused and then spoke confidentially. "You see, I want grandchildren."

"Ma'am, I'm not gay. I'm here to build shelves."

Ali could feel the flush of embarrassment on her cheeks. Even so, she forced herself to push away from the wall and step around Miss Sylvie. This had gone on long enough.

"Mother, leave the poor man alone," she said briskly as she headed for the door. Obviously the only way to get through this incredibly humiliating moment was to ignore the fact that her own mother had hawked her like some used rocking chair at a garage sale. "Harry's helper is here to put up shelves, not be tormented by you."

She stepped onto the porch and smiled brightly. "Hi. I'm Allison Thomas. You've already met my mother."

The day had dawned clear, and the sun was well above the horizon. Light flooded the porch, momentarily causing her to blink as her eyes adjusted. Then she had to blink because Harry's helper wasn't the usual brand of misfit he liked to hire. This guy—she blinked again and had to look up—was way too tall and way too good-looking.

"He doesn't want Rick," Charlotte Elizabeth said cheerfully. "So I guess he's all yours."

chapter two

Ali opened her mouth, but there weren't any words left. It was all too humiliating. To make matters worse, Harry's helper was staring at her as if this was *her* fault. Oh, God. Now she probably wouldn't get those shelves done after all.

Just then something large lumbered through the open back door. Miss Sylvie joined them on the porch.

"This is my pig," Charlotte Elizabeth said. "Miss Sylvie, this is Matt. He's here to help Ali with that messy storeroom of hers. And aren't we happy about that?"

Her last statement came out in one of those "speaking to baby-waby" voices. Ali shuddered. If all this had happened before nine in the morning, what was the rest of her day going to be like?

Take charge, Ali told herself, and stepped to the edge of the porch. "You said your name was Matt?"

"Yes, ma'am. Matt Baker." He touched the toolbelt strapped to his narrow waist. "I'm ready to get started if you are."

"Sure thing. My storage room is this way." She paused and looked at her mother. "Are you staying?" *Please say no.*

Charlotte Elizabeth raised her eyebrows, then touched her chest in a gesture of sincere innocence. "You know I never interfere with your work, dear. We'll be off now. Back to our home." She smiled at Matt. "So nice to meet you. I hope to see more of you later."

Charlotte Elizabeth might be old enough to be the handyman's mother, but Ali knew from experience that she wasn't talking about seeing Matt again another time. When she said more, she meant *more*. As in "Wouldn't it be nice if that handsome young man worked without a shirt?"

All the years she'd spent growing up, Ali had prayed for a normal mother. Not once had God listened. Maybe she should have prayed for patience instead.

She turned her attention to Matt Baker, who kept his steady gaze on her. In another man she might mistake the intensity for some kind of interest. Except Matt wasn't looking at her the way a man looks at a woman. Maybe it was her imagination, but it was as if he didn't see her at all. Or maybe he was terrified she was as strange as Charlotte Elizabeth.

Whatever he might—or might not—be thinking didn't reflect on his face. He was plenty good-looking with dark hair brushed back from a modified widow's peak and brooding brown eyes. The tanned skin and attractive creases in his forehead and at the outside corners of his eyes told of long hours working outdoors. He was muscled, if a bit too thin.

She gave him a quick smile, to which he didn't respond. Not the friendly type, she decided. No smiles, no chitchat. All right, she could *not* talk, too. After all, she wasn't looking for a new best friend. Just shelves. Right after she gave him his instructions, she wouldn't say another word.

"The storeroom is this way," she murmured, turning back to the building and stepping inside.

Matt followed. He walked quietly for a big man. Make that a tall man. While he was a couple inches over six feet, she doubted there was an ounce of fat on him. She wondered if the thinness was by choice or circumstance. If it was the latter, Harry would make sure his helper was well fed. The old man had probably already given Matt a place to stay. Harry tended to attract transient types who worked for a few weeks, then moved on. Ali hoped that Matt would stick around long enough to finish the shelves.

"Welcome to my life," she said, coming to a stop in the center of the storeroom. It was a disaster. She'd been using old bookcases to hold most of her supplies, and they didn't come close to providing enough shelf space. Two picnic tables served as a workspace in the center of the room. The linoleum floor was old, but clean, and needed replacing.

She motioned to the chaos surrounding them and smiled. "I've always thought of this place as a metaphor for who I am inside. A combination of unrelated parts that can be as magical as chocolate or as practical as business supplies." She paused. "Okay, I'm kidding about being practical. At least for now. It's a goal, eventually."

She put her hands on her hips and turned in a slow circle. "What I want is a cabinet for my office supplies. Something out of the way, maybe on that far wall."

She pointed to her right.

"The rest of the area should be open shelves for kitchen stuff. Sugar, flour, chocolate." She glanced at him and smiled. "You may have noticed the sign in front. This is Decadent Delight—a gourmet chocolate shop."

No response. Okay, so he was a good-looking mime.

"In the center, I want two rows of tables. We do lots of mail order and shipping and that requires counter space. There should be shelves underneath. Maybe one deep one on the right side and two on the other side. Paint the walls before putting up the shelves and replace the floor. What do you think?"

Matt glanced around then nodded. "Not a problem."

He speaks!

She walked over to the far corner where a long cardboard tube stood tucked between a bookcase and a plastic bin of flour. "I have plans. I got that far with Harry's last assistant." She opened the tube and spread the papers out on the picnic table.

Matt moved closer and looked down. Ali was surprised to inhale a whiff of clean masculine scent. Not aftershave, but the essence of the man himself. It was very, very nice, and when her stomach growled, she had a bad feeling it wasn't all about missing breakfast.

He traced the simple design for the shelves, then flipped to the second page. "Easy enough," he murmured, not looking at her. "With replacing the floor and the painting, we're talking about a week's work." He glanced down at the floor and kicked at the linoleum. "Maybe an extra day to get this stuff off."

"There is a complication," Ali said, hating that she kind of liked standing next to this guy. She could practically feel the heat radiating from him. Which was insane. He was a person, not a furnace. "I can't give up my whole storeroom. The job has to be done in halves because I need the space. I've got people tracking in and out of here all the time."

She held up a hand and began ticking off on her fingers. "My mother and Miss Sylvie." She grinned. "Scary, but true. Then there are my employees. I have part-time help in the store and in the kitchen. Then I've got two college kids who do the packing. The customers won't be a problem. Most of them don't come back here, although the locals often use the back door."

He frowned. "I'm surprised you're so busy."

"Hey, this is Saint Maggie. Between the wineries, the spa, the ocean, a bed-and-breakfast, not to mention the tearoom across the street, we get more than our share of tourists."

He frowned. Ooh, he had a great frown, Ali thought, loving the way his eyebrows drew together and his forehead got all wrinkly.

"Saint Maggie?" he asked.

"Santa Magdelana," she explained. "Saint Maggie is what we locals call the town. So are you still willing to sign up? I mean we're talking about all this work, along with my mother and the pig."

He stared at her. There was something odd about his eyes. They were intense and yet completely blank. As if no one lived behind them. Which made him good-looking but mysterious. A spy, maybe? Oh, yeah, right. More like he was . . .

None of her business.

Ali pursed her lips together. She didn't know what he was. Nor did she care, she reminded herself. Matt Baker was not her problem.

"Can we talk about the pig?" he asked.

For a half-second life came into his eyes, and she thought he might smile. She found herself holding her breath in anticipation that he would, but then the life faded, as did her hope.

"What is there to say? Most people's mothers collect doilies or those dolls from the Home Shopping Network. My mother has a pig. It's a harmless hobby. For what it's worth, Miss Sylvie is pretty clean. The biggest problem is that she's sensitive to the sun, so she has to wear sunscreen." She paused to wait for the smile that never came.

Ali almost told him it wouldn't kill him to be friendly, then reminded herself again, he wasn't her business. All that mattered was her new storeroom. If Harry's helper could take care of that, she would be a very happy camper.

Matt rolled up the plans. "I need to call Harry with a list of supplies," he said.

She pointed down the hall. "Use the office. Oh, and there's coffee in the kitchen. Help yourself."

Matt left without saying anything else.

A jerk, she thought, as she headed after him, then climbed the stairs and locked her apartment door behind her. Good-looking, but not her type. Not that she had a type. But she *could* have a type if she was more organized. One thing at a time.

Welcome to the world of the marginally insane, Matt thought that afternoon as he pried up the ancient linoleum and peeled off a three-foot section. Decadent Delight was not a place for the faint of heart. Since a little after nine that morning, he'd had another run-in with the pig and had been looked over by high school girls who weren't old enough to be looking over anyone, let alone a man only a few years shy of forty. He'd been roped into carrying supplies into the kitchen, lugging a large order out to a customer's car, and moving a display case just a few inches to the right.

The sound of female laughter drifted into the storeroom and he winced. The job was a mistake, he realized. In the past year he'd taken work like this—fixing fences, steps, even doing a bit of remodeling. In the summer, he'd picked fruit and worked in a winery. But all of his temporary jobs had one important denominator—a lack of contact with people. Working in Decadent Delight was like living in a bus terminal—odd folks appearing and disappearing without warning.

A whiff of chocolate drifted to him. About an hour ago two college kids had arrived and were currently cooking something in the kitchen. The sweet scent mingled with the aroma of coffee and was almost appealing. Matt frowned. He couldn't remember the last time he'd enjoyed the smell or taste of food. To be honest, he couldn't remember the last time he'd been hungry.

He tugged at the flooring and pulled off another three-foot section. A dumpster had been delivered late that morning and set on the side of the building, out of sight of the customers. Matt picked up an armful of buckled, stained flooring and carried it outside.

As he walked down the stairs, he couldn't help noticing the perfect September day. The sky was the kind of blue that only exists on the California coast. He could smell the salt from the ocean, and the temperature was a made-to-order seventy-two degrees. In Chicago it would already be—

He shook his head to break that train of thought before it even began. He didn't think about Chicago anymore. As far as he was concerned, it didn't exist. Neither did his business.

He dumped the flooring and returned to the storeroom, pausing only to take a drink from the bottle of water Ali had left for him. She'd been in to see him around noon to tell him he was welcome to take lunch whenever he wanted. After he'd informed her he would rather work through, she'd told him she was going upstairs to her apartment to fix a turkey sandwich and asked did he want one as well?

As he drank the cool water, Matt replayed the conversation in his head. Something about it bugged him. Something . . . He paused in the act of bringing the bottle to his mouth, then frowned and swore softly. She thought he was broke. Her offer of a sandwich had been because she didn't think he had anything to eat.

"Sonofabitch," Matt muttered, then finished the last of the water and screwed on the cap.

So what, he told himself. She could think what she liked. He wasn't going to explain his situation.

"Are you taking a break?"

He glanced up and saw Ali standing in the doorway to the storeroom. She held a tray in front of her and smiled.

"It seemed to be that time of day," she continued, "so I thought I'd bring you a little something. Compliments of the house." She set the tray on the one picnic table he'd left in place.

At some point, before the store had opened for the day,

she'd changed her clothes. Instead of jeans and a T-shirt, she now wore a black calf-length dress and a green apron embroidered with the name of the store. The look was old-fashioned yet it suited her. She'd tamed her long curly hair into a braid, although a couple of corkscrew curls had escaped to brush against her cheek. He turned his attention to the tray.

There was a small plate containing chocolates and a larger plate with lumpy-looking biscuits and tiny triangle-shaped sandwiches. None of the food tempted him, although he wouldn't mind a cup of coffee.

"I thought you just sold chocolates," he said, pointing at the mutant muffins. "Are these a failed experiment?"

"Experiment?"

"What are they supposed to be? Biscuits or something?"

She laughed. "You're right about the 'or something.' They're scones." She pointed to the various decorative bowls and miniature jugs. "This is English tea, my good man. We have scones, cucumber sandwiches, clotted cream, jam, butter." She touched the carafe sitting in the center of the tray. "I'm cheating by offering coffee instead of tea because you don't strike me as the tea-drinking type. So what can I get you?"

He looked over the food. "Coffee," he said. "Black."

"What else?"

"Nothing."

She opened her mouth then closed it. The slight stiffening of her posture told him he'd insulted her, which made him feel faintly guilty.

"I'm not hungry," he added, then wondered why he bothered.

"But you didn't eat lunch."

He didn't ask how she knew. Women just figured out that sort of stuff. "I'm not a big eater."

"I can tell." She drew in a breath, then released it slowly. "You know, Matt, at the risk of being too personal, you need fattening up. How do you think it looks to my customers if you're skin and bones? They'll think there's something wrong with my cooking."

He eyed her cautiously. "So my passing on your food spells economic disaster for Decadent Delight?"

She grinned. "Exactly."

She had a pretty smile, he thought absently.

"Besides, I made the chocolates myself."

He hesitated. He didn't want to insult her, but he also wasn't interested in the food. "Maybe next time."

She pressed her lips together. "Fine. Coffee it is." She poured him a cup and handed it to him.

He took a sip. "It's great. Thanks."

"You're welcome."

Her gray-green eyes studied him. She had that look about her—the predatory gleam of a female ready to start asking questions. What was it about women and information? They needed to know as much as they could about every person they met.

He tried to forestall her by motioning to the floor. "I should finish prying this up today. Tomorrow I'll start prepping the walls for painting."

"Good." She poured herself a cup of coffee, then picked up one of the truffles. "Chocolate hazelnut," she explained. "My favorite." She took a bite and chewed. After she swallowed, she said, "How long have you worked for Harry?"

"About a week."

"And before that?"

He put down the coffee and returned his attention to the floor. "I'll do a good job for you, Ms. Thomas."

He heard a faint sigh from her. "All right, Matt. I won't ask questions. It's just you're not Harry's usual type. You seem . . ." She hesitated. "I don't know. More competent, maybe? Your hands are plenty scarred, so you've obviously been doing this kind of work for a while, but it doesn't suit you for some reason."

He responded with a grunt. He knew exactly what she was talking about, but he wasn't going to tell her what she wanted to know.

"You really don't want any of this, do you?"

He turned and found her pointing at the tray of food. He shook his head.

"Okay." She picked up the tray. "But if you faint from hunger, don't fall into any of my supplies."

"I promise."

She left without saying anything, but he knew she would be back. She'd already offered him food twice in one day, which told him she was the type who took care of people. Just what he needed—a meddler. He would have to steer clear of her. If he wasn't careful, she would weasel all his secrets from him and expose them to the light of day. Then where would he be?

An hour later Matt had nearly finished scraping the floor. Customers had continued to arrive and leave until he barely noticed the dinging sound from the bell over the front door. It was only when he heard Harry's voice that he bothered to listen in on the conversation drifting into the storeroom.

"I haven't seen Charlotte Elizabeth all day," Harry complained. "Doesn't she usually walk Miss Sylvie in the afternoon?"

"Sure," Ali said easily. "Around the pond. It helps her heart. Miss Sylvie's, that is."

"I heard she had a problem. Charlotte Elizabeth must be concerned."

Matt grimaced. They were talking about a pig, not a child. But he kept working and tried to ignore their voices. Unfortunately, now that he'd tuned in to the conversation he found it difficult to tune out.

"Don't suppose she'll be coming by here anytime soon," the old man said.

Ali laughed. "Harry, you're impossible. I'm *not* going to give you an update on my mother's comings and goings."

"I wish you would. Seeing Charlotte Elizabeth is the bright spot in my day. I've had a crush on her since I was seventeen."

"You and three million other men."

Matt peeled off the last few feet of flooring and gathered the stack. Three million men? There was an exaggeration. Even if Ali's mom had been a beauty in her youth, she wouldn't have charmed more than a couple dozen.

"You making your run tonight?" Harry asked.

"Probably not for a couple more days. I was there last night, which should hold them until Thursday."

Matt stopped working long enough to listen. What were they talking about? Then he told himself he didn't care. He'd almost made it to the back door when Harry continued.

"How's Matt working out?"

"He seems to be a hard worker," Ali said.

"I told you."

"That you did. If he does a good job on the storeroom, maybe the two of you can get to the list I've been whining about for the past year. The fence around the parking lot needs painting. I swear, the ocean air seems to feed on wood . . . or at least on the paint. Also, the parking lot needs a new truckload of gravel on it. And that's just here. There's more work at the tearoom and the bed-and-breakfast."

"Not to worry," Harry said. "If this goes good, I bet he'll buy me out before the end of the year. You'll see."

"Harry, you wouldn't sell for a million dollars."

The old man chuckled. "You gonna write me a check?"

"Not in this lifetime."

Matt left the building and headed for the trash bin. The gravel crunched with each step as he rounded the corner. He'd told the old man that he wasn't looking for more than temporary work, but Harry didn't want to listen. Matt was going to have to talk with him again and make things clear. He wasn't sticking around for very long, and he wasn't buying Harry's business.

He dumped the linoleum and headed back to the store. As he stepped inside, he saw Harry and Ali standing by the picnic table. They were discussing the storeroom plans.

Matt stared at his employer. The old man had showered, shaved, and even combed his thinning gray hair. With his neatly pressed jeans and shining face, he looked like an old-fashioned gentleman caller. All this for the infamous Charlotte Elizabeth. Matt realized he didn't remember what the older woman looked like. When he left for the day, he wouldn't remember Ali, either. People didn't make much of an impression on him anymore and that was how he preferred it.

"I've decided I hate your guts," Ali said cheerfully as she lifted her fork and aimed it at her salad.

Clair St. John didn't look the least bit impressed with Ali's announcement. "I'm not surprised. You've always been jealous of me. Hatred was bound to occur. I'm surprised it took this long."

"Strength of character on my part."

Ali eyed the artfully arranged combination of chicken chunks, halved red grapes, and walnuts nestled on a bed of baby greens. Several slices of freshly baked French bread lay on a side plate next to her dessert fork. Then she glanced at the low floral centerpiece gracing the round oak table.

"You made this, didn't you?" she asked.

Clair grinned and tucked a strand of short blonde hair behind her ear. "The salad, the bread, or the flower arrangement?"

Ali groaned. "All of it and don't answer. I already know the truth." She took a bite of the bread, and groaned again. It was perfect with a crisp and slightly resistant crust encasing a soft-as-a-cloud center.

Her best friend of nearly twenty years laughed. "Ali, so I can cook and arrange flowers? You can do all that, too. You can also make incredible chocolate."

"Yeah, I guess. But my mother was throwing you in my face again this morning. 'Be more like Clair,'" she mimicked.

Clair leaned toward her. "You know she's only trying to show she cares."

"No. She's trying to get her way. She wants me married and pregnant."

"Is that such a bad thing?"

"I guess not. It's not that I don't want a husband and children. I *do*. It's just . . ."

Ali glanced around the dining alcove off the St. John kitchen. Arched windows offered a view of the extensive gardens lit by floodlights in the cool evening. Martin St. John, Clair's husband of six years, had lived in the house all his life. The winery had been a family business for two generations. The gracious adobe house had been built by a Spanish nobleman over a hundred years before and modernized several times. The original lines had been preserved, along with the thick walls and worn tile flooring.

"You're one of those together women for whom everything falls into place," Ali said, then took a sip of her wine. It was a crisp and fruity Sauvignon Blanc, produced on the property. "Six weeks out of school, you meet Martin and fall madly in love. You have two perfect children and a third on the way. While I have a mother who keeps a pig, a business destined to make me fat, and an inclination to date men who are . . ."

She let her voice trail off. How did she describe the men who had populated her life?

Clair dropped her right hand to her swollen belly. Always put together, tonight she wore a navy-and-white shirt over navy leggings. She looked crisp, cool, and perfectly suited to her surroundings.

"Outsiders," Clair said firmly. "You avoid the mainstream and date men who are a challenge. Like what's-his-name. That artist guy."

"Byron." Ali sighed. "He was very gifted."

"Granted. But he was also selfish and self-centered. His art was everything. You could never compete with that."

Ali nodded. She *had* always been second in Byron's life. "Okay, but he needed me. Someone had to keep his life in order."

"And pay for everything when wall-size portraits of buses turned out not to be wildly successful."

"*My* point is," Ali said, ignoring her friend's point, "that I'm starting with a handicap. You have everything you want right now."

"My life has flaws," Clair said. "The kids fight, bugs infest the vineyard, the board on the charity disagrees with me on a regular basis. Don't you think there are times when I wish I was single and completely free to do whatever I wanted?"

"No," Ali said flatly, then smiled. "Wanna trade?"

"Only if you'll be pregnant for the last trimester. It's the worst. Still willing to take it all on?"

Ali eyed her friend's belly. Her own midsection felt small and empty by comparison, and not in a good way. Somehow the dream of having children seemed more unlikely than ever. "In a heartbeat."

Clair shook her head. "You need to find your own path. That won't happen by living my life."

"I hate it when you act mature," Ali grumbled. "So where are Martin and the kids?"

"At the movies. There's a new Disney release, and he took the boys into town to give me a break. Thanks for driving all the way out here to have dinner with me."

"My pleasure."

A coyote called in the distance. The sound was instantly followed by several dogs barking at once.

Ali rose to her feet and started for the back door. "My babies are calling to me," she said as she slipped outside and was instantly engulfed by four dogs.

Her friend followed her. "Martin said I'm not allowed to take any more of your rescued strays. He's being very firm about it this time."

"Yeah, yeah, like I haven't heard that before."

Ali settled on the back step and embraced the animals. Sasha, the German shepherd mix, had been abandoned by the side of the road while she was just a puppy. Misha, a part-Doberman, part who-knows-what, had been a stray hit by a car. He'd shown up limping and bleeding at Ali's back door about eighteen months ago. The two little ones had come through friends of friends, discarded by their owners.

With time and love, all four of the dogs had healed. Clair and her family offered a haven, while the open grounds around the house gave the animals plenty of room to run.

"At least I'm popular here," Ali said, ducking a doggie kiss on the cheek.

"We all love you," Clair told her.

Ali knew that was true. Her friends cared about her, as did her mother and brother. But even though she felt selfish, she didn't always think it was enough.

♥

Thursday night Ali pulled her black Toyota 4-Runner up to the small gate at the east wall of the spa and parked. It was nearly midnight. There were few lights here, and no sound. Overhead the stars were bright in the clear September night, and she could see a half-dozen dark shapes pacing back and forth in front of the gate. Sweatpants and light jackets made them appear like bulky specters.

"Hi. I'm back," she called as she slid out from behind the wheel and circled around to the rear of her vehicle. "How is everyone surviving their week?"

"Shh," someone hissed from the darkness behind the gate. "They'll hear you."

Ali chuckled. "I'm selling chocolate, not drugs. This isn't illegal."

"I know, but—" The woman stopped talking.

Ali nodded in understanding. The instructors at the spa were strict. Meals were provided according to a posted schedule. An extra hour of aerobics was rewarded with a piece of fruit for dessert. When people were treated like children, it was hard not to act childlike. Hence the secret meetings at midnight instead of a visit to her store or even a regular delivery in daylight.

Guests arrived at the Seaside Spa on Saturday and brought with them a commitment to fitness and weight loss that bordered on a religious calling. But by late Sunday or early Monday they were feeling the lack of sugar and caffeine. All the herbal tea in the world wasn't going to help. There was only one cure—chocolate.

Ali unlocked the gate first. She'd had her own key for years, ever since someone climbing the thick adobe walls of the spa to meet her had fallen and broken a leg in the process. While the staff didn't approve of her late-night runs, allowing her easy access was safer for everyone.

Tonight's group of seven consisted of six women and

one man who swore the chocolate was for his wife. Four of the spa guests had come out for her run earlier in the week, but three were new.

As Ali opened the rear of her 4-Runner, she began to detail her inventory. "I have three kinds of coffee, and several boxes of chocolates. Truffles, chocolate-dipped strawberries, pralines, as well as squares of solid chocolate. Everything is handmade and sells by the pound. Except the coffee, of course. That's a dollar fifty per cup."

Two of the women moaned. One tall woman with short blonde hair pushed her way to the front. Her gray sweat suit added bulk to what looked like a nearly perfect body. "Coffee," the woman said. "And a square of chocolate. To start," she added. "I need the sugar in my system before I can think straight."

As Ali opened a green box trimmed with gold, the blonde lunged for the stack of mugs nestled in a cloth-lined basket. The gleaming black coffee dispensers each had a label that explained "Amaretto," "Hazelnut," or "Dark French Roast." The woman poured a mug full of the French Roast and, her hands trembling, brought the steaming liquid to her lips. She swallowed a mouthful and made a sound that Ali hadn't heard since back in high school when she and Clair had stolen and watched an X-rated movie from Clair's parents' private library.

She offered the woman the box of chocolate squares. The woman looked inside, grabbed two, and shoved them both into her mouth. Then she moved aside to let her fellow inmates take their fill.

Twenty minutes later the feeding frenzy had slowed enough to allow conversation. A middle-aged redhead in wire-rimmed glasses leaned against the bumper of Ali's

Toyota. "These are the best chocolates I've ever had," she said, then took another tiny bite of the handmade champagne truffle. "I mean that, and I've done my share of tasting." She patted her ample hip.

"I'm glad you think so." Ali reached into her jacket pocket and pulled out a stack of business cards. "Decadent Delight is on the main road of Santa Magdelana. You'll pass the store on your way back to the freeway, so feel free to stop by before you head home. I make all the chocolates myself, and I'm happy to ship anywhere."

There were murmured promises as she passed around the cards and followed them with a tray of pralines.

A petite gray-haired woman stared at the swirls of chocolate and pecans. "I've lost two pounds," she murmured.

"Oh." Ali drew the tray away. "Sorry. I brought some jelly beans with me. I don't make those, but they're sweet and only four calories apiece. Would you prefer that?"

The woman bit her lower lip. "I shouldn't . . . I can't." Her body swayed, then she swept four pralines into her hand. "Oh, screw the diet, I'll get liposuction instead."

As she gobbled the pralines, she bought a pound of the chocolate squares. "A little something for later," she murmured, causing the other guests to buy for the remaining day or so of their spa experience.

Ali totaled the sales, took cash from the man and four women, and filled out credit-card receipts for the other two.

"You have my business card if you need anything else," she said as she slammed the hatch of her Toyota.

"Hey, Ali."

Ali turned and saw Gerald, one of the spa managers, standing by the small gate. He held a flashlight in one hand. Despite being close to sixty, Gerald had the body of a twenty-five-year-old swimmer, and he liked to show it off in tank tops and bicycle shorts. Although it was fifty degrees outside tonight, Gerald's exposed tanned skin gleamed in the moonlight.

The guests paused and stared, trapped like mice before the cat. Gerald motioned with his flashlight. "Come on, folks. It's late, and we have a sunrise hike in the morning. Get on back to bed."

They slunk past him like guilty toddlers.

Gerald waited until the last of them were safely inside the gate, then turned to Ali. "You're an evil pied piper. I know you don't do this for the money."

"You're right," she said with a laugh. "I do it for the look of sheer bliss on their faces when they take that first bite. That and the fact that spa guests have been some of my best customers. You'd be amazed at how much repeat business I get, even if it is mail order."

Gerald shook his head. "Can't they just eat a salad if they're hungry?"

"You're missing the point." But then that was probably why Gerald had spent his life looking like a Greek god while the rest of America battled an additional ten, twenty, or thirty pounds. "It's not about hunger, it's all about indulging yourself."

"Speaking of indulging," he said, looking her up and down. "You think anymore about that exercise program we talked about?"

"Not even for a second." As if she had time. "I have my mother's legs, or so she informed me earlier in the week. They're actually very nice."

Gerald looked disgusted. "It's not about how we look, Ali. It's about being healthy."

"Which is why you're running around in bicycle shorts and a tank shirt in the middle of the night."

Gerald grinned. "That's different."

"Yeah, right. And in my next life I'm going to be just like you." She started to climb into her 4-Runner so she could head back to her store and bed.

Gerald hesitated, then moved close to the driver's door and tapped on the glass. "Ah, Ali?"

She looked at him, then chuckled and lowered the window. "You're nothing but a hypocrite," she said as she reached for the small bag of truffles sitting on the passenger seat. "Here. Dark chocolate only, exactly one quarter of a pound."

"You're the best."

"So I've heard." Unfortunately, every time someone said that, he meant her abilities in the kitchen. "See you next week."

But Gerald didn't answer. He was too busy savoring his chocolates to even notice her drive away.

chapter three

Matt woke to a warm but smelly bedmate. He rolled over to escape the odor and bad breath, only to have the stink follow him. He opened his eyes and found himself nose to muzzle with the ugliest dog ever born.

"Get out," he muttered low in his throat.

Wide brown eyes regarded him solemnly, then Lucky gave him a doggie smile. A warm pink tongue swiped at his face. Only then did the dirty one-eared mutt scramble off the cot that served as Matt's bed.

Matt swore to himself. When Harry, his boss, had offered him room and board as part of his pay, he'd explained that the back room wasn't much to look at. As Matt glanced around at the rickety furniture and the narrow cot, he told himself he should have paid attention to the warning. Paint that had once been blue, or maybe even teal, had faded to gray, except where it had peeled off completely. Two large cracks ran down the center of the single window, and he had the feeling that only grunge held the pieces of glass together. No, he couldn't complain that Harry had misrepresented the place, but what his boss had failed to mention was that his mongrel dog also considered the room his home. Lucky and Matt tussled over possession of the cot, of the blanket, and even who walked through the doorway first. While Matt won the two former arguments, Lucky generally won the latter.

"Damn dog," he muttered as he rose to his feet and stretched.

Lucky did the same, but from a four-legged position, pushing his front paws in front of him with a moan of pleasure, then sticking out first his right, then his left rear leg, reaching until the individual toes quivered. While Matt slipped on jeans and a worn but clean shirt, Lucky set about the serious business of licking his doggy butt. By the time Matt had pulled on socks and boots, washed his face, shaved, and brushed his teeth at the small sink in the corner, Lucky had finished his ablutions as well and waited by the door.

Matt started to pass through the open door, but as always Lucky beat him to it. They headed for the kitchen where the smell of coffee and frying bacon caused both of them to sniff the air.

"Morning," Harry said when they appeared.

Matt nodded and poured himself a cup of steaming coffee. He sipped it and willed himself not to think about other mornings or other cups of coffee shared with company very different from the grizzled old man standing at the stove.

While Harry wasn't as ugly as his dog, he was a man ill treated by life and time, and the ravages of both showed on his face. Like his dog, he was slightly bowlegged and walked with an attitude belonging to a much larger male.

Lucky barely cracked forty pounds, and Harry stood less than five-feet, six-inches tall.

Harry might not look like much but Matt didn't care. Harry had given him a job without asking questions or checking ID, and he paid in cash.

When Matt had finished his first cup and started on his second, he moved to the table. Harry had already set out eggs and bacon and was currently buttering toast. Lucky munched from the bowl that had been waiting for his arrival. Harry did take fine care of that damn dog.

"How are things going at Decadent Delight?" Harry asked as he took a seat. He motioned for Matt to do the same.

Matt pulled out a chair and settled, but he didn't bother with any of the food. "Good. The old floor is up, and the new one is in. I've painted. Today I'll be working on the shelves. They took a little longer to dry than I thought, but I used enamel paint so they'll be washable."

"Good idea," Harry commented as he scooped eggs onto his plate, then took four slices of crisp bacon. Matt felt a faint rumbling in his stomach. He ignored it.

"You know, once the storeroom is finished, Ali has a whole list of other things she needs done," Harry said casually. "Saint Maggie looks like a small town, but there's plenty to keep a man busy. We don't get much bad weather, but the sea air takes her toll on houses and fences."

Matt rose to his feet. "Forget it, Harry. I told you before, I'm not interested in buying your business. I appreciate the job, but that's all I want. Work for a couple of months before I move on."

Harry's blue eyes narrowed. "You don't strike me as the kind of man to settle for day-labor jobs."

Matt stiffened. "You unhappy with my work?"

"Not at all."

"Good. Then I'll collect my tools and head over to the store."

"You don't like to answer questions, do you?"

"No, but I don't ask 'em, either."

Matt left the room. He was happy to stay in town for now, but if Harry started digging, it would be time to move on.

"It's Saturday," Ali announced when Matt showed up at her back door promptly at eight-thirty.

"Harry has a calendar in the workshop," he told her as he stepped into the storeroom.

Ali stared up at the man who had been working on her storeroom for the past five days, then she planted her hands on her hips. "You don't eat my food, you don't talk much, you don't play well with others. I can't figure out if your comments are truly lacking in social grace, or if you have a really dry sense of humor. I want to give you the benefit of the doubt, but you're not helping."

Matt looked at her for a long time. She'd gotten used to his intense gaze and the echoing emptiness she saw in his eyes. She'd about given up on ever making him smile. Oddly enough he reminded her of an abandoned dog who desperately needed to be taken in and given a home, yet promised to bite anyone who tried to help.

A dangerous train of thought, she reminded herself. After all, she'd sworn to stop playing the rescue game, at least with men. All it ever brought her was trouble.

"I know it's Saturday," he said at last. "Will I be in the way if I work?"

Before she could answer, Charlotte Elizabeth tapped on the back door, then entered without waiting. "Morning, all," she called.

Ali moved to let both her mother and Miss Sylvie enter. Between the half-finished shelves and the supplies, there wasn't anywhere for her to go, except to crowd up against Matt. If Ali hadn't known better, she would have sworn Charlotte Elizabeth had timed her entrance for just this reason.

Worse, standing close to Matt wasn't a bad thing, Ali thought grimly. She rather enjoyed the clean scent of him, not to mention the heat she'd noticed that first morning. He was nice looking, albeit on the thin side, and not unintelligent. But he was obviously not interested in making friends, at least not with her.

"How are we this morning?" Charlotte Elizabeth asked as she held the door open wider to accommodate her pig. "We just did our usual hour around the pond. Ali, I see you're dressed for your customers. You look lovely, dear, but I'm sure Matt already told you that." Charlotte Elizabeth beamed at them both. "It's Saturday."

"Ali already informed me of that," Matt said dryly.

Ali held her breath. Was her mother commenting on the day of the week for any particular reason? *Please God, let her forget it's my birthday*, Ali prayed fervently. She did not want a lecture on the horror of being thirty and single. With a little luck, Charlotte Elizabeth would say her good-byes and head off for L.A. without remembering a thing.

"Matt told me that Harry kept a calendar in the shop," she said by way of a diversion. "The implication being he did not need others to inform him of the date."

"Date," Charlotte Elizabeth said thoughtfully. "Why that's exactly what I wanted to talk to you about, Matt. Do you have anything scheduled for this evening?"

Ali felt the rush of heat on her face, which meant she was turning the very attractive shade of a ripe tomato. There was no point in mentioning *her* plans for the evening. Charlotte Elizabeth wouldn't consider Ali's dinner engagement with her stepbrother any competition for a real live date.

She moved in the small space and tried to find an escape. The good news was that, for the moment, her mother had forgotten her birthday. The bad news was she was bent on humiliating her daughter. Life was a compromise.

"I have chocolate melting," Ali said. "I have to get back to the kitchen before it scalds."

But neither Miss Sylvie nor Charlotte Elizabeth moved, leaving Ali trapped between Matt and the shelves.

Matt settled his toolbelt more firmly on his hips. "Ali made scones yesterday, Mrs. Thomas," he said, neatly sidestepping both the question and the pig. He reached for the door, then pulled it toward him. "You might want to offer Miss Sylvie one with her coffee."

And then he was gone, disappearing into the safety of the parking lot.

"He's good," Ali murmured.

"I'll agree." Her mother's gaze turned speculative. "There's more to that man than meets the eye," Charlotte Elizabeth said, speaking more to herself than Ali. "I wonder where Harry found him. I'll ask him when I get back. I'm off to Los Angeles. I just came by to say good-bye. Have a nice weekend, dear."

"You, too."

Ali hugged her mother, watched her leave, then headed for the kitchen. She'd been telling the truth about the chocolate. She really *did* have to make sure it wasn't ruined.

But the spring in her step wasn't about cooking. Charlotte Elizabeth had forgotten and she, Ali, had escaped. It was going to be a very good day.

By noon Ali had nearly sold out of her freshly made chocolate walnut fudge. Her new line of products—ice cream toppings in flavors based on different liquors—was selling briskly as well. So far the phone hadn't stopped ringing with mail orders, and all of her assistants were on the run with customers. Saturdays were always busy.

Looking around the bustling store gave her a feeling of pleasure. She'd started with little more than a few cooking classes and a dream. Now, five years later, she'd made a success of her life. Well, the business side of it at least. But that was more than a lot of people could say.

As for her Mr. Right—apparently he'd decided to settle for someone else.

The bell over the door tinkled, interrupting her thoughts. Her brother walked into the shop. Lean and elegant, he had mussed blond hair and a ready smile. The face of an angel, with just enough hint of the devil to make the average woman swoon. Ali had watched nearly all her friends fall for him.

He saw Ali and held open his arms. "Who's turning thirty today?"

She laughed, then launched herself at her favorite person in the whole world. "You remembered."

"I'm a dilettante. I have time to remember the important stuff." He pulled her close. "Where's Mom?"

"L.A. A play opening, I think."

Rick laughed. "She forgot your birthday, and you're a happy camper."

"Exactly."

"Then I'll have to torment you for the both of us." He picked her up and swung her around in a circle. "How's my best girl?"

"Happy to see you." When he set her down, she stared up into his familiar puppy-dog eyes. Rick had the winning smile and smooth tongue of a born shyster. He could charm his way out of just about anything. Growing up, she'd always been the one in trouble. Never Rick.

She adored him.

When Charlotte Elizabeth had married Richard Thomas III, Ali had been all of five. At first she'd been thrilled to be getting a father. But when she'd found out there was a big brother in the deal as well, she'd nearly wept with joy.

"I made fudge," she said. "It's almost sold out, but I saved you some in the kitchen."

Rick patted his flat, muscled stomach. "I have to watch my girlish figure, but I might indulge in a little." He put his arm around her. "We're staying the night, then heading into the wine country tomorrow. You have left this evening free, haven't you?"

"Of course. Our birthday dinners together are a tradition." She glanced out the open front door. "Where is your significant other?"

Rick shrugged. "Checking us into the bed-and-breakfast. I trust we have a good room."

Ali grinned. "You'll love the Jacuzzi."

"Eh, Rick, the room, it is fantastic," a male voice announced. His thick pseudo-French accent made the word come out "fan-tas-tique."

Ali untangled herself from Rick's embrace and moved toward her brother's latest "friend." David was small and dark, as lean as Rick, but not as elegant, and all of twenty-three. Which made Rick the older man in the relationship. Rick said that David swore he was from France, but Rick had yet to be convinced. Still, they'd been together for nearly three months, and he made Rick happy, so that was all Ali cared about.

Ali held out her hand. "Nice to meet you, David," she said.

"And you. But my name is pronounced the French way. Da-vede. You know, rhymes with Swede." David chuckled at his joke as they shook hands.

"How very cosmopolitan," Ali said, holding in a grin. Later she would ask her brother where he'd found this boy-toy. Ask and then tease unmercifully.

"Ali, you wanted me to let you know when I was positioning the shelves."

She glanced up and saw Matt standing at the rear entrance to the shop. "Sure. Be right there." She turned to her brother. "Go get settled, and I'll see you around five, okay?"

But Rick wasn't looking at her. His attention was focused on the doorway at the rear of the store. "Who's the guy?"

"One of Harry's helpers. And he's straight."

Da-vede took exception to her comment and moved close to Rick. "We are not interested in a threesome, no?"

Rick laughed. "I didn't mean for me." He turned his

oh-so-blue knowing gaze on her. "Mom didn't tell me you'd hired a looker."

"It's not what you think. He's nice. He works hard."

"Uh-huh. He's downtrodden, in need of a helping hand. Perfect." He patted David's arm. "My sister specializes in rescuing both people and pets."

"Not anymore. I've given that up for Lent."

"Ali, Lent ended at Easter."

She headed for the storeroom. "Whatever. Leave me alone to work, and I'll see you tonight."

It was nearly five that afternoon when a man Matt didn't recognize walked into the storeroom.

"Hey, toolboy, where can I find Allison Thomas?"

Matt carefully finished nailing the shelf into place, then straightened to look at the man standing on the rear porch.

"She's in front. Probably working the store."

"Yeah, and half the county is in there with her. I don't want to be bothered. Could you go get her for me?"

The man was short, heavy, and annoyed. He wore a suit that had seen too many cleanings and a tie that needed one. Thick glasses slid down his nose.

"And you would be?"

"Andy Grant. I write for *Star Gazer* magazine." The man shrugged. "I gotta do this piece on Charlotte Elizabeth Thomas's million-dollar baby turning thirty. Like anyone gives a rat's ass, but it's a job, right?" He jerked his thumb at the shelves Matt had nearly finished installing. "You do menial work so you know what I mean. A buck's a buck."

Matt narrowed his gaze. "I'll tell Ms. Thomas you're here and ask if she wants to see you."

Andy Grant snorted. "Oh, sure. Like there's a question. Who doesn't want to be in our magazine?"

Matt was sure he could come up with an impressive list if he was given a little time. *Star Gazer* was a supermarket tabloid that specialized in sleaze. What on earth would they want with Ali? And what had the man meant by Charlotte Elizabeth's million-dollar baby?

Matt shrugged off the questions and made his way to the front of the store. It was nearly three in the afternoon, and he found Ali behind the counter, measuring out chocolates by the pound. The three clerks helping her were busy as well, but then there had been a steady flow of customers in and out all day. For a small business in an out-of-the-way town, she did very well. Based on what he'd observed, he would guess her retail sales were less than sixty percent of her total sales. The rest of her business was in mail order.

Every afternoon two college kids spent several hours packing up chocolates to be sent across the country. Ali joked that her monthly FedEx bill was nearly as high as her rent. At first he'd thought there had to be a cheaper way to deliver the product, but the chocolate was perishable. Judging from the hungry, salivating expressions on the customers waiting in the store, he doubted the people buying it mail order were interested in waiting any longer than they had to.

He paused in the rear entrance until Ali noticed him, then motioned for her to come over. She spoke to one of her assistants, then walked toward him.

Afternoon sunlight spilled in through the sparkling clean windows. It illuminated her pale skin, highlighting the trail of freckles going from cheek to cheek across the bridge of her nose. She'd long since chewed off her lipstick, and the rest of her makeup was so light as to be nonexistent.

She had a chocolate stain on her apron and additional smudges on her hands. Leigh would have been mildly appalled by Ali's mussed state, but he thought she looked pretty good. She was the kind of woman who—

Down boy, he told himself. He was just the hired help.

"What's up?" Ali asked, her smile ready, her voice cheerful.

Matt stared at her. It took him several seconds to process the question and remember why he'd needed to see her. Then, when he couldn't, he said the first thing he thought of.

"You should order custom mailers."

"What?"

He motioned toward the back room. "You have custom boxes for the candy, but you're using standard boxes for shipping. You could order custom containers the exact sizes you need and skip the filler products. The chocolates would be more secure that way."

She blinked at him. "Do you know how much that would cost?"

"No. Do you?"

She opened her mouth and closed it. "Not exactly. It has to be expensive."

"You won't know if you don't check into it."

"I guess." She tucked a loose curl behind her ear.

"No, you're right. It's a good idea. I'll start calling around on Monday." She paused expectantly. "Is that what you wanted?"

His brain reengaged. "No. There's some guy here who wants to talk to you. A reporter from *Star Gazer* magazine. His name's Andy Grant. Something about the million-dollar baby turning thirty."

Ali flushed bright pink, then ducked her head and sucked in her breath. "Damn, damn, damn. As if turning thirty isn't bad enough."

Matt didn't see the problem, but her distress was real enough. "You want me to tell him to go away?"

She looked at him. The color had faded from her skin, leaving her even paler than usual. Her gray-green eyes seemed to have doubled in size. "More than you can ever imagine. Unfortunately, men like him don't disappear. They haunt. It's generally easier to just get it over with." She touched his arm. "Just don't leave me alone with him, okay? Because this kind of thing makes me crazy, and I'll need to talk to you later to find out how much I screwed up."

"You'll be fine." He reassured her automatically, even though he had no idea what they were talking about.

"Thanks. You're lying, but I appreciate the effort."

She walked over to one of her clerks, murmured something to her, then returned to Matt's side. "Go back and tell him I'll be right there." She began unfastening her apron. "Did he bring a photographer?"

"Grant seems to be alone."

"Good. They'll take a picture out of their archives. I don't think they have any really hideous ones. At least I hope not."

She slipped the apron over her head, then started toward the kitchen. "I'll be less than five minutes, I promise."

Matt hesitated. "What is this about?"

"My mother."

"It's not her birthday."

"Right, but thirty years ago she gave birth to me."

"And the world stood still. What does this have to do with anything?"

Ali laughed. "So you *do* have a sense of humor. I'm relieved. My mother is Charlotte Elizabeth Fitzwilliam Thomas."

The name was familiar. Sort of. He'd heard it— "The actress?"

"That's her. Oscar-winning movie star. When I was born, she had to pull out of a movie. It was a big deal." She glanced toward the storeroom. "Let's not keep Mr. Charming waiting too long. Reporters tend to get impatient. Which never translates into anything good in print."

"Okay." Matt turned away, then glanced at her over his shoulder. "Hey, Ali?"

"Yes?"

"Happy birthday."

"Thanks."

Matt returned to the storeroom. Andy Grant stood with his back to the room, staring out the screen door.

"Ms. Thomas will be right with you," Matt said and reached for a hammer.

Grant spoke without turning around. "What a dump! This town is so small, mosquitoes would starve to death. How do you stand it?"

"I move around a lot."

"You'd have to." He pointed to the bed-and-breakfast across the street. "My editor told me to make a weekend of it, if I wanted. They'd pick up the tab for the night. I told her she was crazy. What's there to do around here but eat chocolate and go crazy? Must be a chick thing, ya know? Me, I'm heading back to L.A. ASAP."

Matt didn't respond. He didn't like Andy Grant very much, and he wanted the man to leave. Barring that, he wanted him to shut up.

"It could be worse," Grant grumbled. "At least I don't have to talk to Charlotte Elizabeth. Although that broad has class. She was some looker in her time, but now she's just old."

"I'll be sure to pass along the compliment," Ali said as she carried a tray of coffee and chocolate into the storeroom. "Good afternoon, Mr. Grant. I'm Allison Thomas. How nice of you to make the drive to see me."

chapter four

Ali had more patience than a saint, Matt thought twenty minutes later. Andy Grant wasn't conducting an interview so much as using the time as an excuse to be rude and insulting. If Matt had been the one Grant had come to see, the reporter would have already found his butt in the dust. But Ali seemed perfectly calm and in control.

As the kitchen and shop were chaotic, they'd decided to conduct the interview in the storeroom. Matt had brought in three chairs and now shifted uneasily in his.

"Your mom working much these days?" Grant asked, sipping the coffee Ali had brought. So far he'd ignored her truffles.

Ali crossed her legs and smiled at the reporter. "My mother retired several years ago. She enjoyed her time in Hollywood, but now she has a different kind of life."

Grant glanced around at the under-construction storeroom and grimaced. "Yeah, the boring kind."

The three of them sat around a makeshift table of

wood stretched across two sawhorses. Ali picked up her coffee but didn't drink.

"It's the kind of world your readers inhabit," she said calmly. "Are you implying their lives are boring?"

"Absolutely. Otherwise they wouldn't be reading *Star Gazer*, you know?" Grant took another gulp of coffee. "Okay, so you're saying that nothing's changed since you turned twenty-five. Figures. We coulda phoned this one in, but no, I had to drive all the way up here just to hear the news." He stared at her. "No wild affairs, no alien abductions?"

"Sorry, no." She smoothed her skirt over her knees. "Actually there has been a big change in my life. Five years ago I had high hopes for starting my own business, but it was all still a dream. Now it's a reality." She motioned to the building around them. "My own private empire, right here in the heart of Saint Maggie."

"Yeah, you're a real tycoon."

Ali seemed to bristle at his sarcastic tone, but didn't otherwise respond. Matt thought about picking the guy up by his shirtfront and tossing him out. There was an unfamiliar tightness in his chest and a heat in his body. It took him a minute to figure out he was angry. His fists ached to plant themselves in Grant's face.

Grant pulled a notebook out of his jacket pocket and jotted down a couple of lines. "Quite a comedown for the million-dollar baby," he mumbled as he wrote. "I'll bet your mother expected a whole lot more for her money."

Matt no longer cared about staying out of it. He half rose to his feet. Ali looked stunned and motioned him back into his seat. "What my mother wants is for me to be happy. In that, I have fulfilled her wish. My life is very complete, and I'm content."

"With this dinky store? You're not even married, Ali. You're thirty now. You've read the statistics. You're more likely to get abducted by aliens than find a man."

"If aliens come for me, I'll be sure to give you an exclusive," she said evenly. "Wouldn't that be fun? I might even make the cover."

Grant considered her comments. "Maybe. If you had real proof. I gotta come up with some kind of headline for what we got now. The article is going to be stuck in the back, anyway. I mean none of this is interesting."

Ali's expression hardened. "How sad that you had to waste your time."

Matt sensed the annoyance building in her. He caught her gaze and jerked his chin at Grant in a "want me to take care of him" gesture. She shook her head. Instead she held out the plate of truffles.

"You haven't tried one, Mr. Grant. I've been told they're worth a plane trip from New York, so just maybe they'll make up for your two-hour drive from Los Angeles."

Grant looked skeptical. "I've got some chocolate in the car."

"It's not the same thing," Matt said before he could stop himself. "If you haven't tasted Ali's truffles, you haven't lived. I take half my paycheck in candy rather than money. Seriously, they're amazing."

Matt reached for the one closest to him and popped it in his mouth. Grant looked interested, and Ali looked stunned. He couldn't blame her. She'd spent the past five days trying to feed him, and he had refused every offer. Here he was—taking food voluntarily.

He bit into the confection. The outside was smooth, rich milk chocolate—just hard enough to make him wonder if it was solid all the way through. Then he hit the softer center. A whipped combination of more chocolate and hazelnuts. But the two had been blended together into a creamy ambrosia that seemed to explode on his tongue.

He'd often heard women go on about the perfection of chocolate, even though he'd never understood it himself. Suddenly, it was clear. Ali's truffle wasn't just a food, it was an experience. Sweet and tempting and possibly the most delicious food of his life.

Grant stared at him, then shrugged. "Okay, I'll try one." He grabbed a truffle and shoved the whole thing into his mouth. After he'd chewed a couple of times, he swallowed and shrugged. "Not bad. Maybe I'll take some with me."

"Of course," Ali said kindly. "I'll wrap them up."

Matt followed the sound of metal objects being thrown into a metal sink. Ali had disappeared after the reporter left, returning, he'd assumed, to the store.

He'd gone back to work as well, trying to lose himself in shelves and nails and the details of construction in an effort to forget about the restorative powers of a single bite of chocolate. He'd not only eaten Ali's food—he'd nearly gotten involved in her life! Temporary, he reminded himself. His stay here was temporary. And then he was moving on.

He entered the kitchen and found Ali tossing spoons, dishes, and metal bowls into the huge double sink against the wall. She'd changed her clothes, discarding her prim workdress for a more casual black sweater and slacks. The new outfit emphasized her breasts and hips, making him aware for the first time that she had curves—the serious kind worthy of a "slippery when wet" sign.

He swore silently, wondering if it was the outfit that had made him notice, or something more sinister. Eve had been tempted by an apple. Was a single truffle to be his downfall?

He leaned against the doorjamb and crossed his arms over his chest. "You okay?" he asked.

She glanced up and shook her head. "No, I'm not all right. I wish that disgusting excuse for a human being had never come here. I wish I'd let you beat him up or whatever it was you'd planned to do when you started to stand up. And please—" She held up a hand as if to stop him from interrupting. "Don't tell me you were simply going to excuse yourself. At this point in time it would be the last straw."

"I wasn't going to excuse myself," Matt told her. "I wanted to throw him out on his butt."

Her hair was a loose tangle of curls tumbling down her back. She wore more makeup than usual, and the smoky shadow made her eyes appear large and mysterious. When she smiled, as she did now, her face transformed from merely attractive to exceptionally lovely.

"Thank you," she breathed. "Even if you're lying."

"I'm not."

Shadows collected outside the oversized kitchen, and he knew he should make his way back to Harry's. He told himself what had happened with the reporter was none of his business, that he wasn't really interested. Except he was interested. Because curiosity was a whole lot safer than many other emotions.

"What was all that?" he asked. "I'm not trying to be

insulting, but why does anyone care that your mom gave up a movie contract when she got pregnant?"

"I find the interest baffling as well." She leaned against the metal counter and sighed. "You know, my mother forgot it was my birthday. She left town without saying a word."

Matt looked at her. Was it just him, or had she changed subjects? "Is that good or bad?"

"I don't know. Which is crazy. I should be thrilled." She shrugged. "You don't know my mother, but her entire goal in life is to make me crazy. I swear, it's her job and she's really good at it. Right now she wants grandchildren. Specifically she wants me married and pregnant. Today, if possible."

"You've got six hours."

Ali gave him a wan smile. "Gee, how very supportive." She paused. "You're probably wondering what my mother making me crazy has to do with your question about people caring that my mother dropped out of a movie deal thirty years ago."

"It did seem to be a non sequitur, but I didn't want to complain."

"Gee, thanks." Ali looked at him, her smile fading. "My mother was a famous beauty who had dozens of affairs through her twenties and thirties, but never found true love, at least not until she hit forty. But before that, she got pregnant. She'd just been offered a role, at the outrageous sum of one million dollars. That was a lot of money back then."

"It's a lot of money now."

She nodded. "Agreed. The thing is the press made a huge deal out of the amount. Then Charlotte Elizabeth turned up pregnant. She'd always wanted children so she was thrilled. However, the women in her family had a history of difficult pregnancies, so she couldn't work *and* have me. When the producer and director refused to delay filming, it came down to a choice between the baby or the role."

"She chose you," Matt said.

"And the press had a field day. From that moment on, I was the million-dollar baby, and the media loved it. I was six before I figured out that other kids didn't have an army of reporters attending their birthday parties."

She smiled, but he sensed she didn't find the situation very funny.

"As I got older, I had more privacy," she continued. "My stepdad did what he could to protect me, and my mother retired from the movie business. I certainly wasn't interesting enough to warrant a story on my own. So now one or two reporters show up for milestone birthdays. It's not so bad."

"Grant was an ass."

This time her smile was genuine. "I agree completely. But I've learned that it's best to be polite. Otherwise, angry words are taken out of context."

Matt couldn't imagine that kind of invasion of his personal life. "You could refuse to meet with them."

"I tried that one year. They wrote an article anyway, and it was very unflattering. Not just to me, which wouldn't have been so bad, but to my mother."

"I thought she made you crazy."

"She does, but I still love her. I don't want her hurt."

There was also the issue of the one million dollars. Matt wondered what it had been like for Ali as a child.

Had she grown up haunted by the money Charlotte Elizabeth had given up?

"My brother, Rick, teases me that at least my kids will cost less than I did," Ali said.

"So you want children," he said.

Ali shrugged. Her gray-green eyes darkened slightly. "Sure. I adore them. Don't most women? But on my time, not my mother's. Which is something of a problem. You may have noticed her desire to get me married off. Richard always sort of kept her vaguely normal, but with him gone, she's taking over the world. Or at least trying to run my life."

As she spoke, color crept into her cheeks. She ducked her head, as if she was embarrassed. Matt thought about Charlotte Elizabeth's not-so-obvious comments about them going on a date that evening.

"I noticed," he said, "but don't worry that she's offending me."

"Do your parents matchmake as well?"

"Not exactly."

"What do they do?"

She looked innocent, but he recognized the fishing expedition. He liked Ali enough not to want to be rude so he prepared himself for the onslaught.

"What do you want to know?" he asked.

"Everything. Where you're from, what you used to do there, why you're hanging out in St. Maggie." She pulled out a stool from under the metal counter and plopped down. "I'm all ears."

"My father currently lives in Italy. My mom died when I was ten."

"Oh. I'm sorry."

"Thanks, but it was a long time ago."

"Anything else?"

"I'm from Chicago."

"And?"

"And that's enough for today." He didn't want to talk about the past. Not his, anyway. "What about you? I know your mom lives here."

"Part-time. She has a place in Los Angeles, as well. I'm her only child—my brother, Rick, is her stepson. She married his dad when I was five. I don't see my biological father very much. He's an actor." She shook her head. "Still dating the starlet of the month. Don't get me started on him."

"All that acting in your blood, and you were never tempted?"

"Yuck. Never." She hesitated. "Okay, I tried it for a few months in high school, and I was a complete failure. I couldn't memorize, I hated being the center of attention, and I don't have a good face for the camera." She spoke the last half of the sentence with an English accent.

He thought she had a pretty nice face. "So you went into chocolate?"

"Sort of. I tried dog grooming for a while. I'm a pet person. But I couldn't handle the smell of wet dog all day." She wrinkled her nose. "I avoided anything fashion related because I don't have the 'what goes with what' gene. Charlotte Elizabeth kept that for herself. I'd always liked to cook. One day I had a taste for fudge. I bought some at a specialty store in L.A. and didn't like it. Then I tried a couple of different places. None of them were quite right. So I set to work in my own meager kitchen, perfecting recipes until I found one I liked."

"And a merchandising giant was born."

"Not exactly. But I like this." She motioned to the building. "I belong here." She straightened and smiled. "So, Matt, what did you do in Chicago?"

He glanced at his watch. "Gotta go, Ali."

"That's not even subtle. Can't you give me a hint?"

"No."

She thought they were playing a game, but he was deadly serious. He didn't want to deal with his past. He couldn't. There was no way to make peace with what he'd done. If she knew . . . but she didn't, and she wasn't going to find out. Not from him.

She rose to her feet. "Fine. Be difficult. You're probably crabby because of low blood sugar. You want to take something home? I've got scones and muffins. Or what about a box of truffles? They're guaranteed to fix what ails you."

She meant well, he told himself. She was being kind.

"I'm fine," he said. "It's late. I'd better be going."

"Okay. But don't forget it's Sunday tomorrow. I'll accept you working on Saturday, but you need a day off. Don't you dare show your face here until Monday."

He wanted to protest. Didn't she understand that he needed to work? It was all that allowed him to forget. The mindlessness of his tasks got him through each day, made him tired enough to sleep. Work had always been his refuge.

Which was part of the problem. When would he learn?

But she looked so earnest, standing there in her tight sweater, giving him maternal advice, and acting sincere and caring. Except Ali didn't act—she simply was all she appeared to be. God save him from kindness. It would be the death of him.

"Monday," he promised and left. There was a liquor

store he passed on his walk back to Harry's. He had enough cash to buy a decent bottle of Scotch. It was a good night for a man to get drunk.

Ali curled up in a corner of her floral-print sofa and surveyed her stepbrother. Rick sat in the melon-colored club chair, his feet propped up on the matching ottoman, her cat sprawled across his lap. They'd finished dinner at a steakhouse in town, then Rick had left David at the bed-and-breakfast, with a promise to return within the hour.

"She's shedding," Ali said, pointing at Domino, whose purr of contentment could be heard clear across the room.

Rick continued to stroke the cat's sleek coat. "You can dehair me before I leave. Because you're my best girl, aren't you sweetie?"

He spoke in a low, gentle voice, directing the words to the cat, but Ali's sweet-faced, black-and-white Domino never looked up. She had been born deaf.

"Did you tell David they have Nintendo for rent at the front desk?" Ali asked with mock innocence. "Just to keep him busy until you get back."

Rick didn't answer. Instead he reached behind him and drew out one of the floral-print pillows nestled at the small of his back, then tossed it toward her. The pillow sailed past her head, without coming close to hitting her.

"Very funny," he said.

"I thought so."

"You usually think so. You're your own best audience."

Ali grinned. "Aren't we all?"

Rick glanced around the room. "Do you have brandy?"

"Yes. You want some?"

Her brother shook his head. "Not really. Just thought I'd ask."

"Testing my hostess abilities? I promise I have clean sheets on the guest bed and fluffy towels in the second bath."

She waited for the snappy comeback or a change in topic. Normally her brother was a fun-loving, witty companion but tonight something was different.

She looked at the man who had been one of her two best friends for most of her life. Rick had always been way more interested in clothes than she'd ever been. Tonight he wore deceptively casual khaki slacks and a dark purple shirt. Both garments bore a designer label and had cost more than a normal family of four's food bill for a month. His watch was more expensive than a Ford Taurus, and she didn't even want to think about what he'd paid for his handmade Italian loafers. Not that it mattered. Richard Thomas III had left his only son a sizable fortune in cash, real estate, and business holdings. All Rick had to do for the rest of his life was figure out how to spend the money after he cashed his monthly check.

"What's wrong?" she asked. "You're restless. Did my birthday take you away from some lovely European destination?"

"No. It's not you, Brillo pad." He flashed her his best grin, the one that sent the ladies to swooning and had brought around more than its share of young men as well.

She fingered her wild curls and remembered being a fifteen-year-old desperate to fit in. She'd wanted long, straight, *blonde* hair. Years of bleaching and straightening had left her hair short, frizzy, and orange. When she'd turned seventeen, Rick had talked her into letting it go natural. He'd told her that her curls were sexy, in a Brillo pad kind of way.

"Then what?" she asked. "Is it David?"

"Maybe."

"I thought you liked him. He's very—"

"Don't go there," he growled in warning.

She raised her eyebrows. "I was going to say 'nice.' Not 'young.' "

"He is young," Rick admitted. "Too young. There's ten years between us, and it's a big ten years. I don't know what I'm doing with him."

She wasn't about to disagree. "If he was a girl, he'd be waving pompoms. Why do all men go for young and pretty rather than—"

"Older and smart?"

She glared at him. "Older at least."

Domino shifted onto her back, exposing her soft tummy. Rick rubbed her belly. "I don't know about always wanting young and pretty. So far I haven't found the right guy, and I get tired of being by myself. David isn't perfect, but he works for now."

"I guess we're both stuck looking for Mr. Right, although in my case I'd settle for Mr. Normal," she said glumly. "At least you don't have Charlotte Elizabeth on your back."

"That's true. I'm in the fortunate position of being unable to provide her with blood-related grandchildren. However, she's quite insistent that you start doing your bit to procreate."

"I've heard. More than once."

He offered a sympathetic smile. "Just stay away from that guy helping out around here. What's his name?"

"Matt." She frowned. "Stay away from him how?"

"Mom says he's exactly your type. That's not good news."

"I can't believe the two of you have been talking about me," she grumbled. "Whatever she's said is wrong. He's not my type. At least I don't know him well enough to know if he is or not, which means Mother doesn't know that either. I wish she'd stop bugging me. I'll get married eventually."

"I believe she wants to insure that your 'eventually' occurs within her lifetime. Don't underestimate her. Mom is the queen of stubborn."

Ali propped her elbow on the armrest and settled her chin on her hand. To Rick, Charlotte Elizabeth was always Mom, but to her, she was Mother. The two names highlighted the differences in their relationships with Charlotte Elizabeth. For Rick, it was simple. They liked each other and that was it. For Ali, there always seemed to be a maze to work through. She didn't know why Rick got along better with her mother. Maybe it was because Rick was male, or because he was the stepson, or it could just be a giant cosmic joke.

"Regardless," she said. "Matt is not the one."

"*Au contraire,* sister of mine. The handsome and mysterious Matt is very much your type. First, he's unemployed."

"No, he's not. He works for Harry."

Rick dismissed her comment with a flick of his hand. "He works as a part-time handyman. Hardly someone on the fast track to upper management. Second, he's obviously in trouble."

She could almost accept the unemployed part, but in trouble? "How do you figure?"

"He won't talk about his past."

"You can't know that."

"Of course I can. I know you, and you'd be pumping him on the first day. If you don't have his life story at your fingertips, he must not be talking."

She sniffed. "I'll have you know that we've had several," *or one,* she thought, "very personal conversations. He's from Chicago and his father lives in Italy. His mother died some years ago. So there!"

"I'm impressed."

"You should be."

Ali wasn't going to admit it, but she actually agreed with her brother on the subject of Matt Baker. There *was* a mystery. He seemed well educated and well spoken. Not the usual kind of man looking for a job with Harry.

"I still think he's a man with a problem," Rick continued. "You can't resist them."

"No. I *couldn't* resist them in the past. I've given up mending people."

Rick laughed. "Not in this lifetime, Sis. Once a missionary, always a missionary. What's the song? 'Rescue Me.' It's perfect."

He hummed a few bars, then moved his lean body in time with the tune. Unamused, Domino glared at Rick, then jumped to the ground. Ali tapped her foot on the floor to get her cat's attention. When Domino looked at her, she patted her thighs. The cat stretched, then sauntered over to jump up on Ali's lap.

"Wouldn't it have been great to be Diana Ross?" he asked, pausing at the chorus.

"I never much thought about it," Ali said honestly, rubbing her cat's head. "Diana Ross?"

"Sure. Beautiful, talented, a great life."

Ali eyed her brother. "We'll ignore that you are neither black nor a woman."

He stretched. "Must be nice to be someone else, even for a little while." He brightened. "Maybe I could be in one of those drag shows and just play Diana Ross."

"Uh, Rick?"

"Yes, my sweet?"

"She didn't sing the song. Fontella Bass did 'Rescue Me.'"

He frowned. "How do you know that?"

"I'm a repository of useless information. It's a gift." She tucked her hair behind her ears and stared at her brother. Was it her imagination, or were there dark shadows under his eyes? "Rick, are you sick?"

"Are we talking mentally or physically?"

Her stomach tightened. "I'm being serious. Is something wrong?" Something—a euphemism for a disease she didn't want to think about.

He smiled at her. Not the charming smile, or the devilish one, but the smile that spoke of his affection for her and the familial bond between them. "I'm fine," he promised. "I'm careful with my health and my lovers, and I get tested regularly. You can worry about a lot of stuff with me, but not that, okay?"

She exhaled in relief. "Okay. It's just that you seem tired."

"Not tired. Bored. My life lacks direction. I can't believe I actually care, but I do. I'm not sure what to do about it."

"Get a job."

He raised his eyebrows. "That's so not me. Maybe I should get a dog."

"It would be a start. Although I'm not sure that's going to help you with establishing purpose or direction."

"You have a point." He crossed his legs at the ankle. "Do you know the worst part about being gay?"

"You both having stubble in the morning?"

He tossed another pillow in her direction. She ducked out of the way.

"I'm being serious," he informed her.

"Fine. I'll be serious, too. What's the worst part?"

"Keeping the relationship going. Guys don't talk. Think about it. In most heterosexual relationships, it's the woman who maintains the connection. She's the one who brings up what's wrong and keeps things in line. Guys know there's a problem, but we don't usually volunteer to talk about it. We keep hoping the other person will do it. Much of the time nothing gets talked about. The problem only gets bigger until it's unmanageable. And then it's too late."

"I've never thought about it that way," Ali said honestly. "Is that what's happening with David?"

"David and I are light-years away from being that close. The problem with my relationship with David is David. . . . Or maybe it's me. I don't know."

"Is there anything I can do to help?"

He leaned his head back and looked at her over his nose. "Maybe."

"What? Do you want to come stay here for a while or should I . . ."

"Money," he said simply. "Give me money."

She stared at him, then blinked. Finally she threw a pillow back at him. Her aim was high, and it sailed harmlessly over his head. "You're a real toad, Richard Thomas the fourth, and I don't like you very much. Money. You have way more than me."

"Way," he agreed with a grin. "My point, little sister," he continued as he dropped his feet to the floor and leaned forward, "is that, except for refusing to give me money, you're still a sucker for someone in trouble. Matt Baker is intelligent, good-looking, and definitely out of place here in Saint Maggie. He's one hundred percent your type. I don't want to see you hurt or used."

"I'm not at risk." Ali didn't want to have this conversation with her brother. There wasn't any point. Okay, maybe her afternoon chat with Matt had been fun. It was nice to know the man had a sense of humor, but she wasn't interested in him. "I told you, I've given up guys like that."

"You said that before. And three days later you met Jason."

Ali clamped her teeth together. She would *not* discuss Jason with her brother. "You know, someone dating a man like Da-vede shouldn't throw stones."

"Fair enough," Rick said with a chuckle. "Just remember that Jason was a lot like Matt. This is where I remind you that he ended up stealing the cash from your till, along with your American Express card. In the three days it took you to figure out it was gone, he'd charged over twenty thousand dollars on it."

She felt the heat on her face and tried to ignore her humiliation at the memory. "Jason and Matt have nothing in common. I'll admit I was stupid where Jason was concerned." She'd been seduced by a pair of sad eyes and a butt worthy of cult status. She'd been able to count her lovers on the fingers of one hand, while he'd been a practiced gigolo. She hadn't had a chance against him. "This is different."

Rick sighed in exasperation. "Not from where I'm sitting. I worry about you, Ali. Please be careful with this guy. At least promise me that much."

"I will," she said grudgingly. "I love you, too."

"I know. I want to see you happy."

"I am happy," she told him. "My life is great. I have a wonderful business that's successful. I enjoy every part of my day."

Which was true. What she didn't tell her brother—mostly because she didn't want to admit it and somewhat because he already knew—was that the days *were* great. It was the lonely nights that were slowly killing her.

chapter five

"I'd bet a month's pay that you feel worse than you look, and you look like crap," Harry said helpfully, his voice only slightly louder than the pounding in Matt's head.

Matt squinted into the bright morning and saw the old man sitting on the top step of the porch. Lucky lay stretched out on the grass nearby. It was a testament to the power of alcohol that Matt didn't even remember if the mangy mutt had crept onto the cot last night or not.

He winced as he took the three steps to the edge of the porch and settled down next to his employer. "I don't believe in doing things by halves," he said, ignoring the way the words made his teeth hurt.

He held in a groan as sunlight pierced his bloodshot eyes. Two cups of coffee hadn't done a thing for his hangover. Even so, he remained hopeful as he took a long swallow from his third.

Harry took a drink from his own mug of coffee. "Want to talk about what's bothering you so much you gotta drink like that?"

"No."

Harry nodded without seeming offended. "I didn't think so."

They sat in silence for several minutes. Matt absorbed the warmth of the sun, letting it bake out the last of the alcohol in his system. While he didn't enjoy physical pain, he didn't try to avoid it, either. It was preferable to the ache of a wound on the inside. That he would do nearly anything to avoid. Even drink enough Scotch to give himself alcohol poisoning.

"He lived up to his name last night," Harry said, motioning toward the dog sleeping on the lawn. "I've already had two calls from upset ladies around town. A dog fitting Lucky's description was seen with both their purebreds." Harry grinned. "I don't know how he does it, but that dog has a gift for finding the ladies in heat. I can't tell you how many puppies born in Saint Maggie look exactly like Lucky."

Matt eyed the flea-bitten mutt and grimaced. More dogs like Lucky? Say it wasn't so. "There's no accounting for taste."

"He's a charmer," the old man continued. "Even Miss Sylvie likes him."

It took Matt a minute to place the name. "The pig?"

"Yup. They're great friends. Sometimes Lucky joins her and Charlotte Elizabeth when they walk around the pond."

Harry continued to talk about Lucky and his many companions, but Matt tuned him out. Instead he looked around the yard at the rear of Harry's house.

The grass was green, but that was more because of a couple of days of rain than any lawn maintenance. A chain-link fence encircled the property. It didn't keep anyone out or Lucky in because the rear gate was missing. In the far corner several rosebushes bloomed, despite years of obvious neglect. To the left of the house was Harry's workshop, where he kept his supplies and his tools.

"Ali's real pleased with your work," Harry said as he finished his coffee and set the mug on the porch behind him. "You're careful and real tidy. That's a plus with the ladies."

"Gee, thanks." Was Harry giving him advice on more than his work habits?

"Where'd you learn to install shelves and put down a floor?"

Matt eyed the old man. Everybody had questions. "My grandfather. He had a workshop out behind his house. He restored old pieces, made one-of-a-kind rocking chairs, that sort of thing."

"Was it his line of work?"

Matt thought about the family business and nearly smiled. "Not exactly. It was more of a hobby. I spent summers with him, and he taught me what he knew."

"How much longer do you think it's going to take to finish things up at Ali's place?"

Matt stared into his coffee as if the answer could be found there. At least his brain was functioning again. "Two, maybe three days."

"Ali's got that whole long list of stuff she needs done. The pay's good. You interested?"

Matt wasn't sure, so he didn't answer.

"She's easy enough to work for," Harry continued, as if trying to sell Matt on the job. "One of the local wineries gave me a call on Friday. They need some fencing replaced. I thought you could keep working for Ali, and

I'll hire a couple of day laborers to take on up to the vineyards. With two jobs going at the same time, I'd give you a bigger cut."

Matt could see where this was headed. "I can't say for sure. I've been thinking that maybe it was time to move on."

He felt more than saw Harry's expression of surprise. "I thought you were going to stick around for a few weeks. That's what you said when I hired you."

Matt nodded in agreement. He'd intended to stay through the end of the month, maybe longer. But now he felt the need to push on, although he couldn't say to where. Not that he disliked working at Ali's store. It was just . . . complicated. She asked too many questions. Her life was too strange.

Which reminded him. "Some reporter stopped by yesterday," Matt said. "He wanted to interview Ali for a tabloid."

Harry nodded. "Must be near her birthday. They come from time to time, wanting to check up on her. It's because of Charlotte Elizabeth."

"Ali mentioned that. Her mother gave up a million-dollar contract to have her?" Talk about carrying around a need to prove one's self.

"She's an amazing woman," Harry said, his tone nearly worshipful.

Matt frowned. "Ali?"

"No, Charlotte Elizabeth." The old man gazed up at the sky and smiled. "I was seventeen the first time I saw her. I don't remember the name of the movie, but she wore a silver-blue dress, one of those formal kinds. It was cut so low that my breath got stuck in my throat. I kept praying she'd pop right out of it, which she didn't. Or if she did, they cut the scene. I spent the entire two hours with a hard-on—praying my date wouldn't notice, or if she did, that she would think it was for her."

Matt chuckled. "Ali's mom was pretty, huh? I don't think I've seen any of her movies."

"You should." Harry frowned. "Pretty doesn't come close to describing that lady, son. She is the most beautiful, elegant, charming woman to ever grace the planet. And to think she lives here, now." He sighed. "Heaven on earth, that's for sure."

Matt wondered what it would be like to live such a simple life, that one's pleasures could be so easily defined. He personally aspired to simple. Although just Friday morning he'd been disgusted when he'd realized he'd nearly picked up the business section of the local newspaper. For a second he'd thought about reading it, just to find out what was going on in the world. But then he'd caught himself and put it back untouched. The business world wasn't allowed to matter anymore. And he was going to make sure it never mattered again.

"Did Ali move here because her mother was here, or was it the other way around?" he asked more to distract himself than because he cared.

"Ali's got a good friend, Clair St. John, who lives on one of the wineries up in the valley. Ali used to visit her a lot. One day she got to driving through St. Maggie and found the house she's in now. It was in need of fixing up, but she liked the looks of it and the location, so she bought it. Then her mother moved to town, and all my prayers were answered."

"Good for you."

Harry stood up and stretched. "It's nearly noon. I was

thinking of grilling a couple of steaks for Lucky and me for lunch. You want one?"

"No, thanks."

"You gotta eat sometime."

"I eat."

"Not enough to keep body and soul together." The old man's gaze sharpened. "You trying to kill yourself or something?"

Matt stared up into the sky and was pleased when his headache didn't worsen. "Don't worry. I'm not trying to kill myself."

Harry took a couple of steps toward the back door, then paused. "Just because I don't ask a lot of questions doesn't mean I don't have them."

"I appreciate that."

"You think about sticking around for a few more weeks. There are worse places than Saint Maggie, and I could use your help."

Matt nodded, but made no promises as the old man stepped into the house. He wasn't sure what to do. The weather was pleasant now, but it would soon cool down. He didn't think he would like spending his winter up north. He didn't even own a decent coat. Or rather he did, but it was back in Chicago, and he wasn't about to go get it.

What would Harry say if he knew the truth about Matt? What would anyone say? He knew what questions he'd have if he were in the old man's position.

He stretched out his legs and relaxed, letting the sun heal his physical maladies. Eventually, the pounding in his head eased some. Lucky stood up and stretched, then made his way over to the steps. He leaned into Matt and placed his ugly one-eared head on Matt's thigh. Without thinking,

Matt reached down and patted the dog. Lucky looked up in doggy surprise. Matt was a little surprised himself, then decided that patting a dog didn't mean anything. But just to be sure, as soon as he finished Ali's shelves, he would pack up and leave Santa Magdelana. For good.

"Oh, Ma-att!"

Matt paused in the gravel parking lot of Decadent Delight and tried not to cringe at the sound of that particular voice drifting across the morning with a sing-song lilt. He'd hoped, just this once, to make it inside without being confronted by the formidable presence otherwise known as Charlotte Elizabeth, but it was not to be. *Just twenty feet shy of my goal,* he thought as he longingly stared at the sanctuary that was Ali's back door.

Slowly, with the inevitability man often feels in the presence of a force of nature, he turned toward the approaching woman and her pig.

Charlotte Elizabeth moved with the regal grace of a woman trained in dance. Even though it was well before eight in the morning, she was already dressed and made-up. Today there was a slight nip in the air and her clothes reflected that fact. She wore a colorful knit sweater over black leggings. Ankle-high boots emphasized the curve of her calves, still youthful like the rest of her, despite her sixty-plus years.

Even as she approached, Matt found it difficult to believe she was Ali's mother. Not that they didn't look alike—there were similarities in the color of their hair and the shape of their eyes—but Charlotte Elizabeth didn't appear the least bit maternal.

"Good morning," he said, bracing himself for Miss Sylvie's enthusiastic greeting. For reasons that were not clear to him, the pig had an unnatural fondness for his shoes. She snuffled them and snorted until he wondered if she was going to rip them off his feet. Ali had sworn she did that to everyone, but Matt had the feeling that somehow his shoes earned special attention.

"Matt. How lovely to see you. Did you enjoy your day off?"

Enjoy? The hangover? The solitude which gave him too much time to remember? The afternoon hike he'd taken in an effort to exhaust himself so that he would sleep? "Sure," he said politely. "And yours?"

"Miss Sylvie and I went down to Los Angeles. The new theater season began."

He stared at the pig who wore a jaunty blue scarf over her collar and tried to imagine what the opening-night crowd thought of Charlotte Elizabeth's date. "Did you two like the play?"

"Yes, of course. Charles and I . . ." Her voice trailed off and she playfully tapped his upper arm. "I didn't take Miss Sylvie with me, Matt. She stays at the townhouse. I put in a video for her, and she's very happy to be on her own."

He almost wanted to know what kind of video her pig preferred, but then decided whatever he imagined would be better than the truth.

"Have you decided to stay or not?" she asked. "Harry said you were thinking of moving on."

"That's right."

He frowned. It was only Monday morning, and he'd talked with Harry the day before. If Charlotte Elizabeth had spent the weekend in Los Angeles, how had she known about his conversation with his boss?

He glanced at her, but she only gave him an enigmatic smile.

"Ali has more work that needs doing over at the tearoom and the bed-and-breakfast. I can't keep it all straight. Something about painting and wallpaper." She tilted her head as she regarded him. "So, what do you think of my daughter?"

He went on instant alert. "She's very nice."

Charlotte Elizabeth wrinkled her still-pert nose. Her green eyes—the color of fresh money—bore into his. "No woman wants to be nice. We prefer exotic or dangerous."

He grinned. "I don't think either applies to Ali."

"I suppose not." She sighed. "More's the pity. But she's very attractive, don't you think? All that curly hair, which she gets from her father." Charlotte Elizabeth smiled at a distant memory. "He was something of a snake, but a handsome man and very good in bed. It just never occurred to me I was going to get pregnant. You see, I hadn't before. Not for want of trying. There were so many men around, and I was something of a bad girl in my day." She grinned.

Matt found himself wanting to smile back. He didn't doubt Charlotte Elizabeth had been wild in her day. She probably still howled at the moon on occasion.

"I'm going to work now," he said.

"Nonsense. I'm sorry if I made you uncomfortable talking about my love life. Although it was over thirty years ago, so I don't see how it could be upsetting to anyone now. I'm simply saying that when I found out I was pregnant with Ali, I was thrilled. And sick. The women in my family suffer terribly. We have three stages of being with child, as they say. Sick, sicker, and sickest. I had to stop work immediately and retire to my bedroom where I spent nine months feeling like death." She paused dramatically. "And then my angel was born. Such a sweet child. So even tempered, so intelligent, so colicky. But that soon ended."

Matt was hoping she meant the colic and not Ali's intelligence.

"I'm not like those women who deliver babies like a barn cat having kittens. If only I had, I would have dozens of children now and even some grandchildren." She paused significantly. "I *want* grandchildren."

Ah, so they were finally getting to the point of this tête-à-tête. "Mrs. Thomas, I'm not really interested in Ali that way. I'm going to be moving on and I think—"

"Good," she said, cutting him off. All the humor fled her face. Her mouth straightened, and her eyes glittered with warning. "You see, Mr. Baker, I thought about this a lot over the weekend, and I've changed my mind about you. I don't know who or what you're hiding from, but whatever it is, it can't be good for my daughter. Unfortunately for all of us, you're exactly her type. Ali's a lovely young woman, but she has appalling taste in men. I want her married and happy, but if she can't be the former, I'll settle on the latter. You're not happy material."

She didn't know anything about him, yet she'd figured it all out, right down to the darkness of his soul. He wasn't in a position to make anyone happy.

"Ali's lucky to have you," he said stiffly. "But don't worry about me."

"Thank you."

She tugged on the pig's leash until the animal gave up

its investigation of the glory that was his shoes and trotted after her like a large pink dog. They were quite a pair, he thought. Who would have thought someone like Charlotte Elizabeth would live in a place like this?

"Oh, Charlotte Elizabeth?"

She paused to glance at him. "Yes?"

"You forgot your daughter's birthday. It was Saturday. Rick was here, though," he added helpfully.

Ali's mother sputtered, then she shook her head in resignation. "And here I'd promised myself I wouldn't do that again." She stared at him. "I suppose I deserve this for butting into your business. All right. Thank you, Matt. I appreciate you telling me."

"You're welcome."

He watched her go. When she was out of sight, he turned toward the shop and paused. Sunlight reflected off the curtained windows facing the parking lot. At one time the house had been a Victorian reproduction. Probably built in the twenties or thirties. There was a wide porch, both in front and in back. Someone had updated the place, opening walls to give the rooms a more spacious feel. Ali had remodeled again so that she could turn the upstairs into a self-contained apartment and use the downstairs for her business. He didn't know much about her past, but the little he did know made him wonder how difficult it had been for her to find the peace she had now.

The back door opened, and Ali stepped onto the porch. She held a cloth-covered tray in her right hand. It looked innocent enough, but she had the light of battle in her eyes, and he knew he was in trouble. Tag-teamed by mother and daughter.

"Don't think I didn't notice," she said when he was

within speaking distance. "Saturday afternoon you ate one of my truffles, and you actually liked it. I saw it in the look on your face. So don't for a minute think I'm going to let you get away with ignoring my food any longer." She whipped the cover off the tray, exposing two steaming mugs of coffee and a plate of fluffy croissants.

"Almond-and-butter flavored," she said. "I made them myself, and let me tell you, croissants are a pain in the butt to make. So I don't expect to hear anything from you except 'thank you, Ali.' Is that understood?"

He looked from her to the tray and back. She fed him because she thought he was too poor to buy food. And because, for reasons her mother hadn't bothered to explain, he was her type. Whatever that meant.

He didn't want to be her type. He didn't deserve to be anyone's type. He didn't deserve to still be alive, either, but he was. And for the first time in nearly a year, he was hungry. Down to the bone starving. And there was only one thing that was going to satisfy him, damn them both to hell.

"Don't look so fierce," she said lightly. "It's just breakfast. You're not selling your soul to the devil."

She was wrong, but he couldn't tell her that. Nor could he resist. With fingers that nearly trembled, he reached out and plucked one of the still-warm croissants from the plate. Then he took a bite and tasted the promise of paradise.

"Office supplies," Matt said, opening the built-in cabinet door. He pointed to the shelves. "The top three are adjustable. And that should about do it."

"I can't believe it," Ali said, turning in a slow circle. "I was here the entire time and saw what you were doing, but I never realized how great it was going to turn out. Thank you."

The messy room had been transformed. The walls and ceiling had been patched and painted with cream enamel, and new flooring gleamed underfoot. New, bright, fluorescent lights illuminated the two fifteen-foot-long worktables covered with, of all things, granite. Matt had found the two pieces discarded at a hardware store. They didn't match, and there were a couple of flaws in the coloring, but she didn't care. Granite would wear well and be easy to keep clean, and the size was perfect.

Built-in shelves lined three of the four walls. He'd installed clear-topped bins for her bulk supplies, dividers to separate her mailing boxes and labels, and drawers for the paper-lined foil that went on top of the chocolates in her fancy boxes. He'd even replaced the window and put up a new miniblind.

Matt shifted his weight from foot to foot. "You really like it?"

"Absolutely. All your improvements are terrific. I wouldn't have thought of them myself, but now I can't imagine how I could survive without them."

A smile tugged at the corners of his mouth, and an impish light danced in his eyes, but all he said was, "Good."

To Ali he appeared to be a man who wasn't allowed to enjoy the moment. He was proud of what he'd done, and he wanted her to say all the right words, but he seemed to be trying to stay disconnected. As if caring about a job well done wasn't permitted.

It was after six, on Wednesday. The store was closed,

and her employees had left for the day. Matt had been hard at work installing the last of the shelves. He could have left her to find the finished product on her own, but he hadn't. He wouldn't admit to caring about the job, yet he couldn't just walk away from it, either. He was a mass of contradictions.

"Speaking of good ideas," she said, leaning against one of the tables and tucking her hands into her apron pockets, "I've been doing some checking around. Those custom mailers you mentioned?"

"I remember. I thought they'd be better for your chocolates than the boxes you were using."

"Exactly. Well I've found a couple of companies who specialize in just that sort of thing. If I buy in bulk, they're the same price as what I've been using. Not only will the chocolates arrive protected, but I won't have the expense of the extra packing material."

"Good."

Matt lounged against the opposite table. His posture was relaxed, as was his expression. In his worn workshirt and jeans, he could have been any one of Harry's part-time helpers. Except he wasn't like most of them. Matt spoke and acted like a well-educated man. Someone used to being in charge of a lot more than a small building project. Someone used to fixing things.

"Thanks for the suggestion." She paused, then decided to test her theory . . . the one that said he was much more than he appeared. "Do you have any others?"

"Sure. Get thee to the Internet," he told her. "I know setting up a halfway decent website is going to cost some money, but there's a whole world passing you by. Not only will your existing customers be able to impulse-order more quickly, it will be easier for them to send their friends to check you out."

"Hey, I just got an 800 number last year." She gave a little laugh. "I'm not sure I'm ready for anything more high-tech."

He shoved his hands through his hair in an impatient gesture. "You've got to do it, Ali. Your business is perfect for the web. You already do a substantial amount of mail order anyway. It's what, forty or fifty percent of your sales?"

She stared at him. How had he guessed that? "Close enough. But what makes you think my customers shop that way?"

He pushed off the table and walked to the window. "Look at this town. It's Yuppie heaven. You've got the wineries, the ocean, and the spa." He turned to face her. "All three things draw consumers with plenty of disposable income. Especially the spa-and-wine crowd. Didn't you tell me that most of your mail-order customers are former spa clients?"

She nodded.

"Trust me. They're all on the Internet. This is a huge, untapped market." His face tightened with intensity as his brown eyes darkened with an excitement she hadn't seen before.

"We're talking about billions of dollars being spent on everything from books to airline tickets to candy. Why not your chocolates? They're the best I've ever tasted."

"Why, thank you, sir," she said, trying to keep her tone light, all the while feeling as if she'd just stepped into a tornado. He was moving way too fast for her.

He paced to the table, then made the return trip to the

window. "It's not the wave of the future anymore, Ali. It's the present. If you don't do this, you're going to go under."

"Actually, my store will be just fine."

"You won't grow."

"Maybe I don't want to grow."

He faced her and planted his hands on his hips. "This place has great potential. You could franchise—become the next Mrs. Fields. You could be a chain."

He was pushing just like her mother. She hated being pushed. "I don't want to be a chain, I like being just a link, thank you very much."

He shook his head in obvious frustration. "I'm not kidding about this. You could—"

She held up her hand to stop him. "You're not hearing me. I don't want to be a chain or a franchise. I might look into a website. Thanks for the advice, but I like being small."

He glared. "We're talking serious money here. If you did some projections you could—"

"No! I said I don't want to. I'm very happy with my store. This is all I want."

"You have to want more. Everyone does."

"No, they don't."

They stared at each other for several seconds. Finally Matt drew in a deep breath. "Fine. Be shortsighted."

Ali smiled. "Ah, a gracious loser. Always a charming quality in a man."

"I don't lose," he said simply. "It's number one or not at all."

"I don't share your philosophy. There are dozens of places besides number one, and some of them are very worthwhile." She tilted her head. "Who are you, Matt Baker? Number-one handyman? What are you doing working in my storeroom? Why did you leave Chicago?"

Surprise widened his eyes, then the familiar shutters came down, and she couldn't tell what he was thinking. His posture changed. He stopped glaring, stopped pacing, stopped everything until he was once again the withdrawn stranger who had first walked into her life.

He'd forgotten, she realized. Whatever it was that had sent him on this journey had momentarily disappeared from his mind. He'd become himself—whoever that was—dropping his guard. The contrast between the two sides of the man intrigued her. It also sent up warning signals. She didn't need any more trouble in her life.

"Just some ideas for you to think about," he said.

So he wasn't going to answer her questions. She pulled a piece of paper out of her apron and unfolded it. After smoothing it down on the granite worktop, she looked at him.

"There's this list," she began. "I have a financial interest in the tearoom and bed-and-breakfast across the street. They both need work. Also, the fence around the parking lot needs painting. Harry is still convinced you're buying his business from him, while my mother has informed me you're going to be leaving town soon. I won't even ask how you came to have a conversation with my mother." She paused.

She'd been hoping for a smile, but his closed expression didn't change.

The next part of her speech wasn't going to be so easy. She cleared her throat. "I have two questions. Actually if the answer to the first one is no, then you don't have to answer the second."

"What's the first question?"

"Are you staying around for a while?"

"What's the second question?"

She resisted the need to put a little more room between them. "Is the reason you're hiding out in Saint Maggie because you committed a violent act?"

He actually smiled. A real smile. Lips curving, teeth exposed, crinkles by the corners of his eyes. It was beautiful. It made her stomach lurch in a way that made her want to gasp out loud and wonder if she'd lost her mind. No way was she attracted to this guy. Not her, not ever. No. Absolutely not. He wasn't her type. Or worse, he was her type, and she'd sworn to avoid that type no matter what.

"Are you asking if I've killed anyone lately?"

She raised her hand and waved vaguely toward him. "Lately, ever, that sort of thing. Killing, maiming, just violence in general. I'm not in favor of it."

He folded his arms over his chest. Oddly enough, the gesture seemed to tug at the shoulders of his shirt in a most interesting way. Had it always done that, and had she not noticed?

"Me, either," he told her. "No violence, Ali. I swear." His gaze shifted away from her. "I'll admit that I've switched gears in the past year or so, but it was a personal choice. I didn't do anything illegal."

The news brightened her considerably. "Oh, good. I believe in giving everyone a second chance, but I'm not into prison reform right here on the premises." She drew in a breath and shrugged. "So, are you staying or what?"

chapter six

No, I'm not staying, Matt thought as he continued to look at Ali. She was still dressed for work, in a dark red, long-sleeved dress with an apron over the top. Her hair, free of its constraining braid, tumbled over her shoulders and around her face in a riot of silky curls. She had big eyes and a full mouth. She was the kind of woman a man dreamed of kissing . . . all over.

He found her attractive, and she took care of him. Those two insights should have scared the crap out of him, but they didn't. Because wanting her was meaningless, and Ali took care of everyone. She hadn't singled him out. If he were to walk away, she would simply turn her social worker's beacon light on someone else. It wasn't personal—what she did for him, not the fact that he found her good-looking and sexy. They were both experiencing knee-jerk reactions.

"Matt?" Her gray-green eyes widened slightly as she spoke his name.

Move on, a voice in his head instructed. It was the safest course for everyone. If he stayed, there would be trouble, although he wasn't sure he could say why.

He shrugged. "I guess I'll be around for a couple of weeks more."

The words surprised him. He'd meant to say no. What had happened?

"Good. Do you want to go over my list now or in the morning?" she asked.

What he wanted was to walk away, but apparently he'd committed himself to a few more days in her company. "Let's do it now," he said. "Then I can talk to Harry and tell him what supplies I'll need."

She led the way to the back door and pulled it open. "I heard he's starting a big job up at one of the wineries," she said as she stepped out into the twilight. The sun had set and there was a distinct nip in the air.

Matt pulled the door closed behind him. He could smell the promise of fall along with the salt from the ocean. Winter in this part of California was mild when compared with the Midwest, but the temperature could still drop to close to freezing at night.

"Harry's hired a couple of guys to help him replace some fencing. It should take about three weeks."

She smiled up at him as they walked across the gravel parking lot. "Multiple employees. Harry's practically turning into a conglomerate."

Matt didn't respond to her teasing. Instead he looked at the trees on the north side of the parking lot. Streetlights illuminated their branches and the dying leaves still clinging there. Leaves, cooler temperatures. Dear God, why hadn't he realized the time of year before now?

"First, I want the parking lot spruced up," Ali was saying. "The fences need painting, and we need more gravel. I think Harry ordered two truckloads last year. I want the gravel in before the rainy season. Otherwise this place turns into one giant mud puddle."

He calculated the date and stumbled to a stop. Nearly a year. Can it have been that long? A year? And he'd almost forgotten. Damn. He'd been a bastard before. He wasn't better now, he was worse.

"The customers don't appreciate that, I can assure you," she was saying.

But Matt wasn't listening. He couldn't. All he could do was try to breathe through the pain searing his chest. A year. Why hadn't he realized? Why hadn't he known?

He started walking. Faster and faster. Every part of his body ached, as if he'd just had a close encounter with a truck. He was battered and broken, and it had been a year.

"Matt?"

He paused long enough to glance over his shoulder. Ali stood where he'd left her, staring at him as if he was crazy. "I can't do this now," he told her. "Tomorrow."

And then he was running into the rapidly darkening night. Running until the pain in his chest deepened and the sound of his shoes on the street echoed. Until—in his mind—he wasn't in Saint Maggie anymore. There was no smell of the sea. There was only the chill of the season's first snowfall. The tiny flakes melting quickly on the coffin being lowered into the grave.

His fault. It had been his fault from the very beginning. But he'd been too self-centered to see it. Too involved in work. He'd killed her—just the way his father had killed his mother. He had always hated his father for that. He couldn't forgive the old man, and he wouldn't forgive himself.

Leigh.

He remembered the past, feeling the people around him, hearing their voices saying they were sorry. How shocking. So fast, so young, so very gone. They kept saying trite meaningless things until he wanted to scream at them to shut up. He wanted to hit them and make them as dead as she was. Their friends, her parents. The faint whisper of someone saying how sad it was they'd never had children.

All he could do was watch the coffin disappearing into the cold dark ground and tell himself that wasn't Leigh. She wasn't dead. It was a mistake. The doctors had been wrong about everything. But it wasn't a mistake and she was gone and it was all his fault. Because he'd turned into a heartless bastard who took whatever he wanted—even someone else's soul.

Suddenly he was running then as he ran now. Running from the graveside, from the cemetery. Running and getting lost in a city so big it had swallowed him whole. Running until his sides ached and his lungs and legs wouldn't let him take another step. Then walking until he stumbled into a bus station and bought a ticket.

Like he had that night nearly a year before, Matt ran. He cursed the darkness that was his most constant companion, moving until his body betrayed him with pain and he had to stop.

He didn't remember much about the bus ride. He'd been numb and empty. His most constant thought had been that he should have been dead instead of her. He'd deserved to die.

"Leigh," he gasped, his breathing ragged. He leaned against a fence post and stared up at the sky. As if calling her name in that direction would mean she heard him.

"I'm sorry."

The words came out on a breath, barely audible and completely meaningless. What did being sorry matter now?

A full moon had risen over the horizon. Full and fat—a hunter's moon. There had been no moon when Leigh had died, no moon when he'd boarded the bus. He didn't know if there had been clouds covering the light or if the moon itself had been absent. All he knew was that he'd stared out of the bus window and seen only darkness. It had swallowed him up, and he'd welcomed the blackness.

He'd walked off the bus all those months ago because of what he'd done. He existed in this half-life, not where he'd been before, but not anywhere he wanted to go, either. He kept moving because if he didn't, he was going to have to face what he'd become. He didn't look back because he couldn't stand to, and he wouldn't look forward.

Matt didn't know how long he stared up at the sky as if he could find absolution there. Instead all he got was a crick in his neck. He called to her, silently and aloud, but there was still no answer.

Finally he stopped gazing at the heavens. Looking around he realized he was completely lost. There were lights in the distance, but around him were fenced fields and grapevines. He'd never been this far out of town.

Before he could decide which way to go, a small shape moved out of the darkness. The shape became a dog, and the dog turned into Lucky. The mutt stared at him for a couple of seconds, then started walking away. Matt followed.

It took nearly two hours for them to make their way back to Harry's. When they arrived, Matt stumbled into the back room and collapsed on the cot. He was tired to his bones. A cold, soul-numbing exhaustion sucked at his spirit until he knew he couldn't have moved even if the house was on fire. Then he closed his eyes and slept.

In his dream he had a sense of something warm curling up by his stomach. Something he should probably push away. Instead he pressed into the heat and drew sleep-filled comfort from the sound of another living creature's heartbeat.

The next morning, when Ali headed downstairs to start coffee for her mother and Miss Sylvie's postwalk visit, she told herself that Matt wasn't going to show up. Last night had been weird, even for him. Something was definitely wrong with that man.

She told herself it was for the best if he disappeared from her life. That the tea shop and bed-and-breakfast had survived without repairs this long, and they would continue to prosper, even without benefit of sprucing. In time, Harry would hire another assistant, and the new man would complete the work.

She nearly had herself convinced, too, so there was absolutely no reason for her heart to flutter in her chest when she saw a tall, dark shape lurking outside her back door. In fact, the fluttering made her nervous. She didn't need another handsome misfit in her life. She'd already had her share, and more. What she needed was stable, reliable, and normal. From what she'd seen so far, not one of those words applied to Matt Baker.

She opened the door and leaned against the doorframe. Matt stood on the top step. He wore faded jeans and a plaid workshirt. Both were clean. His hair was still damp from his shower, and his face looked freshly shaved. Still, something lonely and black lurked in his brown eyes, and she could see lines of pain around his mouth.

"You're not at your best," she said bluntly.

"I've been that way for a while," he replied, shoving his hands into his pockets. His direct gaze locked with hers. "Sorry about last night."

"You ran out, literally, while I was in the middle of a sentence. If I wanted that kind of inattention from a man, I could start dating again."

One corner of his mouth twitched ever so slightly. Unfortunately her heart noticed and did a few steps of what felt like a tango across her chest.

"You want to talk about it?" Ali asked.

"No."

"Good. Me neither. Are you sticking around, or are you leaving?"

"I said I'd be here a couple of weeks. I'll be here."

She glanced at her watch. "You have two choices. You can come inside and have a cup of my delicious coffee. The price of that is my mother and Miss Sylvie will be over in about ten minutes. Or we can walk briskly toward the tea shop, and I can show you what needs doing. That way you'll miss your coffee, but you'll also avoid a close encounter with the meddling insanity that is Charlotte Elizabeth."

This time he did smile. "I've never been much of a coffee drinker," he said as he stepped off the porch. "I'm ready now if you are."

She chuckled. "Coward. Not that I blame you."

The morning air was just crisp enough to make her grateful for her jeans and sweatshirt. Their feet crunched in the gravel as they walked side by side.

"I'll talk to Harry about placing an order," Matt said, kicking at the small stones. "You said two truckloads?"

"That's what I've always done in the past. It seems to work."

He nodded, then glanced toward the painted white fence bordering the parking lot. "I'll sand the wood down before putting on another couple of coats. Should only take a day or two."

"Sounds good."

They stepped onto the sidewalk and reached the corner. Once there, Ali paused. Her store was behind them, the tea shop in front of them. She pointed to the low one-story building. Blue shutters and trim accented the white exterior. A wide porch surrounded the structure. Hanging plants spilled out of baskets while shrubs lined the wide walkway.

"Obviously that was once a private residence," she said. "I don't know the original date of construction, but I'm guessing it was back in the 1920s. The corner property is the bed-and-breakfast."

She pointed to the two-story clapboard house, painted a sunny yellow. Round towers and dormer windows made the roofline look like a three dimensional rendering of Switzerland. Balconies jutted out from oddly shaped doorways.

"There's a second building on the other side of the house," she said. "Those upstairs rooms have a view of the ocean. The original bed-and-breakfast was only the first building. Kasey added the second one about four years ago."

He looked at her. "Do you own these businesses?"

She hesitated. "No. I have more of a financial interest in each."

They crossed the street. To the right, a green park stretched out for several acres, narrowing at the far end to become little more than a meandering bike path. In the center of the park was a duck pond. It was late enough in the year that the darling baby ducks were now indistinguishable from their parents.

Ali paused to point to the hand-carved sign above the doorway welcoming them to "The Tea Shoppe—Restaurant and Store."

"You might want to prepare yourself," she said as she glanced over her shoulder at Matt. She fitted her key into the lock and turned it to the right. "It's not exactly a guy kind of place."

He followed her inside, then paused in the small foyer and visibly shuddered. Ali couldn't help laughing. Matt was over six feet of lean muscle. He had a butt that would turn heads on both coasts, and a smile that stopped female conversations dead. But he couldn't have been more out of place unless he'd showed up for an exam at an ob/gyn office.

The walls of the restaurant and antique shop were covered by pale silk fabric. Fancy casserole dishes stood on top of an old-fashioned metal stove. There were coat racks covered with shawls, tables with linens and dishes, baskets with soaps, lotions, and gels. Exotic tea filled built-in shelves, aromatherapy candles scented the air with vanilla and cinnamon—and all that was just in the foyer. Poor Matt still had to make his way through the maze of round tables all covered with lace cloths and set with floral-covered plates. His big feet narrowly missed a floor display of a stuffed rabbit family. The dolls, all heavily weighted with buckshot, were both functional as well as decorative doorstops.

"Women come here for lunch or tea, and to shop," Ali told him. "We have a wonderful menu of little sandwiches, scones, cakes, and tea."

"Sounds great," he said, his voice completely insincere.

She laughed. "You are lying and doing a bad job of it. Not that I blame you. Men hate places like this."

"I wonder why," he muttered. "Couldn't you have had part interest in a sports bar?"

"Sorry. My friend Sara Gattling bought the house. It had already been converted into a restaurant by the previous owner, so her expenses were mostly for decorating. The kitchen was in great shape." She motioned to the antiques. "Sara has a degree in something like restaurant management and a lot of experience, but the bank didn't want to give her any more credit." Ali smoothed the front of a vintage lacy dress displayed on an old-fashioned headless mannequin. "I happened to have good credit, so the loan wasn't a problem for me. We joined forces."

He looked at the wood floor, the beamed ceiling, then at the two dozen or so tables waiting for their customers. "What do you get out of it? Free tea?"

"I've never been much of a tea drinker," she admitted. "We share inventory. I make scones, muffins, and croissants. Sara does lunch food like quiche and sandwiches, along with cookies, brownies, and the most amazing cakes."

His interest quickened. "Those five-layer chocolate jobs in the display case at your store?"

"One and the same."

He looked around at the pictures, hats, and trays displayed on the wall, then fingered the price tag of a handmade quilt neatly folded over an oak quilt rack. "You didn't answer the question. What do you get out of being part owner of all this? Even during the summer, I'm guessing your busiest months, you're not getting rich off a place like this."

She didn't ask him how he could guess that, although she doubted it would be difficult for anyone to figure out. "Sara works hard. This place is her dream. When the bank wouldn't take a chance on her, someone had to. She's divorced and raising two kids. Her ex does his best with child-support payments, but he's had financial troubles over the years. Her kids are great," she hurried on before he could interrupt.

If her mother were here, Charlotte Elizabeth would roll her eyes. Rick would accuse her of taking care of the world again. What neither of them seemed to notice was that the world was in serious need of care, and no one else was volunteering.

"Marti and Joey, Sara's two little ones, spend their afternoons and evenings here with her. When they're not in school."

"Uh-huh." Matt didn't look impressed.

"Which is why you're here," she continued, gesturing toward the door leading to the back. They walked past the double doors that went into the kitchen and instead stepped into a square hall. There were two bathrooms and a third door marked "Private."

"It's through here," she said, entering an office.

Beyond the space containing two desks, filing cabinets, and a phone was a storeroom. Boxes and a couple of broken chairs leaned against the far wall. One pane of the small window was broken. The center of the room had been swept, and several toys rested on a worn blanket.

"Reminds me of Harry's place," he said, looking around. "You want me to clean out the storeroom?"

"Yes. Most of this stuff is junk and can be tossed. I want it converted to a playroom. Sara has her two children and Dora, she's a maid at the bed-and-breakfast, has a six-year-old. Her older kids are in high school, but little Sally needs somewhere to play."

"Let me guess. Dora's another single mom."

"A widow. Her husband died young and without insurance."

He leaned against the wall and looked down at her. "Let me guess again. You secretly work for Social Services."

"No. I just take participation in my community very seriously. Besides, it's for kids. Who can resist that?"

She was a lady with a cause, Matt thought. He was lucky to have escaped her attention so far. A few meals and cups of coffee hardly counted. No doubt if she had her way, she would reform the world.

"What do you want to do in here?" he asked.

She briefly described a cosmetic remodeling that included fresh paint and a larger window. She also mentioned a box to hold toys and a child-level blackboard. Matt took a small notebook from his shirt pocket and jotted down her instructions.

He looked at the twelve-foot-square room. "Three days, four max. What's next?"

"The bed-and-breakfast. I'll give you the nickel tour so you can get a feel for the place, then show you what needs to be done."

They walked around the corner and up the paved driveway. The parking lot was about half full. The single house was tall and square, and the new addition used the same Victorian style architecture, although the windows were larger and the balconies were less ornate.

Matt paused to survey the bed-and-breakfast. Two sets of French doors stood open, inviting guests to enter a large reception area. Used brick gave the open porch a homey feel. There were dozens of trees, vines, and plants that he didn't have a prayer of identifying. Except maybe roses. He recognized those.

They entered the reception area. Matt took in the tall desk on the right and the taller redhead standing behind it. She looked to be in her midforties, attractive in a stern sort of way, with piercing blue eyes and a full mouth. Her short bob of hair swayed with every movement of her head.

"Morning, Ali," the woman said, never taking her gaze off Matt. "Is this Harry's helper?"

He walked over and held out his hand. "Matt Baker."

"Kasey Johnson."

Her handshake was firm and direct. She didn't look like the sort of person who needed rescuing, but he was sure she had a story of her own to tell.

"Nice to meet you, Matt. Has Ali told you what we want done around here?"

"I was just getting to that," Ali said.

Before Kasey could respond, the phone rang, and she reached for the receiver. While she spoke, Matt looked at the open area beyond the reception desk. There were several comfortable-looking sofas covered in floral-print fabric of green and blue. Three-ring binders promising "Local Restaurant Recommendations" lay scattered on battered wooden tables along with brochures for local shopping, day trips to nearby Santa Barbara, and maps to Santa Ynez Valley wineries. Bookshelves around a fireplace held videos that were, according to a posted sign, free to guests.

"This is the general reception area," Ali said. She pointed to an open doorway at the far end of the room. "Breakfast is served in there, or guests can arrange to have it delivered to their rooms."

They walked into a slightly smaller room set with several tables. A buffet offered fresh fruit, muffins, what he now recognized as scones, juice, and coffee. A young woman in a chef's hat smiled at Ali.

"We're having fresh potato pancakes this morning," the woman said. "And quiche."

Ali looked at Matt. He shook his head. "No, thanks."

"Your loss." Ali smiled at the chef. "Mary is in her final year at culinary school. She's fabulous. The things she can do with eggs and cheese are as close to art as cooking gets."

Mary blushed and ducked her head. "You're being kind."

Ali waved away the comment. "I'm telling the absolute truth."

She led Matt through the small but well-equipped kitchen and into the food storage room. He saw posted menus for breakfast, afternoon hors d'oeuvres, and late-night desserts. Next to the afternoon and evening selections was a list of wines to be served.

Ali tapped the front of a large wine cellar. Through the glass door Matt saw dozens of bottles of wine lying on their sides. Neat white labels hung from each bottle. A three-digit number identified the wine.

"All local," Ali said with pride. "The Santa Ynez Valley wineries around here are coming into their own. We feature different wineries every month. Rick, my brother, does the buying for me. He's spending some time there right now. My friend Clair and her husband own a winery about twenty miles outside of town."

Matt didn't think he'd ever heard of the Santa Ynez Valley before, let alone tasted their wines. "Are they any good?"

"What? You think we want to punish our guests with lousy wine? They're fabulous."

He looked from the bottles of wines to her. "You loaned Kasey money, too?"

Ali cleared her throat. "Like I said, I have a financial interest in things. I met Kasey right after I bought my house. The building needed a lot of remodeling, what with me wanting a store downstairs and the apartment upstairs. I stayed here while the work was done. We became friends. I offered to help."

He frowned. "How could you have helped her with a loan when you were just starting your own business?"

She shrugged. "I just did."

"Yeah, right." There was something she wasn't telling him. "Is there anyone in town you're not helping out?"

"My mother. According to her, I'm in danger of destroying her life by not having children."

He could tell he was making her uncomfortable. Reluctantly, he returned to the business at hand. "What's next on the tour?"

She turned and walked out of the room. After moving down a back hallway, they entered a room that held linens, cleaning supplies, and maids' carts. From there they circled around to the front desk, and Ali grabbed keys to several empty rooms.

"The B and B is a small setup," she explained. "There are five rooms overhead. In the next building there are a total of fourteen rooms, seven up and seven down. The top-right two rooms are a suite. A few of the rooms need to be refurbished. Painting the bathrooms, changing wallpaper, that sort of thing."

She led the way outside, then up a side staircase. When they reached the second floor of the second building, Ali turned to the right and walked to the end. "There are two smaller bedrooms," she explained as she unlocked the door. "This one and the one below. Kasey and I have been talking about converting them from regular bedrooms to parlors. That would mean having three suites instead of just one."

"But you'd cut down on your total number of available beds for the night," Matt reminded her.

"True." She stepped into the room and turned on a light switch. "However, these small rooms aren't as nice as the others in the facility. Kasey has received a lot of complaints about how tiny they are. By converting them, we can charge as much for the suite as for the two bedrooms separately. If we need bedrooms rather than suites, the parlor can be closed off."

He moved into the bedroom. A four-poster bed dominated the tiny space. A canopy of red-and-black fabric hung down each of the four posts, and the mattress was high enough to require a step stool. Rattan furniture added to the romantic air of the room, as did the lace curtains and floral-print wallpaper.

Everything matched, he thought, trying not to be horrified. The bedspread, the wallpaper, even the throw rugs on the polished hardwood floor. Three quarters of the way up the high walls was a narrow shelf filled with knickknacks. Baskets and hats and plates and stacked tins. Nearly a dozen pillows covered almost half the bed. Like the tearoom, it was female paradise.

"Very nice," he said at last, because Ali seemed to be waiting for a comment.

"I think Kasey's done a beautiful job, but you can see how crowded it is. Even with everything scaled down. The bed is only a queen, not a king. The dresser and chair are smaller than in the other rooms. At least the bathroom is decent."

While he stuck his head in there, she disappeared out the front door. Matt took in clean white tiles and a tub big enough for a committee meeting. He noticed the showerhead was high enough for him to stand under. Over the past year or so, he'd missed that. Most of the showers he used spat out water at chest level on him. He'd grown tired of having to limbo to wash his hair.

He studied the floral wallpaper, wondering what it was about places like this and flower prints. There was a silver tray by the sink. Bottles, boxes, and tubes offered floral-scented promises. The towels were white, huge and soft looking. He hated the bedroom, but he wouldn't mind the bathroom—even with the wallpaper.

Back in the bedroom Ali opened a connecting door and motioned for him to come into the second bedroom. As he stepped through the doorway, he instantly understood the problem. Despite the similar canopy bed and too many frills, this room was spacious. There was room to walk around the bed, and there was a small sitting area in front of the window.

"With a sofa, a second TV, and maybe a small dining table, we would make much better use of the smaller room," she said.

Matt glanced back at the doll-size room. "I agree. No guy is going to be comfortable in that place the way it is now. Too many feminine gewgaws in too little space."

She laughed. "Tell me about it." She glanced at her watch. "I need to go get ready to open the store. I'd like you to start with the playroom next door at the tea shop. Then work on the individual rooms here. The renovation of the two small bedrooms into parlors should be last."

"Fine." He made a few notes on his pad. He'd have to talk to Harry about ordering wallpaper and paint. He doubted the local hardware store stocked what Kasey and Ali would want.

"There's one other thing," she said.

Her tone alerted him. He glanced up to see that she wasn't looking at him. Instead, she was staring at something just over his left shoulder, as if avoiding his gaze.

"What is it?"

She pressed her lips together, then shrugged. "Nothing really. It's just I know you're staying at Harry's. Probably in that horrible back room with Lucky. As these small rooms are going to be done last, and this isn't our busy time so they're not going to be rented out, I thought maybe you'd like to stay here." She held up her hand to stop him from interrupting. "I'm offering this because I'm trying to persuade you to stay long enough to finish the work. Nothing more than that."

She still wouldn't look at him. Matt was uncomfortable

with the idea of accepting such blatant charity. He didn't know why she'd made her offer. He doubted it was as simple as bribing him to stick around. But what other reason could there be? Maybe she felt sorry for him.

That rankled. He was a man used to generating envy, not pity. "Ali, I don't think it's a good idea."

"Why? The décor is probably not to your liking, but the bed is comfortable, and there's plenty of hot water."

The mention of water reminded him about the big tub and high shower. That was nearly enough to tempt him.

Her gray-green eyes finally settled on his face. He studied her pretty features—the generous shape of her mouth, the slender nose, and pointed little chin. The mass of dark curls tumbling down her back. As he stared at her, he felt a flicker of something in his chest. An awareness, maybe?

"Say yes."

Suddenly he wanted to see her smiling at him. He wanted her warm and open and nothing like the darkness he was used to.

"Yes," he said before he could stop himself.

She smiled. An instant curving of her mouth. Pleasure lit her eyes, and she rolled forward onto the balls of her feet.

"You're gonna love it. By the time we're through with you, Matt Baker, you're going to actually like floral-print wallpaper."

"I doubt that." He took a step toward her. "Ali, don't try to rescue me."

"I'm not doing that."

"We both know you are. I'm not the guy for you."

"Who said I was—"

A knock on the open front door distracted them both. Kasey stuck her head inside. "Ali, Rick called. He's on his way back with several cases of wine. He said to keep tonight free for dinner."

"Thanks." Ali jerked her head toward Matt. "Our plan worked. He's accepted the offer of the bedroom, and we now have him in our clutches."

"Great." Kasey grinned. "Now that you've accepted we can show you the real list of everything we want done. Did Ali mention the new roof?"

Matt thought about the high peaks on the multilevel structure. "I don't do roofs."

"Kasey, you're the worst." Ali handed Matt a key. "The roof is fine. You can move in anytime you'd like. Dora will be by about seven-thirty in the morning with your breakfast. You're welcome to borrow any of the videos. There's a VCR under the television in the armoire at the foot of the bed."

He took the key. Kasey called out a quick "Welcome" and left to return to the front desk. Ali headed back to her store. Matt walked into the small bedroom that would be his home for the next few weeks.

He looked around at all the frills and furniture and knew Leigh would have loved it here. From the lace to the step-up to the bed. She would have wanted to stay for a long weekend, exploring the countryside, having romantic dinners by the fire. Except he would have been on the phone with a client, or hunched over his laptop. She would have tried to get his attention, first by talking and later by attempting to seduce him. When neither worked, she would have retreated to read or watch television. And he would have let her. Because, as he'd told Ali, being number one was everything.

But he'd been wrong about that. Being number one wasn't everything. It *cost* everything.

chapter seven

"It's just crazy," Ali said, placing the pieces of fudge into a box. "Does Matt really think I'm interested in him?"

Clair leaned against the counter and smiled. "Apparently. If he's warning you off. But to me the more interesting question is why he thought he had to."

"That's what I want to know, too," Ali grumbled.

She set the box on the scale, then read the weight. She cut one more piece and dropped it into the small candy box. Every time she thought about what he'd said, what he'd *dared* to say, she wanted to scream. Or throw something. Worse, thinking about it made her blush.

She glared at her friend. "What kills me is that I was being nice. That's all. Just nice. As in 'Wouldn't staying at the B and B be so much nicer than Harry's back room?' But instead of saying thank you, he tells me he's not the guy for me. As if I was looking for something more."

Clair grabbed a piece of fudge before Ali could close the top on the box. She nibbled on the corner. "Aren't you looking? Or have you given up on men completely?"

Ali sniffed. "I haven't given up. I'm looking. Just not for him."

She wrapped the box in white-and-gold paper, then handed it to Clair. As they were the only two in her shop, Ali came out from around the display case and led her friend to a couple of chairs in the corner.

"What's wrong with him?" Clair asked. "You told me that there's more to him than meets the eye."

"He seems pretty nice," Ali admitted. "He's smart, and I found out he does have a sense of humor. But there are mysteries in his past and that makes me nervous."

"Maybe he's normal," Clair said kindly. "Maybe he's not like your usual type and that scares you to death."

"I don't know what he is, but I deeply resent his assumption that I want some kind of relationship with him."

"Because you don't."

"Right."

Clair laughed. "You're lying."

"I'm not. He's pushy. He wants me to get on the Internet."

"Oh. Well, you didn't say that. Obviously he should be shot at dawn."

Ali sighed. "You're not taking this seriously. I will not be pushed around."

"Are you on the Internet?"

"Of course not."

"So he made a suggestion and you didn't take it. End of story. No pushing at all."

"Maybe."

Clair made everything sound so logical and sensible when Ali knew it wasn't. She felt weird inside. Kind of unsettled. And why had Matt said that, about him not being the right guy for her? As if she'd asked him to be.

"I hate this," Ali muttered. "I don't want the complications."

Clair leaned toward her and grinned. "But isn't this way more fun than your regular life?"

"I approve," Charlotte Elizabeth said, holding up her wineglass. Lamplight illuminated the buttery Chardonnay. "I've always enjoyed the Foley wines."

"I know." Rick leaned close and patted her hand. "That's why I bought an extra half case for you, Mom." He looked at his sister and raised his eyebrows. "What do you think, Brillo pad?"

Ali leaned back in her chair and grinned. "A friendly wine. Open, but not pretentious."

Rick shifted in his chair so he could turn his back on her. "Mom, Ali's being a brat. Make her stop."

Charlotte Elizabeth, resplendent in a vibrant purple silk shirt worn over matching tailored slacks, shook her head at them both. "I've always looked forward to the day when the three of us could sit down and enjoy a meal together as adults. I'm still waiting."

Ali laughed. "All right. I'll be nice. Yes, Rick, I agree with Mother. The wine is lovely. I'm sure everything you bought will be perfect."

Her brother, with his puppy-dog eyes and charming smile, turned and blew her a kiss of forgiveness.

The three of them sat at Ali's small glass table in her alcove dining room. Despite having to stay at the shop until closing, she'd managed to find a clean peach tablecloth *and* matching napkins. If it had just been Rick, she would have told him to dig out plastic placemats and be happy, but Charlotte Elizabeth was a great believer in elegant dining. She claimed that beautiful surroundings made her eat less. Ali had found the theory didn't work for her. She could chow down as much at the latest Chez Whatever restaurant as at McDonald's.

She'd also had to tidy up her apartment. Charlotte Elizabeth had graciously agreed to cook, but she had insisted her daughter act as hostess. So here they were, in Ali's small apartment.

"I've already put the wines into inventory," Rick said. "They're on the master list. Most of the whites will be ready to drink within the year. The reds need some aging."

"I hope they don't take too long," Charlotte Elizabeth said with a small pout. "I would hate to miss out."

The implication being that Charlotte Elizabeth might not live forever. *Unlikely,* Ali thought humorously. *Forces of nature do not die.* But the reality was her mother was sixty-five. Although looking at her tonight, no one would guess it. Charlotte Elizabeth wore her dark hair in a windswept disarray of curls. Wide eyes, artfully made up, seemed to reflect light all the way down to her soul. A few lines by her mouth and eyes hinted that she had lived past forty, but her skin glowed with youthful health, and her hands were smooth and pale.

The good news was that she had inherited some of her mother's gene pool, Ali reminded herself. It probably wasn't going to be enough to keep her looking as good as Charlotte Elizabeth, but then who did?

Ali studied her plate of wine-poached chicken and pasta in a light cream sauce. Freshly grated parmesan dotted the plate, along with a sprig of basil for garnish. Her mother had invaded Ali's kitchen and whipped up the dish, along with salad and fresh bread, when she'd heard Rick was back for the night. Charlotte Elizabeth was a woman of many talents. Domino sat in the corner, patiently awaiting any scraps that might be tossed her way—more than willing to offer her feline opinion of the meal.

Rick expertly twirled a length of fettuccine on his fork. "Isn't someone going to ask?" He raised his eyebrows and waited.

Ali touched a napkin to her mouth. "You mean why, when you and David went off to the wine country together, you returned with the wine but without your friend?"

"I know you're interested," he said.

"Actually, it never crossed my mind."

He glared at her in mock anger. "My life is much more exciting than yours. Of course you thought about it."

"Tell us what happened," Charlotte Elizabeth said, leaning close to her stepson. "I'm sorry I missed meeting David when you arrived last week. Ali said he was quite charming."

Ali looked at her. "No, I didn't."

"Didn't you?" Her mother frowned delicately. "Hmm, perhaps I simply assumed that's what you would have said."

"He was a baby," Ali said. "With an IQ hovering around his chest measurement."

"He wasn't stupid," Rick said quickly. "Just . . ."

"Young, conversationally challenged, too pretty?"

"They can never be too pretty," Charlotte Elizabeth protested. She tucked a small dark curl behind her perfect ear. The movement caught light to reflect off her diamond-and-amethyst earrings and matching bracelet.

Ali glanced down at her serviceable watch—the lone piece of jewelry she bothered with on a regular basis.

Even Rick had better taste than her. Sometimes she felt like a changeling—a baby left on the doorstep rather than actually being born of her mother.

"He was too moody," Rick said. He sipped his wine. "I guess it had something to do with age. He was pissed off from the second he found we'd be having dinner with Ali to celebrate her birthday. The trip went downhill from there. He finally got a rental car and drove himself back to Los Angeles."

Charlotte Elizabeth straightened in her chair and glared at her stepson. "You don't have to rub in the fact that I forgot my daughter's birthday, for which I have already apologized."

"You forgot your *only* daughter's birthday," Rick added helpfully. "But I wasn't trying to rub it in. Amazingly enough, the conversation wasn't about you at all."

"But it should be."

Mother and son laughed together. Ali joined in with a weak smile even as she wondered where she and Charlotte Elizabeth had gone wrong. She never teased her mother like that. If she tried, Charlotte Elizabeth took offense, or was hurt. Somehow they just kept bumping into each other on the curves.

"Are you going to see him when you go home?" her mother asked.

"No point," Rick told her. "He wasn't right for me. I knew it from the beginning. Still it was easy, and better than being on my own. At least that's what I thought at the time. Now I'm going to take a break from the whole relationship rat race."

"It could be worse," Ali offered, spearing the last bite of chicken with her fork. "At least you're getting out there and dating. The last time I went out with a man there were still woolly mammoths roaming the frozen tundra."

And she wasn't looking, she reminded herself. Despite Matt's comments to the contrary.

"You're too picky," Rick informed her and brushed a lock of blond hair off his forehead.

"I'm not picky. All I want is a normal man. Maybe a teacher or a guy who works for the phone company."

Charlotte Elizabeth blinked at her daughter. "While I question your choice of a mate, I will remind you that sometimes love comes later in life. I was close to forty when I met Richard." She reached out and touched Rick's hand. "Your father was a treasure and very much worth the wait." She returned her attention to Ali. "Life is not predictable. And speaking of that, has Mr. Baker moved on? He mentioned he was going to be departing Saint Maggie soon."

Ali shook her head. "Actually he's moved into the bed-and-breakfast. He's going to be doing more work for me."

Wide, beautiful green eyes glared at her. Charlotte Elizabeth set down her glass of wine. "You can't be serious. The man told me he was leaving."

"He changed his mind."

"And how much did you have to do with that?" Her mother slapped her hands, palm down, on the tabletop. "I swear, Allison, it was difficult enough when you persisted in bringing home every stray dog or cat in the neighborhood. But the day you graduated to people, the situation grew entirely out of hand."

Ali felt like a twelve-year-old being lectured for bad grades or not cleaning up her room. "Matt isn't a stray."

"What would you call him? A pillar of society? The man is obviously on the run from something or someone.

He is working for Harry, for God's sake. Is this the man you want as the father of your children?"

"You're making a pretty big leap, Mother," she said, forcing herself to remain calm. Why did everyone assume she had a thing for Matt? "The man is going to be painting fences and putting up wallpaper. Nothing about that implies any responsibility toward my yet-to-be-conceived children."

Charlotte Elizabeth shook her head. "*Now* it's just wallpaper, but what will it be in a few days? I know you, Allison. You can't resist the type. I don't understand the appeal of men like him, but you seem unable to help yourself. You have dreadful taste, and you seem to attract men in need the way magnetic north attracts a magnet. I've thought about this quite a bit, and I've decided you are simply putting the wrong message into the cosmos. If you expect failure, that's what you'll get."

Ali didn't know how to answer that. "I don't expect failure."

"Of course you do. You never pick the kind of man who would succeed. The question is, why?"

Actually the question was more like why couldn't she have had a more normal mother. "Where do you get these ideas?" she asked.

"Daytime television, of course," Charlotte Elizabeth told her. "There's a wealth of information to be had there."

"Stop it, Mom," Rick said, reaching for the wine bottle and topping off all their glasses. "Give Ali a break. She's old enough to make her own decisions. However foolish."

"Gee, thanks," Ali grumbled.

"He's probably an ax murderer," Charlotte Elizabeth announced.

"As none of us are axes, we're safe," Ali murmured before taking a drink of her wine.

"Is this where I mention Jason of the American Express card incident?" Charlotte Elizabeth asked, ignoring her daughter's comment.

Ali wanted to bang her forehead against the table. One ex-boyfriend steals her credit card and charges several thousand dollars on it and would anyone let her forget it? Noooo.

"That could have happened to anyone," Ali said.

"Yes, but it didn't. It happened to you," her mother reminded her.

"Can we please talk about someone else's personal life?" Ali pleaded.

"I don't have one anymore," Rick reminded her.

"And I don't discuss mine with my children," Charlotte Elizabeth said. "However, speaking of children, I've been thinking of breeding Miss Sylvie. I think she would be a wonderful mother. What do you think?"

Matt forced himself to step out of the shower when he figured he was in danger of turning into an amphibian. The endless supply of hot water was a far cry from life at Harry's. The old man had been pretty outspoken about what he saw as Matt's uppity ways, announcing that he wasn't going to give him a raise to support his new luxurious lifestyle.

Matt dried off using one of the thick, white towels on a heated rack by the tub, then slipped into a guest robe so fluffy, he felt like a cat.

After rubbing the steamy mirror so that he could see his reflection, he dug through the small plastic bag that served as his shaving kit, then pulled out his shaving cream and razor. When he'd finished shaving, he combed his wet hair while dismissing the complimentary blow-dryer left neatly on a shelf by the mirror. Ali and Kasey had thought of just about everything.

Before Matt could start getting dressed, there was a knock at his door. He opened it to find a petite dark-haired woman holding a tray filled with food.

"Good morning. I'm Dora," she said as she eased past him and walked to the small table by the window. "Miss Allison said breakfast at seven-thirty, so here it is."

The woman, dressed in jeans and a long-sleeved shirt with a tiny embroidered logo of the bed-and-breakfast on the left front pocket, set down the tray and turned to smile at him. She was in her midforties, barely five-feet tall, and looked perfectly maternal.

Her dark eyes studied him, then she shook her head. "She told me you needed fattening up, and I can see she's right. You're too skinny. You don't have the excuse my Willie has. He's still filling out. But you're a grown man. Eat more." She flashed him another smile. "I know, I know. Not your business, Dora, you want to tell me. Maybe so, but you should still eat." She glanced around his room. "You're tidy. That's nice. Miss Kasey said you'd be staying here for a while. I won't disturb your things when I clean."

She started toward the door. "Willie, my oldest, works here, too. He's in college. You'll meet him tonight. He takes care of the front desk in the evening. Miss Kasey and Miss Allison don't mind if he studies. He's always good with the guests. If you need anything, you tell Willie or me. All right?"

Matt stared at her, not sure what to say. He would have guessed that Charlotte Elizabeth was the only force to be reckoned with in Saint Maggie, but he would have been wrong. Tiny Dora could give the ex-actress a run for her money.

"Thanks, Dora," he said.

She winked. "Eat your plate clean. You hear me?"

And then she was gone.

Matt stood in the center of the room for a couple of seconds. He'd spent the last year surviving by keeping to the fringes of life—not allowing himself to get involved or fit in anywhere. When he was at risk of getting comfortable, he moved on. But here, in a matter of days, he'd gotten involved in too many lives. The sensation of connecting—even on the most basic level—made him uncomfortable.

He turned toward the tray. It occurred to him that he would be better off just ignoring the food. But when he inhaled, the tempting aroma of the breakfast made his stomach growl. Maybe just coffee, he thought as he walked to the table.

There were several dishes and bowls, along with the menu printed on a small card. Fresh fruit (in this case cantaloupe slivers, orange-and-grapefruit sections, and grapes, dusted lightly with pecans) something that looked like berry cobbler but was instead called blueberry crumble, scones (lemon and white chocolate, orange and raisin) a bay shrimp and artichoke-heart omelet, and coffee. A single rose nestled in a tiny silver bud vase and a copy of *USA Today* completed the tray.

His stomach growled again, accompanying a sharp hunger pang. Matt sat on the straight-backed chair by the window and picked up his fork before he could stop himself. He took a single bite of the omelet and nearly moaned aloud. The delicate flavors blended together perfectly. The eggs were fluffy, the shrimp plump and fresh.

It had been so long since he'd done anything but simply go through the motions of surviving that he'd forgotten what it felt like to enjoy anything. But now that he was slowly, painfully coming to life, he didn't know how to make the process stop.

In an effort to distract himself from his disquieting thoughts, he opened the newspaper. Automatically he thumbed through to the business section and scanned the headlines as he continued to eat. From there he noted the list of all the business articles, then flipped to the pages listing closing prices for various stocks. He looked for companies which had gone public in the past couple of years and noted how they were doing, then searched for companies that should have gone public in the past year. Of the four he was interested in, only two were there. And their prices were lower than he would have expected.

Matt frowned. What had happened? Both firms, one a high-tech software designer, the other a major supplier of home furnishings to low-end retailers, had been well on their way to successful Initial Public Offerings a year ago. He'd known that both of them would—

Matt rose from the chair so quickly, it wobbled, tipped, then bumped into the wall. He tossed the paper down as if it had caught fire in his hand. What the hell was he doing? Reading the business section? Caring about his company? As if nothing had happened?

He stepped away from the table and stared at his nearly finished breakfast. The food sat uneasily in his stomach, a heavy weight that illustrated his betrayal. He couldn't go back to his old life. In the nearly twelve months he'd been gone, he'd never once read a newspaper, let alone the business section.

He closed his eyes and balled his hands into fists, trying to think of anything but Birmingham International. But his brain didn't cooperate. Instead his head filled with questions about what had gone wrong with the two IPOs, and what would have been different if he'd been there to shepherd them through.

By one-thirty Matt had cleaned the junk out of the tea shop's back room. He'd stacked the toys in Sara's office and was prepping the walls for painting. Harry would be by first thing in the morning with the supplies he would need, including a larger window and the tools necessary to install it.

Even though he was in the back of the building, with a hallway and office between him and the restaurant itself, the sound of female laughter still drifted to him. He heard the clink of teacups on saucers and imagined tiny sandwiches and desserts in the middle of an ocean of lace and candles. He shuddered.

"I know how you feel, and I'm gay. All those women clucking and tittering. All those frilly things and rickety antiques. It's alien country out there."

Matt straightened and turned. He saw a man lounging in the doorway of the storeroom. A tall, well-dressed man with the easy good looks of a soap-opera actor. Something about him was familiar. Matt knew he'd seen him before, but he couldn't make the connection.

"I'm Rick Thomas," the man said, stepping forward and offering his hand. "Ali's stepbrother. I was here last Saturday to help Ali celebrate her birthday."

"Right." He shook the other man's hand.

Rick's expression turned speculative. Matt wondered if the crack about being gay was a test. Unless Ali's brother planned to make a pass at him, he didn't give a rat's ass about the man's personal preferences. In fact one of Matt's closest friends, Jeff, was gay. At least they had been close before Matt had ducked out on his life.

"I have to warn you," Rick said, walking around the room, then staring out the cracked window. "Sara always tries to pass off her leftovers on the staff. The sandwiches aren't too bad, even though they're so tiny that it takes three dozen to even begin to look like a meal. But the little pink cakes are pretty nasty. Too sweet and spongy. What is it about women and sugar?"

Matt grinned. "It's a relationship we'll never understand."

"Don't I know it. Ali always had a secret stash of chocolate in her room. When we were both at home one summer, I made the mistake of stealing it once. She came at me in the middle of the night. I swear, I thought she was going to kill me."

Rick turned around and leaned against the wall. He wore a long-sleeved navy blue shirt tucked into black slacks. The clothes might be casual, but Matt recognized the quality of the fabric and the tailoring. If Rick was slumming, he did it in style.

He motioned to the empty room. "What's Ali's latest project?"

"A playroom," Matt told him. "For Sara's children and someone else's." He paused, then shook his head. "I can't remember."

"Dora," Rick offered. "Her oldest two are in college, but her youngest is only six. A girl, I think."

"Yeah, that's right. Ali wants a bigger window, fresh paint, even a blackboard."

Rick folded his arms over his chest. He wore his blond

hair to the bottom of his collar. He was the kind of man who attracted attention from both genders. "So what do you think of my sister and her bleeding-heart impulses?"

Matt easily sidestepped the pit. "I just work here. She tells me what to do and I do it."

"Really?" Rick regarded him thoughtfully. "What did you do before you were Harry's handyman?"

"I spent the summer picking fruit."

"That isn't what I meant."

"But it's what you asked." No way was he going to get trapped into talking about his past. What was he going to say? "Gee, Rick, I own a multinational, multibillion-dollar company. So what's new with you?" Instead Matt motioned to the can of caulking compound and the putty knife. "Speaking of work, I need to get back to this."

"Don't let me stop you. I'm lazy enough that I enjoy watching people work. It calms me." Rick smiled. "I'm being completely honest."

Matt didn't doubt that. He'd met men like Rick before. Born charmers whose most difficult decision was what to wear and where to dine. Most of them annoyed him, but not Rick. Rick hadn't interrupted his day to be difficult but to check out the stranger in his sister's life. He was playing big brother. Matt knew it wasn't necessary but doubted the other man would believe him.

Rick paced the length of the room and returned to the window. "This is just like Ali. We were talking at dinner last night that it was a lot easier to deal with her tendency to pick up strays when she stuck to pets. Once she graduated to people the situation became complicated."

"I can imagine," Matt said, patching another hole. He smoothed the putty knife across the wall, packing in the compound. It would be dry by morning. He would sand the repaired patches, then put on the first coat of paint.

"I remember one Christmas when Ali brought a teacher home. The poor man had lost his wife over the summer, and this was his first Christmas without her. Ali hadn't wanted him to be alone." Rick smiled at the memory. "Charlotte Elizabeth and my father were celebrating with us that year. The house was full of Hollywood types and business moguls. Ali's teacher—I can't remember his name—was so out of his element. I think he forgot to be sad. At least most of the time."

He turned to Matt. "She has her heart in the right place."

Matt knew that Rick wanted a response to the tender story, but he couldn't speak. He was too caught up in his own past. Last Christmas had been the first one he'd spent without Leigh. He remembered little of the day, mostly because he'd spent it drunk. All he'd wanted was to wake up and have the holiday over.

He looked at Ali's brother. "You think I'm one of her strays."

"What else would you be?"

"Just a guy who's here temporarily. Don't worry. I'll be moving on before long."

"I'm not worried," Rick said as he headed for the door. "You're not like Harry's usual guys. I doubt the past you're running from is going to be a problem for Ali."

"Why is that?"

"Ali tends to collect men who need her. There was some artist—she not only took care of his loft, she supported him financially. There was also a guy running a halfway house. Ali took care of an entire herd of runaways with him. Talk about caretaker heaven. And then there was Jason. He was her most recent significant other, and he was the worst. He managed to steal her American Express card and clean out her till, all in one day. By the time AmEx notified Ali about some unusual charges on her account, the bastard had rung up over twenty thousand in purchases." He paused. "You're nothing like Jason."

"How do you know?"

Rick smiled again. "You can take one look at me and guess I'm not ever going to push myself to earn my living. Hey, it works both ways. When I look at you, I see a man who isn't interested in finding someone to take care of him. You don't strike me as the type out to scam my sister." His gaze turned speculative. "If I had to guess, I would say you have a life somewhere and eventually you're going back to it."

"Maybe," Matt said, knowing the other man had figured him out too easily.

"Just don't break her heart," Rick said, then waved and walked out of the playroom.

Break Ali's heart? Matt frowned. How could he? They weren't involved, nor were they going to be. Sure, she was attractive. She had a great smile and the kind of body that . . .

Heat filled him. Nearly forgotten and powerful. It brought with it an ache he hadn't felt in what seemed like forever.

"Well, hell," he muttered as blood rushed south and pooled low in his groin. It had been so long since he'd had a hard-on, he would have sworn he'd forgotten how.

Now, physically uncomfortable, but oddly pleased with his body's response, he returned to work. Okay, so he found Ali sexually appealing. She was caring and smart, as well. None of that mattered. Because he'd already been down that path and it had ended in disaster.

chapter eight

Matt finished the first coat of paint in the storeroom shortly before six on Friday. He put the lid back on the paint can and carried the dirty brushes to a sink in the rear utility room. Somehow he doubted Sara would appreciate him washing up in her kitchen.

The new, larger window had gone in more easily than he'd expected. If he finished the second coat of paint in the morning, then he would be able to—

"Whattcha doin'?"

Matt looked up and found himself staring at two children. They were small—a boy and a girl—neither of whom came higher than his waist. Both blond and blue-eyed, wearing matching quizzical expressions.

They were dressed in jeans and sweatshirts, the latter bearing animal pictures. A pink elephant for her and a dark green camel for him.

"I'm washing brushes," Matt said, stating what he considered the obvious.

Sara's children, he assumed, then wondered if the

woman knew where they were. Whether or not she did, he hoped she would soon appear to rescue him from the conversation. He turned the water on harder, in an effort to clean the brushes more quickly.

"He's the man makin' us a playroom," the girl informed her brother.

"I know," the boy said. He looked a little smaller and possibly a year or two younger than his sister.

"I'm Marti," the girl said. "This is my brother, Joey. What's your name?"

"Matt." He worked faster.

"What color are you painting the room?" the girl asked. She wore two butterfly hair clips just above each ear. As she spoke, she swung her arms back and forth, in front of and behind her body.

"White."

She wrinkled her impossibly small nose. "White's not a color. I want the playroom to be yellow and green and purple."

Matt didn't know much about decorating, but the thought of that combination made him shudder.

"And blue," Joey added.

"I have white paint," Matt said firmly.

"At day care we have animals on the wall," Marti told him. "And clouds. Can you make us giraffes and clouds? And zebras." She looked at her shirtfront and giggled. "And elephants and camels, too."

"I've never painted animals."

"You're a grown-up. Can't you learn?"

"Yes, but I don't want to."

Her lower lip thrust out in a pout. Joey stared at him

bewildered. "But you hafta want to," he insisted. "Don't you like us?"

Matt was saved from answering by the arrival of the children's mother. Sara swooped into the utility room and gave a sigh of relief.

"There you two are. Didn't I tell you to stay in my office?"

"We wanted to meet the man painting our playroom," her daughter said.

"I'll just bet you did." Sara smiled. "Sorry, Matt. I hope they weren't too much trouble."

"Not at all," he lied.

The petite woman, blonde like her two children, set down several large notebooks, then gathered her children close for a hug.

"I know you're making Matt crazy, aren't you?"

Marti smiled. "Maybe just a little."

"I knew it." Sara straightened and motioned to the books she'd set on the counter. "Matt, are you going back to Ali's store when you're done here? Can you take the accounting books? She needs to look them over."

He hadn't planned on heading in that direction, but it wasn't much of a walk. "No problem."

"Thanks."

Marti tugged on her mother's hand. "Matt is gonna paint clouds on the wall of the playroom. And animals and—"

"Na uh," Joey interrupted. "Clouds go on the ceiling."

Sara looked impressed. "What a great idea! Plain walls are more practical, I'll admit, but I love graphics to brighten up an area for children. I suppose the clouds would be easy enough—you could use a piece of sponge to make those. But the animals are more complicated. Will you get stencils from the hardware store or will you draw them freehand?"

Matt hadn't been this neatly trapped since the last time he'd played chess with Jeff, his second in command at Birmingham International.

He glared at Marti, who only smiled back, a picture of innocence. "I haven't decided," he said at last.

"I look forward to seeing the finished product," Sara told him, then took each of her children by the hand, called good night, and disappeared with them into the front part of the shop.

When he finished washing the brushes, Matt set them out to dry. He checked that he'd put away his supplies and tools, then gathered the accounting books Sara had left for him and headed toward Decadent Delight.

He wasn't going to paint any animals on the wall, he grumbled to himself as he walked across the street and up the sidewalk. Stencils or no stencils. Okay, maybe white was a little sterile for a playroom. He could do the second coat in cream or even beige.

As he walked across Ali's parking lot, he noticed that the store itself had already closed. The front of the restored Victorian house was dark. But lights spilled from the windows in back and even from nearly fifty feet away, he could hear the beat of loud music.

Matt paused at the back door. He knocked, then pounded on the door with his fist. There wasn't any response. Then he realized he knew Ali well enough to figure she would leave the door open . . . even when she shouldn't. Sure enough, the handle turned easily and he walked inside.

The music hit him with the subtlety of a car doing fifty. It was loud and vibrated through the house. He followed the trail of light and found himself standing in the doorway to the kitchen.

The music poured from a portable boom box set on the counter. A country band bounced through a song about supermodels and long-legged women. Ali—no longer dressed for work, but instead wearing jeans and a purple sweater—bebopped in time with the beat, removing long trays and a big double boiler from under-the-counter cabinets. Her thick hair had been pulled back into a ponytail that swayed in counterpoint to her movements. Her feet, in ragged sneakers, danced and tapped with the drum and bass.

She looked different wearing casual clothes, he thought as he watched her. Good. Very good. His blood began to pump in time with the music.

Matt frowned and wondered what it meant that his body had returned to life. He felt guilty, because after his wife died, wasn't all his desire supposed to be dead, too? If nothing else, he owed her his loyalty, now more than ever.

Ali dumped a flat of strawberries into a colander and ran water over them. When she was done rinsing, she placed them in a single layer on several large trays covered with paper towels.

She moved with an easy grace, her movements quick and sure. She was curvy—different from Leigh who had always been model thin. His wife had looked terrific in clothes. He would bet twenty bucks that Ali looked great naked.

In an effort to distract himself, he looked at the tall

cabinets and long, gleaming metal counters. The CD moved on to a song about a woman named Amie. Against the opposite wall was a bookshelf containing dozens of cookbooks. They were all about chocolate and desserts, and they all looked well used. There were stacks of handwritten recipes as well. From what he could tell, Ali adored her work. She lived and breathed her cooking with a passion he remembered from his old life.

There had been a time when his company had been as important to him. Too important. He'd been obsessed with the numbers, the hunt, the potential for success. The risk and glory of winning had made the long hours worth every minute.

His chest tightened, and he realized that he ached for those days. He missed his work more than he would have thought possible. Which made him the most stupid man alive. It wasn't enough that his love of his work had turned him into the one thing he loathed. Now he had the balls to miss it? He was going to have to—

Out of the corner of his eye, he saw Ali turn. She caught sight of him, jumped back a foot, and screamed. One hand pressed against her chest, the other flipped off the boom box.

"You nearly scared me to death," she said, her voice low and breathy. "How'd you get in?"

He jerked his head toward the back door. "You didn't lock it. You should."

"I thought I did. Obviously not, though." Her gaze then settled on the books he held, and she grimaced. "Not the accounting books. Please say it's something else."

He waved them in the air, then set them on the counter next to him. "Sorry. Sara asked me to bring them over."

She groaned. "Why does she do that? Numbers are *so* not my thing."

He looked at her and had a sudden thought. "You don't even open them, do you?"

"Of course not. They don't make sense. Why would I bother?"

His fingers suddenly itched to flip back the cover. He wanted to study the lines of columns and see what she was doing right or wrong. Whatever it was, he could either fix it or make it better. Instead he tucked his hands into his jeans pockets.

"You might want to know how your investments are doing," he said. "Of course the accounting ledgers are pretty old fashioned. Did you know you can put all this information onto a computer program? It will generate much more comprehensive reports that are easier to understand."

"So I've heard." She returned to her strawberries and continued laying them out on paper towels. "However ledger books don't crash, and they're very mobile. They work for us."

"You're acting like you're caught in the 1800s."

She glanced at him and grinned. "Yes, but if I ever travel back through time, I'll be prepared."

"I could . . ." He hesitated. "I know something about setting up accounting books. I could help."

Her gaze narrowed. "First was your suggestion about the custom mailing containers, although I'll admit it was a good one. Then it was the Internet, and now it's computerized accounting. You have something of a flair for business, Mr. Baker."

"Maybe," he admitted.

"And a strong desire to meddle. Well, tonight I refuse to discuss anything that serious. It will give me a headache. Instead I'm going to be making a fabulous chocolate confection." She motioned to a stool in the corner. "You are welcome to pull up a seat and keep me company. But only if you do so with an attitude of reverence and awe."

"Reverence and awe? That's a pretty tall order. I'll have to see what I can do."

The invitation was harmless, he told himself. And it wasn't as if he had a pressing engagement. He settled on the stool while she finished washing the last of the strawberries.

"These arrived this afternoon," she said. "They're hothouse grown and impossibly expensive, but I couldn't resist." She glanced at him and smiled. "Do you like strawberries?"

"Sure."

"Covered in chocolate?"

He drew his eyebrows together. "I don't know. I don't think I've had chocolate-covered strawberries before."

"They'll change your life, and for the better," she said confidently. "But first the fruit has to dry. Want to help me check inventory?"

Without waiting for an answer, she led the way into her candy shop. He followed. Shades had been pulled down over the front windows and glass door. Ali flipped the light switch, illuminating the square space. She walked behind the display cases in front by the main counter and pulled out a clipboard.

"Different chocolates sell at different speeds," she said as she glanced at the board. "They also require different kinds of storage. For example, the white and plain chocolate truffles need to be refrigerated. I keep them in the kitchen unit, in boxes. They'll last for about two weeks, but they have to be kept separated by layers of baking parchment. The truffles covered with nuts are stored outside the refrigerator, also for two weeks. The cakes and muffins have their own requirements and shelf life."

"How do you manage your inventory?"

She glanced up from the paper. A single dark curl had escaped the ponytail and brushed against her face. She smiled, making the skin crinkle around her gray-green eyes. "If you're asking when do I know what to make and how much, I wing it. I have a sense of what sells and what doesn't, but I'm wrong as often as I'm right." She shrugged, apparently unconcerned. "Sometimes I cook whatever I'm in the mood to cook. It can also depend on what surprise things arrive. Like today. One of my suppliers came by and offered me several flats of strawberries. They're out of season. I bought more than I would in early summer because people are going to be tempted by the thought of fresh, delicious, sweet, chocolate-dipped strawberries in the middle of fall."

She made a few more notations, then led the way back into the kitchen.

Matt trailed after her. He didn't know what to say—mostly because Ali was doing so much wrong, and he knew he didn't have a prayer of making her listen. She was a free spirit and wanted to do things her way. The fact that she was successful was a testament to the quality of her product and perhaps luck. It sure as hell didn't have spit to do with business sense.

"You've gotten all quiet and disapproving," she said, half buried in the large metal refrigerator by the door.

It was a side-by-side model, about double the size of a normal refrigerator. She pulled out boxes of candy and checked the dates on the label against the clipboard she'd brought with her.

"You can't be so haphazard about your inventory," he blurted, walking closer to the refrigerator.

She handed him three boxes and motioned to the counter. "Of course I can. It's what I do. I've always worked this way, and it's fine. Yes, I'm sure I could be more efficient, but this is fun."

"It's expensive. If you cooked on a schedule you could—"

She cut him off with a stare that spoke volumes. She was less than impressed with his theory. What he wanted to tell her was that he billed out for several hundred dollars an hour to give small companies this kind of advice. It was what he did.

"I don't want to cook on a schedule," she told him, then returned her attention to the refrigerator. She dug around in back, then called, "Wow, look," and produced a small, plastic-wrapped plate.

He stared at the dark squares partially obscured by the covering. "What is it?"

"Only the best fudge on the entire planet. I thought it was all gone." She smiled at him. "I had a small incident with this fudge last week. My mother and Rick were over for dinner. By the time they left, I was in serious need of a pick-me-up, so I indulged. It's fabulous, if I do say so myself. Try some."

Before he could start to pull off the plastic wrap, she thrust three more boxes at him, then drew out a large tray of tiny sandwiches. "Sara brought these by this afternoon. Are you in the mood, or are you all tea-sandwiched out?"

He didn't get a chance to answer. She grabbed two more boxes and one more tray, bumped the door closed with her hip, and set her armful on the center island.

"Well?" she asked.

He didn't know what he was supposed to address first. He put the boxes and plate she'd given him next to her pile and studied it. "Are you planning to eat all this?" he asked.

She pulled off the plastic wrap from the fudge, then handed him a piece. "No. We'll snack on what we want, and the rest of it gets picked up by a local food bank in the morning. They come by twice a week. I'm sure the shelter residents would rather have something more substantial than chocolate and muffins, but the food bank keeps taking our donations, which makes me happy."

He bit into the cool fudge. The creamy chocolate melted against his tongue. The smooth texture contrasted with the nuts. "I can already feel the sugar pouring into my veins."

She grinned. "Isn't it great?" she asked, then took a piece for herself. "Do you want sandwiches? You never answered."

"Sure. I didn't have any lunch."

"What is it with you and food?"

"Nothing. I had a big breakfast. Dora delivered it this morning."

"Doesn't Kasey have the best chef? I know she's still in training at the culinary school, but I think she's already fabulous."

As she spoke, she uncovered plates and boxes, exposing tea sandwiches, little cakes, and truffles. She grabbed a handful of the latter and walked to the counter by the sink where she checked her drying strawberries.

Matt put several sandwiches on a paper towel and returned to his stool. He noticed a pad of paper by the phone. He pulled a pen out of his workshirt pocket and drew the pad closer.

"Tell me what sells the best," he said, beginning to write notes. "Which truffles, what kind of fudge?"

She poured water into a pot and set it on the stove, then opened a box of chocolate and broke it into small squares. "Variations on chocolate sell the best in the truffle world. Milk chocolate, chocolate hazelnut, champagne. Next would be the fruit-filled. Fudge is always a big seller. The plain and walnut sell the best, followed by rocky road, and whatever other flavor I'm in the mood to make."

"Does fudge sell better than truffles?"

He looked up at her as he spoke. She'd dumped the broken squares of chocolate into a smaller pot that she put inside the one already heating.

"I don't know. Maybe. Sometimes." She glanced at him and shrugged. "If you want hard-and-fast details, you'd have to look at my sales receipts. Although they're going to reflect inventory rather than preference. Obviously I can't sell what I don't have."

"What about mail order? Is there a catalog your customers order from?"

She stirred the melting chocolate. "Sort of. It's more of a brochure. A few pictures and a listing of what's available. I kept it general so those items would always be in stock." She smiled. "If someone has a taste for a specific kind of truffle or fudge, they can get pretty hostile if it's not available."

He finished the initial list of her products, then started asking questions about her supplies. "I've seen your supplies, so I know you buy in bulk. How are the orders placed? Do you order the same amount at specific intervals?"

"No. I order when I'm getting low on something. Basically I walk through the storeroom and check. We're getting into a busy season so I'll order a little extra of certain things I think we might need." She pulled out several large trays and began tearing off lengths of waxed paper to use as a liner. "It's not wildly scientific, Matt. I listen to my gut."

"Is your gut ever wrong?"

She laughed. "Of course. There is the entire low-fat muffin fiasco as proof."

He made a few pen strokes, drawing lines between inventory and suppliers. "You need to get all of this on a computer," he said, making several small boxes—the beginning of a flowchart. "With perishable product, you have to keep a tight control on inventory. A database of what you sell and what each requires for production would be a start. You can hook it all up to your suppliers."

"I don't think so," she said.

"You could make certain chocolates on certain days. Using previous sales records, you can get a sense of what sells when and match that information to your cooking schedule. You wouldn't have to rely on guessing to know what you're going to need."

"Matt, I don't want to."

He ignored her statement. Instead he turned the pad toward her so she could see his rudimentary flowchart.

"It wouldn't be difficult. I know you're not a fan of the modern age, but you could get one of the college kids you have in here helping to do it for you. They've got to be computer literate."

She brought a tray of washed and dried strawberries over to the center island. She put the pot of melted chocolate next to the tray and proceeded to dip a large, luscious berry into the creamy chocolate.

"You're not listening. I don't want to deal with inventory control and computers. I want to be able to take advantage of a surprise delivery of out-of-season hothouse strawberries. A computer won't let me do that."

"We could build in flexibility. It's still your business. You call the shots."

"Which is what I do now."

She held the chocolate-dipped strawberry by the stem, with her free hand cupped under the treat to catch any drips. Then she walked purposefully toward him and stopped directly in front of his knees.

"Taste this," she said.

He looked at the strawberry and saw that a single drop of chocolate had fallen onto her palm. Involuntarily he opened his mouth. She placed the smooth, still-warm strawberry between his teeth. He bit down.

There was an instant contrast of warm, sweet, melted chocolate and cooler, slightly more tart strawberry. The flavors combined in his mouth. He pulled the stem free and continued to chew.

Ali smiled at him, then licked the drop of chocolate from her hand. "That," she said, "is what this store is all about. Not computers, not flowcharts and inventory control. It's about taking a few quality ingredients and making magic."

She stood close enough that he could see the different colors of green and gold that made up her hazel irises, and the light dusting of freckles across her nose. As he looked at her curly hair, her big eyes, and her full mouth, he felt an emptiness that had nothing to do with food and everything to do with hunger.

Her breasts filled out her sweater in a way that made his fingers itch. The single loose curl by her cheek cried out to be tucked neatly away. Laughter danced in her eyes and teased at the corners of her mouth, making him want to share the joke, even if it was on him.

And suddenly he was lost and confused and not sure what to say. Ali seemed to be waiting for a response. He stared at the strawberry stem in his hand, then at the pot of chocolate on the counter behind her.

"If you eat like this all the time, why aren't you fat?" he asked because it was the best he could come up with.

She tossed her head, sending her thick, curly ponytail flying and returned to her strawberries. "I'm not skinny," she said. "Compared to a fashion model I'm a lumbering elephant, but I don't care. The good news is that while I wasn't blessed with my mother's beauty, I did get her metabolism. For the most part I can eat just about anything I like and stay at this weight. However, I do try to watch it on the real high-calorie stuff."

Her last couple of words came out as a mumble over the chocolate-dipped strawberry she'd nibbled.

"As least I get to do what I love," she said when she'd finished chewing and had swallowed. "In a location I adore."

"Surrounded by family."

She grimaced. "Not always a good thing." She shook

her head. "No, that's not fair. I love my mother, even when she makes me crazy. And most of the time I'm really happy to have her living so close."

"What about your brother? I met him earlier. He doesn't live around here, does he?"

"No. Rick is very cosmopolitan. He has a home in Bel Air, but he travels a lot. I wouldn't mind if he moved to Saint Maggie, but I don't see it happening. Maybe when he settles down." She grinned. "Geez, I sound like my mother. Charlotte Elizabeth wants me married, and I'm talking about Rick needing a life partner."

"You're very comfortable with him."

Ali leaned against the counter. "He's my brother."

"He's also gay. Some people would have a problem with that."

"I don't. Do you?"

"No. I have a close friend who's gay."

Interest sparkled in Ali's eyes. "Oooh, information from the mystery man's past. I want details."

"There's not much to tell. We met through work. About six months later he told me he was gay. I was twenty-four, and it made me crazy. Mostly because we'd been hanging out, watching sports together, that sort of thing."

Ali grinned. "Touching?"

He shook his head. "I'm ignoring that. Anyway, I lost it for about two days and then I realized nothing had changed. I still liked Jeff, I still wanted to be his friend. So I apologized for being a jerk and we were fine."

"Is he single? We could fix them up."

Some of Matt's good mood faded. "Yeah, he's single."

Jeff hadn't been, though. He'd been seriously involved for nearly five years before losing Zack to AIDS. Jeff had taken a leave of absence so he could be with his lover while he died.

Ali watched different emotions flash through Matt's eyes. She wanted to ask what he was thinking, but she couldn't bring herself to spoil the easy mood between them. Besides, if she pushed too much, Matt would probably stop answering her questions.

Still, there was so much she wanted to know. She continued dipping strawberries into the melted chocolate. She wanted to ask what he loved in life. And how he'd come to know so much about inventory control and flowcharts. She wanted to know why he was hiding out in Saint Maggie and how long he would stay.

She studied him from under her lashes. He wore faded jeans and a plaid workshirt. The clothes fit him better than they had when he'd arrived less than three weeks before. All her urging him to eat had paid off by filling him out a little. He still had a way to go before he moved from skinny to lean, but if his current body was anything to go by, it would be worth the wait.

Who was he, this mystery man who had invaded her life? She wondered what he would say if she asked. Then she decided that she would do better with a topic that was more of a sure thing.

"How's the work at the tea shop coming? Did you start the painting yet?"

Matt shifted uncomfortably on his stool. "I finished the first coat today," he said, then paused. "But I've been thinking. If it's going to be a playroom for kids, maybe white isn't the best color."

She set the dipped strawberry onto the waxed paper and reached for another piece of fruit. "I hadn't thought about it, but you're right. I have an account at the hardware store. It's only a few blocks away. Let's go there on Monday, and you can pick out whatever you think is best. Or you can ask Sara. She might have some ideas."

"I've already heard from the most interested parties." He told her about meeting Marti and Joey.

"Marti had some very definite ideas about colors and décor," he said.

"Marti is going to grow up and rule the world. Frankly, I think we'll all be better for it."

Matt stood and walked over to the sink. She watched while he washed his hands and dried them on a clean towel. Then he moved to her side. "If you're planning to dip all the strawberries on those trays, you're going to be here all night. Want some help?"

"Sure."

He stood close enough that if he'd been wearing cologne, she would have been able to smell it. But he wasn't that kind of man . . . or at least he wasn't in this life. She didn't know enough to comment on his previous life. He was tall, several inches taller than her own five feet, six inches. As she passed him the pan of chocolate and went to melt some more, she felt a tiny flutter low in her belly. Something that might . . . under different circumstances . . . be thought of as interest.

Don't go there, she told herself. Don't even think about it. Matt Baker was fourteen kinds of trouble. He didn't talk about his past very much, which probably meant he had something to hide. Not a good quality in a man, although she liked what he'd told her so far.

"So what's the million-dollar baby doing home alone on a Friday night?" he asked lightly.

Ali grimaced. "Do *not* call me that. I hate it. Charlotte Elizabeth's Million-Dollar Baby. It gives me the shudders."

"Okay. What's an attractive woman like you doing alone on a Friday night? Why are you here making candy when you could be out with an MBA or a lawyer, doing the town?"

"Fascinating questions," she said lightly, to hide her confusion. He thought she was attractive?

"Good, because I have one more. Why aren't *you* an MBA or a lawyer?"

Her, a lawyer? Was he serious? She could never have . . .

Ali realized she wasn't sure what she could or couldn't have done if she'd wanted to. The thought of achieving something so tangible had never occurred to her. Maybe it was a legacy from her actress mother.

"What about you?" she asked. "What could you be if you put your mind to it?"

"You didn't answer my question," he said.

"Fair enough. I'm not out with a lawyer because I don't know any whom I would want to date. My business lawyer is a woman. My mother's lawyer is older than civilization. Besides, Saint Maggie doesn't have much to do on any night let alone Friday." She paused to check the consistency of the melting chocolate. "Although I understand there's a fascinating lecture on back health and avoiding common injuries over at the spa."

She turned off the heat and lifted the top pan free. After carrying it over to the island, she positioned herself opposite Matt and pulled a tray of clean berries closer. She felt his steady gaze on her.

"What?" she asked finally, glaring at him. "Why are you staring?"

"I'm trying to figure you out. Why aren't you married with a bunch of kids and dogs."

"I have a cat. I rescue dogs, then pass them along." She dipped the first strawberry into the chocolate, then set it on the waxed paper. "As for why I'm not married, I'm just not."

Matt didn't say anything. The silence between them grew. Ali told herself she wasn't going to be the first one to break it. He was trying that "silence as power" tactic on her, and it wasn't going to work. In fact—

"Growing up as Charlotte Elizabeth's daughter was wonderful," she said, hating herself for being weak. "But it was also strange. She has an interesting personality—which I'm sure you've noticed."

"I have."

She paused and stared past him. Memories from her childhood seemed to fill the room. "It's not that she didn't care about me. It was just that there were so many other things going on. I felt loved, in a remote kind of way. She was sweet, but distracted." Ali paused and laughed. "I'm not explaining this very well, am I?"

"You're doing fine."

"I used to plan summers for Rick and myself. Trips, visits with friends. All the while I kept secretly hoping that Richard and my mother would fly back and just be with us. Like a regular family. I always wanted normal, which Richard was, but Charlotte Elizabeth took a lot of his time. As I grew up, I decided that if I couldn't go back and change my past, I would influence my future. I wanted to marry a regular guy—like a teacher or a phone-company installer. We'd get married, settle in the suburbs, and have kids, dogs, and a motor home."

"So why didn't that happen?" he asked.

Ali swirled another strawberry through the melted chocolate. "I don't know. I suppose a lot of it is my life never lent itself to that. I was sent to a private girls' prep school. From there I spent a couple of years in Europe at finishing school. I might know diddly about flowcharts and computerized ordering, but I can prepare dinner for ten on two hours' notice and know fifteen different ways to start conversations at a cocktail party. There weren't many normal guys in my world."

"That's a real good story, kid, but I don't buy it," Matt said flatly.

Ali was stunned. She blinked at him. "What do you mean?"

He planted his hands on the metal counter and leaned toward her. "You don't want normal. If you did, you'd have it." He motioned to the kitchen around them. "You built this out of nothing. Your background didn't lend itself to this as your destiny. You picked a direction and went to work. Now you have a successful business. If you'd wanted to meet that kind of man and have children and dogs and a motor home, you would have done it. So if you don't want normal, what do you want?"

She couldn't answer the question, mostly because she couldn't speak. He was wrong. He had to be wrong. All her life she'd been waiting to find the right man—someone ordinary and as far removed from her own private insanity of famous and rich parents and exclusivity as possible. There was no way that Matt was right, that she'd *chosen* this path and had therefore also chosen not to find the man of her dreams.

"You could not be more wrong," she managed at last.

"I have made numerous attempts to find the kind of man I've always wanted. It just never worked out."

He finished the last strawberry on his tray. "Yeah? Tell me about one time you found a normal guy and went out with him."

She opened her mouth and closed it. "There was the, ah, man who . . ." Her voice trailed off.

She didn't have a single example. Despite her protestations of wanting someone far removed from her world, she hadn't once dated someone like that. She barely knew any. Was that her fault? Had she been talking about wanting one thing while subconsciously making sure it never happened?

Matt wiped his hands on a towel. "It's getting late, Ali. I should be going."

She was still caught up in his possible revelation and what it meant. "Um, sure. Thanks for helping." She wiped her hands on the same towel and walked him to the door. "Tomorrow's Saturday. You don't have to work if you don't want to. I mean if you want to take the whole weekend off, it's fine with me."

He stared at her. Despite their earlier teasing and pleasant conversation, he suddenly seemed tense and ill at ease. What had happened to change his mood?

"I'll work," he said quietly.

"But you don't have to."

His dark gaze turned troubled, and she knew that he was thinking about whatever he'd left behind when he'd run from his life.

"Yes, I do," he told her and left.

chapter nine

It was nearly ten Saturday night when Matt walked into the reception area of the bed-and-breakfast. There was nothing on television he wanted to watch, and he was too restless to sleep. Maybe a movie would help. He remembered the wall of videotapes by the reception desk and had decided to investigate.

"Evening."

He turned toward the voice and saw a young man smiling at him. He was tall and lanky, with shaggy brown hair and tanned skin.

"I'm Matt Baker. I'm in—"

"I know who you are," the young man said from behind the reception desk and held out his hand. "I'm Willie, Dora's oldest."

They shook hands.

Willie shoved his too-long hair out of his eyes and jerked his head toward the wall of videos. "Help yourself. Saturday's a dismal night for television. I know." He pointed to the small set tucked under the high counter.

Currently the screen was blank. Then he held up a college textbook. "Of course that's good news for me. I need the study time."

Matt moved closer to the counter. He'd only caught a glimpse of the book's title, but it had seemed to be about business marketing. "What are you studying?"

"I'm a business major at U.C. Santa Barbara," Willie said. "Senior year. I have a big project due for my senior studies class."

"May I?" Matt asked as he picked up the book.

It was a comparative assessment of marketing plans in Fortune 100 companies, an expansion of the theory that every industry had two major competitors which took up the lion's share of the business, while a few small firms fought over the crumbs.

"The Coke and Pepsi argument," he said, returning the book to the counter.

"Yeah," Willie agreed. "I'm doing my case study on the airlines. Are there just two big competitors? Some of the regional airlines are growing pretty fast. Then there are the discount airlines, like Southwest, expanding all across the country. I want to explore the issue of public perception of the large carriers versus the reality of growth in different sectors."

"Sounds impressive but challenging," Matt said.

Willie shrugged. "I'm motivated. The best papers often get circulated around at recruiting meetings. I need a good job when I graduate. My mom has worked real hard to get me through college, and I have two younger sisters I want to help in return. That's going to take some money." Willie grinned. "Plus, I want to be a tycoon. That takes starting out on the fast track."

"What are your grades like?"

"All A's, except for two B's, both in nonbusiness classes." Willie made a dismissive gesture with his right hand. "Those general education classes can be killers. Social reform in the 1800s. What was I thinking?"

Matt smiled at the younger man. "You're smart and personable, Willie. You'll do fine during your interviews."

"I hope you're right." He nodded at the bookcase full of movies. "You going to pick one?"

"I think so."

Matt turned to study the different titles. Then he noticed the small sign asking guests to limit themselves to three titles at a time. He'd been about to reach for a video, but he froze in place. Guests.

He wasn't a guest, he was one of Ali's charity cases. He who had always given generously, even if it was with a check rather than with time. Now he was on the receiving end of someone else's good deed. He didn't much like it.

He picked an action movie because they were always a distraction, then waved good night to Willie and made his way back to his small, froufrou room. Once there he pushed the video into the player and settled himself on the bed. But even the opening explosion couldn't capture his attention.

Should he tell Ali the truth, he wondered. Or at the very least pay Kasey for the room? He didn't have an answer to either question. Then there was the matter of Willie. A bright enough young man who probably deserved a chance at the success he wanted. Matt knew with just one phone call he could have Willie interviewed by a half-dozen firms willing and able to consider him for their fast track. The success or failure would be Willie's responsibility, but the opportunity to be in the running often came through connections.

Matt glanced at the phone, then forced his attention to the movie. Several commando types seemed ready to board a grounded plane. The wheeling and dealing part of his life was over. He'd put it behind him the day he'd walked away from Leigh's funeral, and he'd promised himself he wasn't going back. If he made that call, he would get sucked into a world he was determined to forget. Although Jeff would tell him—

Jeff. Matt adjusted the pillows behind his head. He missed his friend about as much as he missed his work. Had Jeff given up on him, assuming he would never return? Matt knew his friend would be mad as hell. Jeff was big on taking responsibility, and he would see Matt's disappearance as quitting before the game was over. He wasn't sure Jeff was wrong. But he had his reasons.

His gaze shifted from the television screen to the newspaper folded neatly on the small table by the window. Since his first morning here, he'd avoided looking at the business section. He wasn't about to slip up again.

Yet the pages called to him, a determined siren promising information. Information he no longer needed to know, he reminded himself. He returned his attention to the movie.

Ten minutes later he swore as he turned off the movie and grabbed the paper. He'd kept the previous two days' business sections as well. Knowing he was a weak-willed bastard, he dug out a pad of paper and a pen, then opened the first newspaper.

Despite the fact that it was mid-October, the ocean breeze was warm as it flirted with the Sunday afternoon beachgoers. Ali strolled through the stalls at the arts-and-crafts fall festival, savoring her lone day off. She'd marked her calendar with the Sunday event nearly a month before and had come armed with an empty backpack, a list, and plenty of money. If she was very lucky, she could make a dent in her impressive holiday shopping list.

Ali paused by a display of handmade wind chimes. The metal and ceramic pieces danced together in the soft breeze. Ali touched a wind chime made of slender copper flowers. Her mother might like it. Of course Charlotte Elizabeth was somewhere at the craft fair and could decide to buy it herself.

Ali glanced around as if she might catch sight of her mother and Miss Sylvie. No doubt they were the center of attention somewhere. She didn't spot either of them and felt a quick surge of relief. She wasn't exactly in the mood for her mother's brand of wisdom.

From the edge of the stall where she stood she could see the fair stretching along the boardwalk for nearly a quarter mile. There were more booths across the street. To the west was the beach and the pier, and beyond them, the blue Pacific Ocean. It was a perfect fall day, Ali thought contentedly as she strolled to the next booth. Warm and clear, with the air smelling sweetly of water and salt and freshly popped popcorn.

She looked over a display of knit Christmas stockings. Each was topped by a different kind of animal. There were bears and dogs and cats and birds.

"Are you looking for anything in particular?" the gray-haired woman manning the booth asked. "We have more inventory in boxes."

Ali considered the stocking. "I don't suppose you have one with a pink pig?"

The woman frowned, then nodded slowly. "I think I made one like that. Although people don't usually think of pigs at Christmas. Unless they're having ham."

She smiled at her slight joke, then bent over and reached into a box under the long folding table that displayed her wares. Ali waited, wondering if a Christmas stocking was an appropriate gift for Miss Sylvie. Then she reminded herself that her mother expected her to get her pet a gift, and it was unlikely Miss Sylvie already had a stocking of her own. Frankly, Ali didn't think the pig really cared about what was under the tree for her. Unless it was edible, Miss Sylvie wasn't much interested in the process of exchanging gifts.

The older woman straightened and handed Ali a red knit stocking with a pink pig at the top.

"I know someone who would think that was perfect."

Ali turned toward the voice and saw Matt standing beside her. Instantly her body began to tingle in a most peculiar way. She felt oddly nervous and almost tongue-tied. Which was crazy. "What are you doing here?" she asked.

He looked around, then returned his attention to her. "I'm not allowed to work on Sundays so I thought I'd take a walk. I came down to the beach and found this going on. And you?"

"Christmas shopping," she said, then smiled at the woman. "I'll take it."

She passed over a twenty. While she waited for her change, she slid off her backpack and tucked the pig stocking inside.

"I'm almost afraid to ask," Matt said, "but who is that for?"

Ali took her change and a receipt, then tucked both into her pocket. "Who do you think?"

Together they slowly walked to the next booth. "Not your mother's pig."

"One and the same. Charlotte Elizabeth insists that Miss Sylvie be remembered at the holidays. The good news is Miss Sylvie also gives gifts. I must say she has excellent taste. Last year she gave me an Hermès scarf that was exquisite."

Matt raised his eyebrows. "You don't seriously think she picked that out herself?"

"I don't know. My mother swears they shop together online and that she buys whatever seems to get Miss Sylvie's piggy attention."

"Insane," he said with a shake of his head.

"I agree, but would not dare admit that to my mother, even under the threat of torture."

She noticed that Matt wore his usual workday attire. Jeans and a long-sleeved shirt. His clothes were worn, but clean. As he moved around a mother pushing a stroller with two seats side-by-side, Ali allowed her gaze to linger on his butt. The man might still need a little fattening up, but parts of him were amazingly perfect.

He returned to her side and lightly touched the backpack. "Looks like you're serious about your shopping."

"I have a huge list, including family, friends, and employees. As you can imagine, Rick and my mother aren't the easiest people in the world to buy for. Charlotte Elizabeth has, over the years, received some amazing gifts, and Rick believes in indulging himself, so I'm always on the lookout for something unique. Although my mother said she was coming to the fair this year, so I'm going to be cautious about buying her something. With my luck, she'll have picked up one just like it earlier in the day."

She realized she was babbling . . . almost as if she were nervous, which made no sense. But then little about her relationship with Matt did.

They explored several booths offering jewelry, nature-sound CDs, handknit sweaters, and candy. The latter offered samples. Matt took a piece of chocolate and ate it, then leaned close.

"Not nearly as good as yours," he assured her. "You have nothing to worry about."

His breath fanned her cheek, and his arm brushed against hers. She shivered as heat spiraled out from the center of her chest. Yikes! No way on this planet was she going to find Matt Baker attractive or even the least bit sexy.

They passed by a large family buying T-shirts with catchy sayings. Ali recognized the owner of the hardware store and called out a greeting.

"That's the fifth or sixth person you've greeted by name," Matt observed. "Is there anyone you don't know in Saint Maggie?"

"Sure. Dozens of people. But I have made a lot of friends here."

"Why?"

She looked at him, but he wasn't teasing. His brown eyes looked serious. "Because I live here. When I moved here five years ago, I didn't know anyone. So I introduced myself to people. I went to different civic meetings, joined a couple of clubs, volunteered. I wanted this to be home, so I had to fit in."

"Is it home?"

"Yes."

"You're good at a lot of things," he told her.

His statement surprised her and made her laugh. "I

wish, but that's far from true. It's taken me years to figure out what I wanted from life. Until I was twenty-four, all I did was mess up. I tried a half-dozen career paths and failed at them all."

His dark eyes studied her. "Trying and finding out something isn't what you want isn't failing. Failing is not trying."

"That sounds good, but it's not how it felt at the time. So when I stumbled into candy making and found I both liked it and could do it, I was hooked. Speaking of which, the strawberries sold out yesterday," she said. "Um, thanks for helping."

"You're welcome."

"So it's your turn."

"For what?"

She pressed a hand to her chest. "I've just spilled my guts about something incredibly personal, and now you have to do the same. After all, we're having a conversation."

"Ali, a conversation is talking about the weather or the stock market. Gut sharing is something else entirely and completely voluntary."

"Fine," she grumbled. "Don't share. I'm not the least bit interested in your past, anyway."

"Liar."

She ignored him. "Besides, it wouldn't be worth it. You'd just give me the death look for invading your privacy and then get quiet."

Matt took her arm and drew her in between two booths. "The death look?" he asked, his voice low and teasing. "What exactly is that?"

"You know. It's the look Darth Vader gave people before he killed them."

"Darth Vader wore a mask."

"Yeah, but he got this strange look. You get it, too." She smiled.

He smiled back, then his mouth straightened. "I know I keep things to myself. It's not personal. Okay?"

It wasn't an apology, nor was it a confession of his deepest, darkest secret. Even so, she felt a little better. "It's fine. We all have our weirdnesses. They're what make us special." She moved back into the crowd and he followed.

"To completely change the subject, I've been thinking about what you said the other night," she said, watching a running toddler scurry by. A harried-looking mother raced after the child. "About my not really wanting a normal guy because if I did, I'd be living a different kind of life."

"It was just an observation," he said. "Don't take it too much to heart."

She looked at him. "But I think you might be right. I've been talking and talking about what I want, but I haven't *done* anything to make it happen. Which means I've been fooling myself. That doesn't make me very happy."

"I think you're making the problem bigger than it is."

"Maybe." She stopped to admire several hand-carved desk accessories. "If Rick actually spent time at a desk, these might be nice. But he doesn't. He has a financial planner who handles all his bills. He's not a letter writer. Come to think of it, I'm not sure my brother owns a desk." She moved to the next stall.

"My point is," she continued, "I have to figure out what I really want. Have I put all my emotional energy into a goal that I have no intention of making happen?"

"Only you can answer that."

"I know. It's close to the end of the year. I think I'll make it a resolution or something."

"Sounds like a plan."

She paused to finger several linen napkins. "Do you like your room at the bed-and-breakfast?" she asked.

"Yes, it's great." He lightly touched her arm to steer her out of the way of three teenage girls walking with their arms linked.

She felt the heat of his fingers all the way to her toes. Ali sighed quietly. Obviously she'd been way too long without a man. Even she was not usually reduced to swooning like an eighteenth-century maiden.

They moved back into the walkway.

"I've been thinking that I should move back into Harry's place," Matt said. "I don't want to occupy a room you could rent out."

Ali turned to look at him. "I told you, we're not going to rent out that room, we're going to convert it. Besides, does Kasey's place feel full to you? This isn't exactly our prime season."

"You're too soft-hearted for your own good."

"Maybe. But it hasn't hurt me so far."

"It will." His gaze was steady and sure, and he spoke as if he could see into the future.

She wanted to know what he saw there and have him confess all his secrets. Was he telling her that *he* would hurt her? Ridiculous, she told herself. That would require more of a relationship than they had.

The path wound to the left. They circled around the parking lot and through a grove of trees. The breeze shifted, and Ali inhaled the scent of freshly baked tortilla chips. Instantly her stomach growled.

"Do you smell that?" she asked with a small moan and pointed across the street. "Riviera Cantina. I adore their food. Have you had lunch? Want to join me? They make the best Mexican food, and their margaritas are to die for."

Matt looked from the restaurant to her. "Sure, but only if I get to buy. You've been feeding me since I arrived. I want to return the favor."

"I'd like that," she told him. "Thanks."

They headed out into the street, then walked across the sidewalk and into the cantina. The pretty, young hostess seated them at an outside table that offered a view of the festival and the ocean beyond. Ali slipped off her backpack then settled into a chair.

"Chips," she said. "Chips, salsa, a margarita, and one of their wraps." She leaned toward him. "You have to try the wrap. It's not exactly a taco or an enchilada. It's better than both. I get chicken, which comes with avocado and bacon and this sauce that is practically a religious experience."

Matt laughed. "Is there any food you don't like?"

"Of course, but why eat it?"

A waiter appeared. Matt ordered a pitcher of margaritas for them, along with two wraps. Both chicken. The waiter was back in less than five minutes, bringing chips and salsa along with a pitcher of margaritas.

"So," Matt said as he poured them each a drink. "Is this the only business in town you don't own?"

Ali chomped on a chip and wrinkled her nose at him. "I only own one business. I'm simply a partner in a couple of others."

"Yeah, right." Matt didn't look convinced. He leaned back in his white plastic chair and took a drink of his margarita. "You probably have entire city blocks in your portfolio of establishments. You're setting yourself up to take over Saint Maggie."

"Ah. You've discovered my secret plan. Now you'll have to be eliminated."

He smiled at her. As had happened before when he was distracted, Matt's eyes cleared and the shadows faded away.

Their round table was shaded by an umbrella. Beyond the bright pink protection, the sky was a vivid shade of California blue. She'd purchased Miss Sylvie's Christmas present, not always an easy task, and was about to eat a delicious lunch. These were the simple moments that made up a perfect life.

"Why do you do it?" he asked.

She blinked at him. "Do what?"

He picked up a chip and dipped it into the salsa. "Get involved," he said before taking a bite.

"You mean with the businesses and people's lives?"

He nodded.

Ali rested her forearms on the plastic tablecloth. Conversations drifted around them, combining with the call of the seagulls. She considered Matt's question, not sure how to give him an easy answer.

"It's something I've always done," she said slowly. "I don't know any other way to live. I can't make a major impact on the world, but I can influence individual lives for the better. I like to think that all the small changes add up to big ones eventually. It's important."

"Is that why you hired Willie?"

Ali sipped from her glass. The drink was tart, sweet, and salty. Perfect. "That wasn't my decision. Kasey handles all the day-to-day activities at the bed-and-breakfast."

"I don't buy that. I think you had something to do with him getting the job."

She traced a random pattern on her paper napkin.

"Maybe. He's a smart kid. Dora saved enough to put him through college, but it was tough, and he has to work part-time to help with a few household expenses. I know he's responsible enough to handle the front desk so I recommended that Kasey give him a try. The evening hours are quiet so he has plenty of time to study. It's an ideal situation for everyone."

Matt didn't look convinced.

"It all comes back for the better," she said earnestly. "People have given Willie help. When he's successful, he'll remember and do the same. It continues the cycle."

"What do you get out of it?"

"Satisfaction. I know I'm doing the right thing."

His dark eyes turned thoughtful. "Dora is a struggling widow with three kids. Sara is a divorced mom with a couple of kids of her own. I don't know Kasey's story, but I'm guessing she has one. Don't you have anyone normal in your life?"

She laughed. "Matt, that *is* normal, at least for most people. We all have tragedies and difficulties, and we learn to cope with them. Usually that's an easier process when it's shared. Life is complicated and messy."

"How much of this is about your mother?"

Was it just her or had the temperature dropped?

Matt leaned forward and put his hand on her arm. "Sorry. That was out of line. I apologize."

She sighed. "You don't have to. It's a reasonable question. Am I living a life of service because my mother lost a million dollars to have me? Maybe. Do I feel guilty because she never completely returned to her career after I was born? Of course. Do I hate the way she pressures me to have children because it adds to the guilt? After all she gave so much, is having a couple of children for her to spoil such a big deal?"

"Ali, we don't have to talk about this."

"I know. I'm just saying that occasionally the pressure gets to me. When I'm doing for others, I feel better about everything. So it works."

He studied her. His fingers still brushed against her arm, which made it hard to concentrate.

"I've never known anyone like you," he said.

"Don't get all that excited," she said. "Some of my efforts are pretty feeble."

The waiter delivered their food.

"I wouldn't describe your efforts as feeble," Matt said as he picked up his wrap. "You're changing people's lives. I respect that." He took a bite of his food.

His words made her glow. She felt special and bubbly. And the wrap was as delicious as ever.

"Good choice," he told her. "I like it. So who's left on your shopping list?"

"My friend Clair and her family. Kasey, Dora . . ."

"Willie and every other stray in your life. Yeah, I know." He laughed.

Ali suddenly found it difficult to breathe. The man was getting under her skin, and she didn't know a single way to make him stop. Jason might have been a lowlife who had stolen her cash receipts and her American Express card, but Matt could turn out to be a lot more dangerous.

He just might have the skills necessary to steal her heart.

chapter ten

Monday morning Matt hesitated in front of the paint display. "Which one?" he asked, staring at three quart-size cans of blue paint.

Ali laughed. "It's your sky, big guy. I would not presume to dictate the right color."

Matt glared at her, but she didn't seem the least bit intimidated. She just wiggled her eyebrows and told him not to forget sponges. "I've heard if you cut them up and dip them in white paint that they make the best clouds."

It was barely eight-thirty on Monday morning. As promised, Ali had brought Matt to the hardware store to pick out the rest of the paint for the playroom at the tea shop.

He picked the medium blue color and placed it in their narrow cart, then he consulted the list he'd made the previous evening. "Grass green and an assortment of animal colors, depending on which stencils we get."

This morning her hair was loose and shiny. She shook her head, and the long curls swayed with the movement, brushing back and forth over her shoulders in a slow, lazy motion.

"No, Matt. 'We' aren't buying anything. This is your project and your responsibility. I do not want my name associated with your ark mural."

"I'm not doing an ark. Just a couple of animals on the wall." Although staring at all the paint choices, he was starting to have second thoughts.

She leaned close and lightly touched his arm. "I must tell you, though, in all seriousness, I'm very impressed that you're willing to take this on. I don't have an artistic bone in my body when it comes to decorating. And there are professors in Switzerland willing to testify to that fact."

"You should wait to see how everything turns out before you start throwing around compliments," he said. "After all, we could end up with two-headed giraffes or monkeys with wings."

"I have every faith in you. Besides, you did a lovely job on my parking-lot fence on Saturday."

"It's hardly the same thing."

Her hazel eyes were wide and teasing. Her mouth curved up in a smile. She'd shown up dressed for work in a long-sleeved blouse tucked into a navy velvet skirt. She looked delightfully feminine and alluring.

He stiffened slightly. Alluring? Women weren't alluring, at least not anymore. He barely noticed them. Or at least he hadn't until Ali had captured his attention.

They'd spent the previous afternoon together. First walking around the street fair, then at lunch. He'd enjoyed her company and had been reluctant to leave. But he'd forced himself to head out as soon as they'd finished eating. Because if he'd stayed any longer, their time together could have become something more than coworkers sharing a meal.

He'd promised himself that he wouldn't let that happen. So he ignored the sweet scent of her body and focused on the business at hand.

"I need to look at stencils," he said.

"They're over here."

She led the way down the narrow aisle and motioned to the bottom drawer of a worn metal filing cabinet. He had to sidestep a couple of customers before he could pull open a drawer. The hardware store, with a big sign proclaiming it to be Saint Maggie's finest, was nothing like he'd imagined. He didn't spend much time shopping for home improvement items, but when he did, he generally went to the large discount warehouses.

By contrast this place was crowded and cramped. Too much merchandise sat on too-small shelves. Upon their arrival, they'd been greeted by the owners—two old guys about fifteen years past retirement age—and a "young" clerk in his fifties.

Matt squatted down and pulled out the rusty drawer. It creaked and screeched and came open with a sudden rush. Dozens of stencils lay nestled together in no discernable arrangement. He flipped through flags and Christmas trees until he found a circus tent followed by several animals, including a seal with a ball balanced on its nose.

He looked up at Ali. "What do you think about the circus as a theme?"

She pressed her full lips together as she thought. "That could work. If you used primary colors, it would be bright. Better than painting grass and trees freehand if you ask me."

He picked out half a dozen stencils, then returned to the paint selection and chose several pint cans in bright colors.

Finally done with their shopping, they walked to the front of the store. The two old guys sitting at the counter studied Matt with interest.

"Good morning," Ali called as she drew her credit card out of her wallet. "This is Matt Baker. He's Harry's new helper. Matt, meet Elvis and Leonard. They own the hardware store."

"Gentlemen," Matt said and nodded.

Both men were stoop-shouldered and white-haired, dressed in matching plaid shirts and overalls. They looked like twins. Old twins. Their sharp blue eyes took in everything about him.

"You're working out at the tea shop now, aren't you?" one of the men asked. Matt didn't know if it was Elvis or Leonard. "Finished at Ali's place?"

"Uh, yes. That's right."

Ali leaned close. "Don't worry about it. They know everything. One of the joys of living in a small town."

"So, young man. Are you going to buy Harry's business?"

The second of the brothers asked the question. Matt couldn't be positive, but it seemed to him that the hardware store suddenly grew quiet . . . as if everyone within earshot was listening. He shifted uncomfortably, then started taking paint out of the cart and placing it on the already crowded counter. He pushed aside a small display of pet tags to make room for the stencils.

"No," he said at last. "I'm not the entrepreneur type. I don't have Harry's business sense."

The elderly man nodded. "Not many do. It would be a challenge to make that business more successful than it is now."

Matt wasn't sure if they were pulling his leg or serious. He looked at Ali for guidance, but she was too busy holding back a smile to be of any help.

She shrugged helplessly, and he felt his lips turn up in an answering grin. Morning sun drifted through the bright windows and reflected off her dark hair. The curls were like a halo around her face. Her skin was clear, almost luminous. Her long lashes made her eyes seem huge.

Ali handed over her credit card. The elderly man who took it grumbled about newfangled contraptions and carefully slid it through the strip in the cash register.

"You should carry cash," he scolded Ali as he handed back her card. "You know the bank robs us of two percent every time you use that thing. Out-and-out stealing, if you ask me."

"No one asked," his brother said. "You think these young people give a hoot about our problems? They're too busy running around, living the good life. It's just you and me, Elvis. Lord knows young Pervis is likely as not to quit and go work at that danged new grocery store."

Matt was pleased to now know who was Elvis and who was Leonard. He also wondered at their concerns that young Pervis, fifty-five if he was a day, would leave a job he'd obviously had all his life.

Leonard slowly placed the paint cans into a paper bag, then handed it over to Matt. "Watch your back. That bag's heavier than it looks. Not that a young lad like yourself is going to listen to an old coot like me. I know what you're thinking."

Matt was amazed that men like Elvis and Leonard still existed, and he doubted that was what Leonard thought he was thinking. Still he smiled and nodded his thanks.

"Bye," Ali called as they turned to leave.

"Mind you watch that stop sign at the end of the drive," Elvis called after her. "Don't go out of the parking lot thinking you're in a drag race because you're not."

Matt was still grinning when his gaze fell on an old-fashioned gas-station calendar by the front door. The top half was a photo of a smiling man pumping gas into a '55 Chevy. But that wasn't what captured Matt's attention. Instead he noticed the date.

It was as if the sun had disappeared from the sky, and every bit of air had been sucked into a black hole. He couldn't see, couldn't breathe, couldn't do anything but realize that tomorrow would be a year since Leigh died.

"Matt?" Ali called. "Are you all right?"

He wasn't but he forced himself to leave the store and walk toward her 4-Runner. He loaded the bag into the rear of the vehicle and silently slid into the passenger seat. But he wasn't really there. A part of him was back in Chicago, listening to a nurse tell him that Leigh was gone.

It was tomorrow. One year tomorrow. Pain ripped through him and with it the realization that he was never going to forget or forgive himself. He couldn't.

"Horses don't look like that."

Matt didn't have to turn around to know that his silence had been invaded by two pint-size critics.

He pointed overhead. "How do you like the sky?"

Marti bent down and stuck her head under his outstretched arm so he was forced to look into her freckled face.

She grinned. "It's very pretty. I like the color, and the clouds are nice."

Finally, because he knew that he wasn't going to get any work done while they were around, he set down his brush and wiped his hands on a rag. Then he sat on his butt and looked up.

"They're not too bad," he admitted. Marti instantly plopped on his lap. Joey remained standing, but leaned against him. All three looked up at the bright blue ceiling and the clouds scattered across the flat surface.

It had taken Matt a couple of tries, but he'd finally gotten the hang of cloud making. The sponge had to have plenty of paint so the white showed, but not so much that it dripped and ran. He learned that it was better to make a couple of passes over the cloud than to try to get it right the first time.

"See how I put a couple right by the corner where the ceiling and wall meet?" he asked, pointing toward the far wall. "I thought it would look nice to have them on the top of the wall as well. Kind of like the edge of the world."

"The edge of the world," Joey breathed. "I wanna go there."

"It's not a real place," Marti said importantly, then looked up at Matt. "Is it?"

He shook his head. "Not anymore."

She wrinkled her tiny nose at his response, but didn't say anything. Matt felt awkward with her on his lap and Joey leaning against him but didn't know how to make them move without being rude. Joey's elbow was digging into his shoulder, and Marti had the boniest butt he'd ever encountered. Still, he stayed where he was. Despite the obvious discomfort, their small weights weren't too horrible.

He was surprised they were so accepting of him, but then what did he know about children? He'd been an only child who rarely saw other kids outside of school. None of his friends had started the family thing yet. Or at least they hadn't the last time he'd spoken with them.

Marti turned her attention to the pictures on the wall. Matt braced himself for the criticism. In theory, stenciling should have been a snap, but life wasn't about a theory. Obviously he didn't have the stenciling skill required for anything to look normal, although the circus tent wasn't too bad.

Marti tilted her head as she stared at the horse.

"Horses aren't green," Joey told him.

"I know. I was trying to blend colors to make brown, but I seemed to have missed the mark."

"What's wrong with his face?" Marti asked.

"I'm not sure." Matt stared at the painted horse. As far as he could tell, the smooshed face was the least of the animal's troubles. The creature had a blurry rear leg and was wildly swayback. "He needs some work."

Footsteps sounded in the hallway. Both kids instantly pushed away from him and headed for the door. Sara caught them before they could escape. The harried blonde mother shook her head. "There you are."

Marti and Joey each cast him pleading glances, then slipped around her and disappeared down the hall.

"I'm sorry," Sara said. "I told them not to bother you."

"They weren't any bother."

He was telling the truth. The kids distracted him from

his thoughts, which was something he needed. As the day progressed, it was as if he'd found himself trapped inside a massive clock. He could hear the ticking of time as it marched on, closer and closer to midnight and the anniversary of Leigh's death. He'd dreaded the thought of having to relive that day, but he knew there was no way around it. He would simply have to hunker down and endure.

Her gaze took in the colored ceiling and the odd-looking horse. "The clouds are very nice," she said politely. "As is the circus tent."

Despite the ache inside of him, he couldn't help smiling. "But you're not going to mention the horse."

"I think it would be better to let that one go." She leaned against the doorframe. "Thanks for taking so much time with the room. The kids are really going to love it."

He rose to his feet. "I'm glad. Except for the mutant horse, I think it's going to be fine."

He'd thought she would leave then, but instead Sara lingered. She studied the cloud-covered sky, then folded her arms over her chest. "How was your weekend?"

The question surprised him. He wasn't used to idle chitchat. "Fine."

She didn't say anything more, but her expression turned expectant. Obviously she wanted more.

"I, ah, went to the craft fair by the beach."

"Really?" She smiled. "So did I. This was one of the weekends the kids were with their dad. I know it's important for them to see him, but I never know what to do with myself. The rest of the time I'm constantly scrambling to meet their needs and with work. When I suddenly find myself having a few unstructured hours, I get lost."

Matt nodded vigorously because he didn't know what

the hell to say. Why did women always want to talk about personal stuff?

Sara laughed. "Sorry. Didn't mean to dump on you like that. I guess it's been on my mind."

"No problem."

Which was a lie. He resisted the need to grind his teeth together. Was she sharing, or did she want the problem fixed? And why come to him? He had enough to deal with having Ali in his life. He didn't—

His brain froze. The last full sentence replayed in his brain until he couldn't think about anything else. *Ali in his life.* No. She wasn't in his life. He worked for her. Actually he worked for Harry, and she was just . . . someone he had to deal with, or something. But they didn't have a relationship. They weren't involved. She wasn't—

He couldn't think anymore. The walls were closing in on him. They had been for hours. Since he'd remembered about tomorrow.

"Excuse me," he said, brushing past Sara and heading for the back door. He had to get outside, or he wouldn't be able to keep breathing.

Sara walked into the shop a little after four on Tuesday. Ali plucked a single white chocolate truffle from the display and held it out. "You look like you need this," she said.

Sara took the candy and nibbled on the smooth coating. "Thanks. It's been one of those days. I ran out of the special before twelve-thirty, and I couldn't sell the mushroom quiche to save my soul. Most of the time I can guess right on the quantities, but every now and then I completely mess up."

"I know what you mean," Ali said. "I'm still trying to pawn off low-fat muffins on anyone who will take them. Miss Sylvie finally stopped eating them. You know you've hit rock bottom when a pig refuses your cooking."

Sara smiled. "I hadn't thought of it that way. If it wasn't for her heart problem, I could test the mushroom quiche on her. But I don't think Charlotte Elizabeth wants her eating that many eggs."

Ali didn't know if Miss Sylvie's condition would be aggravated by eggs, nor did she want to have to consider the fact. It was enough that she'd bought the creature a Christmas present.

Sara finished the truffle. When she'd swallowed, she drew in a breath. "Maybe I'm being weird, but have you seen Matt today?"

Ali came out from behind the counter and wiped her hands on her apron. "No. He's supposed to be finishing up the playroom at your place."

"That's what I thought but I wasn't sure," Sara admitted. "I spoke with him yesterday. He'd started stenciling. We talked and he left. I thought maybe he was taking a break or something. I didn't think about it again until he didn't show up this morning. When I checked, the playroom was exactly as he'd left it yesterday. The paint cans were open, the brushes just lying around. He never came back yesterday to clean up, and he didn't show up this morning."

A knot formed in Ali's stomach. Something was wrong—she felt it to her bones. Then she reminded herself that she could be completely wrong. Matt had certainly acted strangely more than once.

"Let me check with Harry. Maybe he knows something."

She walked into the kitchen and found her small, tattered phone book, then looked up Harry's number. After dialing, she waited, listening to three rings before a familiar, craggy voice muttered, "Hello?"

"Hi, Harry, it's Ali. Have you seen Matt?"

The older man coughed. "Why on earth would I have seen him? I've been working at that damn winery, replacing fences. You know how many acres of grapes those folks got up there? You know how much fencing I gotta replace? And just to make my professional life more hellish than it is, we got rain today. I'm wetter than a sea snake."

Ali turned to glance out the window. The morning's dark clouds had given way to sprinkles. She had her doubts about the "wetter than a sea snake" remark, but she wasn't going to worry about details right now.

"I thought maybe he'd come to help you today. He didn't work on the tearoom."

"Maybe he's at the bed-and-breakfast. He's spending his nights there now, living like royalty. I guess my spare room's not good enough for the likes of him."

Ali sighed. When Harry got into one of his moods, there was no talking to him. "All right, thanks. If you see him or hear from him, would you ask him to call me?"

"What? Now I'm his goddamn answering service?"

Harry hung up without saying good-bye. She turned and saw Sara standing in the entrance to the kitchen.

"Harry didn't know anything," Ali told her friend. "Did you check with Kasey? Maybe he got involved with something there."

"She said she hadn't seen him all day."

Ali didn't like the sound of that. "I'm going to go check

to see if he's sick or something. Can you watch the store for a few minutes?"

"Sure."

Ali grabbed an old windbreaker to protect her from the rain and headed out the back door. She ran across the gravel parking lot and then crossed the street. Light rain dampened her hair and face. She jogged across to the entrance of the bed-and-breakfast, pushing open the front door as she entered.

Kasey sat behind the front desk. She smiled quizzically at Ali. "Hi. What's going on?"

"I'm not sure. Matt didn't show up at Sara's today, and Harry doesn't know where he is. Maybe he's sick. Would you mind if I checked his room?"

"Go ahead. You want me to come with you?"

"No. I'll be fine." She took the key Kasey offered. "Of course if I'm not back in five minutes, call the police."

"Will do."

Ali left the office and headed toward the second building. At the far end she paused in front of Matt's door and knocked loudly.

"Matt? It's Ali. Are you all right?"

Her heart stopped when she saw the "Do Not Disturb" sign in place. She knocked again. After several minutes, she knew she didn't have another choice so she put the key in the lock and turned the doorknob.

She half expected to find a dead body sprawled across the bed. But Matt wasn't in the room. She leaned against the doorframe in relief. Her mind had offered all kinds of reasons as to why he wouldn't show up at work, and none of them had been especially good.

Now she stepped into his room and looked around.

The place was a mess. There were newspapers scattered everywhere, as if he'd started reading the pages, then had tossed them around in anger. The sheets and blankets were tangled, attesting to a restless night. His morning breakfast tray was untouched. But there was an empty bottle of Scotch in the wastebasket. And a picture of a woman on the small dresser.

Ali's heart began to pound as she studied the photograph. The woman was pretty, with long blonde hair and blue eyes. She leaned against a low wall in a garden somewhere, laughing at the camera, or the photographer. She was slender to the point of boyishness.

Who was she? Matt's wife? His ex-wife? A girlfriend? Was she the reason he'd walked away from his oh-so-normal life? Ali didn't have any answer, but her gut told her that the woman in the photo had something to do with Matt's disappearance. She crossed to the bed and sat on the edge, then she picked up the phone.

Kasey answered on the first ring. "Everything all right?"

"It's fine. He's not here. I think he slept here last night, but he didn't eat breakfast. Can you connect me with the police?"

Kasey's breath caught in surprise. "You think there's something wrong?"

"I'm not sure. It's too soon to report him missing, but I want them to look out for him if they can."

"Okay. Just a sec."

There was silence, then a click and a voice said, "Santa Magdelana Police Department. How may I help you?"

Ali identified herself and explained the problem. "I don't think he's a missing person, but I'm concerned that he's out wandering around. If someone on patrol sees him, could I be notified?"

The woman took down Matt's name and a description, then asked for Ali's name and number. She promised to pass the information along.

Ali closed the shop promptly at six. It had been two hours, and she still hadn't heard a word about Matt. Kasey had promised to phone if he showed up. So far it had been quiet . . . too quiet.

Ali knew there was something wrong. Something terrible. She knew that Matt's disappearance was related to his past, but she didn't know how. She retreated to her upstairs apartment, but for once the soothing colors and overstuffed furniture didn't make her feel better. She paced, tried to watch television, then paced some more. If Matt wasn't found, it was going to be a really long night.

By quarter to eight, she'd nearly worn a hole in her rug. She forced herself to sit down and watch television. But ten minutes of flipping channels had her ready to scream and even stroking a purring Domino didn't help her mood. By now it was raining harder, and the night temperature was dropping rapidly. Did Matt have a coat? Was he out there drunk? Alone? Sick? Dead?

She closed her eyes so she wouldn't have to picture him lying in a ditch, then she opened them because the image was all too clear.

The front doorbell to the shop rang, startling her. She put her cat on the floor, then jumped to her feet and raced downstairs. Two people stood on the covered front porch. Actually one stood and the other leaned precariously.

Ali jerked open the door.

Lynn Ellison, a patrol officer and an acquaintance of Ali's, motioned toward the man draped across her shoulder. "I heard you were missing someone who matched this guy's description. Is he yours?"

At the sound of her voice, Matt raised his head. "Hey," he said, and swayed toward Ali.

Ali didn't know what to do. She stood immobilized, staring in shock. "Ah, yes, Lynn. I know him. I thought he was lost or something. Where did you find him?"

"On one of the back roads out by the wineries. Way the hell away from here. I don't know how he got there. If it hadn't been so cold and raining, I would have left him wandering down the road, but I figured I'd better bring him home."

She unlooped Matt's arm from her shoulder. "You ready to stand on your own, Mr. Baker?"

"I'm fine." He took a few steps, then offered Lynn a broad smile. "Thanks for the lift. Really. It was great."

Ali reached out and grabbed him by the front of his shirt. "You'd better come inside." She looked at the other woman. "Thanks for finding him. I was worried."

Lynn helped her get Matt inside. He collapsed in the wooden chair by the door. "You sure you want him around? He's not much of a prize."

"I know. It's not like that. He works for me."

"He'd better be damned good." She touched the tip of her cap, then left.

Ali closed the door behind her. She looked down at a wet and slightly drunk Matt. Anger surged through her.

"What were you thinking?" she demanded, even as she knew it was doubtful he was paying attention. "You scared me to death. I thought something had happened to you."

He startled her by rising to his feet and wrapping his arms around her. She was too stunned to move away. "I couldn't help it," he said, sounding surprisingly sober. "I'm sorry. It's just that I didn't know how else to walk through hell."

Then he kissed her.

chapter eleven

Matt's mouth was warm and gentle against her own. Ali was too shocked to step away, or even respond. She told herself that this wasn't really happening, it couldn't be. Matt Baker kissing her? In what lifetime?

Then she began to notice the little things . . . like the heat of his body, despite his damp clothes, and the way he tasted of expensive Scotch. She'd never been much of a Scotch drinker, but she was starting to see the appeal. He hadn't shaved that morning, and the stubble burned her face, but she found she liked the friction against her sensitive skin.

He wrapped his arms around her and drew her close. She went willingly, probably because she was too startled to protest. Okay, maybe a little because it felt nice to be in a man's arms. It had been a very long time. She'd forgotten what it felt like to be pulled next to a hard, hot body and for the moment feel completely safe.

Slowly, knowing she was crazy, or he was, she raised her arms and wrapped them around his neck. His clothes were wet, dampening her dress. Her low heels gave her an inch or so of extra height, but even so she had to raise her chin to continue to meet his mouth.

His kiss was slow and sensual, his lips brushing against hers over and over. He didn't attack or press her too soon. When his tongue swept against her lower lip, she had the feeling he was exploring rather than insisting. He traced the shape of her mouth, then made her shiver by nibbling at the very corner.

She supposed she should pull away before things got out of hand, but she found she didn't want to. As his hands slid up and down her back, she shuddered slightly as nerve endings began to come to life. When he reached lower and cupped her rear end, she instinctively arched against him, bringing her belly up against the hardness of his arousal.

She'd expected him to be interested in the proceedings, but she hadn't thought he would be so very *ready*. The information was just one more shock in a list of many, but in a good way. She found herself wanting to rub up and down, feeling the length and breadth of him. Her hips thrust forward in an age-old invitation she couldn't control any more than she could stop breathing. A sound caught in the back of her throat. She parted her lips to let it escape . . . and at the same time allowed Matt to enter her.

His tongue swept inside her mouth. He went from tender explorer to masterful seducer in less than a heartbeat. There was something about the way he kissed, or the taste of him, or maybe it was an unexplained chemistry between them. She didn't know and, at this moment, she didn't care about what it was. She only knew it was happening, and she never wanted him to stop.

He brushed against her, exploring, tempting, exciting. First the soft skin of the inside of her lower lip, then the sensitive places that made her breathe his name. She pressed harder against him, trying to remember the last time she'd really kissed a man and been held and had felt the hot, sharp prickling flow of arousal.

Even though her body had been sexually asleep for over a year, it came back to life with the subtlety of a rocket launch. Heat and need and desire exploded through her, making her gasp. The hands on her rear tightened, then one moved up to get lost in her hair.

"I want you, Ali," he growled low in his throat. "I need you." He pressed sweet, wet kisses to her chin, her throat, then licked the sensitive skin behind her ear.

Ali didn't know what to think. They were standing in the middle of her shop. Matt was drunk, although obviously not too drunk. They couldn't do this, and if they did, they couldn't do it now . . . here.

"Matt, we have to—"

But she never got to finish her sentence. There wasn't time before he brought his mouth back to hers. As he kissed her, he cupped her face in his big, strong hands. He held her tenderly, masterfully, and oh, dear God, it had been so very long since a man had held her that way.

One of his hands slipped lower, down her neck and shoulder, sliding along her side, then over to her breast. Even as his tongue moved against hers in a rhythmic dance that made her ache inside, his hand cupped her. Forefinger and thumb found the tight bud of her nipple and gently teased the sensitive point.

She gasped. Only by sheer strength of will did she keep from begging. Dormant feelings sparked back to life, and a direct line formed from her breast to that magical place between her thighs.

She buried her fingers in his thick hair. She sucked in air because she was in danger of losing consciousness from the absolute pleasure of him. All this and she still had her clothes on. What on earth would happen if she was naked?

It was as if he read her mind. The hand on her breast moved to the buttons at the front of her dress and began to unfasten them. One by one they slipped free. No fumbling, no uncertainty. This was a man who knew exactly what he wanted. A small voice in Ali's head murmured this might not be a really great idea. She mentally slammed the door on the sound of reason. She didn't want to be thoughtful or intelligent or responsible. She wanted to feel. She wanted to know that she was still alive.

She reached for the buttons on his shirt.

"Yes," he breathed, looking into her eyes. "Want me back."

How am I supposed to resist that? she thought as her bones began to melt. Her thighs trembled, her heart fluttered, her panties grew damp. She kissed him back, allowing herself to fall into a sexual frenzy of need.

She was shaking so much she had a difficult time with his buttons. Their arms kept bumping. Finally he pushed her hands away and finished unfastening her. He pulled apart the front of her wool dress and shoved the fabric down her arms. But he didn't pull it off, and the tight cuffs wouldn't let her slip out of the sleeves. She was trapped.

She moved her hands behind her to fumble with the fastening at her wrists. The movement pushed her chest up against him. He was hard to her yielding, broad and everything she could ever want. One of the buttons came free, but she couldn't undo the other. He kissed her again. As his mouth took hers, he unfastened the front of her bra. Instantly cold air hit her breasts. But before she could protest or even care, his warm hands cupped her. He circled around her then let the weight of her curves fill his palms. Then he broke the kiss, bent his head, and took one of her nipples in his mouth.

A single, slender line of tension coiled down through her belly. She clutched his head with her free hand, curling her fingers through his hair. It was impossible to stay standing. She was shaking too hard . . . it felt too good. They had to . . . to . . .

Then his mouth was on hers. He wrapped his arms around her and pulled her close. He pressed himself against her, thrusting and rubbing and making her whimper. As his tongue swept into her mouth, she sucked on it. He growled low in his throat and grabbed her hips. Heat filled her. Blood flowed hot and heavy. She wanted to rip off her clothes and feel him inside of her—anything to ease the pressure building as she swelled and prepared for that blessed moment of entry.

He broke the kiss and swore. "We have to—" He glanced frantically around the room as if just realizing where they were.

Her apartment was upstairs but that seemed an impossible distance. Matt must have agreed because even as he moved her backward, he tugged on her dress, trying to pull it off.

"I'm caught," she said, showing him the wrist still trapped in fabric.

He unfastened the button, then grabbed her hand and

pulled her over to the small, sturdy table she used to display sale items.

With one sweep of his arm the packages of chocolate and scones went tumbling to the floor. Ali found she didn't even care. He walked to the rear of the store and hit the light switch. Instantly the room faded into shadows with only the lights from the display case providing illumination.

Ali nearly had time for second thoughts. They were obviously both crazy. They couldn't do it on her sale display table. That was insane. That was—

But then Matt was back in front of her. He lightly kissed her mouth, then her nose, her temple, her cheeks, and her chin. His fingers teased her nipples until the mindlessness returned, and all that mattered was how it felt to be close to him, having him touch her.

She reached out to finish the job she'd started before. There were only two buttons left. She unfastened them, then pulled his shirt from his jeans. Matt shrugged out of the shirt. He stood before her in the semidarkness, lean and masculine, looming above her. She pressed her fingers to his chest and felt warm skin and crinkly hair.

Then they were kissing again. Deep, soul-touching kisses that made her feminine parts weep with wanting. He shoved down her dress. She stepped out of her shoes and kicked them away. As he stroked her breasts, she shrugged off her bra, while he unfastened his jeans.

She stalled on her panties, suddenly unsure of what they were doing. She broke the kiss to look up at him. "Matt?"

Instead of answering, he reached a hand between them and slipped inside the protective layer of silk. Warm fingers tangled in curls, then reached beyond for that single point of pleasure. He found it on the first try.

A single stroke nearly brought her to her knees. She had to clutch his shoulders to keep from falling. A moan slipped out and her entire body shuddered. He circled the spot, nearly ignoring it but moving close enough that she practically begged for him to touch her again *there*. Then he did. Over and around, over and across, over and over again until she was panting.

Tension filled her. She was so wet, so hot, so ready. Each stroke of his fingers was heaven and torture. She shifted, parting her legs to make it easier on both of them.

Suddenly he pulled his hand away. She cried out in actual pain as the need grew to an unbearable pitch. He pulled the panties to her knees, then helped her onto the table. He bent over her and as his mouth found her nipple, his fingers found that secret place again. He moved in tandem, circling and nibbling and touching and moving faster and lighter and making her cry out and tense until she wasn't in control, until she didn't have a choice.

And then she was at the edge. Her knees drew back, her hands hugged him close. She breathed his name as the explosions began.

A thousand perfect contractions filled her being. Even as he continued to circle and touch, taking her higher, even as she reveled in her release, he pressed a single finger inside of her. She convulsed around him. Intense pleasure, so wonderful she didn't know how she'd survived without it all this time, filled her.

Her orgasm went on and on, finally slowing and leaving her feeling lethargic and contented. Matt raised his head. She smiled at him. "That worked."

He didn't answer. Instead he fumbled with his jeans, then shifted so that he could kiss her. As his tongue entered her mouth, she felt something masculine probing where his finger had just been. She reached down and encircled him, guiding him inside.

As he entered, stretching and filling her, the lethargy vanished. The first thrust reawakened her nerve endings, and the second started her on the path to completion once again.

She was wet and hot, and Matt didn't think he could hold back. The needs of his body were too strong. He wanted her with a desperation that made him shake like a teenager doing it for the first time. He'd been dead inside for so long that coming back to life was almost painful. The brush of her skin against his was exquisite torture. He filled her again and again, never wanting this to end but knowing that he couldn't hold out very long. Not when Ali offered such temptation.

She was full-breasted and curvy. When he cupped her breasts, her long hair brushed against the back of his hands. Need raced through him, making him groan as he pushed into her and felt her contract around him.

He opened his eyes and stared down at her. She was so damn beautiful.

"Ali," he breathed.

Her body moved beneath his. He felt her muscles convulsing, reacting to their joining, the movement of him inside of her. She gasped and came up off the table, clutching at him. Strong rippling movement massaged him as she found her own way to paradise. The sight and feel of her combined to push him over the edge.

As the pleasure began to overwhelm him and he reached the point of no return, he knew that what was supposed to bring him closer to all he'd lost had instead pushed him further away. He had no doubts about the woman beneath him. As he gave that final push and felt himself falling out of control, he found he couldn't regret this act of joining even if he might be sorry later.

And then he couldn't think at all. He could only be in her, lost in the pleasure of his release. He bent over her, kissing her face, murmuring her name. "Ali. Sweet Ali."

With an awkwardness that made Ali wince, they made their way upstairs to her apartment. She clutched her clothes to her chest and tried not to let the humiliation overwhelm her. Although, at the moment, it seemed to be a likely prospect.

What on earth had she been thinking? Of course the real answer was that she hadn't been thinking and would now have to suffer the consequences.

She opened the door at the top of the stairs and turned on the living room light. Trying not to think about the fact that Matt was several feet behind her and staring at her bare butt, she hurried through the furniture-filled room toward her bedroom.

"Ah, make yourself at home," she called over her shoulder. "I'll just be a second. I want to put on a robe."

She practically flew into her bedroom and slammed the door behind her. She would have leaned against the paneled wood, but it was cold and made her shiver. Instead she tossed her clothes onto the bed and dug in her messy closet for her robe.

Two minutes later she was securely wrapped in yards of terry cloth. She checked her reflection in the mirror, groaned at the tangled mess that was her hair, and ignored the faded makeup. She didn't know what she was going to say when she walked out into the living room, but she refused to hide away in her bedroom until she came up with a witty opening line. Better to stumble over the words than to give Matt a chance to disappear without saying good-bye. She didn't particularly mind if he left, but she didn't want him sneaking away.

She found him sitting on her sofa. He'd dressed—rather he'd pulled on his jeans and shirt, leaving the latter open. His feet were bare. She caught sight of his boots and socks placed neatly by the front door.

Domino, as much a sucker for Matt's male charms as Ali had been, draped herself across his lap. He rubbed the top of the cat's dark head, making her purr with ecstasy.

Ali paused awkwardly in the doorway and tried to smile. It was a surreal moment that didn't make any sense. Her body still quivered from their recent lovemaking. Her face felt hot where his stubble had scratched her skin. She was nervous and contented and very, very confused.

"I've made a friend," he said, still looking at her cat. "What's her name?"

"Domino. Because she's black and white. Not very original, but it suits her." Was she babbling yet, or did she get to look forward to that happening in a few minutes? "She's deaf so you have to stomp on the floor or flick the lights to get her attention."

"She's pretty."

"Yes, she is. So, ah, how about some coffee?" she asked when he finally looked up at her. "Although this is more a champagne and truffle moment, I'm guessing you've had enough to drink tonight."

Matt rubbed his forehead. "Coffee would be great. You need help?"

He set the cat on the sofa cushion next to him and rose to his feet before she could stop him. When she headed for the kitchen, he trailed after her. They were silent as she filled the coffeepot and flipped the switch.

"Well, then," she said and tried to fake a smile. She had a feeling she failed.

He pulled out a chair and sat at her round oak table. His hair was mussed, his eyes dark with shadows. As she studied him, she realized the shadows weren't about his lack of sleep but instead had everything to do with ghosts.

Fear tightened her chest. Fear about his past and what or *whom* he was running from.

"I, um . . ." Her voice trailed off. She leaned against the counter and tightened the belt on her robe. The hot liquid dripping into the coffeepot sounded loud in the lingering silence. "Are you sorry?" she blurted out, then hated herself for the question.

The darkness faded from his eyes as he smiled at her. "No," he said, quietly. "Are you?"

"Of course not." Her voice was high and bright, as if a change in tone could hide the lie. Sorry? She was confused and disconcerted. She wouldn't know if she was sorry for a couple of days.

The tile floor was cold on her bare feet. She glanced down at her toes. My Lord, they'd just had sex! How had it happened? Had she been so incredibly starved for a man's touch? She had a momentary flash of the passion that had filled her. Where had it come from? Had she done it with Matt because it had been a long time and she'd had physical needs? Or had it been more scary than that? That she responded because she might actually, sort of, kind of, maybe *like* the man?

"I need a third alternative," she muttered.

"What did you say?" he asked.

Ali waved away the question and turned to check on the coffee. While the steaming liquid filled the air with a welcoming scent, she pulled open the cupboard and collected two white mugs.

She turned to face him. "The thing is, Matt, I can't do this. I'd promised myself that I wasn't going to get involved with someone like you ever again."

He leaned forward and rested his arms on her table. She tried not to notice the expanse of bare chest and stomach, or the way she suddenly wanted to press herself against his warmth and be held.

"Define someone like me?" he asked.

She shrugged. "Men with pasts. Men on the run."

He grinned. "You make it a habit to get involved with men on the run?"

"You know what I mean. You have secrets."

"Everyone has secrets, Ali. Even you."

"Maybe, but you have more than most, and they drive you. I don't want to do that anymore. I want someone normal. You are many things, but you'll never be that."

The coffeepot grew silent. Ali turned toward it, then poured them each a mug of the steaming brew. Gathering her tattered bits of dignity and courage, she picked up the two mugs and carried them over to the table. She placed one in front of Matt and took the seat opposite him. As she sat, she was careful to make sure her robe stayed closed from collarbone to toes.

Matt took a sip of the coffee. "You say you want normal, but that would last about fifteen minutes. Then you'd be bored to death."

"Maybe, but it's my choice."

"It's the wrong choice. What you need is . . ." His voice trailed off.

She waited, suddenly daring to hope that someone, somewhere, was going to tell her what she needed. She'd been trying to figure it out for herself nearly all her adult life, and she'd never once come close to being successful. Maybe Matt had the answer.

The fact that they were talking about what she needed and not what they'd done didn't escape her. Obviously they were going to have to dance around other topics before they got to figuring out where they went now.

He smiled suddenly. "I can't tell you. You're going to have to figure it out for yourself."

She wasn't impressed. "You're being coy because you really don't know."

She had him there, Matt thought, but he wasn't about to admit the truth. Because what he wanted to tell her was what she needed was him. Which made no sense. Hadn't he already screwed up enough in his life? Hadn't he learned that he didn't have whatever it took to make a relationship work?

Ali leaned her elbows on the table and stared at him.

The overhead light reflected off her dark curls. Her hair was a mess, all loose and tumbling over her shoulders and down her back. The disarray suited her.

She was different from Leigh in so many ways. Her terry-cloth robe was functional rather than fashionable. Leigh would have preferred to catch pneumonia than be seen in one like that. Ali was mouthy and curvy, and she kissed like a dream.

She tossed her hair over her shoulder and drank her coffee. She had a way of holding her mug firmly with both hands, all the while sticking out her pinkies. It was a charming mannerism.

She made him hurt inside, mostly because being around her made it too easy to forget what he'd done.

"This is all your fault," he said wearily, finally feeling the effects of spending the previous night both awake and drunk.

She set down her mug and laced her fingers together. "The sex?"

Despite his conflicted feelings inside, he grinned. "I think we have equal responsibility in that."

"Then what?"

Her eyes were wide, her skin luminous. He stared at her lovely face, at the freckles visible now that her makeup had faded, at her swollen mouth. Her skin was red, probably from his scratchy beard. He rubbed his jaw and felt the stubble. "Sorry about the burn."

"No big deal. It'll be gone by morning."

He told himself it was time to make noises about leaving. She shifted in the chair, and her robe gaped open about two inches. He couldn't see any cleavage, but that didn't stop the heat and blood from rushing to his groin.

"Ali?"

He didn't sound like himself at all. He sounded animalistic, almost in pain. Questions filled her eyes, followed quickly by a woman's answers. He wanted her again. Before he could stop himself, he was on his feet, circling the table then bending low to kiss her.

"We can't," she protested, even as her lips moved against his, offering, healing. She opened for him, inviting him to taste her, to please her again.

"Do you want me to stop?" he asked, pulling back just enough to allow him to look into her wide eyes. Her irises dilated, and the corners of her mouth trembled.

Slowly she rose to her feet. For a split second he thought she was going to walk him to the door. Disappointment clattered to the bottom of his stomach, and his blood quickly cooled.

But instead of showing him out, she took his hand and led him through the living room and from there down a short hall into her bedroom. She touched the light switch on the wall, and three floor lamps sprang to life. He had a brief impression of male hell . . . light pinks and roses blended with cream. Dozens of lacy, fluffy pillows covered a queen-sized bed. Lingerie tangled and half-spilled out of an open drawer in a stenciled dresser. There were candles on most of the available surfaces and floral paintings on the fabric-covered wall. Everything about the place set his teeth on edge, yet it was so perfectly Ali.

She stopped in the center of the room and turned to face him. "This is crazy," she said. "We don't have anything even close to a relationship. I'm not sure why I'm doing this."

"Maybe because you want to," he offered.

She drew in a deep breath. "I guess that's as good a reason as any."

She went up on her tiptoes and pressed her mouth to his. The desire was as immediate as it was powerful. His blood heated back to boiling. His erection flexed painfully, and he knew if he didn't have her in the next several minutes, he would explode from the longing.

As his mouth pressed against hers and his tongue found new favorite places to taste and explore, he reached for the tie on her robe. The knot unfastened easily, and he pushed the heavy terry cloth to the floor.

She was naked instantly. Even though it was probably rude and insensitive, he couldn't help stepping back so he could look at her. She shivered slightly but didn't try to cover herself as he gave into his need to study the perfection before him.

The mass of dark curls covered her shoulders and teased her breasts. Dark pink nipples puckered under his scrutiny. He could see her collarbone and the faint shadow of ribs, but not the sharp outline visible with Leigh. Ali's waist tucked in neatly before flowing out to curvy hips. Her belly rounded delightfully, just enough to make him want to press a kiss to the pout of her belly button. Long legs curved gracefully down to slender ankles and feet.

He dropped to his knees and pressed his mouth to her stomach. She shivered when he dipped his tongue into her belly button and tickled her there. As his mouth moved lower and his hands cupped her hips, she clutched first at his shoulders, then buried her fingers in his hair.

"Matt," she breathed when he reached the soft, dark curls hiding her feminine secrets. "What are you doing?"

He chuckled. "What do you think?"

He parted the curls and dipped his tongue inside to taste her. The sweet saltiness was better than he'd imagined. He searched for then found the small point of her pleasure. Two flicks of his tongue had her trembling. He could actually see the muscles in her thighs quiver with each stroke.

"Get on the bed," he told her as he stood up and shrugged out of his shirt. As she did, he shoved down his jeans and moved to join her.

She'd shifted to the center of the mattress, leaving him enough room to settle next to her. But he wasn't interested in that. Instead he knelt between her legs, parted the protective curls, and continued what he'd begun.

Ali arched into the pillows at her back and told herself to keep breathing. The problem was all she wanted to do was focus on the feel of Matt touching her that way. She didn't care if air didn't fill her lungs. What was breath at a moment like this?

She tried to tell him how she felt . . . what she was feeling . . . but she couldn't speak. She could only part her legs more and pray that he never stopped.

His tongue was everywhere, circling her most sensitive spot, teasing where he'd entered her before. He licked over, then around. Fast, slow. He sucked, he nibbled, he retreated only to begin over again. When she arched her hips toward him in an involuntary thrust of passion, he chuckled low in his throat.

Passion overwhelmed her. Passion and need and so much confusion. What were they doing? Who was this man? The questions swirled through her brain right up until he slipped a finger inside her. Then she couldn't think at all, she could only feel the wonder. Her heels dug into the mattress and her head dropped back. Tension grew, spiraling higher and higher until control passed from her to him, and she lost herself in the vortex of her release.

She knew she cried out. She gasped, she called his name, she begged. He continued to touch her, and she continued her climax until her body had given up the last drop of completion. She was still trembling when he shifted forward and entered her.

Another climax ripped through her, catching her off guard. She hadn't expected that she could . . . not so soon. She opened her eyes and realized something was wrong. She couldn't see Matt clearly. It was only then that she figured out she was crying.

As he kissed away her tears, she wrapped her arms around him and drew him closer. He thrust in and out of her, taking them both to the edge of wonder and sending them soaring across to the other side.

chapter twelve

Ali whisked the hollandaise sauce in the small saucepan and listened for both the sound of the toaster and any noises from the bedroom. The shower had turned off about ten minutes before. It wasn't as if Matt had a bunch of fashion choices. He could put on what he'd been wearing the night before, or he could wear a towel.

She heard a faint creak from the floor and glanced over her shoulder. Matt, dressed in his jeans and shirt, walked into the kitchen and sniffed the air. "You're cooking," he said.

"Amazingly enough, I know how to make more than chocolate." She motioned to the table where they'd sat the previous evening. "Have a seat. Everything is nearly done."

As if proving her point, the toaster popped. Ali pulled the saucepan off the heat and kept stirring. With her free hand, she lined up ingredients, then pulled out two plates and set them on the counter. She put two English muffin halves on Matt's plate and one on hers. Warm ham slices went next, then a poached egg, all topped with the creamy, rich sauce. She scooped fresh strawberries onto each plate and garnished them with a sprig of mint from the plant that refused to die regardless of how little she watered it.

She carried the plates to the table and set them down. She'd already poured ice water and coffee. "That should do it," she said as she took the seat across from him and plastered a smile on her face. She had a serious case of "the morning after" complete with a knot in her stomach and a bad case of the shakes. She hadn't had tons of experience with situations like this, and she never knew what to say.

Matt stared at his plate. "Impressive."

She tried for a smile. "Yes, well, as I've mentioned before I had a couple of years at a Swiss finishing school. The cooking classes were my favorites. I can also fold a napkin into about any shape you would like. The trick is starch. Most people forget to starch their napkins, or they use too little. My teacher used to tell us that there was no such thing as too much starch in a napkin. I listened so I had the perkiest boats and flowers on the table."

She pressed her lips together. She was babbling. But the man made her nervous. After all, they'd crossed the line from friends and work associates to the more uncomfortable label of "lovers."

Ali tried not to flinch from the memory. They'd made love twice more, the last time just before dawn. Worse, she'd initiated that one, still half asleep, reaching for him. The fact that he'd been eager and willing didn't make her feel any less slutty. What had she been thinking?

She hadn't been thinking, she reminded herself. That was the problem.

Matt took a bite of the Eggs Benedict. He chewed slowly and swallowed. "Great," he said with a genuine smile. "Thanks for going to all this effort."

"No problem." She tried for a sophisticated, airy tone but doubted he was fooled.

The breakfast did look good, but her stomach wasn't ready for food. So she chased the strawberry halves around her plate and hoped he didn't notice. She was confused and contented and uneasy and worse, slightly aroused. Now that she knew how good it was between them, she wanted to keep doing it. To make the situation even more intolerable, she was only wearing her robe. Which meant her imagination could provide the picture of her tossing off the robe, shoving the food onto the floor, and draping herself across the table by way of invitation.

What would she do if he said no?

The horrifying question kept her in place and quiet until he'd finished eating. When he pushed his plate away and reached for his coffee, she looked up at him.

Their gazes locked. She noticed that some of his shadows didn't seem to be in residence. In fact, despite the fact that they hadn't gotten much sleep the previous night, he looked surprisingly rested.

"I know what you're thinking," he said as he set his coffee cup on the table.

She doubted that because she didn't know what she was thinking. But all she said was, "Oh?"

"You're wondering about last night."

Actually she'd been feeling confused and slightly stupid. But "wondering" was okay, too. "What about last night?"

He gave her a slow, masculine smile. It spoke of wanting and possession and great contentment. It forced her to swallow and ignited fire all through her body. Unfortunately the need wasn't all sexual. Some of it was emotional. She wanted to be held by Matt and talk to Matt, watch him laugh, share dreams.

Ali closed her eyes and suppressed a moan of dismay. This was when she really hated being a woman. Men could go do it with any willing female and walk away without a second thought. Some women had that ability as well, but most didn't and she fell into the latter category. There was something so incredibly biologically intimate about admitting a man into one's body. The act of opening up, of lying defenseless, of *trusting*, set a woman up to get stupid. And she'd fallen right into the trap.

"Last night you saved me," he said, then shrugged. "I know that sounds melodramatic, but it's true. The past year has been hellish."

"Why?"

"I had a life before I came here," he said.

"I sort of assumed that."

"What it was isn't important," he continued. "What *is* important is that a year ago my wife died."

Ali opened her mouth, then closed it. She hadn't been expecting that. His wife? He'd been married? Of course he'd been married. Men like him didn't stay single forever. Not that she knew what kind of man he was, but still. Married? And a widower?

"I'm sorry," she managed to mumble past suddenly numb lips.

"It was a year ago yesterday."

The words caught her unexpectedly, like being side-swiped in a car accident. She never saw it coming, so the impact hit her all the harder.

Ali gasped. "Last night was about her?"

"No," Matt said swiftly. "Never. I swear."

She wasn't convinced. "Is that why you left Chicago? Because she died?"

He nodded. "I felt so damn guilty. After the funeral I walked away from everything. I didn't know what else to do. I just got on a bus and when it stopped I got off. I've been making my way from one place to another, and somehow I ended up here."

She shifted in her seat, then tugged on the belt of her robe, making sure it was tight. Despite the thick fabric covering her body, she suddenly felt exposed and very foolish. Her stomach turned over, and she was grateful she hadn't eaten.

Matt stared into his coffee. "It was cancer. Melanoma. It worked fast. She was diagnosed in the summer and died last October."

He paused. Ali tried to speak, but couldn't. Her throat was tight and raw. Her face burned, but she didn't know if it was from embarrassment or from Matt's stubble.

"She was young and beautiful, and she had everything to live for," he said at last. His voice was low and harsh, still angry with fate. "It was my fault."

"It can't be. You didn't give her cancer."

"No, but because of me, she lost the will to live. I—" He turned away. "Our marriage was a business arrangement. We'd agreed to be sensible. Ours would be a relationship built on friendship and mutual respect. Then she went and changed the rules. She fell in love, but I couldn't love her back."

Ali was struggling to keep up. "That's sad but not a death sentence."

"She refused treatment," he said flatly. "After the first round of chemo, she gave up, came home, and died. If she'd had something to live for, she would have tried harder."

"You can't know that."

"Actually, I can."

Ali couldn't remember ever feeling this empty and confused. It was as if someone had stolen her very soul. Coolness seemed to seep into her bones. She couldn't take in all he was telling her.

"What was her name?" she asked, forcing the words between stiff lips.

"Leigh."

She swallowed. She had to ask, because she had to know. Even if it was bad . . . especially if it was bad. "Are you sure last night wasn't about connecting with her?"

He leaned across the table and took both her hands in his. "I know I'm a bastard, but even I wouldn't do that. Last night was about being alive and very specifically being with you. If I was a better man, I probably would have tried to think about her, but I didn't. I'll have to live with that as well."

She pulled her hands free, desperately wanting to believe him. But she wasn't sure she could.

"Matt, there's no reason to feel guilty. You drank too much on the first anniversary of Leigh's death. That means you cared about her."

"No, it doesn't," he said quietly. "I wish it did." He studied her. "Are you okay with all this?"

"I'm fine," she said, forcing a cheerful note into her

words. How could she have gone from silly and happy to shaken and horrible in such a short period of time?

He was looking at her expectantly, as if he wanted more. She took a sip of coffee. "Well, I guess that clears everything up. I, ah, suspect the best course of action is to keep this turn of events to ourselves. I mean between my employees, Sara, Kasey, the kids, and my mother, it could get really complicated."

"Is that what you want?"

"Oh, yeah. Absolutely." She glanced desperately around the kitchen. Her gaze settled on the clock above the stove. It was a little after seven. "And look at the time. You should probably get to work, and I have to shower and get ready to meet my mother. She and Miss Sylvie are usually here by eight. Besides, there's a table display downstairs that needs rearranging."

Had they really done it on a table? In her store? She bit back a moan.

Matt didn't move. "Are you sure you're okay?"

"Never better. After all that sex, I know my sinuses are clear." Did she sound as stupid as she felt? Could God be that cruel?

"You didn't eat."

She glanced at the congealing sauce and eggs on her plate. "I'm not much of a breakfast person."

His dark eyes brightened with momentary fire. "I'll remember that."

"You don't have to. I mean that was your point, right? This was about the anniversary of your wife's death." She couldn't bring herself to say the woman's name. "You've gotten through that, and there's no need to repeat the one-time event."

He stood up slowly. "It wasn't one time, Ali. And it wasn't insignificant."

"Great. For me, too." She rose to her feet. "I, ah, guess you know the way out."

She turned on her heel and hurried toward her bedroom. Once there she slammed the door, headed for the bathroom, and dropped to her knees in front of the toilet. Seconds later her stomach lurched, and she threw up the single cup of coffee she'd drunk that morning.

When the retching finally stopped, Ali shifted into a sitting position and leaned against the tub. She closed her eyes and wondered how she could have done it again. After all this time, after all the lectures to herself and the promises, she'd gone and fallen for yet another man who needed saving more than he needed her.

Matt wasn't out of work or a thief, but he was just as unapproachable. He was a man trying to escape from the guilt of his past. When the guilt was gone, he would be, too.

"I worry about Rick," Charlotte Elizabeth said as she set a cut-up scone on the floor next to Miss Sylvie's morning cup of coffee. "He's had several difficult relationships, and now he's talking about just getting used to being unhappy and alone."

Ali, still reeling from all that had occurred in the previous twelve hours, struggled to pay attention to her mother's chatter. "You know he goes through stages where he swears he'll end up living above somebody's garage, just him and some old dog, like in the pet-food commercials. That's so not him, Mother. Rick will find someone long before I do."

Her mother, resplendent as always in an emerald jogging suit that perfectly matched her eyes, sighed heavily. "Both my children are looking for Mr. Right. You don't know how many times I've prayed that you don't find him in the same man."

Despite the trauma in her life, Ali couldn't help smiling. "I'll second that. Mostly because in a competition like that I suspect Rick would win, and I doubt my fragile ego would survive the defeat."

Charlotte Elizabeth settled on one of the tall stools in the kitchen and sipped on her coffee. "I want to tell you you're wrong, but I'm not sure you are, darling. Please don't take that in a bad way."

"You mean there's a good way to take it?" Ali teased, with a lightness of spirit she didn't feel. Even as she spoke with her mother, part of her brain was still mulling over all that Matt had revealed that morning. Words and phrases flashed through her brain.

He'd been married and his wife had died. He felt guilty about not loving his wife when she'd loved him. He felt responsible for her death. Ali felt badly for Matt and all he'd been through, which was good, but she also felt badly for herself, which was immature and selfish.

"You're not listening, dear," Charlotte Elizabeth complained.

"Sorry," Ali said as she poured herself a cup of coffee and pulled out the stool next to her mother's. She settled on the seat and glanced around the kitchen. Even though her personal life was in the toilet, she still had her career. That was a small comfort.

"What are you thinking?" her mother asked. "Is it Matt?"

Ali didn't want to ask how she'd guessed. She considered blurting out the truth. But the momentary relief of getting it off her chest would not be worth the trauma of having her mother meddling in her personal life.

"Even I know that Matt would be a big mistake," she said, telling the complete truth. Unfortunately last night she hadn't thought about him being a mistake. She hadn't thought about anything but how he'd made her feel warm and safe and so very alive in his arms.

"I'm glad you see that." Her mother leaned toward her. "I want you to be happy."

Only Charlotte Elizabeth could ever look graceful on a stool, Ali thought. She probably just looked awkward. "I appreciate that. I want the same thing for you." She paused and decided that a version of the truth wouldn't be out of line to share. "I've been thinking about my longtime goal of dating someone normal. I've recently realized that, despite all the times I've said that's what I want, I've never once bothered dating a 'normal' guy."

Charlotte Elizabeth frowned. Delicate eyebrows drew together as her bee-stung mouth thinned slightly. "You're right. You haven't. Why is that?"

"Good question. The theory is that I haven't wanted to. I know there have been regular guys in my life from time to time. One or two must have found me reasonably attractive. Yet I never encouraged them. I've been wondering if my stated quest for normal has simply been a way of avoiding what I really want."

Her mother clasped her hands together. "How very clever of you, Ali. I think that's exactly right."

Ali figured this wasn't the time to share that the initial concept had originated with Matt. "Unfortunately I don't know what to do with the information now that I have it."

"It's obvious. You start going out with normal men and see if that's what you want. We can make a list of all the single men in Saint Maggie." Charlotte Elizabeth paused, then tucked a loose strand of dark hair behind her ear. "Well, perhaps not *all* the single men. We don't want old men like Harry on the list. Or those brothers who own the hardware store. But there have to be men your age whom you would like. And what about the Internet? Isn't everyone meeting their soul mate there? I've been hearing about that all over those television talk shows."

Ali felt as if she had to duck out of the way of a steamroller. "Thanks, but right now I just want to get used to the idea that I have some influence over who I date. I need to put off the actual dating for a while."

At least until she got over Matt.

"Whatever you think is best," her mother told her. "You know, I love you very much, and I will always be proud of you."

Ali swallowed, fighting sudden tears. What was it about sex that made her all weepy? "I feel the same way. I love you, too." She slipped off the stool. "I have to get the store ready to open," she said, thinking of the sale table, the contents of which were currently on the floor.

"Then Miss Sylvie and I will head home." Her mother stood, then moved close and hugged her. "I'll always be here for you, Ali. You know that, don't you?"

"Sure."

Ali hugged her back, then watched her mother call for her pig. They were an odd pair, she thought as she turned toward the main showroom. She came from a very interesting gene pool. Both her parents had been famous actors. Her biological father, an aging film star still dating starlets in their late teens, supplemented his residual payments by doing voice-overs for commercials shot and shown overseas. They'd met a few times over the years, but he'd never shown much interest in his only child, and Ali didn't know him enough to care if they had a relationship or not. Richard, Rick's father, had been all the father she'd needed.

She walked into her store and turned on the light. The point was she didn't come from ordinary people, which probably explained why—

She stumbled to a stop in the center of the room. Instead of finding boxes and baskets scattered across the ground, the sale table was exactly as she'd left it. Matt must have straightened things before leaving.

Matt. She crossed to the window and pulled the blind, then stared across the parking lot to the two businesses across the street. He was over there now, beginning his day. Was he thinking about her, about what they had done the previous night? Had he used her deliberately, or was she just handy?

The pain in her stomach hadn't gone away. She told herself it would be best for them both if they just forgot what had happened between them. And if they couldn't forget, then to pretend. The problem was she'd never been much good at pretending.

Matt took a lunch break that day. He didn't usually, but he had several things he wanted to get done. When he told Sara he would be back in an hour or so, she handed him a plate with several tiny sandwiches, a slice of quiche, and a piece of pink cake. He passed off the latter to Lucky the second he spotted the mangy dog in the parking lot. Together they crossed the street and headed for Ali's store.

Matt circled around back. He had no intention of speaking with her. At least not yet.

He left Lucky on the back steps and moved into the rear of the building. He walked through the storeroom and into the kitchen where a couple of college students worked. One was making candy, and the other was hand-printing mailing labels for the day's orders. They both looked up and smiled at Matt. He nodded and headed for the small office at the rear of the kitchen.

He told himself what he was doing wasn't wrong. Or if it was, it was for the right reason. Then he reminded himself that if Ali thought her books were private, she should at least put them in a drawer.

But as he entered the office, he saw the green ledgers were where he'd left them the last time he'd been by here. Sitting right on top of her desk. He grabbed them, along with a pad of paper and a pen. In his pocket was the list and chart he'd made the previous week while she'd been cooking. He figured he could get his proposal together in about an hour.

Fifteen minutes later he'd finished his lunch and had everything spread out on the desk in his small bedroom at the bed-and-breakfast. He had a momentary wish for his laptop, then reminded himself people had been doing this sort of thing longhand for centuries. He could tough it out for an hour.

He flipped open the first ledger and scanned her accounts receivable. But instead of seeing the numbers, he saw Ali lying naked, writhing as he touched her. He was hard in a second.

If someone had told him yesterday he would make love with another woman, he would have called that person a liar. If that same someone had said not only would he not feel especially guilty, but that he would spend the following morning humming like a fool, he would have figured insanity ran in the family. But that was exactly what had happened. He couldn't get Ali out of his mind, and he found he didn't really care. He wanted to think about her, about what they'd done together.

He wanted to do it again.

Ali turned the sign in the window so that it read "closed," then pulled down the shades covering the window. For a while she'd thought the day might never end. She was tired, not just because she hadn't gotten any sleep the night before, but because she felt as if she'd had a close encounter with an emotional flash flood. She felt battered, bruised, and completely flattened. All she wanted was to crawl into bed—alone—and sleep.

But the effort of locking up the rest of the building, not to mention climbing the stairs, seemed too much to contemplate, let alone do. She leaned her forehead against the wood-framed front door and sighed. She hadn't thought it would be like this, she admitted to herself, even as she wasn't sure what the "it" was. The sex? A potential relationship with Matt? The realization that once again she'd made a hideous mistake that was going to have huge ramifications in her life?

If only it could just be about what she'd claimed earlier—sinus-clearing sex. If only she could see last night as a coming together of two anonymous bodies who pleasured one another and then moved on. Maybe in her next life she could cultivate that ability, but currently she was stuck with a brain and heart that got all mushy as soon as she got naked with a guy.

She turned and headed for the rear of the store. Just to make her life even more interesting, she had the added bonus of being unsure of her feelings. She didn't think she loved him—*I mean come on! Love?* After a night of great sex? But if not love, then what? And why did she have a strong sense of needing to suddenly prove herself with him?

The feeling had started shortly after he'd told her about being married before. Ali felt as if she were in competition with a dead woman—in competition and losing badly. As she entered the kitchen, the back door banged shut, and she heard footsteps in the storeroom. Heavy footsteps. Masculine footsteps. Instantly her heart began to pick up the beat, and her thighs trembled. She knew who it was even before Matt walked into the kitchen.

She was happy to see him. Happy and giddy and suddenly weak with desire. *Jeez.* She had it worse than she'd thought.

He smiled at her. A real, great-to-see-you kind of smile. "Hey," he said, moving close and kissing her on the cheek. "Quit leaving the back door open. Anyone could walk in."

"So I noticed."

Her skin burned where he'd kissed her. She had a strong and painful desire to throw herself into his arms and hold him close until all her uncertainties faded. Which could take months. They would die like that, embracing, then in time, their bare bones would fall to the floor like so many pick-up sticks.

"Have a seat," he said, pulling up one of the kitchen stools. He grabbed a second one and settled himself on it. "I want to talk to you."

She plopped onto the seat. Talk? That sounded promising. She envisioned an emotional conversation about feelings and future plans. Maybe he was ready to tell her more about his mysterious past. Maybe he was ready to admit that she really mattered to him and that—

"It's about the business."

She blinked, then almost laughed. How typical. She was thinking hearts and flowers and he wanted to talk numbers.

It was only then that she noticed he was holding ledgers in his hands. She looked closer. *Her* ledgers. She took them from him. "What are you doing with these?"

"I borrowed them."

She flipped through the pages that listed everything from her cash receipts to her depreciation schedule. "This is private."

"Not when you leave it out on your desk for anyone to find." He took the books from her and set them on the counter. "That's not what I want to talk about." He leaned close and took her hands in his.

He felt warm and strong, she thought, momentarily distracted by his touch. She looked at him and realized that for the first time since she'd met him, the ghosts were gone from his dark eyes. He still wore worn jeans and a threadbare flannel workshirt, but he'd changed. Did he sit a little straighter? Was there more of an air of confidence about him?

"I didn't work this afternoon," he said. "At least not

at the tea shop. Sorry. I'll finish that up first thing. I got involved with your books instead."

"Why?"

"Ali, you're sitting on a gold mine. I still want to talk to you about getting a website, but that can wait. The first thing is your cooking schedule. You're wasting time and money doing things the way you do. If you scheduled cooking sessions—making certain candies on certain days—you could streamline your supply-ordering process and get a better handle on your inventory control."

He released her hands. After opening one of the ledgers, he pulled out a long sheet of paper. He'd taken several pages from a yellow tablet and taped them together. There were boxes and lines and arrows. She peered closer. The man had made a flowchart of her cooking schedule.

"You can't be serious," she told him.

"Of course I am. I went through your different supply invoices and called your suppliers. You're not taking advantage of bulk discounts. Worse, your suppliers are all online and give a second discount for using their automated system. If you cooked on a schedule, we could set up a database. It would link to your suppliers. When you used something, all you'd have to do is enter the amount. The computer would automatically order when supplies ran low. You would only have to get personally involved for seasonal items."

He looked as proud as the football captain after a championship season. Ali stared at him and wondered how the species had survived as long as it had. She had been hoping for romantic phrases and flowers, and he wanted to talk about inventory control. She worried that she might have connected with him in a way that was emotionally dangerous to her well-being, and he'd spent the afternoon designing a flowchart so she could have a cooking schedule. Men and women weren't from different planets—they were different life-forms. She was carbon-based, while he had a heart of silicon.

"I really don't want to talk about this," she told him honestly. "I'm tired and I don't want to cook on a *schedule*."

Matt brushed aside her comments with a flick of his hand. He turned over the paper. There was more writing on the opposite side. "You need to offer more prepacked candy. All the big candymakers do. Yes, there are individual choices in the store, but everywhere else customers buy prepacks. Currently customers can order anything they'd like, in any quantity. That's not cost efficient. Too much time is spent on the packing, plus it messes up your inventory. One big phone order can deplete any one item." He thrust the paper toward her. "You're actually making less money on some of your mail orders than on store sales."

Ali struggled with the tension growing inside of her. He was picking apart the one part of her life that worked. She felt the first sparks of annoyance. "Matt, I said I don't want to talk about this."

"Then don't talk. Just listen."

"No! I don't need you butting into my life like this. Having sex with me does not give you the right to take over. You don't own this company. These are my choices, not yours. I don't want to change how I do business."

He drew his eyebrows together. "I'm not saying I own the company. What I'm saying is that I know a hell of a lot more about business than you do. Chocolates, sports equipment, cars. Retail has a lot of similarities. There are a few basic principles that need to be followed, and you're not following them."

She couldn't believe it. "You're comparing my truffles to basketball or hockey equipment?"

He seemed to recognize the very deep, dark pit he'd wandered perilously close to. "I didn't mean that, exactly," he hedged. "Just that you could be a lot more successful if you'd listen."

"Great. I'm getting business advice from my handyman."

His gaze turned intense. "Ali, I know what I'm talking about!"

"How?"

Matt shifted on the stool, then stood. "I have an MBA from Harvard. Is that good enough for you? I may not know the specifics of a candy store, but that doesn't matter. Most business truths are universal. You're doing well for someone self-taught, but you could be doing better. Look."

He flipped open one of her ledgers, then turned pages until he found a loan repayment schedule. She was still reeling from his blithe statement that he had an MBA from Harvard. She had two night classes on small-business management from the local community college.

"You started with a dream and a loan," he said pointing to the top of the page. "You made regular payments and got your business going."

"Why is that so bad?" she asked defensively. "That's the main function of a loan. Borrowing money, then paying it back."

"Yes, but you paid it back too soon." He looked at her

as if she was cute but not very bright. "The interest is deductible. As soon as you had the cash, you paid off the whole thing."

"I don't like owing money."

"That's my point. You *want* to owe money. Your interest rate is reduced by the effect the interest deduction has on taxes. Which means your real rate of interest is substantially less. You'd be better off continuing to make the monthly payments and use the increase in cash flow to expand the business or make improvements. Now, to do that, you'll have to take out a second loan. Not that it will be a problem. You're not heavily leveraged. The bank will see you as a dream client, although the interest rate will probably be a little steep."

She slid to her feet and slammed the ledger shut. She didn't know which made her more furious—the fact that he was trying to run her business or that he knew what he was talking about.

All her life she'd fought against feeling inadequate. She could never measure up to being Charlotte Elizabeth's million-dollar baby. She hadn't had what most would consider a traditional education, given the napkin-folding lessons and the like. Nor had she had a clue as to what to do with her life. She'd made a small success of an equally small business, and Matt wanted to tell her she'd been doing it wrong.

"You will not destroy this," she told him angrily. "This is my business, and I'm running it my way."

She'd spent the previous night making love with the man standing in front of her, and she didn't know anything about him. Her eyes began to burn. She blinked back the tears, swearing to herself that she wouldn't lose it in front of him. To distract herself, she grabbed her ledgers and clutched them to her chest.

"I don't care about expanding," she said clearly and slowly. "I don't want to change how I do things. I like my business the way it is. As for paying back a loan too soon or getting another one, what your investigation failed to turn up is there is no bank loan, there never was."

Matt frowned. "I don't understand."

"That would be my point. What your MBA from Harvard failed to tell you is that I borrowed the money *from myself*. My mother was a very successful actress and my stepfather a multimillionaire. Between them I have a trust fund well into seven figures. I could open ten stores if I wanted. I could open a damn mall if I had the inclination. It was never about the money, it was always about making something from nothing. I wanted to prove that I could. I don't need to be a chain or on the Internet. This store is all I've ever wanted."

He didn't even blink. "But you could be so much more."

"I *am* more." She tossed the ledgers onto the floor, then pulled off her apron. "This conversation is over."

"No, it's not."

She ignored him and started walking toward the back door. "You have two choices. You can walk out of here now and keep your job, however meager that might be, or you can stay here and argue. In which case, I will fire you and then call the cops to come take you away for trespassing."

Matt's expression turned icy, but he didn't try convincing her again. He turned on his heel, walked past her and out the back door. It slammed shut and she was finally alone.

As victories went, this one was pretty pitiful.

chapter thirteen

Late the following Tuesday afternoon, Ali, Kasey, and Matt sat in the bed-and-breakfast office discussing the renovations. Actually, Kasey and Matt were talking while Ali sulked.

She'd tried to come up with a better term for her reluctance to participate in the conversation and her incredibly strong urge to puff out her lower lip. Unfortunately, "pouting" described it completely.

"You sure you want roses?" Matt was asking, passing Kasey a wallpaper sample. "I don't think the color matches the swatches you've already picked for the bedspread."

Ali glared at them both, but they didn't seem to notice. She really hated that. She focused her anger into a laser beam and tried to bore a hole through Matt's forehead. Unfortunately she didn't have any psychic power, so nothing happened.

Damn the man! It had been a week since they'd done *it.* She spent her days trying not to think about all that had happened, which was almost the same as *only* thinking about what had occurred. She hadn't been sleeping and when she did finally drift off, she had long, involved, very sexual dreams about being with him and touching him. She generally woke up in an uncomfortable state. Last night she'd made her usual spa run, which always cut into her sleep time. She was tired, cranky, and feeling particularly left out of the loop.

Matt, of course, looked perfect. Rested, alert, fit. As if all he'd been waiting for was a couple of rounds of the wild thing to heal him. He'd gained a few more pounds . . . all in the form of muscle. His already impressive body had filled out perfectly. He still had a high, tight rear that made her fingers itch every time she looked at it.

Since their *discussion* in her store last week, they'd barely spoken. He'd apologized the following morning, promising to stay out of her business. She'd accepted and waited for him to fall at her feet and beg for a second chance. He hadn't bothered. Damn the man. Nor had he swept her up in his arms, telling her that she was the most amazing thing to have happened to him. Instead he was polite and cordial, in a businesslike sort of way, with not a single flowchart in sight. It was as if she didn't exist for him anymore. What was she supposed to do about him? Not that he seemed interested in the fact that she felt she had to do something.

"What do you think, Ali?" Kasey asked, holding up two different wallpaper samples. "Matt says the floral print is better than the plain roses. I'm not sure."

Ali raised her eyebrows. "Wallpaper opinions from a man who can barely walk through the tea shop without shuddering. I'm impressed."

Kasey looked surprised at her catty tone. Matt didn't

seem to have noticed. Ali was instantly ashamed of herself. She was behaving like a thirteen-year-old. She knew better. Yes, making love with Matt had upset her in more ways than she'd realized, but that was no excuse to let her feelings spill over into the rest of her life. This was about business.

"Aren't you refinishing the sofas as well?" she asked. "Why don't we put the wallpaper samples next to the bedspread and sofa swatches? Then we can judge the overall look of the room."

"Good idea," Kasey said. She rose from behind her desk and reached for a thick folder tucked into the messy bookcase against the wall behind her. "I have it right here. We can—"

The door to her office opened abruptly. Willie stuck in his head. "Sorry to interrupt, but there was a call from the hospital. Harry's been hurt."

"From what we've been able to piece together," the doctor was saying, "Harry was fixing fences at one of the local wineries. He took a tumble down a steep incline. He has a few cuts and bruises and a broken leg. We've sutured the two deepest lacerations and given him a tetanus shot. The bone is set. As long as he rests for a couple of weeks, it should heal. Our concern at this point is the bump on his head. He lost consciousness for a while, but no one knows how long."

Matt stared at the doctor, a thirty-something blond guy in a white coat. "You're thinking he has a concussion?"

"We're not sure. He tested clear on any internal injuries, and his vitals are strong. We're doing a few more tests now. Even if they come back normal, we'd like to keep him overnight to observe him. After we release him, he's going to need looking after until he's up and around."

Ali folded her arms over her chest. "That's not a problem."

The doctor nodded. "Good. I'll speak with you this evening, if there's a change in his condition."

"Thank you, Doctor," Matt said. The two men shook hands.

Ali watched the doctor leave and sighed. "I know it's important he stay here, but I wish they weren't keeping him. He's going to hate spending the night here."

She was nervous and upset. Matt wanted to put his arm around her and pull her close, but nothing about her body language told him that would be welcome. She looked as prickly as a cactus. He hadn't realized her hazel eyes could turn so cold, but he would swear he felt ice forming at the back of his neck every time she looked at him.

"It won't be so bad," Matt told her. "I'm going to stay with Harry. I checked with a nurse while you were in talking with him. They let families use a cot in the room."

"But you're not family."

"She doesn't know that."

Ali stared at him. "You lied?"

"It was for a good cause."

She still wore her workclothes—today's outfit was a red corduroy jumper with a long-sleeved white turtleneck underneath. She'd caught her long curls with a ribbon at the nape of her neck. She looked beautiful, and more than a little lost. He wanted her. More than that, he wanted to be friends with her again. Something fundamental had changed between them, and he hated that.

Things had gone very wrong after they'd made love. He knew that, but didn't know what to do about it. Somehow he'd screwed up. He probably shouldn't have told her about Leigh. Or maybe he should have. . . . Hell, he didn't know.

If only they'd stayed in bed. He and Ali had been perfect there. He'd never experienced anything like it. But later, when he tried to help her. . . . He shook his head, still not sure what had happened. One minute he was the hero, the next she'd thrown him out on his ear.

To add insult to injury, she'd had the last word when she'd mentioned her trust fund. Although as soon as she'd told him about it, he'd realized he should have been able to figure it out all on his own. Ali didn't act like the daughter of a rich family, but Rick had been a walking, breathing clue. Not to mention Charlotte Elizabeth's jewelry choices.

"Ali?"

She shook her head. "I guess I'd better go. I have a few people to notify, arrangements to make for when he's released."

"Ali, don't." He put his hand on her shoulder. "Why aren't we talking?"

"We are. This is a conversation. I have to go."

She turned away and left. He watched her walk down the hallway, then disappear around a corner. He headed toward Harry's room. Halfway there he realized the smells of antiseptic, sickness, and the dinner that had been served a few hours before mingled into a remembered perfume.

Past and present blended, then bent, sending him tumbling back to a time when his life had revolved around the pain ripping through Leigh's slight body. Her only chemo treatment had left her gasping for life. She'd been so sick, a frail skeleton who had begged him to take her home. She'd wanted to die in their bed, away from the equipment and coldness of the hospital.

He remembered how he'd resisted taking her home because he hadn't wanted to have to stay with her, listening as her breaths became gasps and then stopped altogether. True, he hadn't loved her the way she'd loved him, but he'd never wished her ill. He hadn't wanted to watch her die. He'd been such a damn coward. As often as he could, he'd stolen away to the refuge that was his work. He'd allowed himself to become caught up in the company and in the end, she'd died alone.

What had those last hours been like? He would never know. They hadn't made peace, they hadn't talked. There had only been the phone call from the day nurse and incredible guilt.

Something soft brushed against his shoulder. Despite his intense guilt and sorrow, Matt felt a surge of relief that Ali had returned. He desperately needed her right now. But when he opened his eyes, he saw an unfamiliar nurse smiling at him.

"You're Matt, right?"

He nodded.

"Harry's back from his tests, and he's just fine. You don't have to worry. In fact you can go see him now if you'd like."

"Sure. Thanks."

Matt followed the nurse down the hallway. His body ached as if he'd taken the tumble instead of Harry. She paused in front of an open door, then waved him inside.

Matt pushed away all his unresolved feelings and stepped into the room.

Harry lay on a hospital bed. He had a bandage around his left hand and forearm, a swollen jaw, and a cast on his elevated left leg.

"You look like you were in a bar fight," Matt told him.

Harry grinned. "I feel like it, too." He pushed a button on the bed and raised the back so he was in a reclining position. "I just saw the doc. He says I'm the hard-headed type, which worked in my favor. They'll let me out in the morning." His smile faded. "But I'm going to have to rest for a while."

The older man paused. Matt moved closer and settled in the visitor's chair. "It won't be so bad to take a few days off."

"I guess." Harry picked at the light blanket covering him, then looked at Matt. "I was almost finished with the fence, too. I've already let go the extra help, figuring I'd rather take a couple extra days and keep the money. But I'd promised it would be done by the end of the week. I know you're involved with Ali's stuff. But do you think you could see yourself clear to finish the fence job for me? Ali'll understand."

"I'm sure she will." Matt leaned forward. "Just tell me where to go, Harry, and I'll take care of it. There's no problem."

"Great."

He gave Matt instructions on where the last of the fence lines were and what supplies to use. Matt noted everything on the small notebook he kept in his shirt pocket.

A nurse appeared and checked Harry's pulse, blood

pressure, and temperature. She looked into his eyes and asked him questions about double vision or a headache. Harry grumbled through the examination.

"Do you know what places like this charge?" he asked when the woman had left. "An aspirin is five or ten dollars."

Matt looked around at the plain room. Three beds took up most of the floor space, although only Harry's was being used at the moment. The television bolted high on the wall was ancient. The medical equipment looked old, if well maintained. This place was a far cry from the state-of-the-art facility Leigh had been in. Still, it wasn't cheap, and Matt would bet his company's fourth-quarter earnings that Harry didn't have medical insurance.

He told himself Harry's finances weren't his problem. He told himself not to get involved. He told himself that he had to do what was right for him, not anyone else. He knew he was whistling in the dark. He was going to do exactly what he shouldn't.

"I have to go get a few things," Matt said, rising to his feet. "I'll be back in about an hour."

Harry pretended to scowl. "I'm not some young pup who can't be left on his own. I don't need a damn nursemaid."

"I know, but I'm spending the night here anyway."

He made the decision impulsively and more for himself than Harry. He'd done everything wrong with Leigh. He wasn't going to make the same mistakes again. Not if he could help it.

Harry looked pleased, but instead of thanking Matt he only grumbled. "You probably snore. If you keep me awake, I'm gonna make them move you to another room."

Matt grinned. "Sure thing, Harry. See you later."

He waved, then left the room. On his way out, he circled around to the admissions department. The woman on duty looked up when he presented himself in front of her desk.

"Yes? How may I help you?"

Matt hesitated. He knew what he should do, what he was going to do, but still he questioned the wisdom of his actions. Once he did this, used a credit card and left an electronic trail, he would set in motion circumstances that he couldn't control. People from the company would be able to find him. Knowing them as he did, he knew they hadn't stopped looking.

"Sir?" the pretty brunette said. "Did you want something?"

"I'm here about a patient," he said. "I'm Matt Baker. I want to take care of the bill."

He gave the woman Harry's name and room number. She typed on her keyboard, then studied the computer screen. "There's no insurance listed. Are you going to give me that information?"

"No. I'm going to pay the bill."

She raised her eyebrows. "Sir, the bill could be several thousand dollars."

"I know." He reached into his back pocket and pulled out his wallet. He drew out one of his credit cards. American Express—platinum. It didn't have a limit.

She took it from him and studied the card. "Matthew Birmingham. I thought you said you were Matt Baker."

He held out his wallet so she could see his Illinois driver's license. She studied the license, the signature, and the picture, then she looked up at him and nodded. "Thank you, Mr. Birmingham. I'll run this through right now."

Matt appeared at her doorstep the next day, just as she was opening the door. Ali glared at him through the glass door and thought about not letting him inside. However, the gesture seemed childish and counterproductive. He'd spent the night at the hospital, and she wanted to know how Harry was this morning.

She unfastened the lock and turned the sign. Then she forced herself to open the door and smile pleasantly.

"Have you just come from the hospital?" she asked, turning to go back into the store.

"Yeah. I saw the doctor this morning. Harry seems fine. They're going to be releasing him in a couple of hours."

"That's good," Ali said, being careful not to look at Matt. She busied herself with tidying a display that was already pretty perfect, then froze when she realized it was the sale table—the place where they'd lost control and first made love. Heat flared on her face. She moved over to the shelves on the wall and rearranged several jars of chocolate-fudge sauce, careful to keep her back to him.

"I've made arrangements to pick him up," Matt was saying. "He's going to need someone to check on him for the next couple of weeks. I thought it would be easier if I moved back into his place. There's also the fence job he was doing at one of the local wineries. Harry asked if I would finish that for him. He'd promised the guy to have it done this week. That means I won't be able to work at the bed-and-breakfast for a few days, but I didn't think that would be a problem."

Ali drew in a deep breath. She was angry and confused and didn't know what to say to Matt. The events of the previous week stood between them like a partially open box that neither of them was going to talk about.

"It's already being handled," she said at last. "I was on the phone last night with my mother and a few others."

"I don't understand."

She put down the jar of fudge sauce she'd been moving around like a chess piece and turned to face Matt. He stood in the center of the room, his hands shoved into his back pockets. He'd showered and shaved recently. His jaw was smooth and his hair still damp.

"Harry isn't going home. He's going to my mother's. She's volunteered her guestroom for him. It's big and, even more important, it's downstairs. Lucky is already there."

Matt shook his head. "I forgot all about that damn dog."

"For what it's worth, I did, too. Charlotte Elizabeth is the one who remembered. She drove over and picked him up. He gets along fine with Miss Sylvie, so there's no problem there. You're welcome to go finish the winery fences, but the rest of it is taken care of."

His dark gaze met hers. "I'm impressed."

"Don't be. I might not have an MBA from an Ivy League school, but I'm at least mildly intelligent and can organize a thing or two."

"I've always thought you were very intelligent."

She felt the tension returning to her body. "You don't always act like it. You act like you're the king of the universe, or at the very least, used to being in charge."

"Ali, I—"

"Speaking of charging," she said, cutting him off, "I

called the hospital this morning to ask about Harry's bill. He doesn't have insurance, and I thought I would take care of it for him. However a very pleasant young woman informed me someone had already done that. Amazingly enough this mystery person had put Harry's bill on a credit card. You wouldn't happen to know anything about that, would you?"

Matt shifted awkwardly from foot to foot. "Ali, it's not what you think."

"Then what is it? You've been living in Harry's spare room like you're practically homeless, and you have credit cards with limits high enough to pay entire hospital bills? Where are you going to get the money to pay the bill? What are you doing here? Who are you?"

The last question was the most important, she realized. But she already knew he wasn't going to answer her. And being lovers for a single night didn't give her the right to pry.

"Ali, I can't."

"I know," she told him, even though she didn't. He couldn't what? Tell her the truth? Say that it mattered? Believe that he cared?

She felt achy and tired, and it was barely ten in the morning. "I'll make you a deal," she said turning away so he wouldn't see the tears filling her eyes. Why was she crying? She never cried. "You take care of the winery, and I'll deal with Harry. Maybe if we don't see each other for a while we'll stop fighting so much."

"Are we fighting?" He sounded genuinely surprised. "I knew you were mad at me about something, but I didn't think that was the same as fighting."

She didn't know if she should laugh or scream. Instead

she drew in a deep breath and blinked back the tears. Then she forced herself to smile at him. "We're fighting, Matt. I'm angry and hurt and confused. You're not dealing with any of that. Avoiding me isn't going to make it go away."

He stared at her as if she'd suddenly started speaking Russian. "Ali, I don't understand."

"I know. Just leave."

"But you said that wouldn't fix anything."

"You have to pick up Harry."

"Not for a couple of hours."

"I have to work in the store."

He looked around. "You don't have any customers."

He was being logical. She hated that in a man. "Matt, I can't do this now."

He frowned. "But you're still mad?"

"Yes."

"And you're going to stay mad for a while?"

"Probably."

Confusion settled on his face. "Is this a female thing?"

"I guess it is."

He sighed. "Are we going to talk about it later?"

"Yes."

"Will it make sense then?"

She couldn't help smiling. "Probably not."

"I didn't think so." He opened the door, then glanced at her over his shoulder. "Would it help if I said I'm sorry?"

"Do you know what you're sorry for?"

He hesitated. "Maybe."

Despite the ache in her heart and the weariness settling over her, she couldn't resist smiling. "Yes, Matt, it helps."

chapter fourteen

Matt left the store, paused on the top step, and nearly turned back. He had no idea why Ali was upset with him. It had something to do with the fact that they'd been lovers. That part was incredibly clear, but after that, he was lost. He recalled having this same "what the hell did I do wrong" sensation with Leigh on multiple occasions, and he'd never been able to figure it out.

Was it him? Was it women in general or only the ones he knew? Was this a male/female thing inherent in relationships that caused men to—

He headed for the bed-and-breakfast, then stumbled to a stop. Relationships? Had he thought that? Did he and Ali have a relationship? They'd made love—that counted for something. In fact thinking about them making love made him want to be with her again. Which distracted him from everything he had to do.

A relationship? He couldn't. Because, dammit, he was clueless about how to get it right. God knows he'd had one misstep after the other with Leigh.

Forget it, he told himself. Focus on what's important.

He shook off all extraneous thoughts and walked into the bed-and-breakfast. Willie sat behind the counter.

"Why aren't you in class?" Matt asked.

"I don't have class this morning. Kasey asked me to fill in for a couple of hours." Willie grinned and held up a thick, dark blue management text. "I don't mind. I need the study time."

"I need to use the phone," Matt said, pointing to the phone by the sofa in the reception area.

"No problem," the young man told him.

Willie turned his attention back to his book while Matt pulled out his wallet and removed the Hertz corporate card from its slot. He dialed the 800 number and made arrangements for a four-wheel drive SUV to be delivered to the bed-and-breakfast.

When he hung up the receiver, Willie looked at him. "Mom said that Harry's doing better."

"He is. They're releasing him this morning." Matt thought about his conversation with Ali. "I guess Charlotte Elizabeth is going to keep him at her place for a few days."

Willie grinned. "She's kinda cool, for an old lady, I mean."

Matt assumed they were talking about Charlotte Elizabeth, and he supposed that a gracefully aging sixty-something former actress would still be considered "an old lady" by a kid barely twenty-one.

"I've seen some of her movies," Willie went on. His dark eyes brightened with appreciation. "She was really something. Amazing face and a body." He held his cupped hands out about eight inches from his chest. "I guess she never did a nude scene, which is too bad."

"Have you told her about your disappointment?"

Willie laughed. "No way. She'd slap me. But she was a serious babe back then."

"I haven't caught one of her movies, but I'll have to do it soon," he said. Maybe he would see a bit of Ali in the much-younger Charlotte Elizabeth.

A large truck rumbled into the bed-and-breakfast parking lot. A man in white coveralls climbed down and waved. "Where do you want it? In back?"

Willie nodded and pointed to the rear of the building. He stood up and looked at Matt. "It's the guy with the linen delivery. They've been messing up pretty bad, so I'm going to have to go over this carefully. Would you mind staying here until I get back? Just in case the phone rings."

Matt was already moving behind the desk. "No problem. I've got to wait for my rental car anyway."

"Cool. See you in a couple of minutes."

The lanky college student sauntered down the hall toward the back. Matt took his place at the desk. He glanced at Willie's college text and the page of notes. Then he noticed that the computer was on and logged on to the Internet. Before he knew what he was doing, he'd typed in a few keys and the screen shifted. Seconds later he found himself staring at the Birmingham International website.

His throat tightened as he stared at the familiar logo. He couldn't remember the last time he'd seen it. More than a year—sometime before he'd walked out of his life.

He glanced around guiltily, as if he was doing something he shouldn't do, then he reminded himself he was stuck until the rental car arrived. He navigated through the various pages, then checked his e-mail. The box was empty. No doubt one of the vice presidents took care of that now that he was gone.

He typed more keys and entered a private site that specialized in periodical and newspaper articles. He searched under his company, going back a year. He ignored everything about his disappearance and concentrated on pieces about the fiscal health of the firm. Several caught his eye. Without thinking, he tapped the print key to get hard copies to read later.

Jeff would be doing his best, Matt thought as he studied a press release. Jeff had more brains than any three CEOs Matt knew. But he would be hampered by policy and Matt's absence. Matt tapped on the edge of the keyboard. The company he'd once loved to the exclusion of all else was in trouble. And it was all his fault.

Guilt rippled through him. He shouldn't have left the way he had. He should have made better arrangements for his staff. Except he'd had to leave because the guilt was killing him.

While the printer was still humming and spitting out paper, he typed in two more words for a search. "Allison Thomas."

The screen instantly filled with dozens of articles about Charlotte Elizabeth's Million-Dollar Baby. Matt clicked on one at random and found himself staring at a picture of a very young Ali sitting on top of a fat pony. She couldn't have been more than five or six in the photo. Her dark curls spilled down the back of her pint-sized cowgirl outfit, and her smile was infectious. A much younger Charlotte Elizabeth stood behind her, beaming with maternal approval.

There were more articles, but the number decreased

as she got older. He found a picture of her at her high school graduation. She looked young, but sweet and beautiful. Not to mention innocent. Charlotte Elizabeth was standing next to her with Rick and an older man he thought to be Rick's father. They were the perfect family.

But they hadn't been perfect. Somewhere along the way Ali had decided she had to prove to herself and the world that she was worth the price of her birth. She was still proving herself. He thought about her trust fund, how she'd loaned herself the money to start her business, then had paid back every penny . . . with interest. How many people would have done that?

She could have spent her life in useless leisure. If she'd wanted to dabble in business, she could have hired someone to run the company for her. Instead she showed up for work everyday. She'd found where she wanted to live, and she'd made a place for herself. She rescued those in need and made friends with everyone from an old coot of a handyman to the residents at the local women's shelter.

A black Ford Explorer pulled up in front of the reception area, and a man in a Hertz shirt stepped out. A small car with a Hertz sign on the door pulled up behind him. Matt logged off the computer and went outside.

They finished the paperwork in a matter of minutes, and Matt signed the credit card receipt. He'd rented the SUV for three weeks with the understanding he might want to keep it longer. Then he took the keys. When Willie returned, Matt collected his articles from the printer and slid behind the wheel of the vehicle.

Even though his driver's license was still valid, Matt couldn't remember the last time he'd driven. In Chicago he and Leigh had always used cabs or a limo. He took a couple of seconds to find all the controls. As he started the engine, he pulled the directions to the winery out of his shirt pocket, then headed out onto the main road.

The late morning was bright and cool. He planned to speak with the people at the winery to let them know he would be completing the fences by the end of the week, then drive over to the hospital in time to pick up Harry.

He turned left at the main intersection in town and drove north and east. There was a shopping center, complete with a grocery store and a Blockbuster, then a subdivision. After that, civilization seemed to fade away, leaving behind open acres neatly cultivated with rows of grapevines.

Matt opened the sunroof, then rolled down the windows. The cool air washed over him. He had places to go and people to see. How long had it been since he could say that?

He shifted in his seat, then spotted a flashing red light in his rearview mirror. A patrol car paced him. Matt checked his speedometer, but he wasn't going fast. Was there something wrong with the car?

He pulled over. As he watched in the side mirror, he saw a tall, blonde woman step out of her sedan and start toward him. She wore the tailored uniform of the local sheriff's office.

When she reached the window, she tilted back her hat and smiled at him. She was a California blonde, complete with freckles, blue eyes, and a full mouth. Centerfold pretty, even in her unflattering uniform.

He remembered her from the previous week, when he'd been drunk and in too much pain to pay attention to where he was or what he was doing.

"You're the officer who took me to Ali's."

"Right." She leaned one hand on the open window and shrugged. "You weren't breaking the law. I thought I recognized you and pulled you over to get an update. How are you feeling?"

"I'm not drunk," he told her. "Do you want me to walk a line or anything?"

She chuckled. "Actually, I believe you."

"Good."

Her humor faded. "Is whatever was bothering you fixed now?"

"No, but I'm handling it better."

"Some days that's all we can ask for." She slapped her open hand against the roof of his SUV and motioned to the road. "That's all I wanted to know. Have a good day."

"You, too, Officer."

He shifted into gear and continued toward the winery. He wondered if the deputy had really stopped him to find out if he was all right, or if she'd been concerned he was drunk. Not that it mattered which. But he knew that if they ran into each other again, at the grocery store or somewhere else in town, they would stop and talk. If she was with her husband or kids, introductions would be made. It was the same with Willie or Kasey or Sara or Charlotte Elizabeth. Somehow, without him realizing it was happening, he'd started to make friends in Saint Maggie. He had a life here. This time when he left, there would be people to remember him. Matt couldn't figure out if that was good or bad.

Ali leaned against the wall by the door in Charlotte Elizabeth's guest room and murmured softly, "What's wrong with this picture?"

The "wrong" was the juxtaposition of a gruff, battered Harry settled comfortably in her mother's frilly guest room, his broken leg propped up on fluffy pillows. From the white four-poster bed to the lace curtains, soft peach lacy sheet, and silk and lace bedspread, the room was a woman's paradise. Yet Harry seemed to be, if one could excuse the pun, in hog heaven, what with his beloved Lucky curled up at the foot of the bed and Miss Sylvie sprawled across a thick rug by the small fireplace.

Charlotte Elizabeth bustled into the room, a wooden tray in her hands. "Here's lunch. I hope you like it." She settled the tray over Harry's lap, then carefully fluffed the pillows behind his back.

"Not that it's any skin off my nose if you don't," Ali's mother said cheerfully. "I didn't make any of it. But then I didn't have to. Simply everyone has brought by all kinds of casseroles and platters." She beamed at Harry. "I do so like a man who makes himself a vital part of the community."

Harry looked at the screen idol of his youth and blushed furiously. "Thank you, Charlotte Elizabeth."

The worship in his voice made her preen. Harry had spent the last two nights as Charlotte Elizabeth's guest. She enjoyed playing the role of Florence Nightingale. Today she'd returned to the time of her youth, dressing in a full-skirted shirtwaist dress in a deep emerald green. Pearls encircled her throat and wrist, while pearl studs competed with the luminescence of her earlobes. She was a radiant and still-sexy, upscale version of June Cleaver.

Charlotte Elizabeth pulled up a chair and sat close

to Harry. She took one of his hands between hers and sighed. "How are you feeling, dear man? Any better?"

Even from her place by the door Ali could smell her mother's sensual perfume. Poor Harry must feel like he'd been caught up in a cloud of jasmine and musk.

"I'm feeling a little more like myself," Harry said cautiously. "But still a bit peaked. I'm not sure I'm going to have the strength to get up this afternoon."

"And why should you?" Ali's mother said briskly, patting his hand before releasing it. "You had a terrible accident. You need to recover."

Ali rolled her eyes. She was torn between exposing Harry for the fraud he was and wondering at Charlotte Elizabeth's need to nurture. *It must be a pre-grandmother thing,* Ali thought. Her mother had been loving and supportive, but she hadn't been one for hands-on involvement when Ali and Rick had been growing up. First a pig and now Harry. Who or what would Charlotte Elizabeth take on next? If Ali didn't know better, she would say her own need to rescue was catching—or genetic.

The doorbell rang. Her mother excused herself to see who was there.

Ali pushed off the wall and took a step toward the foot of the bed. "Gee, Harry, if you're still feeling so weak, maybe we should talk to the doctor about readmitting you to the hospital."

Her suggestion earned her a glare complete with drawn-together bushy eyebrows and a firm-set mouth. "You hush up. When do you think someone like me is going to get a woman like Charlotte Elizabeth to fuss over him? So what if I want it to last a little longer. She don't mind."

"I know. I'm teasing." She glanced over her shoulder to make sure they were still alone. "Seriously, are you doing better?"

He fed a piece of meat to an always hungry Lucky. "Sure. I'm sore and stiff, but I've been through a whole lot worse. I remember—"

But his memory was cut off by the sound of voices in the hall. Her mother's sultry tone wasn't a problem, but Ali stiffened when she heard the visitor speak. Matt had arrived to check on his employer. Ali looked around the room, wishing there was a back way out. Unfortunately, she was trapped.

Matt and her mother entered the room. Matt gave her a quick nod, then greeted Harry. Ali tried not to feel slighted. After all, she and Matt didn't have that much contact these days. He was busy working at the winery, and she had her store. She'd been careful to visit Harry when she knew Matt would be busy. Until now she'd been successful.

It had been eleven days, she thought, wishing she weren't still counting it in days. At least she'd moved on from hours. Eleven days since they'd made love, and she'd worried about getting involved with a man who had too many secrets and, despite what he claimed to the contrary, was probably still in love with his late wife. Eleven days of feeling confused and angry and rejected and mostly stupid.

"The fences are finished," Matt was saying. "They signed off on the job this morning. I figured I would get back to work at the bed-and-breakfast."

"That sounds like a plan," Harry said.

Charlotte Elizabeth moved to the older man's side. "Matt, you're going to have to take care of things at Harry's business. He's not going to be able to leave for at least two more weeks."

Ali raised her eyebrows at the news. So Harry was as sick as all that? She noticed that Matt looked equally skeptical.

"Whatever," he said. "I'll run by and check for messages every day or so. You don't have anything else lined up for work, do you?"

"Nah. I thought I'd take a few days off after the fences were done."

Charlotte Elizabeth clapped her well-manicured hands together. "Now you can do that right here in my guest room. Won't that be wonderful?"

Harry's expression said that it was. Ali resisted the urge to gag. She excused herself, saying that she had to get back to the store. It was Saturday, after all, and she had customers to attend to.

She'd hoped to make a quick escape, but Matt was right on her heels as she left. He was quiet all the way out of the house. But as they started down the front walk, he touched her arm to stop her.

The feel of his fingers on her—even through the sleeve of her blouse—was enough to send her heart rate soaring. Her chest tightened, and her legs felt as if she'd just completed an advanced step-aerobics class.

"We have to talk," he said, his voice low.

She closed her eyes briefly as a knot formed in her stomach. "I don't think so. You'll probably expect me to be reasonable, and that's really not my preference."

He circled around her until he was standing in front of her. He released her arm, but then touched his fingers to her chin, forcing her to look at him.

"Let me recap," he said. "Last week you and I spent a wonderful night together making love. When we parted in the morning, to the best of my knowledge, everything was fine between us. I returned later that evening to see you, and somehow the conversation deteriorated to you threatening to fire me."

He paused as if to make sure he had the sequence of events correct. Ali wanted to look away, but the light pressure of his fingers on her chin wasn't something she could ignore. She hated the heat that flared on her face. She was blushing, damn him.

"Since then you've been angry at me, and we haven't been speaking," he continued. "Do I have it about right?"

She sniffed. "I guess."

He lowered his arm to his side. "I understand that you're also annoyed because I paid for Harry's hospital bill."

"I'm not annoyed," she said, cutting him off. "I didn't have any burning desire to pay it. What annoys me, to use your term, is that you *can* pay Harry's hospital bill. It's one thing to have a secret past. It's quite another to flaunt it. Especially when I know you're not going to give me any answers."

His dark eyes gazed at her steadily. "Agreed. I'll accept my responsibility for that, but what about before? After we made love. What happened then?"

You tried to fix me when you should have been telling me how much you adored me, she thought sadly.

"I'm not in the mood to tell you," she said. "At the risk of being a typical female and incredibly immature, if you can't figure it out, then there's no point in having this conversation."

He made a sound of pure frustration low in his throat. He glared at her. "That's not an acceptable response."

"Acceptable to whom? Are you now the conversation police? Do I have to submit my responses ahead of time and get them approved?"

He took a half step closer, trying to loom over her, no doubt. But she'd been loomed over by the best, and there was no way he was going to make her back down. She slapped her hands onto her hips and glared at him.

"If you don't tell me, I can't fix it," he said slowly, as if speaking to a half-wit.

"Did it ever occur to you that fixing was the problem?" she asked, just as slowly.

"What are you talking about? The problem is you're angry. Am I making a mistake in assuming that you want that changed? Are you much more comfortable with me being the bad guy? Does that make everything tidy and safe for you?"

"Maybe," she admitted, even though she didn't want to. Then she sighed. "Go away, Matt. I don't want to do this now."

"I'm not going anywhere until we get this straightened out." He stopped looming and tucked a loose curl behind her ear. "I really want to know."

She didn't know what to say. The truth was always a possibility, but it made her seem so . . . stupid. "I just . . ." Her voice trailed off.

"Yes? You just what?"

She stared at the center of his chest. "You talked about my business," she mumbled, then raised her gaze to his.

Matt stared at her blankly. "What do you mean? You're

mad because I had some ideas about making you more successful?"

"Yes. I didn't want you interfering, but that's not what upset me." She sighed. "You talked about business, Matt. After all we'd done. I didn't want a presentation to the stockholders. I wanted something more . . . personal."

She found herself staring at the center of his chest again. She hated this, and him. Because he'd entered her life and made her forget her promise about not getting involved with inappropriate men. Matt might not be exactly like the other guys in her life, but that didn't mean he was a smart choice. He was going to be moving on, probably without looking back, and she would be left behind. Alone and missing him.

"What exactly did you want?" he asked.

She glared at him. "Look, if I have to tell you step-by-step what to do then just forget it."

"But if you don't tell me, how will I ever learn?"

"You're not supposed to learn, you're supposed to *know*."

He threw up his hands. "Dammit, Ali, that's ridiculous! If you want something from me and I'm not doing it, you have a responsibility to tell me. If I blow you off, then you have every right to get mad at me. But don't you dare get pissed off because I can't read your mind."

"I wanted you to be romantic," she said through clenched teeth. "Okay? I wanted you to hold me and tell me that it had been fantastic and that I was more than a convenient body. That you couldn't wait to make love with me again. That you wanted to start a cult for the specific purpose of worshipping me. Is that specific enough for your pea-size brain?"

He looked as if she'd slapped him. His entire body

stiffened, then relaxed. He moved close. "You're right," he said softly. "I'm sorry. I should have said something personal and romantic. It *was* great. You were great. And a cult is really a good idea." He grinned. "Want to talk about initiation rights?"

That sounded like a fine idea to her. Except . . .

She held out her hand. "Stop right there. While I appreciate the apology, just saying the words doesn't instantly make it better."

He exhaled loudly. "Why not?"

"Because I've been hurt. It's going to take some time to recover."

His hands clenched in frustration. "This is so like a woman."

"Oh, great. The typical male response when you don't instantly get your way on something. I'm sorry my recovery timetable is inconvenient. How like a woman, right? Here's news. I *am* a woman. So why are you announcing the fact? It's not interesting. Next time try saying how like a cat or how like a gecko."

Matt stared at her. His expression told her that he thought she'd just lost her mind. "A gecko?"

"They're lizards."

"I know what a gecko is." A smile tugged at the corner of his mouth. "I've never thought of you as a gecko. They don't have hair like yours."

Now it was her turn to smile. "I don't think they have hair at all."

He moved close and pulled her into his arms. "Okay, I'll accept my responsibility in what went wrong and the fact that you have to forgive me and recover on your own timetable. How's that?"

"How incredibly gracious of you." Her voice came out a little softer than she'd planned.

Matt groaned. "I don't remember any woman being as difficult as you."

"It's part of my charm."

"You *are* charming."

Then he lowered his head and kissed her.

They were still standing in front of her mother's house, in plain sight of anyone inside, looking out, or of any interested passersby. Ali didn't care. Matt felt strong and warm as he held her. She liked the way their embrace was familiar. His mouth was firm and gentle as it brushed against hers. She found herself surging against him, urging him to deepen the kiss.

His tongue swept against her lower lip. She opened instantly for him, welcoming, savoring the taste of him. He brushed against her. Heat spilled through her, moving down to her breasts, then lower still to that place of welcoming. Her thighs tingled, her knees shook slightly.

The sound of a car going by forced her to pull back. "This isn't a great idea," she said. "I really do have to get back to the store soon, and we're fairly public here."

She wanted to say more. She wanted to ask him if he'd been thinking of her as much as she'd been thinking of him. She wanted to know how much she meant to him and have him say that he couldn't imagine being with anyone but her. However, her anger was gone and with it, her ability to say exactly what she was thinking.

He stroked her cheek. "I'm sorry I talked about business," he said. "What we did that night mattered."

He took her hand and pulled her to the porch step, then settled on the brick and patted the space next to him. "The thing is I find business a whole lot easier to deal with than personal stuff."

"So that's why you went weird on me after we, ah . . ." She paused as she sat on the step. "You know."

He smiled. "Yes. I guess it's how I grew up."

"There's a statement begging for an explanation."

She thought he would clam up on her . . . *again*. Instead, he stared into the distance, but she had the feeling he was really seeing into the past.

"My family owns a business," he said. "They have for several generations. It's passed down, father to son."

"What if there aren't any sons?"

He glanced at her. "So far that hasn't been a problem." He returned his attention to the horizon. "I grew up knowing that I was going to take over the company, which was good. I enjoy business. I like getting lost in my work. The thing is there's an expectation of success."

She studied his strong profile. "Isn't that pretty common?"

"Sure, but in my family the expectation is that each generation will do substantially better than the one before. I am, in essence, in competition with every generation that came before."

"How strange. So you have to best your father?"

"Yeah." He shrugged. "It can create tension."

"Did you do better than him?"

He nodded. "My father is a difficult man. He could never figure out what he wanted from me. When I failed, he ridiculed me. When I succeeded, he ignored me. I hated him and as I grew up I was determined to grind him into the dust."

"That's a strong reaction."

He glanced at her. "He killed my mother. Not with a

gun or a knife, but with neglect. She was a sad woman who adored her husband, but he couldn't be bothered. I remember her walking through the house like a ghost. Today she would have been diagnosed with clinical depression, but back then her doctor gave her pills and told her to rest. One day she died."

Ali gasped and touched his arm. "Oh, Matt," she breathed. "I'm so sorry."

"I appreciate the sympathy, but it was a long time ago."

She knew that but doubted the pain ever went completely away. Nothing she'd ever imagined for Matt had come close to the truth.

"My father was in Martinique with his latest mistress when my mother died," he continued. "I never forgave him for that. I celebrated my thirtieth birthday by throwing him out of his own company."

"It beats quality time with a reporter," she said, then slid closer to him and put her arm around him. "I wish I knew what to say."

"You don't have to say anything."

"Your dad's in Italy now, right?"

"Yes. We don't speak."

She gave him a slight smile. "So you're a former tycoon with a grudge against your father. At the risk of being self-centered, it's nice to know that other families are dysfunctional, too."

"We certainly qualify."

She didn't know what else to say. Her heart ached for him and her head reeled with all the new information.

"I appreciate you sharing this with me," she said. "Is there anything I can do to help?"

He looked at her. His expression was more rueful than

sad. "No. It's all old news. I told you because I want you to understand that I didn't mean to hurt you the other day. I wasn't trying to be insensitive when I discussed business after we'd made love. I thought I could help. Once I got into the business mode, it was tough to stop. Like father like son." He leaned forward and rested his elbows on his thighs. "I'm supposed to be pretty smart, but I guess I haven't learned a thing."

"I understand," she said, lightly touching his shoulder. "And I appreciate the information. I might have overreacted to the situation."

"Might have?"

She smiled. "Okay, I did overreact."

He tilted his head toward her and raised his eyebrows. "So it's really all *your* fault."

She pushed his arm. "Stop it."

There was so much more she wanted to know. Things that needed to be said. What was the name of the company? How successful had he been? What was his other life like? Although she was reasonably confident it was nothing like her world here in Saint Maggie.

He glanced at his watch. "I've got to get to work, and I know you do, too. Want to get together tomorrow? It's Sunday. You don't work."

She swallowed her regret. "I can't. I'm going to L.A. It's a friend's birthday. All women, or I'd ask you to go along. I won't be back until sometime Monday."

He kissed her lightly. "Next time, then."

She nodded and rose to her feet. Their conversation felt unfinished to her. She wanted him to offer something else. A date Monday night, except she had her run to the spa. Okay, Tuesday, then. But he didn't say anything, and she couldn't bring herself to suggest it. So she gave him a bright smile and hurried back to her store.

Matt bent over and blew the grit off the windowsill. He rubbed the sandpaper over a rough patch, then slid his fingertips along the smooth surface.

The sanding was the last of the prep work he had before painting the trim in this particular room. After finishing with the paint, he would put up the new wallpaper. Kasey had already ordered the rolls, and they would be delivered to the hardware store by the first of the week. Now that he had wheels of his own, he could pick them up without having to coordinate with Kasey or even Harry.

He smiled as he thought of how the old coot was milking his injuries for all he could, basking in Charlotte Elizabeth's attention. If Harry had his way, he'd probably never leave. He'd already been there nearly a week.

"Matt?"

He turned and saw Kasey walking into the room. She folded her arms over her chest. "Do you know anything about working in retail?" she asked.

He put down the sandpaper. "What do you need?"

"Not a thing. It's Ali." Kasey wrinkled her nose. "She's got the flu or something. I went over to talk to her this morning and found her barfing her guts out. It wasn't an attractive visual, I have to tell you. Wednesdays are her light days for help, so she was threatening to force herself to work. I can't leave the front desk and frankly I don't want to work in her store. If I spend more than a few minutes over there, I tend to start eating everything in sight."

Kasey was still talking, but Matt wasn't listening. "How long has she been sick?" he asked, interrupting her.

Kasey frowned. "I'm not sure. She didn't say."

He'd seen her on Saturday and she'd been fine, he thought, already closing the window and locking it. She was supposed to have driven to Los Angeles for something on Sunday. Since then he'd seen her briefly, but they hadn't had a chance to talk or spend any time together. He'd been planning on going over later that afternoon to invite her to dinner or something.

"I'll take care of everything," he said. He dropped his tools into the open toolbox, then snapped it shut. A quick glance around the room, bare except for drop cloths protecting the hardwood floor, told him the rest of his work here could wait.

"You're sure you want to do this?" she asked. "The store caters to a pretty fussy clientele."

He gave her a quick smile. "I can handle it," he said. "I'll look in on Ali, then get the place open."

Kasey looked doubtful but relieved. "Call me if you have any problems. And I mean that. Call. I'll give as much advice as you need over the phone. Just don't ask me to show up in that den of temptation unless it's an emergency."

Matt eyed her tall, slender shape. She wore a black sweater over black slacks. The dark colors emphasized her model's body. It seemed to him she didn't have anything to worry about.

"I'll be in touch," he promised as he left the room.

Ten minutes later he stood in the center of Ali's living room. She lay curled up on the sofa, a washcloth pressed to her forehead. Her skin was pale. She was on her side, with her knees pulled up to her chest. Every few minutes, her mouth tightened. Since he'd arrived, she'd already bolted once for the bathroom where she'd retched several times before limping back to collapse on the cushions.

"You look awful," he said helpfully.

"Thanks. I feel awful. Now go away. I do misery much better alone." She closed her eyes and clutched her stomach.

He pulled up an ottoman and sat next to her. "Cramps?" he asked.

She shook her head without looking at him. "No. Waves and waves of nausea. When they subside, I feel fine. I don't know." She groaned. "I can't figure out what I ate that would make me so sick. I guess it's a flu bug."

She opened her eyes and blinked at him. "Why are you here?"

"I'm going to take care of the store for you. Kasey would, but she's afraid to be that close to so much chocolate for any length of time."

He stroked her face as he spoke. She wasn't especially warm, so he doubted she had a fever. Just a nasty stomach virus.

"Don't be so nice to me," she said feebly. "All I want is to die."

He stiffened. "Don't say that, Ali."

She frowned, then shook her head. "Sorry. I was being funny, but that was in bad taste."

"No problem. Now you rest. I'll take care of everything."

She narrowed her gaze. "I don't know that I trust you downstairs," she told him. "Don't sell me out to a conglomerate or start a franchise while I'm sick."

He grinned. "Do you really think I'd do that?" he asked.

"In a heartbeat. It's so your style."

chapter fifteen

By Saturday afternoon Ali had given up trying to feel better. She'd had a couple of horrible days, throwing up and generally feeling that death would be far preferable to an existence on her knees in the bathroom. By Friday, however, the stretches between "tossing her cookies" had stretched into hours. She still felt woozy and weak, no doubt from being hungry and dehydrated, but she was more functional.

Matt had plied her with fluids, soup, and dry toast. She'd forced down a banana that morning, and it had almost stayed where it was supposed to. When she wasn't throwing up or feeling nauseous, she actually felt fine.

"Very strange," Ali said as she zipped up her dress, then fastened her hair into a ponytail.

Matt had been by that morning with instructions for her to rest, but that was impossible. She could hear her customers downstairs. She hadn't been in the store nearly all week, and she wanted to see how things were going.

She slipped a dark green apron over her dress and tied

it in back, then shoved her feet into black ballet flats. She checked her makeup one last time and headed for the stairs.

As she descended, the sound of voices got louder. They obviously had a crowd. She hoped that all the college kids had shown up for work. Matt was probably running around like a chicken in there, she thought with a smile as she made her way through the small hallway and stepped into the main room of the store. He would be—

Ali came to a stop just beside the counter. Saturdays were always her busiest time, but today customers stood three deep waiting to pay for their purchases. She saw that all her helpers were in place, assisting customers, ringing up chocolates. But that isn't what shocked her into silence. Instead it was the man holding court in the center of the store.

Matt stood chatting with several women. He held a tray of cut-up truffles in one hand—obviously offering the pieces as a sample. The women, varying in age from eighteen to eighty-one, hung on his every word. And why not, Ali thought with some amazement. He looked as tasty as the chocolates he held.

She stared and blinked, opened her mouth and closed it. She'd only ever seen Matt in jeans and a workshirt, or nothing at all. But the man standing before her wasn't Harry's silent, too-thin day laborer. No, this man was well dressed, well groomed, and glib.

She studied the black slacks he wore, along with the tailored, dark burgundy shirt. Both were deceptively casual, but she had a stepbrother who was something of a clotheshorse so she knew quality when she saw it. Neither article of clothing had cost less than a couple of hundred dollars. His Italian leather shoes had set him back more than Harry netted in an entire month.

Her gaze narrowed as she realized he was completely at home in her store. The front door opened, and three more women entered. Two of them called Matt by name. And to think that when he'd first shown up on her back doorstep he'd been skinny and uncommunicative. She'd actually taken pity on him, feeding him and worrying about him.

Matt looked up and saw her. She told herself to look stern, but when he smiled that bone-melting masculine smile of his, her traitorous body did just what it was supposed to. She was in danger of collapsing and not from the flu, either. She felt both cold and hot, not to mention all tingly. It was a different kind of sick, but no less debilitating.

Ali managed to smile back at him, then she turned to leave the room. She couldn't stand there looking at him. Not just yet. Not when she'd just had a close encounter with the truth.

She'd fallen for him. It was stupid and she knew better. It was worse than stupid, it was self-destructive and she probably needed intensive therapy, but that didn't change what had happened. Somewhere between stuffing him with scones and truffles, and ripping off his clothes so they could do the "wild thing," she'd lost her heart.

She leaned against the wall and moaned. Why did she keep falling for men who couldn't possibly fit into her world? Matt might look different on the outside, but on the inside, he was exactly the same as every other guy she'd had a failed relationship with.

Matt had a life somewhere else. A very successful

life that didn't include her. He'd already been married, and from the little he'd told her, it hadn't gone well. His wife had died, leaving him guilty and confused. He had unresolved issues with his marriage and with his father, although she wasn't really in any position to pass judgment on someone with family trouble. She had plenty of her own.

The problem was that when Matt got his act together, which she was starting to think wasn't going to take all that long, he would be gone, heading back to his world. He was a tycoon. She wasn't. He wanted to rule the world, or at least his company, and she wanted normal. They had nothing in common.

She hugged her arms against her chest. Just once she'd like to get the whole man-woman thing right.

Ali sucked in a deep breath and released it. Not sure where else to go, she headed into the kitchen. The familiar metal appliances and fixtures were of some comfort, she told herself. At least she would always have—

She screamed. Honest-to-God opened her mouth wide and let loose with a high-pitched yell.

She heard footsteps in the hall, then the door behind her opened. "Ali, what's wrong?" Matt insisted. "Are you okay?"

She pointed to the gray and off-white *thing* sitting on the counter. Just sitting there. As if it belonged there. "What have you done?"

Matt came up behind her and put his hands on her shoulders. "You scared me to death."

"Good." She continued to point and stare. "You haven't answered my question."

He laughed and tugged her arm to her side. "Don't be silly. You know what that is. I bought you a computer."

She'd known, of course, but she'd hoped she'd been wrong. "Tell me it's not for the business."

Matt turned her until she was facing him. "Of course it is. Remember, we talked before about getting you into the new century? I've already hooked you up to your suppliers. Even if you don't want to flowchart your cooking schedule—which is still a great idea, by the way—you can order with the touch of a button. It'll be a lot easier. Come on, I'll show you."

She grabbed his arm. "Didn't we have an entire conversation about this just a few days ago? Weren't you groveling in the dust for talking about business when you should have been bringing me flowers?"

"Yeah, but this is different. We haven't made love in a while."

He was clueless, she realized. Completely clueless. In fact he'd lied. Not about being sorry but about knowing what he was sorry for.

"It's not different. It's exactly the same."

"Not at all." He patted her hand on his arm. "Before I was being insensitive. Now I'm being masterful. Besides, you'll love it. Let me show you how it works."

She couldn't believe it. The man was actually pushing keys and making things appear on the screen. She let go of his arm and thought about hitting him.

"Don't you get it?" she demanded. "I don't want this! Not now. Not this way. I have nothing against computers in general. I just don't see the point in changing my business. I like the way it is."

"You're scared," he said indulgently, as if she were a small child afraid of the dentist. "But we can work through your technology phobia."

"I'm not phobic!" She had to hold back a scream of frustration. "I've screwed up enough places in my life. I don't need another one. And that's what a computer is. One giant place to fail."

He touched her cheek. "Not with me around to keep you safe. You'll see. I've entered most of the inventory information already. Along with your revenues for the year-to-date. I still have to get the expenses up-to-date, but that won't take too long."

He looked excited, she thought, still in shock. Excited and proud, like a kid bringing home a crooked, ugly bread box from wood shop. Did schools still have wood shop?

"It's only been four days," she murmured more to herself than him. "You've only been working in the store four days. How did you get this done so fast?"

He led her to the machine. "That's the beauty of computers. They make everything easy."

She stared at the alien intruder cluttering her beautiful kitchen. "This isn't what I want for my life," she said firmly. "No computer, no datalink to my suppliers, no year-to-date anything."

"Ali, don't be a stick in the mud."

"Four days," she repeated. "You did this in four days."

The back door opened with a creak. She glanced up, not sure what to expect next. It turned out to be a surprise, too. Rick strolled into the kitchen. He had a thick, softcover book in his hands.

"Rick?" Ali said in confusion. "I didn't know you were in town."

Her brother glanced at her and smiled absently. "Oh, hi, Ali. I was bored in L.A. so I came up to hang out for a few days. I got in yesterday. Matt told me you were sick, and I didn't want to risk catching anything so I stayed clear." He noticed her gazing from him to the computer and walked up to pat the ugly machine.

"Don't you love it?" he asked. "Matt told me what he's doing with the business. About time you moved into the modern age."

He held up the book he was reading. Ali glanced at the title, then recoiled when she saw it was all about establishing and maintaining a website.

"What are you doing?" she asked in a panic. "Why are you reading that?"

"Matt told me about your plan to get a website up and running. He suggested I think about handling it for you." Rick grinned at his new best friend. "At first I wasn't sure, but then I got this book and I have to tell you, I'm intrigued. The possibilities are endless. They don't even have to be all that expensive. Security isn't much of a problem anymore. With the right graphics and a simple ordering form, you could kick butt."

"But it's only been four days," she moaned softly, almost as a prayer. How could her life have changed so quickly?

"Matt and I have been talking about different ways to grow your business," her brother, the traitor, continued. "I'm thinking of getting a laptop so I can work on this at home. I need to go buy one of those computer magazines and do some research."

Matt patted her shoulder. "I have to get back to my customers. Why don't you get some rest, Ali? You're still not back to a hundred percent. You don't want to have a relapse."

Rick buried his head in the book and waved in her direction. "He's right. You should listen. I came to get your letterhead so I could study it to see if it will work on the website. Then I'm heading back over to Mom's to read more about different designs. I'm in the upstairs guestroom because Harry is still in the downstairs one. Do you know when he's leaving?"

Before she could answer, Rick had strolled out of the kitchen. She heard the rear door open, then close. Matt had left for the store, and Ali was alone with the computer.

"We'll never be friends," she told the blank-faced machine. "I'll never like you, and we'll never get along."

That established, she turned on her heel and left. Once back in her room, she stripped out of her clothes and crawled into bed. It had only been four days, she thought with a whimper. How could she have lost control of her life so quickly?

It was nearly midnight when Matt pulled into Ali's parking lot. He wanted to check on her before he returned to the bed-and-breakfast for the night. Besides, he had a feeling she would be waiting up for him.

Sure enough, he found her hovering at the top of the stairs. She wore black leggings topped with a dark green sweater. Her feet were bare.

"How did it go?" she asked as soon as she saw him. "Everything all right? You know I could have done the spa run myself. I don't feel that bad."

He climbed toward her.

"You were throwing up just this morning," he reminded her, pausing in front of her. "Whatever that bug is, you're not completely over it yet. Until you are, I want you resting and not passing it on to customers."

She folded her arms over her chest and glared at him in mock anger. "Who put you in charge?"

"I've always been in charge." He smoothed her curls away from her face, then cupped her cheeks. Her eyes were wide and her mouth trembled slightly. She was beautiful. Every curve, every curl, every freckle. He wanted to have them all. He wanted her. Now more than ever.

"How do you feel?" he asked. "Your tummy, I mean."

Something sparked to life in her eyes. "Why do I suddenly think you're asking for reasons other than concern?"

"Because I am."

She raised herself up on her tiptoes and brushed her mouth against his. "I feel great. How about you?"

He took her hand in his and pressed her palm against his groin. He was hard and ready. "You would be crazy to get involved with me," he told her, then groaned as she closed around him and rubbed.

"Too late," she told him.

He knew she was right. It was too late. They were involved, and he couldn't find it in his heart to be sorry. He bent his head and kissed her.

For Ali, the scent of him and the feel of him was a chance to relive something wonderful and perfect in her life. She reveled in the feel of his broad chest pressing against her breasts and the way his hands moved up and down her back. It had been two weeks since the night they'd become lovers. Two weeks of wondering if it had all been real and what did it mean to him? Days of wishing it would happen again, of longing to know what he thought of her and what he remembered about that one special night.

And now he was touching her again. Pulling her closer and closer, brushing her bottom lip with his tongue before plunging inside her. She tasted his masculine sweetness. They danced together in a familiar yet oh-so exciting rhythm. She felt her muscles begin to relax, and her bones begin to melt. Her breasts ached as they swelled in anticipation and between her thighs a growing heat caused her to squirm and dampen in readiness.

"Ali," he breathed against her mouth, then pushed back slightly and kissed her cheeks, her chin, her earlobes, and her neck.

She felt like a rag doll. She would do whatever he wanted. It didn't matter how he touched her—there was pleasure to be had from every caress.

Matt straightened and wrapped his arms around her. "Why don't we continue this somewhere more comfortable?"

"Great idea."

She leaned against him as they walked into her apartment. He moved easily through the room, as if he'd grown familiar with the layout of the place. She supposed he had. After all, in the past week he'd spent many hours here, checking on her during her illness, bringing her groceries, cooking her soup and toast. He'd even washed her sheets and changed the bed.

Now he led the way down the short hall and into her bedroom. He flipped the wall switch, illuminating the lamp by the bed. Then he turned to her and pulled her back in his arms. He kissed her slowly, deeply, and with great passion. His hands settled on her hips before circling around to her rear and hauling her against him. She arched into him, wanting to bring her center into contact with his erection. She burned for him, wanting him with a passion she'd never experienced before.

He read her mind. "I want you," he murmured between kisses. "I want you naked and under me. I want to be inside of you. Ali. I want to watch your face change as I enter you. I want to make you writhe and scream and get so lost you'll never find your way back."

His words made her shiver. As he spoke, he began to pull up her sweater. Well-trained fingers searched for then found the hooked closures of her bra. He unfastened them, then moved around her ribs to her chest. There he cupped her breasts and caught her nipples between his thumbs and forefingers.

Exquisite sensation washed over her. She could only gasp as flames of heat licked at her body. With each brush of his teasing touch, her insides contracted. Tension grew—in her breasts, between her legs, all through her body. Involuntarily her hips pulsed in an age-old beat. All thoughts of subtlety and slowness faded. She wanted with a desperation that left her breathless.

"Matt," she gasped as she stepped away. She jerked off her sweater and shrugged out of her bra.

Fortunately he understood her fever. His hands worked as quickly on the buttons of his shirt. He stepped out of his shoes, then bent over to pull off his socks. By the time she'd shimmied out of her leggings and panties, he was shoving down his slacks and briefs.

Ali fell onto the bed. She parted her legs and held out her arms in silent invitation. He moved on top of her, bending down to kiss her.

"Wait," she cried softly. "You have to touch me. You have to know how much I want you."

She needed him to know. If there had been a way to open herself enough to expose her soul, she knew she would have done it. Confusing, conflicting feelings raced through her. She knew that Matt was dangerous to her emotionally, yet she couldn't help needing him desperately . . . and not just in bed.

He did as she requested and slipped his fingers between her curls. She was wet and slick and ready. He groaned in response to her heat. The second he touched that one small, tight place of pleasure, she arched toward him. Her arms went around him and her mouth found his. Her release was as powerful as it was instantaneous. She shuddered and cried out and clung to him.

Deep kisses accompanied the perfect pleasure. She quieted at last, but there was an edge to her peace. There was more for both of them and she wanted that.

His hand moved away and something much thicker and longer probed. She shifted and he slid inside of her. Their gazes locked. She watched the passion flare on his face and knew that he saw the same on hers. He moved and they both caught their breath.

I love you.

The words came from nowhere, terrifying her yet feeling incredibly right. This wasn't the time, and for all she knew, he might not be the man. But she thought them. She screamed them over and over in her mind. They continued to stare at each other, bodies reaching, responding, joining in the most intimate way possible.

She reached for him, pulling him close. He surged into her. She felt the first of the contractions begin deep inside of her and rippling to the surface. She called out his name. He shuddered in response, kissing her, mating with her. For one brief, shining moment, actually belonging to her.

Ali awoke sometime close to dawn. It was still dark out, but there were hints of light at the edges of the blackness. She lay nestled in Matt's embrace. After making love, they'd settled under the covers and had fallen asleep. She liked the feel of him so close in the night. It comforted her.

She breathed in the scent of his skin and the lingering musk of their lovemaking. But while her body was content, her mind raced. She still had no answers to the questions in her head. Did she really love him? There were still too many mysteries about his past. He made her crazy with his fixing, but he also completed her in a way she'd never felt before. With Matt she was content. She didn't feel like she was screwing up all the time.

She wasn't stupid, she reminded herself. It didn't take a degree in psychology to know that between the price put on her birth and the way she'd been raised, with such successful and wealthy parents, that she would grow up expecting to have to earn any love or even affection that came her way. Through hard work and determination she'd done her best to break that cycle, and she'd thought she'd succeeded. But now she wasn't sure. Would Matt prove to be the exception to the rule, or proof that her judgment was tragically and terminally skewed?

She stretched and started to turn over. Suddenly her stomach lurched in the direction of her throat. She groaned and raced for the bathroom. Once there, she assumed the familiar pose and proceeded to empty her stomach over and over again.

When she had finished, she washed her face and brushed her teeth. Quietly, she opened the door to the bedroom, hoping to make her way back to bed without being detected. As she'd feared, Matt wasn't asleep anymore. He was sitting on the edge of the bed, watching her.

He was naked, and glorious, but she doubted he had sex on his mind. Instead he looked worried as he watched her approach.

"What's going on?" he asked.

He *sounded* plenty calm, but the shadows had returned to his eyes.

"I'm fine," she assured him, and now that the nausea had passed, she *did* feel better.

"It's been over a week, Ali. You can't keep going on like this. It's more than the flu. Have you been to a doctor?"

She wrinkled her nose, then walked around the bed and slid in next to him. She rested her hand on his bare back. "I don't need a doctor. I'll get better. Besides, my doctor is in Los Angeles. I don't want to make the drive."

He turned to stare at her face. "I'm worried about you," he admitted. "You're not improving at all. Something is wrong, and you can't put off getting it looked into."

"Matt, you're being sweet, but don't be concerned."

He rose to his feet. "That's not good enough. I'm not going to lose you. Either you go to your doctor today, or I make arrangements."

She appreciated the concern but not the high-handedness. "I don't think so. It's my body and I'm going to be fine. You don't have the right to dictate."

He shook his head, as if he'd expected no more from her, then reached for her phone. He hesitated, then dialed a long distance number. Ali sat up, pulling the covers with her. What on earth was he doing?

After a moment of silence, he said, "This is Matthew Birmingham. I would like to speak with Dr. Welch. Yes, I'll hold."

Birmingham? His last name was supposed to be Baker. Her mind tilted and whirled as a thousand questions flew at her from all directions. She'd found out that he'd used a credit card to pay Harry's bill, but no one had mentioned it had been in a different name. *Birmingham. Why was that familiar?*

"Matt, this isn't a good time to take control of my life."

He ignored her.

"Yes, Doctor. Thanks for taking my call." He paused and his expression turned rueful. "Yes, it *has* been a long time. I'm sorry." More silence. "The reason I called is that I have a friend who is ill."

He went on to describe her symptoms. Ali's shock deepened when he offered to put a private jet at the doctor's disposal. The physician agreed to fly out that afternoon. Matt said good-bye and hung up the phone.

"He'll be here later," he told her. "But you probably heard that." He tried to smile and failed miserably. "Look at the bright side. Now you don't have to make an appointment to go anywhere."

She couldn't speak, couldn't think, couldn't breathe. She could only stare at him. "Who *are* you?"

chapter sixteen

After each customer left, Matt paced by the front windows of the store and watched for the limo that would bring Dr. Welch to Saint Maggie. His stomach was in knots, and he was having trouble breathing. Ali was sick. Obviously very sick, because she couldn't stop throwing up. He couldn't go through this again, he thought frantically. He couldn't watch her die.

He had a brief thought that he was being punished because Leigh's death hadn't touched him the way it should. So now Ali was sick. No, he told himself. Fate wasn't that tidy.

He closed his eyes briefly and saw Ali's accusing expression as she'd asked him who he was. A wave of nausea had saved him from answering. While she'd been in the bathroom, he'd slipped out and escaped to his room at the bed-and-breakfast to shower and change. By the time he'd returned, she'd been waiting for him downstairs. But before he could answer any of her questions, she'd raced off to the bathroom. While he appreciated being able to avoid reality for a little while longer, he would rather face her wrath and have her well.

For the twentieth time in the past hour, he glanced at his watch. It was only one. The doctor wouldn't arrive for at least another hour. Even though Matt was having the doctor flown in on a private jet into the Santa Barbara airport to save time, Chicago was still a four-hour flight from the West Coast.

Hurry! he thought frantically, as if he could will the man to be here now. He had to know that Ali was all right. He had to know that she wasn't going to die.

He was about to turn away from the window when a taxi pulled into the parking lot. Matt frowned. He'd arranged for a limo to pick up the doctor, so it couldn't be him. Had someone from the spa grown desperate or had—

The rear door opened and a tall, sandy-haired man climbed out. Jeff Peterson was lean, with pleasant features and an easy smile that hid the heart of a natural-born tycoon. He was a couple of years shy of forty, brilliant, organized, and the number-two guy at Birmingham International.

Jeff looked around at the store, then shifted his briefcase to his right hand and walked briskly toward the front door. Despite his fear for Ali, Matt couldn't help feeling pleased at seeing his old friend.

Jeff stepped into the store. He took in the two college kids behind the counter, then saw Matt and stopped just inside the door. Matt studied his face and saw that his once close friend hadn't changed all that much. Jeff looked a little older, a little more weary.

"Long time no see," Matt said by way of a greeting. He knew he looked odd, in his casual slacks and shirt, wearing a dark green apron with the name "Decadent Delight" embroidered on the front in gold. Matt couldn't help grinning. "Let me guess," he said as he walked forward and held out his hand. "The hospital credit-card charge. I figured you'd have someone monitoring my American Express account. Success is in the details. Isn't that what you've always preached?"

Jeff stared, looking anything but happy to see him. He also ignored Matt's outstretched hand. "We thought you were dead, or maybe kidnapped," he said without preamble. "The staff went crazy looking for you."

Matt dropped his arm to his side and motioned for Jeff to follow him into the hallway where they could have some privacy. "I'm sorry. I should have called more."

"Twice," Jeff accused. "You phoned twice in a whole goddamn year. The last call was over six months ago." He took a step toward Matt, then seemed to bring himself up short.

"I know. It was stupid as hell."

"We lost the Datapoint account," Jeff said, ignoring his apology. "Did you read about that? It turned out to be the biggest IPO in history. Bigger than UPS and Martha Stewart combined. That could have been ours. Dammit, it *was* ours, but we lost it when you walked away. The client got nervous and then they were gone. A lot of people worked their asses off, and for what?"

Jeff's anger was a tangible, living thing. Matt didn't know what to say. Guilt and frustration filled him.

"You don't understand," he said, but even to him the words sounded lame.

"Damned straight I don't. Nor do I give a shit." Jeff took another step toward him. Rage burned in the man's blue eyes. "You'd better start by explaining where you've been all this time. Why didn't you get in touch with us? Why didn't you care about the company or the people there? What makes you think you have the right to walk away from everything like that? Dammit, I'm your *friend*. At least I was."

"I know. I can explain."

"I doubt it." Jeff looked skeptical. "But I can't wait to see you try."

Ali stepped into the hallway. "I'm sorry but your explanation is going to have to wait. I was here first."

Matt groaned. Things were not going his way.

"Is he the doctor?" she asked.

Matt shook his head. "Ali, this is Jeff Peterson. He's the senior executive officer at Birmingham International. Jeff, this is Ali Thomas. She owns the store."

Jeff nodded at her, then turned to Matt. "Doctor? Are you sick?"

"No, Ali is."

Ali leaned against the doorframe. She looked from Matt to Jeff. "Birmingham International?" she said, sounding stunned. "You're Birmingham International?"

Just then the front bell tinkled. Seconds later Matt heard a familiar voice asking for him. *Finally,* he thought with some relief.

"Why do you need a doctor?" Jeff asked Ali.

She blinked as if trying to clear her vision. "I, ah, I don't. Matt overreacted. How long have you worked for him?"

The back door banged open. "Guess what I found?" Rick called as he walked into the hallway. "Ali? You're not going to believe it."

Matt ignored the rest of them and hurried to greet the small, gray-haired man waiting in the store. "Dr. Welch," he said warmly and shook the man's hand. "Thanks for coming."

"You didn't give me much choice, Matt. Besides, the flight gave me a chance to catch up on my reading. Where's my patient?"

"In here." Matt led him back into the hallway.

They entered bedlam. Everyone was talking at once. Rick had his computer book open in his hands and was trying to show something to Ali. Ali was talking to Jeff, while Jeff still looked ready to kill Matt.

"Quiet!" Matt called out. There was immediate silence. He looked at Ali. "This is Dr. Welch. Please take him upstairs and let him examine you. All right?"

Ali hesitated, then nodded. She approached the doctor and they shook hands. Then Dr. Welch put his hand on the small of her back. "Come, my dear. Let's get away from all these men, and you and I can have a nice chat about why you don't feel well. I'm sure together we can figure out what's going on."

Matt started to go after them, then stopped himself. Ali would probably feel more comfortable to have her examination in private. Besides, he and Jeff had unfinished business.

"I'm Rick Thomas," Rick said.

Matt turned in time to see the two men shaking hands. "Jeff Peterson." They released their hands slowly and seemed to have forgotten he was in the room.

Rick closed his book and smiled at Jeff. "You know Matt?"

"I work for him." Jeff hesitated. "Just who *is* Ali?"

"My sister," Rick informed him.

Jeff turned his attention to Matt. "Who is she to you?"

Good question, Matt thought, but he didn't have an answer.

Ali sat in her living room, avoiding the gaze of the kindly doctor. He looked like somebody's grandfather, with his gray hair and gentle eyes.

On the one hand, she appreciated Matt's concern for her health. Based on what had happened with Leigh, he would be hypersensitive to an unexplained illness. On the other hand, he was trying to take over her life, which she hated, and he was pushing her around, which she hated even more.

Of course she *had* been throwing up fairly regularly for several days with no sign of relief in sight. Perhaps she should just let the doctor examine her and castigate Matt at another time.

"I've come a long way to see you, young lady," he said. "Matt seemed very concerned about your health. Do you have any idea what's wrong?"

Ali pressed her lips together and forced herself to pay attention to the conversation. "Not a clue. I think I have a stomach bug, but it's not going away or getting better."

Dr. Welch patted her arm. "Not to worry. I'm here now. Why don't we get on with the examination?"

Twenty minutes later he handed her a stick. Ali stared at a pink plus sign.

"I could take a blood test as well, if you'd like, but I've found these tests are fairly accurate," the doctor said. "When combined with your symptoms and the small changes in your body, there's little doubt."

She didn't speak because she didn't know what to say. Her body and mind felt numb, as if she wasn't having a reaction at all. Yet she knew it wasn't that. She knew she was in a state of shock. Soon all kinds of emotions would flood her, and she would be overwhelmed.

"I'm pregnant," she whispered, barely able to believe

the words. Although she should. After all, she and Matt had been completely stupid about birth control.

Dr. Welch studied her face. She knew he wanted to know if she was happy about the news. Ali swallowed and looked at him.

"It's all right," she said. "I'm stunned, but not unhappy." A small glow burst to life inside of her chest and began to radiate outward. "A baby? Really?"

He smiled. "So it would appear."

"Wow. I've always wanted kids. It's the men I have trouble with. A baby!"

She stared at the stick. She and Matt were going to have a child together. *A child!* It was crazy, in the most wonderful way. But . . .

She set the stick on the coffee table. Matt owned Birmingham International, a company even she had heard about. When he'd mentioned a family business she'd thought it would be something like a small retail store. Not a multi-multibillion-dollar, multinational concern. He was rich, successful, and what on earth was he doing in her life?

Dr. Welch moved to the sofa and put a comforting hand on her shoulder. "You look overwhelmed."

"Just a little."

"The good news is you're healthy. Now relax. You have a nine-month journey ahead of you. You're just at the beginning of it, and you're going to need your rest."

He released her hand and opened his bag, then withdrew a prescription tablet. "You need to find a local doctor with whom you're comfortable. Make an appointment right away. In the meantime—" He scribbled on the pad. "Here are the names of a few excellent books on pregnancy. Buy them and read them. They will answer many of your questions."

"My mother had a difficult pregnancy. She was sick a lot."

"Was her life or yours ever at risk?"

"No. She just threw up all the time."

He nodded. "Sometimes that's the way it happens. There's no reason to think you won't carry a healthy baby to term, but again, discuss this with your doctor. He or she can watch for potential risks. But based on how you turned out, I think you're going to be fine."

She was relieved. "I guess I have to worry about what I'm eating."

"Absolutely. Healthy foods." He tore off the sheet and handed it to her. "As for the throwing up, it's caused by an increase of a chemical in your body. Hormones change when a woman conceives. There are many theories about morning sickness. For some women it's exacerbated by stress. Massage, yoga, and relaxation techniques may help. I would suggest you try them. Also, as your body gets used to the new hormones, you'll feel less sensitive."

She nodded, overwhelmed by her situation and by all he was telling her. Except for not knowing how Matt felt about her, and the fact that she was in love with him, and being confused about her life, everything was perfect. She was going to have a baby!

Dr. Welch rose to his feet. "You'll be fine, Ali. Relax, find a doctor to help with your pregnancy, and enjoy the rest of your life."

She smiled at him. "Thank you so much for everything. Especially the advice."

He opened the door to her apartment. Matt, Rick,

Jeff, and her mother spilled into the room. They were all talking. Ali ignored them. She folded up the paper the doctor had given her and tucked it into her pocket. Then she shifted so that she was lying on the sofa, curled up with her head on a pillow.

Quiet joy filled her and with it a contentment she'd never felt before. Whatever happened, she would have a child. The one thing she'd always wanted. She couldn't wait to tell Clair.

Conversation flowed around her. Matt demanded that Dr. Welch tell him what was wrong.

"She's fine, Matt. A healthy, strong young woman. But if you want any more specifics, you're going to have to talk to her."

The doctor left and Matt trailed after him. Ali wondered what she was supposed to say to Matt, to everyone in her life. Pregnant. Who would have thought? But it made sense, she reminded herself. All the times she'd been with Matt, they'd had unprotected sex. Talk about stupid. But she'd been without a lover for so long that she'd gone off the Pill, and she and Matt hadn't used condoms.

There was no excuse, she told herself. She was thirty and she knew better than to act so irresponsibly. Except . . . except she couldn't find it in her heart to be sorry. Matt would probably regret the pregnancy, and everyone else in her life would lecture her, but screw it. While she'd never thought about being a single mother, she figured she could learn what she had to in order to raise a healthy, happy child. She wasn't alone in the world, and she didn't have financial worries. Thousands of women with much less than she had raised children on their own and did magnificent jobs.

"I can't believe Matt called for a doctor," Charlotte Elizabeth was saying. "Ali, you should have told me you were that sick. I could have checked on you more. But you told me it was just the flu."

Ali raised her head and looked at her mother. Worry darkened Charlotte Elizabeth's eyes and pulled her full mouth into a straight line.

"I'm fine," she said honestly, feeling better than she had in days. "Matt got a little crazy, nothing more. Dr. Welch says I'm completely healthy." For a pregnant woman.

Rick peered over to look at her. "What's going on, kid? You gonna croak or what?"

She smiled. "I think 'or what.' I have no plans to die anytime soon."

Matt burst back into the room. "He wouldn't tell me anything. What's going on, Ali? What did he say?"

Charlotte Elizabeth drew herself up to her full five feet, five inches and glared at the much taller man. "That is what I would like to know. How dare you keep my daughter's condition from me? You should have told me she was seriously ill."

"I'm not seriously ill," Ali said, but they weren't listening to her anymore.

"You've been busy with Harry," Matt told the former actress. "Besides, until today I didn't think Ali's condition was a problem."

"There isn't a problem," Ali said calmly, but no one was listening.

She noticed Jeff standing by the door, watching without participating. What must he think of them? Not that she really cared. She was going to have a baby. Her very own child. Someone to love, someone to care about. No matter what happened in her world, she and her child would always have an emotional and biological connection that neither time nor distance could break.

Matt walked over and sat next to Ali on the sofa. Rick herded Charlotte Elizabeth toward the door.

"We'll be waiting outside," her brother said and led the other two out onto the landing. He closed the door behind them.

When they were finally alone, Matt cupped her cheek, then touched the tip of her nose with his index finger. "How are you feeling?" he asked.

"Not too bad."

"Are you going to throw up anytime soon?"

"I don't think so."

He tried to smile, but it didn't take. "Want to tell me what happened with the doctor?"

"Sure." She studied his face. "I'm really fine. You overreacted."

"I know. I couldn't help it. I just knew that I didn't want you to die."

"I appreciate that."

He gently tugged on a curl, then dropped his hands onto his lap. "I thought I could take care of you myself. I thought if I stuck around and handled things, I could make you better."

There was an audible click in her brain. "Because with Leigh, you weren't there enough. You were trying to atone."

"Dumb, huh?"

"No. It's really very sweet."

He looked at her. "I told you before I'm not proud of what I did with Leigh. What I didn't tell you is that I wasn't there when she died. I had a big deal I was closing.

I was too good at what I did, and I thought I was the only one who could do it. That made it easy to sell my soul to the devil."

"We all make mistakes," she reminded him, aching for both his obvious pain and the poor woman who had died alone.

"It wasn't a mistake," he said firmly. "It was unforgivable."

She didn't believe that, but she also wasn't going to be able to convince him of the fact.

"Tell me all about Birmingham International," she said instead.

"You know a lot of it. My family has owned Birmingham International for years. We started out as a small business bank in the late eighteen hundreds, then gradually switched to business investment advice. For the past thirty years, we've focused on taking successful, private companies public. Getting their books in order, polishing their image, getting enough interested investors to guarantee success."

Ali turned onto her back and looked at him. Matthew Birmingham. She'd always known that he wasn't just another one of Harry's hard-luck cases.

"So you're a rich, powerful guy," she said. Someone not in need of a rescue, but she didn't want to think about that right now.

He nodded.

"And now your past has caught up with you. Whatever will you do?"

"I don't know," he said honestly. "What about you? Tell me what's going on. Why have you been sick?"

"An interesting question." She swallowed. "I'm pregnant."

chapter seventeen

The door to Ali's apartment flew open, and Rick and Charlotte Elizabeth stumbled inside.

"Pregnant?" Charlotte Elizabeth exclaimed in delight. "Oh, Ali, this is wonderful news!"

Matt froze in place. There was an explosion of voices around him, but he couldn't hear them. He couldn't hear or see anything. He'd expected something frightening and had tried to prepare himself for the worst. He'd never thought to hear that Ali was going to have a baby.

That made him a father. He stared at Ali, who shrugged. "Yes, well, we were 'busy' several times," she murmured.

He didn't know what to think. Kids. He'd always assumed that someday he'd have a couple. But—

Hot damn! He grinned at Ali. "Are you sure?"

Some of the trepidation left her eyes. "There's no dead rabbit, if that's what you're asking, but I do have a stick I peed on. Want to touch it?"

He barely noticed when Charlotte Elizabeth pushed him out of the way and took his place on the sofa. "Darling, what wonderful news." She cupped her daughter's face in her hands. "A baby of your own and a grandchild for me." Charlotte Elizabeth nearly vibrated with excitement. "Unfortunately the women in our family are generally ill during pregnancy, but it will all be worth it, I promise. Based on your symptoms, I should have guessed. Isn't this amazing. A baby is a joy and brings magic to every life it touches."

She turned to glare at Matt. "With the possible exception of ingrates who don't know to welcome a miracle when it bites them on the ass." She returned her attention to a stunned-looking Ali. "A child is a precious gift. You are so very lucky."

He held up his hands in protest. "I know it's a miracle."

"Are you okay with this?" Ali questioned, her expression concerned.

"Yeah, sure. It's just a shock."

There was an understatement.

Out of the corner of his eyes, he saw something move. Jeff had entered Ali's apartment and stood just inside the door. Reality slammed into him with the impact of a meteor heading for Earth. He was going to have a child. And he was Jonathan Birmingham's son.

Without saying anything else, he turned on his heel and left. He made his way downstairs, then through the kitchen and outside.

The bright sky was its typical California blue, and the air was unseasonably warm. He crossed to the fence marking the boundary of the parking lot and leaned against a wooden post.

A baby. He was both elated and terrified. Because he would cut out his soul if he ever treated his child the way his father had treated him. Yet a year ago he'd realized he was twice the bastard his father had ever been.

But here, in Saint Maggie, he'd changed. He wasn't Matthew Birmingham, tycoon, he was Matt Baker. A regular guy. Here he could forget the past, and here he might just have a chance at being a decent father.

He heard footsteps and looked up to see Jeff approaching.

"You're having an interesting afternoon," Jeff said.

"Tell me about it. I never thought Ali was pregnant. She'd been sick and—"

"You think I give a fuck?" Jeff asked coldly, cutting him off. "You selfish bastard. How dare you walk away from the company the way you did? You had responsibilities."

"You probably want me to say I'm sorry," Matt said.

Jeff shook his head. "That's not even close to being enough, *boss.*" The word was laced with contempt. "I'd always been second in command, with a clear understanding that there were some things I wasn't allowed to do. When you walked out, you didn't change the rules. That means there were accounts I couldn't access and decisions I didn't have the authority to make. You left us hanging in the wind."

Jeff took a menacing step forward. Anger vibrated through his body. "We are all dying now, thanks to you. We've lost contracts and good people. The company is in trouble." He turned away, as if he couldn't bear looking at Matt. "The hell of it is, I could have done it all, but the way you'd set up the company, my hands were tied. I could only watch us sink deeper and deeper. Right now Birmingham International is about five months from going under. Our reputation is in tatters, and people's livelihoods are on the line. All because you had to take some self-indulgent trip to find yourself and deal with your grief."

If only it were that simple, Matt thought. If only he'd run away because he was lost without Leigh. If only he'd loved her with a devotion that transcended death. At least that would be noble.

"What do you want from me?" he asked the man who had once been his best friend. "You're right. I haven't thought about the company, and my actions were selfish. I shouldn't have left that way." No, he should have sold the whole damn place and then walked away.

Jeff spun to face him again. Heat and contempt poured off him in nearly visible waves. "What do I want? How about retribution! You act like you're the only one who has ever suffered an emotional loss. The rest of the world exists in a vacuum and only the great Matthew Birmingham matters."

"It wasn't like that."

"Did you think I didn't know what it felt like?" Jeff asked. "I'd been through it."

"I know."

"I would have listened. You didn't have to leave."

But he did. That was what Jeff didn't get.

"I'll give you the company," Matt said quietly. "Get the lawyer to draw up the papers. You can have it. I'm not interested in it anymore. I'm not going back. Take it."

"You're crazy," Jeff growled.

"Probably, but that doesn't change the validity of what I'm saying. Take the damn company. You've earned it after this past year. Make a billion. Be happy."

Jeff's gaze was dark and angry. "You know what? I don't want it, either. I'm tired of caring. I quit. That's what I came out here to tell you. The company can go to hell for all I care."

Matt tried to figure out if he cared either. He felt a sharp pain inside, but then it was gone. "Whatever you want is fine."

Jeff stared at him. "I don't get it. What happened?"

"I realized I'd won the battle and lost the war. I couldn't stay."

"Then I'm not staying, either. I'll give it another month. Not for you, but for the people still stuck at the company, either because they have nowhere else to go or because they're stupid enough to believe in you. Then I'm leaving."

That suited him just fine. "I'll send you instructions for closing the company. A month should be enough time."

"That went well," Ali said, trying to convince herself that Matt's departure wasn't a bad thing. He'd seemed happy about the baby. That was good. A confession of adoration would have been better, but one baby step at a time.

Her insides felt as if a drill team had used them as a practice field. Her entire midsection hurt from all the vomiting, and the man who fathered her child had just disappeared.

And yet she couldn't find it in herself to be sorry. She pressed a hand to her stomach and knew that whatever Matt decided, she was thrilled to be pregnant.

"He'll be back," her mother said, leaning close and kissing her cheek. "It was a shock, and he needs to think about it. Everything is going to be fine. And even if Matt turns into an idiot and doesn't care about the baby, we're all here. Your family might be small but what we lack in numbers we more than make up for in intelligence, money, and devotion. We will both be here for you."

Charlotte Elizabeth looked at Rick who nodded in agreement. "Barring that," her mother said with an impish smile, "we'll hire a baby nurse."

Ali couldn't help returning her smile. "I'm sure you'll have one picked out by the end of the day."

"I'm sure I will," her mother said sweetly.

Rick walked over and sat on the coffee table in front of the sofa. He looked at her. "How are you doing?"

"I'm still trying to believe it myself," she admitted.

Charlotte Elizabeth glanced at Rick. "At least Matt isn't a loser."

"That's true," Rick said. "And I like his choice in friends."

Ali tried to remember what Matt's friend had looked like, but she couldn't for the life of her recall. She'd been too caught up in waiting for the doctor.

The door to her apartment opened. Matt stood there, looking at her. She tried to read his expression, but failed, which didn't make her feel very good. She'd just spent the last however-many days throwing up because she was pregnant with his child, and she might spend the next eight or so months doing the same. While he'd seemed pleased, he hadn't actually come out and said so.

"We have to talk," he said.

She resisted the urge to roll her eyes and say, "Well, duh." "Fine," was her more mature response. "When do you want to do that?"

"How about now?" he said. "If you two could excuse us?" He stepped aside and glanced at her mother and brother.

Charlotte Elizabeth eyed him cautiously. "Allison is in a very delicate condition. She needs rest and devotion."

"I'll see what I can do," Matt told her.

"That's all I ask." Charlotte Elizabeth paused. "No, that's not true. I'm sure I'll have more to ask later." She headed out the door.

Rick didn't budge. He looked at his sister. "You okay with this? I'll stay if you want me to."

Ali shook her head, although she avoided looking directly at Matt. Now she wasn't sure she *wanted* to know what he was thinking.

"I'm fine," she told him. "We have a lot of things we need to straighten out, and we'll do that better without an audience. But thank you for offering."

"No problem, Brillo pad." He flashed her his best grin, bent and kissed her cheek, then rose to his feet. "I'll be downstairs. Yell if you need anything."

He walked toward the door, pausing when he reached Matt. Rick's puppy-dog eyes hardened. "Be very careful with what you say to my sister," he warned, his voice low and menacing. "If you hurt her anymore, you'll answer to me."

Matt nodded. When Rick was gone, he turned to Ali. "Is Rick going to beat me up?"

She pushed herself into a sitting position, then swung her feet down to rest on the floor. She felt excited and tired and confused. "Maybe. He's studied martial arts of some kind. I could never keep them straight. But whatever it is, he's a black belt. So he could probably take you, and I'm sure it would hurt."

The thought cheered her, and she was able to smile as

Matt settled in the club chair closest to the sofa. But her momentary humor faded when he spoke.

"About the baby," he began. "I didn't use any protection, and you weren't on any birth control."

He wasn't asking a question, but she sensed the real meaning behind his statements. "I didn't do this on purpose," she said quickly. "You're right, I'm not on any kind of birth control. I haven't had a relationship in so long that I finally went off the Pill. I always figured if something happened, I would have enough warning to go back on it."

Matt's firm, sensual mouth twisted into a straight line. "I didn't give you much warning that night," he admitted. "I wanted you desperately."

Sex was the last thing she wanted to think about. It was what had gotten her in this predicament in the first place. "Yes, well, who wanted whom isn't really at issue. The most important point is that I'm keeping the baby." Her voice was clear and firm. "That is not negotiable."

"It never occurred to me you'd do anything else." He leaned forward and rested his elbows on his thighs, linking his hands together. "Ali, I'm really happy about the baby."

It was as if a lead weight had been lifted from her shoulders. She sighed with relief. "You are? Really?"

"Absolutely. I like Saint Maggie. I think we'll do well to raise our child here."

He was saying all the right things, but there was something wrong with how they sounded.

"What about your life in Chicago?"

"That's over. I'm getting rid of the business. I'll settle here. Maybe I'll buy out Harry like he keeps saying."

She blinked several times. Buy out Harry? "But you own Birmingham International. It's huge. You can't just sell it."

"Sure I can. I'll put the money in a college fund."

"Matt, with that kind of money you could educate every child in Kansas."

"Whatever. The point is we're going to have a baby together. Here. In this great town."

It was bad enough that he was talking all about the child and nothing about the parents. But selling his company and buying out Harry? She narrowed her gaze. "What aren't you telling me?"

He shifted in his seat. "Look, I had a life in Chicago, and now I'm going to have a life here."

"No. That's not nearly good enough. What's going on? Start at the beginning and speak slowly."

He was silent for a long time. Domino strolled into the living room and jumped onto the sofa. Ali stroked her and took comfort from the cat's loud purring. She had a bad feeling about what he was going to tell her.

"Is this about Leigh?" she asked, praying he would say no.

"Yes, in part. It's also about my father. I don't want to tell you because it will change things."

"How?"

His mouth thinned. "You won't like me anymore."

"I doubt that. Why don't you start talking. If at any point I start disliking you, I'll warn you so you can stop."

"Fair enough." He leaned back in the chair. "I told you about the competition in my family. The need for the son to do better than the father."

She nodded.

"While I was growing up, my father always told me I could never beat him. He said I wasn't nearly smart enough. When he wasn't insulting me, he was ignoring both me and my mom. He never loved her. They married because she was rich, and he made her think he adored her."

He looked away. Ali had a feeling he was staring into a past that still brought him pain.

"His rejection destroyed her. I told you she died but the truth is, she killed herself."

Ali didn't know what to think, let alone say. She leaned forward and touched Matt's hand. "I'm sorry."

He shrugged. "At least I didn't find her. It happened while I was in school. I'd never much liked my father before that, but after her death, I hated him. I swore I would crush him like a bug. I grew up wanting revenge."

He squeezed her fingers and released her. "So I went to college, got good grades, met the right people, and went into the family firm. As I told you before, I squeezed my father out into the cold on my thirtieth birthday. I didn't crush him, but I let him know I could have. Then I started looking around for a wife. The right kind of wife."

"A blue blood," Ali said, remembering the photo in Matt's room at the B and B. "The right connections, the right family, plenty of money, and straight blonde hair."

Despite the pain in his eyes, Matt chuckled. "You left out the merger. Leigh's father owned a small financial firm that had cachet but no cash flow. We joined the two and I married his daughter. It was the business arrangement that let me destroy my father. As I told you before, Leigh and I had agreed that being friends was enough to build a marriage, but that all changed when she fell in love."

Ali felt those last words stab her clear down to her heart. She didn't want to hear about anyone else loving Matt.

"So it wasn't happily ever after?" she asked.

"Anything but. Leigh decided she wanted a real marriage, and I was too busy to care. I gave her gifts instead of time. She was desperate to get my attention, and I couldn't be bothered. Then she got sick."

He sat forward, resting his forearms on his thighs. "I should have been there more. My God, the woman was dying, and I was busy running my deals. The day she died, Birmingham International was part of the second biggest IPO in history. I was too busy to get home. The nurse had to call to tell me Leigh was gone."

He raised his head and looked at her. "I knew in that second I'd become a man my father could be proud of. I was even worse than him. It wasn't supposed to be like that. I was supposed to be a good and decent man. I was ashamed, and it was too late to change any of it."

Ali knelt in front of him and put her arms around him. "It's all right."

"No, it isn't. That's why I walked away from it all. Because I couldn't stay and continue to be my father. All Leigh wanted was a little time and affection. I couldn't spare her an hour out of my schedule so that I could hold her hand while she died. The nurse told me the last thing my wife said was to tell me that she loved me."

Tears glinted in his eyes. Ali ached for him. She pulled him close and held him. His pain washed over her, making her want to weep *for* him as well as with him.

"You're not that man anymore," she said. "You've changed."

"I want to believe that. And while I'm here, in Saint

Maggie, I can. So that's why I'm selling the company. We'll just live here like regular folks. You want normal," he reminded her. He smoothed her hair back from her face. "How does that sound?"

"It sounds really great."

She knew that with time he would start to care about her, wouldn't he? They would get married and raise their child together. It would be perfect.

So why did it feel so very wrong?

He straightened. "I'd better get back to the store. Who knows what's going on down there. Will you be all right by yourself?"

"I'm fine. In fact I'm feeling so good, I might go see my friend Clair. I want to tell her the good news."

Ali sat curled up on a sofa in Clair's oversized family room, sipping a special tea her friend had sworn helped with pregnancy-induced nausea. She'd just finished telling Clair about Matt's confession.

"So it's all settled. He's going to stay in Saint Maggie. We're going to raise the baby together. At least I think we are. That part didn't get discussed. I should be ecstatic. Why aren't I?"

Clair regarded her thoughtfully. "Maybe because you're finally getting your dream of normal. It's one thing to wish for it, another to live it. I've always suspected that you talked about finding some normal guy because you thought you should, when in truth you were afraid it would bore you to tears."

"That's what Matt said," Ali muttered glumly. "So if I don't want normal, what do I want?"

"Matt. You said you're in love with him."

"I am. And he's happy about the baby, which is more than a lot of men would be. I do want to be with him. All of this is perfect. So what's wrong?"

Clair shifted on the sofa so that she was facing Ali. "Maybe it's that you don't believe he could be happy running Harry's business."

"Worse. I don't think Harry is going to sell to him." She sipped her tea, which tasted like dirty peppermint.

"He can buy the hardware store," Clair said helpfully. "Or maybe a winery."

"Maybe." Although Ali couldn't see it happening. Matt in a leather apron, selling nails? Or picking grapes?

"I should just be happy," she said. "I love him, and he wants to be with me. He hasn't actually said he loves me, but he cares and that's a start. Once he sells Birmingham International, he'll have plenty of money, so I don't have to worry that he's involved with me for mine. I guess all my dreams are coming true."

Ali just wished she felt better about the whole thing.

chapter eighteen

Three days later Ali watched the last of the customers leave the store. She stood alone at the front window of her apartment, staring down into the parking lot. Lights clicked out a short time later. She waited for Matt to climb the stairs to spend the evening with her as he had for the past three evenings.

They would have sensible conversation over the sensible dinner he insisted on fixing for her, because he wouldn't let her put out much more effort than eating and drinking. They would talk about events around town, how she was feeling, maybe watch a little TV, and then he would leave. No sex, no declarations of love, no excitement. If this was normal, she wanted a rain check.

He was acting as if she was made of pixie wings, and he was in his dotage. He'd talked about opening a pet store in the new strip mall going in at the edge of town. It was scary. Worse, it wasn't Matt. She missed the take-charge bully who bought her computers and wanted to put her cooking on a schedule. She also missed her store.

Tonight she was going to tell him that she was going back to work, pregnancy or no pregnancy. She was having a baby, not fighting a debilitating illness.

That decided, she let the curtains fall back in place and walked to the sofa. Two minutes later she heard his footsteps on the stairs. Every sense went on alert. Her stomach dove for her toes, taking her composure with it and leaving her feeling exposed and shaky. It didn't matter that he was making her crazy, she still adored him. In fact she could forgive a lot of his idiosyncrasies if he would just make passionate love with her.

He opened the door to her apartment and smiled. "Hey, gorgeous. How are you feeling?"

"Good."

She took in the height and sheer masculinity of him. His thick dark hair hung to the bottom of his collar and tumbled over his forehead. Stubble darkened his jaw. He still wore a tailored long-sleeved shirt and khakis, but he'd removed the dark green store apron. He was handsome, intelligent, and the father of her child. Ali couldn't help a proud smile. If nothing else, her baby would be starting out with some very nice DNA.

"We need to talk," he said, moving to the sofa.

She closed the door and moved after him. "I agree." She settled onto the club chair at right angles to her sofa and leaned forward expectantly. "Matt, this is crazy. We have to make some changes."

"You read my mind."

Matt set several ledgers on the counter. Ali hadn't noticed them before. Now she frowned as she recognized her accounting books. He opened one and stared at a column.

"It was slow this afternoon," he said, by way of introduction. "I was able to finish going over your books." His dark gaze met hers. "Do you know how much money you're losing everyday? Just for starters, your payroll is insane. You have too many people on your staff. The college kids work crazy hours. From what I can see, you let them show up about whenever they want. I can't find any kind of schedule."

Ali blinked at him. *He wanted to talk about business?* "You know, Matt, a conversation like this is what got you in trouble before."

"I know, but this is important. I want you to be as successful as possible. I have years of experience streamlining businesses, finding every single extra dollar, and putting it to good use."

She swallowed her rising irritation, telling herself that he wasn't being insulting on purpose. This was his way of keeping her and the baby safe. "I don't need this lecture. I'm happy as I am." She took the book he held from him, closed it, and set it on the table. "My business is doing well. As for the college students, I let them work out their own hours. I only ask that they be here on Saturdays."

"That's crazy. You have to be more organized. You have to have a schedule."

"Why?"

He glared at her. "It's just how things are done. I can only imagine the bigger mess at the tea shop and bed-and-breakfast."

Despite her best intentions, her temper started to flare. "Who do you suggest I fire there? Kasey? Maybe Dora and Willie? I'm sure they could find other jobs, and if they don't, there's always the welfare system, right? Or maybe a homeless shelter."

He looked a bit chagrined as he leaned back on the sofa and shifted uncomfortably. "No, of course not. In fact I was thinking about Willie. He seems like a smart kid, so I made a couple of phone calls to get him interviews. There are a few big companies in Los Angeles that I've dealt with over the years. They would have probably been interested in him anyway, but I made sure he was on the slate. The rest is up to him."

She wasn't sure if she should strangle him or laugh. "Matt, you make me crazy. Even while we're having this ridiculous conversation, you're proving my point."

His gaze narrowed. "What point?"

"That this isn't about business, it's about life. I'm not interested in making more money. I do fine with what I have. Decadent Delight was always about having a dream and bringing it to reality. About making an amazing piece of chocolate that could, in a perfect world, change someone's life.

"I only ever wanted to be self-sufficient and give back to the community," she continued. "That's why I hire all those kids. So they can go to college and earn spending money and have fun at this time in their life. I work with the local women's shelter because they were there for Kasey and saved her life when all her husband wanted to do was use her body for batting practice. I don't want to win, I want to belong."

Matt glared at her. "You're wrong. What matters is being number one."

"You don't believe that anymore. You walked away from your company."

"That's different."

"Tell me how."

He sputtered but didn't answer. Suddenly a lightbulb went off in her head and the brightness nearly blinded her. He was doing, fixing, whatever she wanted to call it because that was how men worked. Men who were involved with a woman did things for her. They washed cars, fixed squeaky doors, rotated tires. After they'd made love the first time and she'd felt all mushy and connected, she'd wanted to talk about emotions, cuddle, be romantic. Matt had obviously felt something for her as well, because he'd tried to fix her business. It was his way of offering her a meaningful—if only to him—gift.

He was doing the same thing now. "Fixing" her business to make it do better. If he was a baker, he would have come home with a dozen loaves of bread. If he was a mechanic, he would have tuned her car. But he wasn't any of those things. He was Matthew Birmingham, tycoon.

"And once a tycoon, always a tycoon," she murmured.

"What?"

"Matt, this isn't necessary," she said gently, oddly touched by his ineptness. "I don't need you to take care of me."

"Someone has to do it. You're not going anywhere by yourself."

She ignored the insult. He couldn't help it. He was just being stupid.

"You can't hide from what you are," she told him.

"What I am is the guy who's going to drag you into the modern age."

"No, you're a big-time businessman who is suffocating in this one-horse town."

He looked as if she'd sucker punched him. "No. I'm happy here."

"Are you? Really?"

He avoided her gaze. "Absolutely."

She wanted to believe him because having him around was the best thing that had ever happened to her. But if he didn't belong here, she had to let him go. And then she knew the truth.

"You want to go back, but you're afraid," she said.

He moved to the sofa and pulled her close. "I won't be that man again, Ali. I swear, I'd rather be dead. I was such a bastard. I'm better here."

"Don't you think the kind of man you are today is about who you are, not your location?"

"I can't be sure."

"I'm sure," she said, and she was because she loved him. He made her crazy, and she couldn't imagine a world without him. But not this way. Not with him needing so much more than Saint Maggie had to offer.

"You have to go back," she told him. "You have to make peace with it all. Sell the business, don't sell the business. It doesn't matter what you decide, but you have to face the demons and win."

His dark eyes studied her face. "Come with me."

Come with me . . . not I love you. She told herself it didn't matter, even though she knew it did.

"I can't. You have to figure this one out on your own. I know you'll make peace with it all. If that happens, call me and then we'll figure out who's going to live where. I'm betting you'll be fine."

The shadows were back, haunting his expression. "And if you're wrong?"

She kissed him instead of speaking because she didn't have an answer for that.

Two hours later Ali was still trying to convince herself that Matt would go back to Chicago, figure out his life, realize he loved her, and return to her side in forty-eight hours. She wasn't buying into the story.

Her mind swirled, whirled, and dipped in a dizzying display of overload. There was too much to consider. The baby, Matt leaving, his guilt about Leigh, the baby, Ali's love for him, her own past, the losers she'd dated, and her fear that she would never measure up to her price tag. Plus, she was pregnant!

When Ali couldn't stand it another second, she grabbed her coat and hurried downstairs. Ten minutes later she knocked on her mother's front door, then pushed inside.

"It's me," she called as she shut the door behind her and locked it. Charlotte Elizabeth never bothered with something as mundane as locking her own door.

"We're in the family room, darling."

Ali followed the sound of the cultured voice that had done hundreds of voice-overs for everything from cars to hemorrhoid cream. She walked through the stylishly decorated living room, complete with several Dali originals, past the dining room where a small but elegant Renoir graced the far wall, down the short hall, and into the spacious family room.

Charlotte Elizabeth rested on her knees in the center of the thirty-by-thirty room. A white, oversized sectional sofa sat on the wall opposite the wide-screen television and smoked-glass cabinet with every television surround-sound DVD-video device known to man. An impressive array of clickers lined up neatly on a glass and marble coffee table.

Drapes covering French doors leading to the patio and pool beyond had been pulled shut against the darkness.

Her mother looked up and smiled. "I'm so glad you stopped by," she said. "Miss Sylvie is a little down in the mouth. Aren't you, sweet girl?"

Her mother, a beautiful, award-winning actress and all-around semi-normal person, cupped her pig's face and kissed the spot right between the animal's eyes.

Charlotte Elizabeth returned her attention to her daughter. "She misses Lucky. Harry moved out a couple of days ago and took that ugly dog with him. I don't miss one hair on that mongrel's head, but Miss Sylvie just hasn't been herself. She's barely eating. I'm concerned she's going to fade away."

Ali eyed the impressive build of her mother's pet. "She's got a ways to go before you have to worry."

"I suppose you're right. In the meantime, I'm doing my best to brighten her spirits."

It was only then that Ali noticed the pile of Hermès scarves in a tangle on the floor. As Ali shrugged out of her coat and tossed it over an arm of the sofa, her mother pulled out a length of silk and draped it around the pig's neck. All of Paris would be appalled, Ali thought with a slight smile.

She settled on the sofa and sighed. At least here she didn't have to worry about having an emotional crisis. Her mother would keep the conversation fixed firmly on issues that affected her the most. They would discuss the baby, Rick's lack of a love life, and the latest trend that was sweeping through Los Angeles. Exactly what Ali needed to get her mind off the disaster that was her life.

"I see that Matt left," her mother said, settling on a

blue-and-gold scarf and tying it in a jaunty knot. "He had a suitcase with him, so I'm assuming he's heading back to Chicago."

Ali opened her mouth to respond and found that she couldn't speak. Everything blurred. Suddenly she was sobbing as if her heart had broken . . . which it had. The man she loved had just walked out on her.

"Oh, Ali," Charlotte Elizabeth murmured, moving next to her on the sofa and pulling her close. "My poor little girl."

Surprisingly comforting arms wrapped around her. A familiar scent—of both Charlotte Elizabeth and one of her many perfumes—surrounded Ali, making her feel as if she was eight again and had just found out that the girl she'd thought of as her best friend was making fun of her behind her back.

"He's gone," Ali said, then hiccupped. "He's gone. I sent him away because I'm an idiot, even though it was the right thing to do. What if he doesn't come back? What if he doesn't know he's in love with me?"

"Matt isn't that stupid, darling. Of course he'll realize he loves you." Her mother rocked her back and forth. "Hush, sweet girl."

Despite the pain in her heart and heaviness weighing down her soul, Ali couldn't help laughing. "That's what you said to Miss Sylvie."

"Both my girls are sad."

Ali straightened and managed a watery smile. "I always wanted a sister, Mom, but I never thought she'd be a pig."

But Charlotte Elizabeth didn't respond to the feeble joke. Instead she stroked her daughter's face. An odd expression darkened her beautiful green eyes. "You never call me Mom."

Ali ducked her head. "I know," she whispered. "It never sounded right, I guess. . . ." She swallowed as more tears flowed down her cheeks. She brushed them away with the back of her hand, then looked at her mother. "I can't ever make up for the past," she said. "I'm sorry. I wish I could, but there's no way."

Charlotte Elizabeth frowned delicately. "What on earth are you talking about?"

"The million dollars. Losing that movie deal. It's not as much about the money as the lost opportunity. I know that turning down that role meant you lost favor with the studio. That was a big deal back then." Ali bit her lower lip. "I'm really sorry."

Charlotte Elizabeth reached forward and grabbed her in a firm hug. "Silly, silly girl," she said fiercely. "Is that what you think? Is that what you've thought all these years?" Her mother released her, then took hold of her shoulders and shook her slightly. "Do you think I cared about that movie?"

Ali sniffed. "Didn't you?"

"No. And the reason I didn't work as much after you were born was that I didn't want to. There were dozens of offers and many of them for a lot more money, but they didn't matter. Then I met Richard. So my not working again was never about you. Is that what you've thought all these years?"

"Afraid so."

Ali turned her mother's words over in her head. Was she telling the truth? Could Ali believe that she hadn't messed up everything by being born?

Her mother touched her damp cheek, then her chin. "But even if turning down that movie had meant I never worked again, you were worth it." She smiled that slow, beautiful smile that had won the hearts of millions of men back in the sixties and seventies. "I know you don't completely believe me now, but when you hold your own child for the first time, you'll see what I mean. Every baby is worth a million dollars. Every new life is worth everything. You were a miracle to me. The best miracle in my life. Yes, Richard was my great love, but you, Ali, you were my child. Who would have thought I would be so blessed?"

Until that moment Ali hadn't realized there was a knot inside of her. A small hardness that came from always worrying about being enough. For the first time ever, the knot loosened and slipped away. Peace stole over her, peace and a sense of belonging.

"Thank you, Mom," she whispered hoarsely and hugged her mother tight.

They clung together for a few minutes. When they separated, Ali brushed the lingering dampness from her face. "Are you okay with the baby?"

Charlotte Elizabeth laughed. "I'm thrilled. Although I have a few things to say to Matt when next he shows up."

Some of Ali's peace faded. "I just hope he does come back," she said, looking away from her mother and focusing her attention on a slumbering Miss Sylvie. Her large pig-sister had stretched out on a cashmere blanket by the sofa.

"He'll be here," her mother said firmly. "If nothing else, you have to resolve the logistics of the baby. If he's not already in love with you, a few more weeks in your company will take care of that."

From my mother's lips to God's ears.

Her mother tilted her head. "Of course you didn't tell him you loved him either, did you?"

Ali cleared her throat. "How did you know I cared about him?"

"You aren't the type to sleep around, more's the pity. If you did, you wouldn't take everything so much to heart. But you're not going to change. My point is that you wouldn't have allowed yourself to get pregnant if you hadn't cared."

"I didn't exactly plan this."

"Perhaps not the baby itself, but you were there at the getting-naked part and obviously didn't protest."

No, Ali hadn't even thought about protesting. She'd wanted him too much.

"Matt is a lot like you," her mother said. "He doesn't sleep around, either, so the fact that you were lovers is significant."

Ali wanted to believe her. "You're assuming a lot. Is this where I remind you that he's gone?"

"Oh, he'll be back."

"How can you be sure about that or any of this?"

Charlotte Elizabeth grinned. "Ali, there's a lot to be learned on daytime television. If you'd been watching Oprah, you wouldn't be in half the trouble you're in now."

Ali wanted to tell her mother that she was crazy, but Ali had a bad feeling that, in this case, Charlotte Elizabeth was right.

"I hate waiting," she told her mother. "I want to go after him, but I know that would be wrong. He has to figure this out on his own."

"Young love," Charlotte Elizabeth said with a sigh. "I wouldn't go through it again for a million dollars."

chapter nineteen

Matt paced the length of the United Airlines terminal at LAX. He was a little early for his flight to Chicago. After buying a cup of coffee from Starbucks, he'd gone to the newsstand and picked up the current issues of *Fortune* and *Business Week*. But instead of reading them, he was walking back and forth trying to figure out what to do.

He had to go back to Chicago. He knew that now. Leaving without warning had damaged the company, and he had a responsibility to fix that. He still intended to sell the whole thing, but it would fetch a better price when he'd mended broken bridges with his clients and his employees. He also wanted to talk with Jeff some more. Once the two men had been close. Their relationship was worth saving.

The third time he passed the pay phones, he couldn't stand it anymore. Normally the phones were three deep in people, but this late, they were nearly all empty. Matt took a step toward the nearest one, fishing out his calling card from his wallet as he walked.

He set his bags and magazines on the floor, his coffee on the small shelf, inserted his card, then punched the numbers for Saint Maggie's directory assistance. Two minutes later he heard a phone ringing.

"Hello?"

"It's Matt," he said, leaning against the wall and cupping the receiver between his chin and his shoulder. "Did I wake you?"

Ali sighed softly. "No. I'm not sleepy."

"Where are you?" he asked, imagining her rooms and wanting to place her in one.

"In the living room. On the sofa."

He pictured her curled up in a corner, knees drawn up to her chest, hair long, loose, and curly, Domino stretched out beside her. His chest tightened as he added details to the image.

"Want to hear something funny?" he asked.

"Sure."

"I don't know your phone number. I guess there's never been a reason to call. You shouldn't be listed."

She chuckled. "Why are you still trying to run my life?"

"Because I already miss you."

He heard her breath catch. "Matt . . . me, too."

Something warm filled his chest. This sensation was less about his libido and more about his heart. He liked it. He liked her. A lot.

"How are you feeling?" he asked.

"Okay. I haven't thrown up in a while, if that's what you're asking."

"I wasn't, but thanks for the update. So what are you doing?"

"Reading my pregnancy books."

"Anything interesting?"

"All of it, but I have to tell you that delivery is way more vicious than I would like."

He wasn't ready to think about that. "We have time before it's an issue."

"It's never going to be an issue for you. I'll be the one screaming my lungs out."

He held the phone a little tighter, as if he could somehow close the distance between them. "I had a thought."

"Did it hurt?"

He smiled. "Very funny. It's actually a serious and profound thought."

"Oh, then let me sit up. That way I'll pay attention more."

He pictured her pushing herself into a sitting position, her long hair tumbling over her shoulders, her curvy body moving with a sensuousness that took his breath away. She would be—

"Matt?"

"Huh? Oh, my thought. While I was driving to the airport, I was going over all that we talked about. My past, my relationship with my father. Do you realize all our lives we've both been driven to act because of our parents? For you it was Charlotte Elizabeth and the million dollars. For me it was my father."

"I hadn't considered that. So we have something in common."

"A big something."

"I was thinking, too," she murmured. "Want to hear my earthshaking news?"

"Sure."

His throat tightened. Was she going to tell him that

she loved him? Because he desperately wanted to hear the words. He had to know that all he'd told her about his life hadn't driven her away.

"You've helped me see that I'm okay because of who I am and not what I do," she told him. "The irony is you define yourself by what *you* do. I think you need to learn the same lesson."

The disappointment was bitter on his tongue. "Hey, it's too late for psychological analysis."

She sighed. "I miss you, Matt. I want you gone, but I miss you."

"You want me gone?" he teased, knowing he had no right to want her to confess all when he wasn't willing to do the same. But he couldn't promise Ali anything until he'd made peace with his past.

"You know what I mean," she told him. "You need to do this."

"Agreed. And I swear I'll be back. Then you and I will have some serious talking to do."

"I look forward to that."

"Which means if you go online, no picking up on strange guys."

She groaned. "That's so likely. Me, using a computer?"

"Give it a try. Rick will help. If you're feeling brave, visit the Internet," he said. "I signed you up on AOL. You'll see the icon on your computer downstairs. The password is 'pink pig.'"

She laughed. The low, throaty sound carried over the phone lines and dove directly for his groin. It settled there, making him ache with need.

"I have a vague idea about AOL and no clue as to what

an icon is," she told him. "If I figure that much out, I guess I'll need a password, so thanks."

"It's not too hard. You'll get it."

He heard an airline employee announcing the preboarding for his flight. "That's my flight. I have to go."

She cleared her throat. "You know you can call me from Chicago, right? In fact, it would be a really good thing. Otherwise I'm bound to start thinking that you've forgotten me and then I'll send Charlotte Elizabeth after you. You wouldn't want that."

He touched the telephone, as if the contact would carry across the phone lines. "I promise to call. Try not to rescue the world while I'm gone."

"Try not to take it over."

He heard another boarding announcement for his flight. He drew in a breath. "Ali, I'm going to have to go, but I'll call you soon, all right?"

"Sure."

There was a moment of silence. He had so many things he wanted to say to her. "I know I complain about you rescuing the world, but if you hadn't rescued me, I'd still be lost."

She made a choked sound, as if she were fighting back tears. "You would have found your way home eventually."

"I'm not so sure." He had a feeling he would have spent a long time stumbling around in the dark. She'd been his light. She'd taught him . . . everything.

"Ali, will you do me a favor?"

"Sure," she said without hesitating. "What?"

"Think of me."

"Always."

He hung up with the sound of her promise filling his ear. He picked up his bag, his magazines, and his coffee, then made his way to his plane. After over a year, he was finally going home.

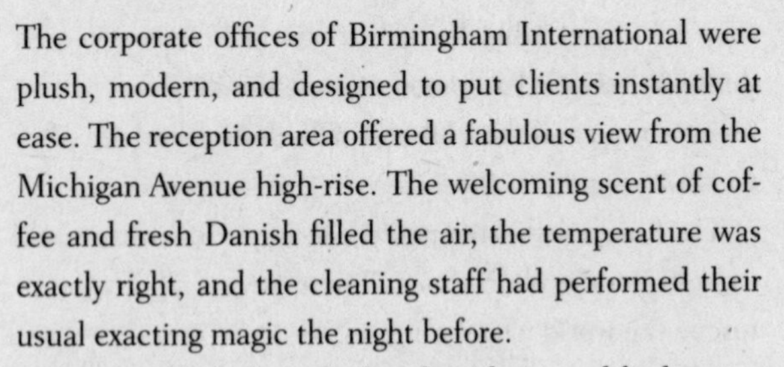

The corporate offices of Birmingham International were plush, modern, and designed to put clients instantly at ease. The reception area offered a fabulous view from the Michigan Avenue high-rise. The welcoming scent of coffee and fresh Danish filled the air, the temperature was exactly right, and the cleaning staff had performed their usual exacting magic the night before.

Matt walked through the glass doors and had an instantaneous feeling that he'd never left. Everything was as he remembered, right down to the receptionist's elegantly coiffured graying hair.

Rita had been with the company nearly thirty years. She manned the front desk with the efficiency and attention to detail of a general planning a strategic battle. She greeted each call and visitor with professionalism and courtesy. He'd never once seen her speechless.

Until today. She looked up, a formal smile in place, then froze. Her mouth dropped open, her brown eyes widened, and she actually spilled coffee onto the cherrywood reception desk.

"Mr. Birmingham?" she sputtered.

"Good morning, Rita. I'm glad you're still here. Is Jeff in yet?"

"I, ah, yes. He's in his office. But Mr. Birmingham, are you back?"

No, he wasn't back. He was here to get his company

ready to sell, then he was going to walk away from the monster. But there was no point in starting rumors with the staff. So he simply smiled and nodded. "I'm back," he said, and headed down the carpeted corridor to his office.

Rita didn't say anything. However, her paralysis must have faded as soon as he was out of sight because by the time he reached the T-intersection that marked the beginning of the executive suite, he could see his own secretary, Mrs. Ferguson, hanging up her phone. There was a slightly dazed expression on her well made-up face. By the time he was within hailing distance she'd managed to control her expression.

"Mr. Birmingham," she said pleasantly as he approached, as if he'd only been gone for the day. "How nice to see you."

She rose and opened his door for him, then followed him inside.

He came to a stop in the center of the room. He'd been gone over a year, yet nothing had changed. The carpeting underfoot, the wide desk, the floor-to-ceiling windows, the view, were all as he remembered. There wasn't a speck of dust or the hint of mustiness to tell him that he'd been gone more than a few minutes. The only physical clue was that his normally messy desk was swept clean of any papers, folders, or notes.

The penthouse condo he'd shared with Leigh had been where he'd slept, but this was home. It was here he'd plotted and dreamed, celebrated successes, and studied failures so as not to repeat the same mistakes.

Ali had celebrated her thirtieth birthday with her brother and fighting off a rude reporter. He'd celebrated his by throwing his father out of the family business and getting drunk right here in this office.

"I'll be right back with your coffee and the *Wall Street Journal*," Mrs. Ferguson said, walking around him and turning on his computer. She paused, questions darkening her bright blue eyes.

She had to be in her early sixties—she'd worked for his father for years before Matt had stolen her from the elder Birmingham. Mrs. Ferguson was a widow and a gossip magnet. She'd never uttered an indiscreet word in her life, but she listened so sympathetically that people couldn't help talking to her. She also didn't keep secrets from her boss, which was probably why complaints were murmured within her hearing. A word whispered to "Mrs. F." eventually came back to the man in charge.

Matt touched her arm. "I'm fine," he said. "Thanks for being concerned."

She worried her lower lip. "You were gone for a very long time, sir. Some people thought you weren't coming back."

"What did you think?" he asked.

She tilted her head slightly. "I hoped you would find what you were looking for. Did you?"

"Yes, I did."

What he'd found was himself, and a way to live in peace. He might never again feel the thrill of the chase and the high of being successful, but he would also never have to look at himself in a mirror and see his father. He would never again be ashamed of himself.

"I know it's very late to be saying this, sir, but I am sorry about your wife," Mrs. Ferguson told him.

"Thank you," he told the older woman.

Mrs. Ferguson smiled and excused herself.

Matt sat behind his desk. The chair felt good . . . familiar. He found himself anticipating reading the paper and wondered what everyone in the company was working on. Not that he cared for himself. He simply wanted to know how profitable the firm was going to be when he sold it.

By the time Mrs. Ferguson returned with his coffee and newspaper, he'd already made a list. "I want a meeting with each of the department heads, starting within the hour," he said. "Tell them to be prepared to give me updates on every account on the books. Where we are, where we're going. This afternoon I want to talk to the vice presidents of Finance and of Human Resources. Tell them no bullshit. I want the truth, however ugly it might be."

Mrs. Ferguson continued scribbling on her pad, then nodded. She finished and looked at him. "Have you spoken with your father, sir?"

"No." And he wasn't going to.

"Look what the cat dragged in."

Matt looked up and saw Jeff Peterson stroll into the room. Matt studied him, trying to judge his mood.

Jeff winked at Mrs. Ferguson, then pulled out a chair in front of the desk and sat down. The secretary walked out of the room and shut the door.

"I heard you were back," Jeff said evenly.

"Are you surprised?" Matt asked, wondering what his second-in-command was thinking.

"Yeah. I didn't think you'd bother." Jeff stared at him. "Now what? Are you here for good or just dropping by on your way to your next retail job? I hear they're hiring at Watertower Plaza. Plenty of good seasonal opportunities there."

He no longer had to guess at Jeff's mood. "You're still angry."

Jeff shrugged. "I shouldn't give a damn about this place, but I do. I guess what they say about teaching an old dog new tricks is true."

"Are you still leaving?"

"Are you still selling out?"

"Yes."

"Then I guess we don't have anything to talk about."

But Jeff didn't move from his seat. Instead he picked up a pen from Matt's desk and turned it over and over.

"Remember Hercules Construction?" Jeff asked.

Despite the tension between them, Matt grinned. "Barry Newhouse. He couldn't decide if he wanted to run the biggest commercial construction company in the Midwest or start a singing career."

Jeff chuckled. "So one night when we'd all been working late, we took Barry to that karaoke bar and got him drunk so he'd sing."

"He was awful," Matt said as he leaned back in his chair, lost in the memory. "He sounded like a cat in heat. Remember the waitress was so shocked, she dropped her tray of drinks."

Jeff pointed at him. "And remember Vinnie—what was his last name?"

"He never said." Matt chuckled. "He claimed to be a former Mafia guy who had 'an unspecified amount of cash' he wanted to invest. He came to us because he figured we wouldn't ask so many questions."

"Right, and then he flew us to New York and sent hookers to our room."

Matt smiled at his friend. "Yeah, and you sent yours over to me."

Jeff shrugged. "I didn't have any use for her, and I figured all straight guys had a threesome fantasy. It was your big chance."

"To think that I blew it by turning those two ladies down."

Jeff continued to play with the pen. "While there isn't a funny story attached, one of my favorite deals was with those small banks."

Matt nodded. "We did some good there."

They'd been approached by a loose collection of small town banks. New banking regulatory laws allowed them to consolidate, and they wanted to take advantage of that to survive. He and Jeff had put in hundreds of hours. He doubted they'd even broken even on the deal. But the IPO had gone off without a hitch, and the financial institutions were thriving.

Matt studied his friend. "I know what you're doing," he said. "You want me to remember the good times so I won't sell."

"It crossed my mind." Jeff looked at him. "You think I don't know what your father was like? We were friends in school, Matt. I saw what he did to you. I heard the things he said. And I was there when you swore on your mother's grave you would take him down."

Matt remembered that, too. "I paid a high price to honor that promise. Maybe too high. What's the point of beating the devil if I simply take his place?"

"It doesn't have to be like that." Jeff leaned toward him and set down the pen. Then he put his hands flat on the table. "Birmingham International used to be a great company. Sure we handled the flashy IPOs and made way too much money, but there was more to it than that. What about the good we did?"

"Maybe." Matt didn't want to remember. His mind was made up. "Anyway, why does it matter? I thought you were leaving."

Jeff shrugged. "I might be willing to rethink that, but only if you're staying. We built this together, Matt. We should see it through."

Matt hated that he was tempted. Everything his friend said hit him directly in the gut . . . and the heart. He'd always loved his job. For a long time the focus had been on destroying his father, and that was wrong. But when it wasn't all about taking down Jonathan Birmingham, it was damn good.

Matt raised his eyebrows. "I thought you were pissed off at me."

"I am, but I guess I'm going to let it go. *If* you make the right decision. If you decide to up and leave, then I'll know you're nothing but a coward and a quitter."

Matt smiled wryly. "Gee, Jeff, tell me what you really think."

"I think you belong here. I think you can lead the company without turning into your father. And I think without Birmingham International, you'll be miserable, and you'll make everyone who cares about you miserable as well."

Matt wanted to tell his friend he was wrong, but then he remembered his compulsion to "fix" Ali's business. How he'd brought in a computer and hooked her up to the Internet when she would rather have eaten glass.

"Maybe," he conceded. "Let me think about it."

"I'm not going anywhere," Jeff said. "At least not for now."

Jeff rose to his feet and left. Matt watched him go. He felt the temptation of his old life, but what about Ali and the promises he made to her to return? What about the fact that he'd never felt about anyone the way he felt about her? What about the baby?

"This is what I found," Rick said two days later as he bounded into the store holding several papers in his hand. "It's all in your head."

Ali whirled to face her stepbrother. It was midafternoon, and the store was quiet. They were alone among the samplings of chocolate. She put her hands on her hips and glared at him.

"Don't even think that, let alone say it. I refuse to believe even one article has suggested morning sickness is all in my head."

Her brother grinned impishly. His well-cut hair tumbled over his forehead, giving him the appeal of Dennis the Menace, while giving her all the exasperation.

"Okay, maybe it's not in your head," he said, stopping next to her and offering the pages. "But there are studies that suggest stress exacerbates morning sickness. The primary cause is an increase in what they call the pregnancy hormone," he recited. "First-time mothers are especially sensitive. In fact—"

Ali held up her hand to stop him in midsentence. She shook the papers at him. "I can read, you know. I can even do math."

"Ingrate."

He flopped down on one of the stools behind the counter. Dressed in dark slacks and an eggplant-colored shirt, he looked casual and relaxed. But despite his outwardly calm appearance, Ali knew that he was part of a plot.

"Why are you still here?" she asked, setting the pages down on the counter and folding her arms over her chest. "I'm feeling much better. You should go home."

"Ouch, and thanks for all your hospitality," he grumbled.

"I know what you're up to," she said, ignoring his complaint. "You and Charlotte Elizabeth have conspired to make sure that I'm never alone. Number one, I'm completely fine. I've also been reading the pregnancy books I bought, and I have a doctor's appointment on Monday. So get off of me. Number two, you have your own life, so go live it. Number three, you're getting on my nerves."

Rick grabbed a sheet of tissue paper from the box behind the display shelves and plucked out a piece of chocolate walnut fudge. He popped it in his mouth and chewed slowly. When he was finished with his treat, he spoke.

"Number one, you need me. Matt told you to check out articles on the Internet, which was a good idea. However, it requires you to actually approach your computer and type on the keys. Something you have yet to do. Therefore, without me, you would not be in possession of that cutting-edge information. Number two." He paused. "I forgot your list. What was next?"

She gritted her teeth and bit back a scream. "You make me crazy," she said.

"You love me and all the attention. You're crushed because Matt's gone, and if I wasn't here cheering you up, you'd spend your entire day in tears."

His words hit a little too close to home. Thanks to her new hormones, which apparently didn't have enough to do by causing her to barf her guts out every few hours, her eyes got watery at everything from the weather report to a cheerful "good morning." She blinked back the sudden tears.

"Jeez, I did *not* want to turn on the faucet," Rick grumbled, even as he came around the counter and took her in his arms. "It's okay, Brillo pad. You're gonna be fine."

"When?" she asked with a sniff. "He shouldn't have left me. I'm pregnant. I'm going to have his baby, and he doesn't care."

Rick tilted her face up and wiped away her tears with his fingers. "This is where I remind you that you told him to go. It was your theory that he had to leave so he *could* come back. You were the one talking about how he had to settle with his past before he could deal with his future."

"Sure, be a guy. Take his side."

She started to pull away, but Rick wouldn't let her. "I'm not on anyone's side. You're my sister and I love you. I'm just pointing out that I don't think Matt has walked off and left you. He's going to come back."

"Maybe I won't want him then," she said with another sniff.

Rick rolled his eyes. "That's mature. I'm so proud."

This time she shoved hard enough to break his hug. "You don't understand."

"I understand everything," he told her in that "I'm so superior" tone of voice that made her want to back the car over him. "You're scared because you're pregnant and in love with a guy who hasn't said he loves you back."

She glared at him. "How do you know that?"

"I know you. You have all the symptoms of someone who has fallen hard." Rick moved toward her and touched her shoulder. "If he'd told you he loved you and wanted to marry you, you would have told the world, and you wouldn't be so upset."

"Maybe," she admitted and sighed. "I know he cares, he calls every night. But I don't know how close that caring is to love."

"I know it's tough to wait, but that's what you have to do. Matt has a lot of his old life to work through."

She knew that. She also believed Matt would return to her. But what was she supposed to do in the meantime?

"I need to distract myself," she said and glanced toward the kitchen. "Maybe you could teach me to use the computer."

Rick clutched his chest and took several dramatic steps to the left. "The shock," he gasped, "is killing me!"

"Yeah, yeah, you're no Charlotte Elizabeth on the stage, that's for sure. So can you teach me?"

He straightened. "Absolutely. Matt showed me how to work the business programs. I've been entering data from the store. After that I figured I'd get started on the tearoom and B and B."

"Yuck. Did I mention I hate the new millennium?"

"You'll adore being computer-literate. You can send me e-mail."

"Why? I see you multiple times a day. It's not like I get a chance to miss you."

He sniffed. "I might just up and leave."

"When?" she asked, but there was affection in her voice.

"You just wait and see," he told her.

Before she could reply, the rumble of a large truck cut through her thoughts. She watched as a white cab and trailer pulled to a stop in front of the bed-and-breakfast.

The sign on the side identified the owners as a construction company in Los Angeles. A smaller truck pulled up behind the first.

"What on earth?" she asked.

"Let's go find out," her brother said as he headed for the door of the shop.

Ali followed, turned the lock, and put up the "temporarily closed" sign. She hurried through the kitchen and joined Rick to walk across the parking lot to the businesses across the street. Kasey and Sara had already collected out in front. Kasey was talking to a man holding a clipboard.

"We've got a work order," the man was saying. "Everything's been paid for. Remodeling, paint, wallpaper, the whole works. So just sign here."

Kasey took the clipboard and studied it.

"What's going on?" Ali asked.

"I'm not sure." Kasey handed her the board. "It lists everything we planned to do."

Ali scanned the list. Sure enough, each of the bed-and-breakfast rooms had a detailed inventory of work next to the room number. She flipped through the pages until the last one, which listed Matthew Birmingham as the name of the person who placed the order.

"Matt did this?" Kasey asked, voicing Ali's confusion.

"Looks like it," Ali said, grinning as she gave the work order back to her friend. Kasey began speaking with the contractor.

Ali didn't listen. She was too busy being happy. Matt wasn't forgetting about Saint Maggie or her. He was taking care of his old business, along with his new. He hadn't just walked away without a second thought or left anyone in the lurch. He hadn't forgotten the work he'd promised to do and was going to make sure it got done.

She rested her hands on her stomach. "Your dad is a very good man," she whispered.

Rick caught her eye and winked. "Maybe now you can keep the faucet off for a couple of days."

"Sure," she said, even as her happiness made her eyes fill up with tears.

"Women," her brother grumbled with disgust, even as he moved close enough to put his arm around her. "I can't wait for Matt to come back and take over."

"Me, either."

chapter twenty

"Don't tell Kasey," Matt said, "but I like the Four Seasons way better than the bed-and-breakfast."

Ali sat on a stool in her kitchen, the phone clutched tightly in her hand. She laughed softly. "Traitor. How can you say that?"

"Because there's not a frill in sight. Just plain walls, a plain bedspread, and no candles."

"You have no soul."

"I happen to have a very old soul. It just hates girly stuff."

"Does it hate me?"

"Oh, no. It has great affection for you. Hating girly stuff has nothing to do with liking or disliking girls. Or women."

"I'm glad to hear it."

Just the sound of his voice was enough to make her feel light enough to fly. Ali wanted to purr with contentment. Matt was calling every day, sometimes more than once a day, doing his best to stay connected.

"How's work?" she asked.

He hesitated. "Complicated. The cleanup is taking longer than I thought. I have disgruntled employees and wary clients."

He launched into a complicated story about an IPO for a company that sold shares in private jets for smaller corporations. Sort of an airborne time-share. Ali listened, not understanding all the details, but intensely aware of the excitement in his voice.

He loved his work. She'd never understood that before. For him, the numbers and possibilities blended together the same way sugar and cream did for her. His magic was a successful IPO, hers was a perfect piece of chocolate.

Fear swept through her. It was cold and dark and made her tremble. How could he turn his back on what he loved? And if he managed to do that, how could he ever be happy?

"Matt," she said, interrupting him in midsentence. "Are you sure you want to sell the company?"

"Of course. It's the right thing to do."

"It doesn't have to be. You're not the man you were a year ago. Maybe there's a way to have it all."

He laughed. "Don't worry. I know what I want. Just give me a little time and I'll be back."

"I hope so," she told him. "I need you."

I love you, but she didn't say that. Because as much as she wanted to speak the words, she'd promised herself she would only say them in person. She wanted to feel his arms around her as she spoke the truth.

"I need you, too," he said. "I want you to miss me a lot. Oh, how's the work going on the B and B?"

She told him about the refurbishing, then they talked

about Rick and her forays onto the Internet. But when they hung up, the fear was still with her. A man like Matt could never be happy in a place like Saint Maggie. Which meant she had to figure out if she could be happy anywhere else.

Matt turned the key and pushed open the front door. He'd been avoiding the condo for nearly ten days, but he couldn't do it any longer. So he forced himself to step over the threshold and enter the last place he'd seen Leigh alive.

He'd already gone looking for some hint of her spirit or essence by visiting her grave earlier that morning, but once he'd arrived and placed yellow roses on the cold, dry ground, he'd realized she'd never been there at all. If he had any chance of finding her to apologize and say goodbye, it would be here—where she'd lived, laughed, loved, and died.

He set his briefcase down and walked into the open living room, with its white-on-white decorations and floor-to-ceiling windows overlooking the lake. The house smelled faintly of cleaning products and emptiness. The weekly cleaning service had continued to look after the place, paid by the accountant who handled all of Matt's personal expenses.

He paused just past the sofa and studied the large framed photos on a side table by the fireplace, the two of them on their wedding day and another of them honeymooning in the Cayman Islands. As he looked at the pictures he saw something he'd never bothered to notice before. Leigh stared at him with adoration in her eyes, while he looked off into the distance.

She had loved him and he had run from those feelings, not knowing how to deal with them. He'd channeled his energy into business, becoming even more successful. He'd ignored her needs, ignored *her*. He'd been such a bastard. She should have left him a long time before she got sick, but that wasn't her way.

Matt turned to his left and headed down the hallway. The last room on his right was the master suite. Thick carpeting muffled the sound of his footsteps. Here the furnishings had an oriental influence. Black lacquered surfaces inlaid with mother-of-pearl. Leigh had always said how much she hated the set. A decorator had picked it out, insisting it was just the thing. Matt had agreed with her, overriding his wife's opinion. Now as he looked at the room of cream, white, and black accented with gold, he realized it was a cold, perfect place. But it could never be anyone's home.

He moved to the nightstand where he'd kept a picture of Leigh. Just in case company ever wandered into the bedroom. He touched the black frame, then traced the shape of his late wife's cheek. He'd never taken the time to know her. He'd sent his secretary out for gifts at birthdays and Christmas, he'd announced their vacation plans when it suited him to travel, and he had enjoyed her body when he'd needed sex.

On the far side of the bed he saw her day runner in its leather binder and a novel she'd been reading. A tattered bookmark indicated that she only had a couple of chapters left. Chapters she would never finish.

Any other reminder of her illness was gone. No hospital equipment hovered in the corner, no hint that someone had died here.

He walked through the sitting area and into the bathroom. Her clothes still hung in the closet. He opened the mirrored doors and stepped into the cedar-lined space. There he could press one of her sweaters to his face and inhale the scent of her. It was barely familiar.

Pain filled him. Pain and guilt and shame. He had never wanted to be the kind of man to treat a woman like that. And yet he had.

"I'm sorry," he breathed into the silence. "Leigh, I'm so sorry. I should never have married you. I should have let you be happy with someone who could appreciate you."

He bowed his head. The worst of it was he'd left her alone to die. He'd been too busy with his work.

That damn company. He had to get away from it before he turned back into his father. He wouldn't destroy Ali the way he'd destroyed Leigh. He couldn't.

He left the closet and the bedroom, returning to the living room. Once there he sat on the edge of the sofa and set his briefcase on the coffee table, then opened it. He stared at the dark-green foil candy box he'd asked Mrs. Ferguson to order shortly after he'd arrived in Chicago. As per his request, she'd used her own name and credit card so that no one would know it was for him.

Now he opened the box of chocolate hazelnut truffles and took out a single candy. He studied the gleaming surface, knowing that Ali had made this particular candy with her own hands. She'd wanted it to be perfect, because she always led with her heart and did her best. He bit into the truffle.

The flavor exploded on his tongue. Sweet and rich and consuming. Suddenly she was with him, in the room, demanding to know if color had been too expensive when they'd decorated their black and white palace. Telling him that he sure as hell wouldn't get away with ignoring her—not if he wanted a relationship. She expected better of him. She was laughing and arguing and alive and vital. She healed him. She made him whole. She would never let him turn into his father. He loved her.

A knock on the front door made him turn around. He saw Jeff standing there.

"Mrs. F. said you'd come back to look things over," his second in command said. "I thought you might want some moral support."

Matt motioned to the open box of chocolates. "Have one. Ali made them and they're terrific."

Jeff crossed to the table and picked up a chocolate. He chewed, then nodded. "Pretty good."

Matt frowned. "They're amazing."

"Yes, boss."

Boss. That's what he was. He owned Birmingham International. It had been in his family for nearly a hundred years.

"I love it too much to give it up," he said, staring down at the open box of chocolates. "And I love her too much to give her up."

"Then keep them both."

Simple words. Was it possible? Matt leaned back against the cushions and thought about how on earth he and Ali could blend their worlds. Dear God, her mother had a pig for a pet.

"She has a life in Saint Maggie. I couldn't ask her to give it up."

Jeff settled in a chair across from the sofa. "Then don't.

I know I'm going to hate myself for saying this, but the company could be relocated." He shuddered. "I'd go, even though I despise California. Or you could commute. Corporate jets and all that."

"Good point."

Matt wondered if it was possible to make it work. Did he have a choice? He loved Ali too much to ever let her go, but without the firm, he would die a little inside every single day.

He pushed the box of chocolates toward Jeff. "If I start acting like my father again, I'm counting on you to tell me. Of course that assumes you'll be sticking around."

Jeff bit into another truffle. "I think something could be worked out."

"I'd want you as my best man."

Jeff cleared his throat. "I'd be honored."

"I guess this is where I have to tell you that there will probably be a pig at the wedding."

"You know, this isn't your best side," Rick said helpfully.

Ali waved him away as she rinsed out her mouth. He didn't budge from his position in the doorway to the bathroom. After she'd finished brushing her teeth and had dried her mouth on a towel, she turned to glare at him.

"Can I please have some privacy? I don't enjoy throwing up every day, and having an audience doesn't improve the experience."

He waved the *What to Expect When You're Expecting* book at her. "Where's the infamous glow? They don't mention crankiness as a symptom of pregnancy. I'm going to have to send them a letter about their oversight."

"Leave me alone," Ali insisted, pushing past him. "I have to get back downstairs. I left Charlotte Elizabeth in charge, which is too scary to think about."

"Mom's fine," Rick told her. "I made the herbal tea Clair recommended. You know that always settles your stomach."

Ali cast a worried glance at the floor, then decided that her store could survive without her for a few more minutes. Although she generally only threw up once or twice a day, it took a few minutes for the queasiness to fade. Clair's tea was her best remedy for that.

"Okay," she said with a smile. "Thanks."

She walked into the living room and sank onto the sofa. Rick disappeared into the kitchen, only to reappear with a steaming mug. When he handed it to her, she breathed in the orange scent and sighed. "You're being very good to me, and I appreciate it."

He waved away the compliment. "I'm a saint. The town council has already approached me about a statue, but I'm not sure. Can a statue really have dignity if the subject isn't riding a horse?"

"What about statues of animals?" she asked. "They're rarely on horses."

He sniffed. "I'm ignoring you. Oh, and speaking of ignoring things, you haven't wanted to talk about this, but I think it's pretty funny that Harry got an offer for his business."

In addition to hiring the construction crew to finish his work at the bed-and-breakfast, Matt had sent a computer nerd who'd spent two days locked up with Rick while they designed her website, a selection of hats for

Miss Sylvie, toys—including an indoor jungle gym—for Sara's kids and the new playroom, and gourmet meal service that delivered hot, nutritious meals to Ali's door every evening promptly at six, when the store was closing. He'd even sent her mother flowers. Now Harry had received a mysterious offer from someone interested in buying his small business.

This was all Matt's doing. How was she supposed to resist the man? And when was he coming back to her? In their nightly conversations, he was decidedly vague about the actual date.

Ali blew on her hot tea, then took a sip. As the steaming liquid slipped down her throat, her stomach began to calm down.

"I miss him," she admitted aloud.

"Speaking of missing," Rick said brightly, "I'm going to be heading out of town for a few days."

"Oh? Where are you going? Europe?"

"Not exactly," he said shifting uncomfortably.

Ali set her tea down and stared. Her sophisticated, charming, always suave brother actually looked embarrassed. "Are you blushing?" she demanded.

Rick glared at her. "Of course not. I'm just going away for a couple of days."

"So you said. But not to Europe."

"No."

She waited. When he didn't say any more, she pressed the point. "Well, where are you going?"

He cleared his throat. "Chicago," he muttered. "Jeff Peterson called and asked me to dinner." Rick shrugged. "I said yes."

Ali blinked in surprise. "Matt's second-in-command?" She had a vague recollection of a tall, good-looking blond man. "Wow. I didn't know you two had talked."

"We had a few minutes together. I'm sure it's nothing, but it's only dinner."

"Well, who would have thought," Ali said softly. She rose and hugged her brother. "I hope everything works out for the two of you. He seemed very nice. Intelligent and successful. Nothing like Da-vede."

"Gee, thanks." Rick turned to leave. "I'll see you in a few days."

"Okay. Have fun."

He walked to the door and paused. Turning toward her, he snapped his fingers, as if he'd just remembered something. "I nearly forgot to tell you," he said, an impish light in his eyes. "You have a visitor. Matt's waiting downstairs."

Ali screamed, reached for a pillow on the sofa, and tossed it at her brother's head. But Rick was long gone, with only the sound of his laughter drifting back toward her.

Damn him, she thought frantically, rushing back into the bathroom and checking her face. She looked the same as always, except for the dark circles under her eyes. Despite spending about ten hours a night in bed, she wasn't sleeping very well. Her wild hormones, the changes in her life, and Matt being gone did not make a restful combination.

She quickly took a gulp of mouthwash, swished it around, and spit it out. Then she applied lipstick and smoothed her hair. Her apron lay where she'd tossed it in her haste to make it to the bathroom nearly a half hour before.

Matt, here! She couldn't believe it. Why hadn't Rick told her right away, the rat. That was so like him. She would find a way to pay him back later, but right now she had to go see Matt.

Just thinking his name made her heart beat faster, she thought as she hurried to the front door of her apartment and started down the stairs. Her legs trembled, her palms were sweaty, and there was a tumbling sensation in her stomach that had nothing to do with being pregnant.

Thrilled, excited, happy, and ready to jump into his arms, she raced into the kitchen. Matt stood by the metal sinks, looking out the window. He had his back to her. She studied him, every part of her hungry to see if he'd changed.

He was still tall, broad, and incredibly appealing. Instead of jeans or even khakis, he wore a tailored dark gray suit. His hair was shorter than she remembered, and there was an air of quiet confidence about him. Whatever demons he'd had before were long since laid to rest.

As if he'd sensed her presence in the room, he turned to face her. Her heart fluttered as she stared at his familiar face. Dark eyes brightened with pleasure. He smiled and she was lost.

"You look good," he said by way of greeting. "How do you feel?"

"Fine. I'm still wrestling with morning sickness, but it's getting better."

He jerked his head toward the front of the store. "Your mother has been giving me a blow-by-blow of your health. She's better than the Internet."

"Charlotte Elizabeth is an amazing woman," she agreed.

Matt's expression softened. "She's not the only one,

Ali. You're pretty amazing, too." He took a step forward. "I've missed you so much. I hated being without you."

She nodded. "Me, too."

"I took care of all the details I'd left behind here in Saint Maggie. All of them, except one. You."

She swallowed but couldn't speak. If her heart pounded any harder, it was going to snap a rib. She couldn't catch her breath or move or do anything but think how much she loved this man. If he wasn't here to tell her he wanted to spend the rest of his life with her, she didn't think she was going to survive.

With a flash of insight she realized that her mother had waited nearly forty years to meet the love of her life and once she had, no other man would do. Ali had a bad feeling she'd inherited her mother's need to love only one man—and for her that man was Matt.

He took a step toward her. The large kitchen island was still between them. Matt moved around it. "You've changed me, Ali. I'm not just talking about healing, although you had a part in that. There has been a fundamental shift in how I view things. You made me see how one person can make a difference. You showed me what it means to have a giving heart. I made a lot of mistakes before I met you. How I got lost in work, how I messed up my first marriage. I screwed up, I was selfish, I didn't listen or try to understand."

He paused, then walked over and took her hands in his. She nearly collapsed at the feel of his warm fingers entwining with hers. She wanted to throw herself at him, but she also wanted to hear what he was saying.

"I love you, Ali. I've never loved like this before. You

own me, body and soul, although I have to tell you I'm not that much of a prize."

Her heart stood still in a perfect moment of joy.

He released one of her hands and cupped her face. "I love you, and I hope you'll understand that my feelings have nothing to do with my responsibilities toward our child. I want to be with you always. I want to marry you and grow old with you. And I want to have many, many babies with you."

Possibly for the first time in her life, words failed her. Ali threw herself at Matt, wrapping her arms around him and feeling him pull her close.

"I love you," she breathed, as tears trickled down her cheeks. "I've loved you for a long time."

"I've loved you, too. I just didn't figure it out until I was ready to leave Saint Maggie. And then I didn't want to say anything until I knew I was coming back." He put his hands on her shoulders and shifted her back so he could stare into her face. "I need you to believe me, Ali. While I'm thrilled about you being pregnant, I'm not doing this because of the baby."

"I know. I love you. For always."

He searched her face. "Are you sure?" He took a deep breath. "Because I have another confession. One you may not like."

When he hesitated, she waited patiently, not afraid anymore. If Matt loved her, she had nothing to fear. She saw the trepidation in his eyes and suddenly she knew.

"You want to keep the business," she said.

"I do. It's in my blood. I wish it wasn't, but I can't walk away. I'm terrified I'll turn back into my father, but Jeff said he'll beat the crap out of me if I ever start, and I'm figuring you'll keep me in line, too." He looked at her hopefully. "I know it's not what you want. You want some normal guy, and I could try owning the hardware store or Harry's business—"

"Harry didn't sell," she said, cutting him off. "I knew his talk about wanting to get rid of it was so much hot air." She reached up and brushed her mouth against his. "Besides, I was mistaken about wanting a normal guy in my life. What I want is you. I suspected you were a tycoon when I fell in love with you, so this isn't a surprise. Keep your company and this time do it right."

He pulled her close and held her as if he would never let her go. "I want to find some land nearby and build new corporate headquarters for Birmingham International. I'll move the company to Saint Maggie so you can still have your store and your family close by."

"You don't have to," she said, pressing herself against him again. "While I still refuse to be a chain, I wouldn't mind having a branch or two. You think Chicago is ready for my chocolates?"

"Absolutely." He hugged her fiercely. "I need you, Allison Thomas. You make me a better man than I ever believed possible. Tell me you'll marry me and love me forever."

She laid her head against his chest and listened to the steady sound of his heart. It was the last thing she wanted to hear every night for the rest of her life. "I do love you, and if you don't marry me, I'll tell my mother and she'll hunt you down and hurt you."

He chuckled. "I don't doubt that for a second."

He bent his head and kissed her. She responded to

him, moving her mouth against his, savoring the familiar taste, the feel of him. Heat began to blossom in her belly and breasts.

"Are you sure?" he asked, his lips still touching hers. "Can you really walk away from Saint Maggie and everyone here?"

"I'll visit," she said. "And the really important people will still be around. You can't for a moment believe my mother won't move to Chicago. After all, her first grandchild is going to be born there." Ali grinned. "I wonder how Miss Sylvie is going to like snow."

Matt groaned. "We're going to have to have a pig-proof house. And knowing you, room for every stray dog and cat in the neighborhood. Not to mention downtrodden neighbors. What a life!"

She looked at him. "Are you sure that's what you want?"

He settled his mouth on hers. "Absolutely."

epilogue

"I can't believe I'm doing this," Matt grumbled as he pushed open the door to the private hospital room and ushered in a very large pig poorly concealed under a beige trench coat.

"You love it," Rick told him as he pushed at the rear of Miss Sylvie, urging her out of the hallway. "If nothing else, it will be a great story to tell when Lynette starts dating."

Matt straightened and glared at his brother-in-law. "My daughter is never dating. Not even when she's forty."

Rick only chuckled.

"What are you two arguing about now?" Ali asked.

Matt turned at the sound of her voice and smiled as a familiar warmth filled him. Then he took in the tiny infant cradled in her arms, and wonder joined his contentment. They'd honestly and truly made a baby together. A perfect, beautiful little girl.

"We're not arguing," Matt said, walking over to the hospital bed and touching first his wife's cheek, then his daughter's. He stared at the sleeping newborn. "Your cousin is here, darling. Fortunately, you didn't take after her side of the family."

"No. She looks exactly like my baby pictures," Charlotte Elizabeth announced, swooping down to join the happy parents. "She's going to be a beauty, just like her very young grandmamma. Aren't you, my love?"

"It's getting a little thick in here," Jeff said, but the tone of a proud uncle tempered his words.

Ali shifted the baby so that she could free one hand. She reached for Matt and grasped his fingers in hers. "Are you scared?"

"More than I've ever been in my life. And more happy." He looked into her gray-green eyes and saw her love reflected there. It was a perfect, giving emotion he could never do enough to earn. He'd been blessed many times in his life, and he was a humble, grateful man.

"Are you going to call your dad?" Ali asked.

"In a little while."

At Ali's urgings, he'd contacted his father a few months back. The two Birmingham men had started talking, the first step to mending fences. They weren't ready to meet, but if his wife had anything to say about it, a reconciliation was inevitable. Matt might never agree with what his father had done, but he could understand it. Matt had nearly been destroyed in the same trap.

A low grumbling sound filled the room. Ali touched her stomach and blushed. "Okay, so I'm hungry. I was in labor for twelve hours, and they didn't let me eat anything."

Charlotte Elizabeth reached for the phone. "Did I tell you I found the most amazing Italian restaurant a few weeks ago? Renaldo, the owner, is quite the charmer.

I'm sure he'd whip up something special for you, darling. What would you like?"

Matt didn't see any reason to point out it was nearly midnight. After all, for Charlotte Elizabeth, Renaldo would probably do almost anything. Just as he, Matt, would do anything for Ali.

He'd been given a second chance, and he'd grabbed it with both hands. His life was so different that sometimes he didn't recognize it. Between the sprawling house in the suburbs, the constant visitors, his mother-in-law and her pig in permanent residence in the nearby guest cottage, he never knew what he was going to find when he came home. Except for one thing—he knew that Ali would be waiting for him, her lips smiling, her heart open. She'd turned out to be the best thing that had ever happened to him.

"What do you say we give this little one a year or so head start, then try for a boy next time," his wife said in a low voice.

His chest tightened. He kissed her. "Have I told you how much I love you?"

"Every day, but I don't get tired of hearing it." Tears filled her eyes. "I love you, too. For always."

Keep reading for a special preview of

The Marcelli Bride

Susan Mallery

Available now!

If Darcy Jensen had known she was going to be kidnapped, she would have worn better shoes. Or at least more sensible shoes. As it was she'd dressed in black strappy sandals that weren't all that comfortable for walking, let alone being dragged across a parking lot and thrown into the back of a van.

She did her best to resist. Screaming was out of the question because they'd already gagged her. And the resisting part went badly, what with her hands tied behind her back, although she did nail one guy with a decent head butt.

Even as she landed hard on the metal floor of the van, she wondered how it all had happened. She'd been in Ann Taylor checking out the new clothes for fall. She'd told Drew she needed to use the restroom.

Traveling with two Secret Service agents meant rarely using a public restroom. Drew had consulted with the manager of the store, who was all too happy to have the president of the United States' daughter peeing in her private bathroom. Darcy had done her business, washed her hands—not only because she always did, but also because people checked on things like that when one was in the public eye—and had started back through the stockroom toward the dressing rooms, where she had a pile of clothes waiting for her.

That's when the men attacked. Four guys in Halloween-type demon masks grabbed her. Before she knew what was happening, they'd slapped tape on her mouth. The hand tying came next, then the dragging.

One of them even remembered to pick up her purse, she thought grimly as she stared at her now-scratched Maxx bag bought on QVC lying next to her on the floor of the van.

The rear doors slammed shut, and the vehicle sped out of the parking lot.

Darcy braced herself as best she could on the ribbed floor as the van bounced, swerved, then turned onto what felt like a main road. Two of her abductors had taken the front seats—she could see them through the small grille—while the other two must have had their own transportation. She was alone in the back of the van.

Alone with her purse.

There were no windows, no way to get anyone's attention. And no one to watch her retrieve the panic button that would signal the Secret Service and send them rushing to rescue her.

She inched her way toward the purse, only to have the van take another corner, causing the bag to go sliding out of reach. Two more slip-slides across the dirty metal floor and she was within reaching distance of her purse . . . except for the small problem of her hands tied behind her back. Could she open the zipper with her teeth? Probably not with the gag in place.

Darcy had done her best to stay focused in the moment. If she anchored herself in the now, the terror wasn't so bad. She could function. But if she allowed herself to think about what they could do to her, how it was national policy to never negotiate with terrorists, then fear would explode inside of her, making her want to scream and beg, despite the tape across her mouth.

No! She wouldn't go there. She wouldn't give in. She was strong and determined, and by God, she would get her panic button and push it until dozens of armed agents came storming through the walls of the van.

She didn't have much choice. Drew had been assigned to her long enough to know that the "trying on" part of a shopping trip could take at least an hour, which meant he wouldn't notice she was missing until the van had enough time to cross a couple of state lines.

If only it wasn't so hot, she thought as she went to work on the zipper. August in D.C. maintained the average temperature of a blast furnace with plenty of humidity thrown in for good measure. The front of the van might have AC, but here in the prison part of the vehicle, no such luck.

She ignored the heat, the sweat, the scrapes and bruises, and bent over her purse. Several more turns, some speeding and three failed attempts later, Darcy had discovered she could not open the damn zipper with her teeth. Which left her to scoot the purse into a corner, turn her back, and try to open it that way.

Easier said than done, she thought as she discovered she couldn't even hold on to the purse, although she did a lovely job of scraping her arm and banging her head. Why did this stuff always look so easy in the movies?

She tried again, carefully lodging the purse against the wheel well, then rolling onto her back and grabbing for the bag with her fingers. This time she got it and turned it slowly until she felt the zipper.

Don't make a turn, don't make a turn, she chanted silently, knowing if they did, she would slide across the van and have to start all over again.

The vehicle stayed mercifully straight.

Inch by inch she pulled the zipper down. Sweat poured down her back and made her fingers damp. Her bare legs stuck to the floor of the van and to whatever crumbs and icky things were scattered there. At last the purse was open. She plunged both hands inside and felt around for the familiar plastic case. Lipstick, wallet, cell phone, pen—

Cell phone? Nearly as good as the panic button. She would have to dial, of course, but she could call the operator and asked to be put through to her father. She could—

Darcy swore. Right. The tape across her mouth would make it difficult to hold a conversation. Back to digging for the panic button.

At that exact moment, the van suddenly came to a stop. Both she and her purse went sliding, although not at the same rate of speed. She had no way to get back to it before the bad guys opened the rear door to find her sprawled in a corner, her skirt up to her waist and the contents of her purse spread all over the floor of the van.

"You didn't take her handbag?" one of the guys asked the other. "Goddamn it, Bill, I thought you were smarter than that."

The recipient of the scolding, a smallish man in a vampire mask, stiffened. "You used my name. Now she knows my name."

The other one, demon-guy, snorted. "Yeah, because there's only one guy named Bill in the whole country. Come on, Einstein, let's get her inside."

Darcy tried to scramble away from her kidnappers, but as she was already in a back corner of the van, there was nowhere else to go. They half carried, half dragged her into what looked like a large warehouse.

She did her best to fight, lashing out at them with her feet. The action caused them to hold on tighter to her upper arms and made her break a heel on her new sandals.

Now she was mad, she thought as they put her into a straight-back chair and began tying her down. They'd screwed with her day, bruised her, thrown her around the inside of a disgusting van, scratched her new leather bag, and ruined the black sandals she'd just bought after waiting four weeks for them to go on sale. There was going to be hell to pay.

She told them so, although the tape on her mouth interfered with the intensity of her message.

"I don't think she likes us," Bill said, stepping back as she tried to kick his shin.

"Gee, I wonder why. Most people love a good kidnapping."

With that, the two men walked off. Darcy tried to hold on to her anger by reminding herself how much the sandals had cost, even on clearance, and how little money she had coming in these days. It worked for nearly a minute, then the fear set in. What were they going to do to her?

She told herself that torture was unlikely. Either they wanted money or something they thought they could only get from the president of the United States. Unfortunately that was a big pool of possibilities, everything from sovereignty to nuclear weapons.

Then there was the matter of the no-negotiation policy. The one that told her she could be stuck here for a very long time, and then she could be killed.

Darcy might not love everything about her life at this moment in time, but she wasn't ready for it to be over. Terror tightened her throat and made it impossible to breathe. She had the sudden thought that she was going to throw up.

Stay calm, she told herself. If she vomited, she could drown in a really gross way. She had to find her Zen center. Not that she'd ever studied Zen, but she could imagine what it was like. A tranquil place. A place where reality was an illusion and all that mattered was the slow, steady beating of her heart.

Deep breaths, she told herself. In and out. No hurry in the air department. Just nice slow—

"Did you hurt her?"

The question came from somewhere behind her as she heard several people approaching. Panic joined fear as she tried to figure out if, in this man's opinion, hurting her would be a plus or not.

"She got banged up in the back of the van," Bill said. "But that's all."

She looked around for some kind of escape. But the huge, empty warehouse didn't offer any places to hide, and being tied to a large, heavy chair limited her options. She tried to scoot and only succeeded in wrenching her back.

"Good. We don't want any unnecessary bloodshed."

Darcy exhaled in relief. Speaking as the kidnappee, she was delighted to know that bloodshed was to be avoided until necessary. Not that she wanted to know what would be considered necessary.

Their footsteps got closer, then three men were standing in front of her. She recognized her two kidnappers, who stood with a new guy, also in a demon mask. He was taller than the other two, and stronger. Something he proved when he turned on the non-Bill one and grabbed him by the throat.

"What the hell were you thinking?" he demanded, shaking the smaller man like a dog shakes something tasty just before he kills it.

Bill danced from foot to foot, although he didn't rush in to help his friend. "We got her, boss. Just like you said. The president's daughter. This is her."

The leader released non-Bill and curled his hands into fists. He stared at Darcy through the slits of the mask and growled.

"Not this one, you idiot. The other one. Lauren. No one cares about this one."

Less than thirty minutes later the van came to a stop. Darcy was still too stunned to react, even as the rear doors opened and the two men reached in to pull her out. One of them cut the bindings on her wrists while the other collected her purse and tossed it on the ground next to her. The broken sandal followed. Then they ran back to the front of the van, jumped inside, and sped away.

She had enough functioning brain left to look for a license plate—there wasn't one—and to note the color and make of the van. Then she sank down on the curb of the deserted loading area at the rear of the mall and rested her filthy arms on her scraped and bloodied knees and her head on her arms.

This hadn't happened, she told herself, even as the truth of it settled around her like a hot, sticky fog. She'd been rejected by kidnappers, which made the event a new high in a lifetime of lows.

Talk about a photo opportunity, she thought grimly. Here she was, battered, bruised, cut up, scraped. Her clothes were dirty and torn, her shoes broken, and she'd just been tossed aside like a used tissue.

Darcy straightened, pulled the tape off her mouth, then gasped as skin tore with the adhesive. That wasn't going to be pretty as it healed. She felt around on the cement until she found her purse and pulled out the panic button. Better late than never, she thought as she pressed down on the bright red button and waited for the cavalry.

Lieutenant Commander Joe Larson had always considered the admiral a reasonable, if distant, commanding officer. All that had changed at 9:18 the previous evening. The admiral wanted someone's head on a stick, and he was gunning for Joe's.

"What kind of half-assed, goddamn asshole . . ."

The tirade continued, but Joe didn't bother listening as his captain got reamed. He could figure out the highlights without hearing them. Besides, the captain would be passing them along personally to Joe soon enough.

Such was the chain of command. The admiral chewed out the captain, the captain chewed out him, and he, well, Joe hadn't decided what he was going to do. Like they said—shit rolled downhill.

He crossed to the window of the office foyer and stared at the activity below. There was plenty of it at the

Naval Amphibious Base. And just beyond the building, the Pacific Ocean sparkled in the bright summer morning. Other careers might offer better pay, but none could beat the location on Coronado Island.

Given the admiral's temper, there was every chance Joe could soon be exploring those other careers. Or stationed on a naval base in Greenland. Screwups came in all shapes and sizes. This one had all the potential firepower of an aircraft carrier. Explaining to the captain that it hadn't been his fault wasn't going to change a damn thing.

Fifteen minutes later, the door to the captain's office opened and the admiral stormed out. Joe stood at attention as the angry man stalked by, then he looked at his commanding officer.

"Come on in, Joe," the other man said in a weary voice.

Joe entered then closed the door behind him. "Sir."

Captain Phillips waved to the empty chair in front of his desk. "You hear all that?"

"Yes, sir."

Phillips, a tall man in his early forties, sighed. "He loved that boat."

Joe didn't respond. The information wasn't news. The admiral had been restoring his nearly eighty-year-old boat for the past five years. The engine was new, and the electronics state-of-the-art, but the rest of it was original, lovingly sanded and varnished by the admiral's own hand.

The man's wife had left him, claiming she refused to come in second to a floating hunk of wood, and his children rarely visited, knowing they would be put to work on the boat. Six months ago the admiral had decided to live aboard.

Then, last night, at 9:18, the admiral's pride and joy had been accidentally blown up by men under Joe's command. They were lucky the admiral hadn't been on board at the time.

"Want to tell me what happened?" the captain asked.

Joe shrugged. "The team was celebrating being back," he said. The Navy SEAL team in question had just returned from six months of hazardous duty out of the country. "They'd all made it out alive. Even Grayson."

"How's he doing?" the captain asked.

"Lieutenant Grayson is still in the hospital, sir. He's recovering from his injuries."

Grayson had been shot on their last op. His men had brought him back and kept him alive until he'd been evacuated to the hospital ship, then brought back home.

Joe remained perfectly still as he continued. "I spoke with the men on the team yesterday afternoon. They'd had six missions back to back, with minimal downtime in between. I suggested they burn off some steam."

Phillips nodded. "They decided on boat races."

"Yes, sir." Made sense. To a SEAL, the water was a second home. "They used small boats and kept within the marina speed limit." Sort of. "Unfortunately their racing course took them over a BUDS training exercise."

The future SEALs had been in their second round of training, learning to dive and work with explosives underwater.

"Last night the explosives were live. Apparently the movement of the boats racing overhead confused a few of the trainees. They're not allowed to surface to get their bearings. Instead of putting their explosives on the target, they placed them on the admiral's boat."

Talk about plain bad luck, Joe thought grimly. "The explosives were small and shouldn't have caused much damage. Unfortunately the admiral had recently refueled his craft. There was a small leak in the engine. When the explosive went off, it triggered a chain reaction that turned the admiral's pride and joy into kindling. At least that's the preliminary report."

Captain Phillips didn't speak for several seconds. "Aren't you going to tell me that the admiral tied up in a restricted area? That he shouldn't have been there in the first place?"

"No, sir." What was the point? Joe had been in the navy long enough to know excuses only made the situation worse. Besides, who would have told an admiral to move his boat?

"You have a great career," his captain told him. "You've worked hard, moved up the ranks. I was confident you'd make it to admiral yourself, before you retired."

Joe had walked into some of the most dangerous situations in the world and lived to tell the tale, but nothing he'd experienced prepared him for the sense of fury that gripped him as he sat there and heard his career talked about in the past tense. The navy was all he knew, all he'd ever wanted.

He'd told the men to go have fun. It was his responsibility. Technically, he could pass the punishment on down, but next in line was Lieutenant Grayson, currently missing most of his right leg and facing a long road to recovery.

No. This time the chain of command stopped here. With Joe.

Phillips flipped open a file. "You've been with the

SEALs nearly ten years, Joe. You're a fine officer and one of the best men I've ever worked with. The admiral wants you punished, and I want to save your career if I can."

"Thank you, sir," Joe said, feeling the first hint of relief.

The captain smiled. "You might want to hold off on your thanks. The best way I know to punish you is to temporarily reassign you to a special project that has nothing to do with the SEALs. The best way I know to save your ass is to get you the hell out of here for a few weeks and let the admiral cool down. As an interesting point of fact, my brother-in-law is fairly high up the chain of command in the Secret Service. I don't think you knew that."

"No, sir," Joe said, not sure what the information had to do with anything.

"You've mentioned you have family here in California," Phillips said. "The Marcellis. They own a winery just north of Santa Barbara?"

"Yes, sir." Joe had no idea what was going on, but he didn't like it. Technically he was related to the Marcelli clan, but they weren't his family.

"What you don't know," the captain said, "is that the president's daughter was kidnapped yesterday."

Joe stiffened as he pictured the attractive, curvy blonde who frequently served as the president's hostess. "Lauren?"

"No. The other one. Darcy. Apparently they grabbed her by mistake—Lauren was their actual target."

"How could they screw that up?" Joe asked. Darcy was nothing like her sister in looks or temperament.

"No one knows. The point is, both women are being taken out of Washington and sent to different locations.

Safe houses, if you will. They'll have their usual Secret Service protection, but until the kidnappers are caught, they need to lay low. This is all confidential, Joe. You aren't to discuss this information with anyone."

"Of course not, sir." Joe had no problem keeping quiet. What he didn't understand was what any of it had to do with him.

Captain Phillips leaned forward. "There is some concern about Darcy. She's not generally cooperative, and frankly no one wants to be locked up in a safe house with her. The thought is if she can be kept safe but still have a semblance of a life, it will be easier for all concerned. Basically a place that is isolated but not solitary. I thought of what you've told me about your family's winery. There's a large house, plenty of room for the team and Darcy. I wasn't sure how I was going to convince you to take this assignment. After last night, I don't have to."

Joe put the rest of the pieces together and didn't like the finished picture. That was to be his punishment. To babysit the president's daughter and spend time with the Marcellis.

"I have a SEAL team heading out in two months," he said. "There's important work to be done."

"Someone else can take care of that, Joe. Right now the president's daughter is your responsibility."

"Sir, sending her to the hacienda is an interesting solution," he said, "but the winery is not easily guarded. There are hundreds of acres, employees, staff. Plus my relatives would have to be cleared for security purposes."

"Already done. You're right about the winery being an open space, but who would think to look for her there? The navy is cooperating with the president at his request,"

Phillips told him. "Unless you want to call the president and explain why you're unwilling to protect his daughter?"

Joe felt the doors of the prison swing closed. "What is my assignment, sir?"

"Coordinate with the Secret Service. Their job is to protect Darcy, but you are to facilitate what they need. Be another pair of eyes. Use your tactical skills to their advantage. When the kidnappers are caught, you'll return here and we'll see if the admiral has cooled off enough for you to resume your duties. In the meantime, do what you can to keep Darcy Jensen happy."

Joe rose and saluted. "Yes, sir," he said and left.

He was completely and totally screwed, sent away in disgrace, his career in jeopardy. He would be lucky to come back as an ensign.

As for keeping Darcy Jensen happy—from what he'd heard, that was a task even a SEAL couldn't pull off.